She woke up married…
and then she ran.

> **"It has come to my attention that I may have engaged in some . . . unfortunate conduct last night."**

"I regret it, truly," Georgette continued, "and I am sure you will agree that the best thing to do is pursue an annulment. You have some skill in legal matters, Mr. MacKenzie, so it seems as if it should be a simple—"

"My friends call me James."

She licked her lips. "James, then . . ."

He raised an imperious brow. "*You* will call me Mr. MacKenzie."

A flash of something—was it anger?—widened her eyes. "I will call you whatever I please," she retorted, lifting her chin. "Rogue. Scoundrel is a good name, and fitting, don't you think?" Her gaze swung southward for a scant moment, lingering a hair too long. "*Husband.* That last one is the most annoying, I will admit."

James suffocated an irrational urge to acknowledge her spirit with a grin. When she stood up to him, she was glorious. Was it any wonder he had behaved so impulsively last night?

He willed himself to remember why he was here and what she was. "It matters not what you call me," he said. James stuffed the instinct to soothe her. Did she think she could bat those eyelashes at him and turn his insides to jelly, the way she had last night?

He wouldn't permit it, not anymore. "I call you a criminal."

By Jennifer McQuiston

WHAT HAPPENS IN SCOTLAND

Coming Soon

BRIGHTON IS FOR LOVERS

JENNIFER McQUISTON

What Happens in Scotland

AVON

An Imprint of HarperCollinsPublishers

AVON BOOKS
An Imprint of HarperCollins*Publishers*
10 East 53rd Street
New York, New York 10022-5299

Copyright © 2013 by Jennifer McQuiston
Excerpt from *Brighton Is for Lovers* copyright © 2013 by Jennifer McQuiston
ISBN 978-0-06-223129-1
www.avonromance.com

First Avon Books mass market printing: March 2013

Avon Trademark Reg. U.S. Pat. Off. and in Other Countries, Marca Registrada, Hecho en U.S.A.
HarperCollins® is a registered trademark of HarperCollins Publishers.

Printed in the U.S.A.

10 9 8 7 6 5 4 3 2 1

To my husband, John.
While my heroes exist primarily in my head,
my imagination is far more vivid when I am with you.

Acknowledgments

LIKE MANY DEBUT authors, I owe an amazing debt of gratitude to an entire herd of people. Not just those who helped me with this, my first published book, but those who have helped me on the entire journey, which spanned three years and five completed manuscripts.

First and foremost, I want to thank my supportive family, without whose love and assistance I could have never conceived of writing a book, much less completed one. My husband, John, deserves a special thank you and probably a three-week vacation for everything the spouse of an obsessed writer must endure. I am grateful for my mom, who made that all-important parenting decision that if I was old enough to sneak her historical romances under the covers, I was old enough to read them. Thanks to my sister Julie Hensley, who provided early critical feedback as I sorted out the business of being a writer, and who isn't afraid to tell her literary genre colleagues I write "those books." Thank you to my beautiful girls for bringing me such joy. I love you dearly, but don't assume every book deal = another new pony.

I owe a very loud shout-out (more of a shriek, really) to Georgia Romance Writers. I value every one of the friendships I have formed in this wonderful writing community and cannot say enough good things about how much they support emerging authors. Thank you to early beta readers—Stacy Heilman, Allyson Reeves, Angie Stout, Colleen Wolpert, Anna Steffl, Laura Disque, Kristina McElroy, Daphne Ross, Terry Brock Poca, Noelle Pierce, Helene B. Chandler Rosencrantz, and Emery Lee—who read some truly awful stuff. Thank you, as well, to published authors Meredith Duran, Courtney Milan, and Vanessa Kelly, who offered charity critiques I was lucky enough to win *and* smart enough to study.

No writer can succeed without amazing critique partners, and I owe a huge thank you to Romily Bernard, Sally Kilpatrick, Tracy Brogan, Kimberly Kincaid, and Alyssa Alexander. These ladies always tell me when I get it right and never fail to point out when I write something too stupid for words. Thank you to Tony Bernard (a.k.a. Boy Genius) for the gift of my beautiful website. To Sarah MacLean, who gave me the loveliest cover blurb on the planet: thank you for your wild excitement and your heartfelt advice; it means the world to me. I want to express my sincere appreciation to the most patient agent on the face of the planet, Kevan Lyon, and to the amazing Esi Sogah and the entire team at Avon Books for making me feel wonderfully welcome. Here's hoping I fulfill your faith in me!

What Happens in
Scotland

Chapter 1

THOUGH SHE WOULD never admit it to polite Society, Lady Georgette Thorold hated brandy almost as much as she hated husbands. So it was the cruelest of jokes when she awoke with nary a clue to her surroundings, smelling like one and pressed up against the other.

As she reluctantly came to her senses, unwelcome scents and fears crowded out lucid thought. In all her twenty-six years, Georgette had never even raised a glass of the amber liquid, much less slept in sheets that smelled as if they had been washed in a distillery. She was used to a feeling of comfort on waking, or at least familiarity. But judging by the stained wallpaper in her bleary line of vision, she was not in her bedroom, and there was nothing of comfort in the pounding of her head.

And, more to the point, her husband had been dead for two years.

A man's warm body was stretched against her back, and she could feel the telltale press of an erection knocking against the base of her spine. She stared down at the muscled forearm that lay across her shoulders, noting its possessive, sinewy strength. For the briefest of moments she considered closing her eyes and going back to sleep in the appealing cage of this man's arms. But clarity punched its way through her murky confusion.

She was in bed. *With a stranger.*

Heart pounding, she wiggled her way free and leaped from the tangled covers, dodging a gauntlet of broken glass and articles of clothing as she scrambled for safety. She sucked in a roomful of air, trying to escape the panic perched on her shoulders.

There were feathers everywhere. On the floor. On the ceiling. On *her.* Horrified by her lack of hygiene and the fear that somewhere in this room there might be a slaughtered goose, she closed her eyes, praying that when she opened them again it would all disappear. But the lack of eyesight proved ill-advised in the mess of the place. She tripped and stumbled against a wardrobe that looked to have survived the Jacobite Risings only to now sit ruined, one door hanging off its hinge.

Despite her graceless clattering, the man in the bed snored through it all. Georgette scrubbed a fist across her eyes, as if she could banish the sight of him, then lowered her hand to cover her mouth. The smell of brandy hovered there on her skin. Had she bathed in the vile stuff? What on earth had she done?

Dear God, she was in a strange room with a strange man, smelling of the same spirits her former husband had consumed to lethal outcome—what *hadn't* she done?

Bile, thick and bitter, rose in the back of her throat. This could not be happening. This was not who she was. Her now-dead husband had been the rake and libertine. She had been the wife who turned a blind, tortured eye. She abhorred the thought that in one night, she appeared to have sunk to the level of debauchery her husband had embraced during their brief marriage.

Nay, she had sunk below it. Because while such behavior was permitted among the men of the *ton*, she was a lady. And ladies did not wake up in strangers' beds, without a clue of how they had come to be there.

She took a step backward, certain her circumstances couldn't get any worse. The wall scorched the bare skin of her shoulders with all the subtlety of a branding iron. Air clawed at her lungs, demanding entrance. Apparently, her circumstances *could* get worse. Because in addition to waking beside a man whom she didn't know, she was undressed.

And the only thing Georgette hated more than brandy and husbands was nudity.

Her heart tripped along in her chest as if she had awakened from a bad dream. Only this was no dream. Dream men didn't snore. Her former husband had taught her that, if nothing else. And dream or no, she needed to locate her clothes and her sanity, both of which seemed as absent as her memory.

She grabbed the nearest item of clothing she could find, which turned out to be the sleeping man's shirt, and shook tiny bits of glass and feathers from it before clasping it against her bare chest. The shirttails came down to her calves. The rustling of fabric released a not unpleasant fragrance, clean soap underlaid with a hint of horse and leather. She felt an answering, instinctive tug in her body's most intimate places. How could she be so brazen? She didn't know this man. She didn't *want* to know this man. Her stomach churned in confusion and embarrassment, and she cursed her body's traitorous response.

Evidence of her bed partner's own state of disarray peeked out from beneath the covers, hinting at their interactions of the previous evening. A muscled calf, scattered with a dusting of dark hair, flexed alarmingly. The sheets shifted as he turned over, revealing a head of brown hair. He sported a full beard that no young man in London would have suffered without a wager first being laid down, but it did not hide the patrician slope of his nose or the sensual slide of his lips. In sleep, his face looked peaceful. Appealing in a masculine sort of way.

And terrifyingly unfamiliar.

"Dear God, what have I done?" she whispered. Clasping the shirt tighter against her body, she picked her way closer and studied his features, trying to jog her memory for some hint of what he meant to her, or she to him. He looked to be in his early thirties. His hair showed a tendency to curl at the edges, and the brightening light of dawn caught the glint of red in his dark beard. His eyelashes lay like a smudge against his lightly weathered cheek, making Georgette's pale, pampered skin feel insipid by comparison. No slice of recognition accompanied her perusal, though standing this close to him brought a rush of heat to her limbs.

Beneath the man's head she could see sheets that looked none too clean. The thought of fleas niggled at her, and her skin jumped beneath an imaginary assault. If she had chosen this room, what had she chosen in him?

"Please, please, at *least* be a gentleman," she muttered, trying to decide if the sleeping man looked more like a footman or a peer. The shirt she held against her was of fine cotton lawn. But most gentlemen of her acquaintance weren't quite so . . . muscled.

She spied her dress in a graceless heap on the floor and stooped to pick it up, then dropped to her knees to look under the bed, searching for her shoes. Shards of glass and rough-hewn floorboards scraped at her knees, and above her the man gave another rattling snore. A thought struck her with blinding horror. If her partner in sin was a gentleman, he might insist on marrying her after what she presumed must have taken place.

And if there was one thing she was determined to avoid, aside from word of this reaching London's scandal sheets, it was another loveless marriage to a man with a penchant for women and drink.

She rose to her feet and yanked her wrinkled gray silk over her head, not even bothering to try to find either her corset or her chemise. A shifting on the mattress sent her panic to new heights, and she abandoned her haphazard efforts to button the bodice and dashed for the door with no thought in her head other than to put some distance between herself and this anonymous, offensive stranger. But the dirt and glass-strewn floorboards sucked at her slippers, and the latch seemed to snag on her hand.

Then she saw it.

The ring on her left hand glittered in a skein of sunlight that snaked its way between the room's lace curtains. Horrified, Georgette twisted her hand, peering at the bit of gold. The symbolic weight of it was as heavy as the weight of her worst fears. She wore a signet ring emblazoned with a family crest, one she did not recognize.

And judging by its position on her hand and the circumstances of her morning, she appeared to be married.

Disbelief settled in her bones. It was not possible. A wedding took planning. A posting of the banns, or a special license, at least. And the logistics of the matter aside, she *couldn't* have done this. Not now, when she was finally shaking off the manacles of two years of mourning. Not now, when she was finally poised to taste the freedom long denied her.

She whirled back to look at the man again. No matter how handsomely proportioned the stranger in that bed might be, no matter how the sight of his muscled calf sent a flutter of expectation in her abdomen, she was certain she could never have wanted this.

Anger flooded her chest, filling the space where fear and uncertainty once held ground. She stepped closer. She needed to wake him, to find an explanation, but the thought of touching him made her fingers curl in trepidation. Cursing her lack of a weapon, Georgette scanned the room. She grasped the nearest object she could find, then turned back to face her still-sleeping bed partner. Hefting the thankfully empty chamber pot on one hip, she reached out a hand and thumped it against his bare shoulder.

"Open your eyes," she hissed in a voice she barely recognized.

The man in question rolled over, stretched, and blinked up at her. Sleepy green eyes the color of apothecary glass focused on her. A seductive smile curled the edges of his lips, revealing even, white teeth.

"Good morning," he said, his voice a rustic, rumbled burr. "I dinna ken why you have left, but I wish you would come back to bed."

His uncultured accent told Georgette as clear as any map where she was, and her heart squeezed tight in her chest. A snippet of memory settled over her shoulders like a heavy woolen mantle. She was in Scotland, where an irregular sort of marriage could indeed be had on a whim.

She remembered now, at least some of it. She remembered planning a holiday, and her hopes for a rebirth of spirit after the terrible circumstances of her husband's death and the endless cycle of mourning. Her cousin had come north to study the fauna of Scotland, hoping to write a treatise on his work, and he had invited her to visit. She remembered thinking, *Scotland is the place*, with its breathy pine forests and pastoral summer scenes and, most importantly, its distance from London's Season. She needed that distance, needed time to collect herself and prepare for the pitying stares that would no doubt accompany her return to polite Society.

Only, never in her wildest imaginings had she considered that return would occur as a married woman. And try as she might, she still could not remember the circumstances that brought her here, to what had to be a public inn, or to this man.

The necessary words, dry as the burnt toast she could smell wafting up from some lower level of the building, stuck in her throat. She forced herself to choke them out. "Who are you?"

A surprised chuckle escaped the man as he shifted and sat up. "*Now* you ask? It didn't concern you last night overmuch."

The slide of the sheet pulled her eyes in a far too southerly direction. His abdomen was a washboard of muscle, layers defined as precisely as a scalpel's blade. She swallowed. This was no gentleman, and probably no mere footman either. Not with a physique like that. The sight of his bare chest brought heat licking against the edges of her body, and the warmth settled with terrible surety between her legs. She was attracted to this man. Shame in her body's inappropriate reaction screamed in her ears.

"*What* are you?" she pressed, her voice a strangled knot.

He chuckled. "What a daft question to ask, after the service I have provided you." He nodded in the direction of her hand, and his smile shifted to a smirk. "I am your hero husband, milady. And you owe me another kiss."

Another kiss? Dear God, she couldn't remember the first one, though a primitive, distant part of her regretted the loss. And though she had suspected it, the confirmation of their circumstances twisted her panic to new, dizzying heights. "Husband?" She licked her lips, desperate for a moment's clear thought.

This man, with his uncultured consonants and eye-pleasing musculature, was clearly a commoner. She was the widow of a viscount. If she chose to marry again— which she would not—it would not be to a man who looked as if he made his living at indecent labor. No matter what this scoundrel thought he had gained, and no matter what manner of shocking intimacy she had forgotten, she would never have done this.

"Do you know who I am?" she demanded, trying to intimidate this man who sent her heart bounding in fear but her body inexplicably leaning toward him.

"I ken you as well as any man can know a woman." He crooked his finger at her and beckoned in a playful, possessive display. "Now bring yourself back, my lady wife, and let us get reacquainted."

His voice was teasing, but his words were damning. This was why she had sworn to never marry again. How *dare* he summon her that way? How *dare* he presume?

His words flung her body to motion. The chamber pot's trajectory was more instinctive than calculated. A certain resolve burrowed beneath her skin even as the sound of crockery on bone sent her feet to flight.

She was no one's plaything, not anymore.

And she would be no one's wife.

Chapter 2

GEORGETTE RUSHED DOWN the dark stairwell of the ramshackle inn, past the public room with its gut-wrenching smells of coddled eggs and smoked kippers, past even the shocked innkeeper, who did no more than call out after her as she plunged through the front door.

The cacophony of the street outside was an assault on her mind and body, as if a giant's hand had flung her against a stone wall. The sun's low-slanting rays hinted at the morning's early hour, perhaps no more than seven o'clock, but the jostling of street vendors and the noise from the nearby market told her the citizens of this modest Scottish town took their mornings seriously. The smell of frying dough wafting from the street corner made her head pound and her stomach turn over in objection, but she tamped down the urge to vomit. Her body's complaints about her raucous night were not chief on her list of things to sort out this morning.

She had struck a man. Had struck her *husband*. She hoped the man—whoever he was—was unharmed, that she hadn't done permanent damage to that handsome profile. She hadn't been thinking, had impulsively given in to a lifetime of frustration. And was it any wonder she had behaved without due deliberation? She could scarcely breathe.

Thinking was out of the question.

She lifted her skirts and hurried down the street at an unladylike jog, determined to put as much space between her and the scene of her shame as possible. She repeated her inescapable new mantra in time with her steps. *Dear God, what have I done?* And after a minute or so, through a dawning sense of panic and confusion, she added a new piece for good measure: *Dear God, where am I?*

She hurried past foreign-looking storefronts, so different from London they made her eyes ache. There was no familiar landmark she could see, no sense of having been here before, no sense of knowing where she was going. Dogs and children, all bearing the ribbed, hungry look of the Scottish hills, scattered before her, and the thick brogue of snatched bits of conversation battered her ears.

She made it five blurry blocks before the exertions of the previous evening caught up with her. Reaching out a hand to brace herself against a brick wall, she leaned over, sucking in great breaths full of air beneath the shade of a shop awning. A pair of young women passed by, their bonnets trailing pink ribbons. They studied her with avid curiosity, putting their heads together to whisper behind cupped hands.

Georgette hated to imagine what she must look like. Heavens, her unbrushed hair alone should be enough to stop traffic, and there was no denying the smell of brandy still polluted the air around her. When she had escaped the inn, she entertained no thought beyond fleeing. But now she stood in a state of dishabille on a public

street, her gown gaping rudely down the partially buttoned front.

She couldn't even remember the last time she'd gone
without the benefit of a corset, and now there were witnesses to her disgraceful, slatternly appearance.

Straightening up, she turned in a full circle, searching
for a safe face or landmark. This time, with the benefit of a moment's rest, she could see more. The striped
awning across the street. The communal pump with its
line of townsfolk waiting their turn to gather water. But
Georgette truly had no idea where she was. The only
person she knew in this town was the handsome, hea-
then Scotsman she had left in her bed.

And the only other person she knew in Scotland was
her cousin, Randolph Burton.

She groaned, slumping back against the wall as she
contemplated the mess her life had suddenly become.
This was supposed to be the start of a two-week holiday at her cousin's house in Scotland. She remembered
arriving three days ago—or was it four? Randolph's ob-
sequious welcome had been a disappointment, as had
the realization that the promised female escort was not
in residence. Worse, she remembered her suspicions that
Randolph's interest in her seemed more calculated than
cousinly, bolstered by a dinner when he had stared at her
over candlelight and she had fidgeted in her seat. That,
unfortunately, was where her memory ended.

"I've brought you a kitten, miss."

Georgette whirled, her heart leaping in her throat.
A man in a bloodstained apron stood a few feet away,
close enough that she could smell the coppery, sweat-
soaked scent of him. He sported a beard the color of

clay, littered with bits of food and other ill-considered things.

Around the burly figure, the business of the town's morning swirled. Children skipped by, and women with baskets headed to the market Georgette had seen a few blocks before. No one seemed to notice or care the man held a cleaver in one meaty hand, and clasped a brown and gray striped kitten by the scruff of the neck in the other.

"Do I know you?" Georgette asked, taking a cautious step back, not even caring that the movement took her into the street.

A smile cracked his lips, revealing a red, jarring hole where his top front teeth should have been. "MacRory's the name. I dinna have a chance to tell you last night while we were getting acquainted."

"I met you last night?" And they were *acquainted*? The man appeared to weigh close to twenty stone, all flesh and gristle. He was either an unhygienic butcher or a murderer. Neither career recommended him as a close, personal friend. He could crush her with a finger as easily as a fist. How familiar could they have become in the brief span of her memory loss?

"You dinna remember? Ach, well, you were on me and off again so fast, I suppose that explains it." The aproned man's voice carried the same rumbling burr of the man she had left in her bed, but the timbre of his voice evoked none of the same soul-stirring reactions. His words, and what they implied, make her neck flush with horror rather than attraction.

"I was *on* you?" Georgette prayed she had misheard him.

"Oh, aye. Wrapped your hands right around my girth you did." His hearty laugh made the stains on his apron shake like windblown curtains. "You knew just how to squeeze."

Sweat pricked the hollows of Georgette's underarms and a racking shiver shook her spine. Her mind's screamed protestations tumbled about until they distilled into a single, inarguable question. "I beg your pardon?"

"Take it, lass." The man gestured toward the squirming tabby with his knife. "You earned it."

Georgette was confused—and alarmed—enough to reach out her hand and snatch the kitten to her chest. It was impossibly tiny, perhaps three or four weeks old. How she was supposed to take care of the thing she hadn't a clue, but some long-dormant nurturing instinct welled up in her chest. She could not give it back, not now. It might end up on someone's dinner table if she did.

The butcher gave her one more gap-spaced grin and then turned and lumbered off down the street. Bile rose in the back of her throat as she watched him disappear into the crowd. Dear God, had she really touched him so intimately last night?

And worse, had she serviced him in exchange for a kitten?

Georgette blinked against the tears gathering in her eyes. She had not cried when her husband had died, though she felt no small measure of guilt for his untimely death. Neither had she cried upon discovering her shameful circumstances this morning, nor upon stumbling about a foreign town in a state of half dress and being gawked at by a pair of young ladies who looked as fresh as pressed flowers.

But now, upon hearing that she might have engaged in disreputable activities with more than one man last night, *now* she was crying? She was as disgusted with herself for her weakness now as for her apparent recklessness last night.

The sound of hooves and wheels pulled her from her self-flagellation, and Georgette jumped in her skin as a black draught horse cut through her thoughts, the driver shouting at her in some unintelligible brogue. She scrambled toward the edge of the street, her slippers grappling for purchase on the manure-slicked paving stones. She almost fell, then righted herself one-handed.

She clutched the kitten against her chest as the cart rumbled by. She shuddered as she considered how close she had come to dropping the helpless creature in her dash to safety. She slipped the kitten down the front of her bodice, then fastened the remaining buttons over it. It curled into a ball, right between her breasts. She would sort out what to do with it later. Right now she needed both her hands.

"Georgette!"

Her cousin's voice, shrill as the hawkers selling their wares on the street corner, sent relief coursing through her body. She turned toward the shout to find Randolph standing a few feet away, his mouth wide enough to catch the dust from the retreating wheels of the wagon that had almost killed her. She had known Randolph Burton since childhood, and he had always been a fastidious sort of person. But this morning, his normally well-waxed hair hung in tufted blond clumps around his face, and his necktie was rumpled and askew.

Georgette had never seen him look so disheveled, or so dear.

He lurched toward her and she welcomed his familiar clasp on her elbow. "Cousin," she murmured, placing a grateful hand in his proffered one.

The touch of skin on skin was jolting. She had left her gloves in the room at the inn, if indeed she had even worn them last night. The reminder of just how far she had stepped outside of propriety, and the realization that she honestly didn't know what she might have done, tightened her fingers in a fierce grip. Just a few days ago she shrank from Randolph's touch, not wanting to encourage his fumbling interest.

Now, she didn't care. She wanted only to lean on someone who could whisk her away from this place and these circumstances. "I am happy to see you," she choked out.

He swallowed, the motion visible between the drooping edges of his en pointe collar. "You . . . you are truly happy to see me? Then why are you crying?"

Georgette swiped at her eyes. "You cannot imagine how glad, Randolph. You are the first familiar face I have seen today. I have no idea where I am, but if you are here, I must presume we are in Moraig."

He swallowed again. "Er . . . yes." His gaze scraped her skin. "Where have you been all night, Georgette?"

Her initial relief faltered at that. She pulled her hand from his grasp. Of course there would be questions. Not even Randolph—bumbling, oblivious man that he was—could accept her appearance this morning without wondering. "I . . ." She wiped her sweating palms on her skirts and shook her head. She could not say. It was too shaming, and far too intimate to share with her cousin.

A man in a top hat walked by on the opposite side

of the street and called out a hullo, to which of them Georgette could not be sure. Randolph raised a hand to the man before turning his attention back to her. "I have looked for you all night," he said, his voice dropping to a fierce whisper. "I was worried about you, desperately so. I was just on my way to the authorities when I saw you in the street."

The thought of her cousin reporting her evening's escapade to anyone, authority or no, made her pulse pound out a terrified objection. Georgette found a false smile and stretched it across her teeth. "No need for that." She willed him to believe her. "Here I am, safe and sound."

Randolph's thin brow rose. "Truly? Where did you spend the evening?"

This was a delicate matter. Clearly, things were not right here, but she loathed revealing the exact circumstances of her morning to Randolph. "I . . . I was hoping you could tell me that," she admitted.

He squinted down, concern flooding the gray eyes she knew matched the color of her own. Instead of answering her, his gaze pulled down in the vicinity of her bodice and lingered there. His face colored, a ruddy confection of capillaries and shock that sent her toes curling inward with shame.

"Where is your . . . er . . . corset?" he asked.

As if on cue, the kitten started to squirm. Georgette winced in mortification as tiny claws punched through the front of her bodice. "I would rather not say."

For a moment he leveled a mystified stare at the space where she had stashed her little passenger. Then his face went from red to white in a heartbeat. "Dear God!" he gasped. "Have you been assaulted?"

She shook her head, despair clutching at her chest as

sharply as the kitten's needlelike claws. "No," she whispered. "I do not think so." Whatever else her mysterious Scotsman's sins, she did not think she had been an unwilling party in the night's festivities, not when her body flushed every time she thought of him. "How did I come to be here?" She sighed, pressing her fingers into her temples.

"On the street?"

"In town!" she snapped.

Randolph stuttered a moment. "Wha-what is the last thing you recall?"

Georgette closed her eyes. She remembered putting on the dress she now wore, a dove gray silk that was only just barely a step above mourning. She recalled struggling with the mother-of-pearl buttons, and her consternation that Randolph had neglected to provide her with the promised maid. Not so much for the convenience of the thing, but the propriety of the matter. She didn't like being alone with Randolph, had wanted the buffer another human being would provide over afternoon tea.

She opened her eyes. "I remember taking tea with you. We had those ginger biscuits." She recalled choking them down with an artificial smile plastered on her face. Hard as river stones, those cookies had been. Although Randolph possessed an almost frighteningly accurate knowledge of the historical and medicinal uses of aromatic herbs, his ability to translate such knowledge into something edible was suspect.

"And what next?" Randolph pressed, looking a sickly white.

She squirmed, trying to sort through the mental fog. A new memory surfaced, clear as daylight on water. Of Randolph twisting nervously in front of her near the hearth, saying, "Dearest Georgette, you are a woman of no small means. Now that you are out of mourning, there will be those who would take advantage. Let me be the one to protect you."

"You asked me to marry you." She remembered the taste of panic in her mouth that had accompanied his fumbled proposal. "And I explained why I could not."

Randolph winced, his eyes squinting owllike over his spectacles. She regretted hurting him then, and she regretted hurting him now. But she had come to Scotland for a respite, not an offer of marriage. That he thought she needed protecting had perturbed her at the time.

That he might have been right shattered her now.

"So *that* you can remember." His voice hung thick with regret.

"Yes." Georgette blew a hot breath between her teeth. "Then . . . nothing." She searched and came up empty. It was a maddening affair, to not know what she might have said or done. Why, anything could have happened. Anything at all.

She almost laughed. It was necessary to keep from catching on a sob.

"We went out," Randolph offered, his fingers gripping her arm to steady her.

"Out?" she echoed.

He nodded. "After tea, we came to Moraig to attend evening services at St. John's."

"But why would I not remember that?" Georgette protested.

Randolph shook his head and took in a none-too-appreciative sniff. "I suspect it is because of the brandy."

Georgette's eyes widened. "I do not like brandy." A warning began to pound in her ears.

Randolph smiled, and for the first time that morning he appeared positively smug. "That did not stop you from having two—no, I believe it was three glasses yesterday evening, before we departed."

She gasped. "That . . . that isn't possible!" Surely she would remember doing something so out of character. Then again, she couldn't remember getting married, or crawling into bed with a deliciously proportioned Scotsman either.

Randolph leaned in, so close she could see the hairs that escaped his nostrils and the lines of exhaustion under his eyes. She had to resist the urge to back away from him. "Perhaps you were upset over our discussion, Georgette. Perhaps you were rethinking such a strong opinion, realizing how positive a match between us might be. I honestly do not know what was trotting around your head—I scarcely ever do. I tried to dissuade you, after the first glass, but you said you had come to Scotland to break free, to try new things."

Guilt squirmed in her stomach. She could sense the disapproval falling off her cousin's thin shoulders. She didn't want to believe it, but this part of the conversation rang all too true. It echoed her secret thoughts and dreams, dreams she had kept hidden her entire life, even during her very proper come-out and the subsequent disappointment of her marriage.

Worse, with Randolph supplying the details, she remembered the first glass, now. And, dear God, it *had* been brandy.

"If it was your first experience with strong spirits," he said, "is it any wonder you can't remember?"

"I . . . I suppose you are right," she breathed, shaken to her core.

"Perhaps it is better to just focus on the future, rather than on the events of yesterday." He covered a sudden yawn with one hand. "Given your appearance this morning, it might be something better forgotten, hmmm?"

Georgette wanted to agree. Randolph was being so nice, so understanding, it quite made her feel worse. He had lost sleep looking for her, while she had been out all night carousing and collecting orphaned kittens and forgetting her corset. But even as she turned herself over to the idea of banishing all thoughts of the man with whom she had awakened, an image of straight white teeth flashed into her mind. Had those teeth grazed her hot skin and nipped at the hidden recesses of her body last night? She had never imagined such a thing, had never even let her husband touch her so inappropriately. Her entire body flushed, as if objecting to the very idea of letting go of the false memory.

She wasn't sure she *could* forget the way her Scotsman had looked on waking this morning. His lips had curved with wicked intent, just a shade higher on the left side than the right. His eyes had been the color of new grass, and just as fresh. No, wasn't sure she could forget him.

Or that she wanted to.

Oblivious to her discomfort or the direction of her inappropriate thoughts, Randolph pulled her toward a waiting curricle. She let him lead, her hand still curved around his. He had not pressed her for more details. Her secret was safe. Relief trailed her, though it did little to lessen the guilt.

"I need only to speak with Reverend Ramsey," Randolph said amiably as they walked, his words as light and fluffy as the clouds crowding the morning horizon, "and we can be married by tomorrow."

Georgette dug her thin-soled slippers into the pavement and pulled them to a graceless halt. It wasn't the words that jarred her as much as the arrogant assurance in her cousin's voice. Panic scratched beneath her skin, panic of an entirely different sort than had sent her fleeing the brawny Scotsman this morning. Whereas that man had set her feet running because she feared her body's unwanted, jolting response to the sight of his bare chest, the thought of intimacy with *this* man made her want to curl into a tight, protective ball that could not be breached. "We shall do no such thing," she choked out. "As I explained yesterday, I have no wish to marry you."

Randolph turned on her then, his gray eyes flashing. "That was before you stayed out all night and drank yourself into a stupor, cousin. Before you did God knows what with God knows who." He pushed his spectacles up the narrow plank of his nose. "That was before Reverend Ramsey called out hullo on the street, and saw us both looking as we do. You have precious little to recommend you except your reputation, Georgette, and you have done a frightfully poor job protecting it. You are lucky I care for you enough to still offer for you, after the evening you appear to have enjoyed. You should be thanking me."

Georgette gasped and pulled her hand from fingers that suddenly felt closer to talons. "I cannot marry you," she hissed. That was not the complete truth, she realized as she stared at a muscle jumping angrily above her cousin's pale brow. She didn't *want* to marry him.

Where was a chamber pot when you needed one?

"You can and you shall marry me." Randolph leaned in, his earlier familiarity escalating from something comforting to vulgar. "Everyone will believe you spent the night with me," he went on, his voice an eager rasp. "Reverend Ramsey will have surely repeated it by now. And when you see how much you have to lose, I imagine you will happily say your vows."

Anger splintered her rising panic. Randolph was the second man this morning who had tried to twist her to his will, the third if you counted the butcher who had foisted the kitten upon her. She was heartily tired of playing the biddable lady and doing what everyone expected of her. And the thought of marriage to Randolph, with all his panting insecurities, filled her with revulsion. She knew of only one way to dissuade him.

"It is too late," she blurted out. Her voice was surprisingly steady, given the shaking of her limbs. "I appear to have gotten married last night."

There. She had given voice to the terrible thing she had done. Randolph would be disappointed, but at least he would no longer be so desperate as to keep asking for her hand. And she felt sure he would not tell anyone *why* they could not marry. He was her cousin. He valued her enough to have offered for her, had only said those terrible things because he wanted to marry her. He would guard her honor. She was sure of it.

"Why do you believe you are married?" he asked, his voice very close to a growl.

"I awoke this morning next to a stranger who called me his wife," she admitted, wishing it did not sound so . . . unseemly. "And there is this." She twisted the ring around on her finger.

There was a beat of silence as Randolph stared down at the bit of gold. While he had been expressive throughout their earlier exchange, he now seemed hewn from granite. Clearly her unflappable cousin was in shock. She knew *she* still was. Why, yesterday he had done no more than wince when she had turned him down, but this morning he was frozen by the news of her evening's escapades. He was no doubt wondering about her sanity, measuring her against the standards of Society and finding her lacking.

She was a proper lady, or at least she had been yesterday.

But she had a sinking feeling she would never deserve that title again.

Chapter 3

"CAN YOU HEAR me, you sodding fool?"

Though better sense bade him not to, James Mac-Kenzie opened his eyes. His brother William loomed over him, as fierce and wild as their ancestors must have looked when they fought against Edward I. William's face held a smirk and his fingers curved around shards of white pottery. Once upon a time, James would have put a fist to his older brother's clean-shaven jaw in response to the insult. But that was a lifetime ago. He was a man now, with a measure of self-control. Besides, something about the oddity of waking to William's none-too-handsome face told him that now was not the right moment for such childish antics.

"Bugger off," James moaned, his head a mass of mangled thoughts and pain. "Can you not see I am sick?"

William hefted the ruined bit of china and dangled it above James's nose. "I confess that was my first thought, but by the looks of things here, it seems you have put the chamber pot to a different use." He frowned a moment, the motion looking more like a grimace. "Injured, is more like it. Did you get in a fight with your piss pot, then?"

James squinted up at his brother, absorbing his words

like water into sand. As a fledgling solicitor, his life was built on seeing the truth behind a set of given facts, but he was damned if William's remarks made any kind of sense. He had spent yesterday bent over his desk sorting out the proper legal precedent for damages over a mixed-breed bull jumping the fence to impregnate someone's prizewinning heifer. His evening had consisted of dinner and several draughts of ale in the local pub house. Now he felt as if he had been hauled in from the knacker's.

What had any of that to do with a ruined chamber pot?

"You don't know what you are talking about." James started to shake his head and then decided better of it. Life seemed so much easier when his brain wasn't bouncing around his skull.

"Oh that's rich, coming from a man who doesn't know where his boots are." William tossed a pair of battered footwear onto the bed. " 'Tis a bonny nap you've had, nigh on two hours since dawn. But the innkeeper insists on your removal now, I am afraid."

"Innkeeper?" James sat up and waited until his chest stopped heaving and the walls stopped bending toward corners. "Is that where I am?" He swung his bare legs off the edge of the mattress and hefted his barer arse off the bed, for once grateful for William's brute strength as his brother caught him in a forward pitch. The floorboards crunched under his feet, and the sharp, sweet odor in the air gave him pause.

Christ, had he smashed a bottle of brandy on the floor last night? He peered around the room, took in the ruined wardrobe, the upturned washbasin. Feathers floated in the air and stuck to the walls. A woman's corset hung from the drapery rod, something plain and demure but oddly beautiful for its lack of adornment. There was no denying the room looked as if a bloody good party had taken place.

"I hope she was worth it, you daft fool," William snorted.

"Who was worth it?" James muttered, grabbing his shirt from the floor.

"The woman you brought up here last night."

James stiffened against the slide of fabric across his chest. The shirt seemed different. It smelled of brandy, and an exotic fragrance that he could not quite name. "What woman?" he managed, starting in on his buttons. "And where in the bloody hell am I?"

"The Blue Gander." His brother chuckled. "And the woman you married last night."

That froze James's progress more efficiently than had his hands been tied. What William was suggesting was impossibly vile. He was not someone who married women he didn't know. "What in the hell are you talking about?"

"Oh, stop your sniveling outrage," William chortled. The obvious glee on his face sent James's fingers curling into a tight fist around the edges of his shirt. "It wasn't a real marriage."

James managed to raise one brow. This, at least, was familiar. He was used to being teased, by William in particular. Perhaps his brother had even cracked him over the head with the chamber pot himself, although that would admittedly be beyond the pale. "Put your wasted Cambridge education to work and attempt to formulate a complete sentence," he growled. "What are you talking about?"

"I am simply telling you what I heard when I stopped

by your rooms this morning looking for you," William qualified. "I don't know what went on last night, but your friend was right full of information and all too willing to share. I came here to see for myself."

"Have you been checking up on me?" Anger spliced through the pounding of James's skull at the mention of his friend. Patrick Channing shared a set of rooms with him on the east side of Moraig, a necessity when you struggled to save every penny your fingers touched. More to the point, Patrick had shared several of those pints he recalled from last night.

But neither explained why his family was poking about his business.

"Someone needs to make sure you don't kill yourself," William retorted. "Channing said you didn't come home last night, so I thought I'd better look in at the Gander. The innkeeper sent me right on up." He tilted his head, a flash of sympathy skirting his usually hard features. "Ah, Jamie-boy. Happens to the best of us. There's no denying you are in a sorry state for having gone sniffing after the wrong woman. You are bleeding all over the sheets."

"The devil you say!" James pushed his hand to his right temple, then immediately regretted his haste as he located at least one source of his discomfort. "Oh! Ow." He sucked in a breath as shards of memory, as fragmented as the bit of pottery in William's hands, danced behind his skull.

"Aye, it's a right fine one she gave you," William nodded.

James's fingers came away sticky with partially congealed blood. He held them up to his eyes and his usually faithful stomach pitched like a child's toy boat in a stern gale. Someone—apparently a *female* someone—had given him a right good rap to the skull. He shook his head, trying to focus the pieces of memory that refused to fall into place as a result of the injury. His remembrance of how he had come to be here was as wrinkled as the shirt he had just buttoned. He could recall his bloody name. His recollections of his past were there too, bright and vivid and lamentable. Even his brother's none-too-handsome face seemed as familiar as his own skin.

He just couldn't remember her.

"Who was she?" James choked out. Whoever she was, the woman appeared to harbor a violent streak. Perhaps he should count himself fortunate to come out of the encounter breathing. But even as he considered the evidence, a ghost of a memory tickled at his anger. Nymph-white hair, dancing in candlelight. Wide gray eyes. A wide, laughing mouth. *On him*. He swallowed hard.

The woman had attacked him. What she might or might not have done before the assault bore no relevance.

"According to your friend Patrick, she wasn't the queen, but about as high and mighty, and twice as pretty. Lucky bastard." William tossed him his trousers. "Although unlucky might be a better title, given how things have turned up."

James struggled into his trousers, one unsteady leg at a time. "Never was one for titles," he breathed.

"Just because you do not have a title does not mean you do not have means, Jamie. 'Tis not your family's fault you were born too pigheaded to see reason, and so determined to make your own way no matter the cost. Besides, this griping about not liking titles could not have helped you with the lady in question. Why, it's no wonder she departed under such questionable circumstances. Couldn't stand the Highland stink of you, I would wager."

James sat down and fumbled to get his boots over his sockless feet. "I . . . I can't remember." The memory that tugged at him was too opaque for clarity, but something told him his partner of the previous evening hadn't objected to his origins in the slightest.

"Getting soused will do that to you."

James fought back a snarl. William's yammering was starting to match the pounding above his temple. "I had a few, but I was not tumbledown drunk, if that is what you are implying." He staggered to his feet and shrugged each protesting shoulder into his jacket. "And I've never forgotten a bloody thing before, not even when I have been falling down in my cups." The throbbing in his skull reached a new crescendo of pain. "I suspect my memory loss has more to do with my crushed skull than a glass too many last night."

"If you canna remember," William retorted, "it matters little either way."

Ignoring his brother, James stepped toward the window, his eye drawn by white linen. The floor crunched menacingly beneath his feet. He wondered if his companion of last night had cut her feet on the shards of glass upon waking. Somehow, the thought did not please him as much as it should.

He peered up at the bit of clothing that had caught his attention. The corset he had spied earlier hung from the drapery rod like a demented flag. Up close he could see the fine stitching and silk ribbons that lined the edges. The edge of an ivory busk peeked out of the center pocket, tempting him with a hint of engraving. He lifted the entire garment from its mooring, tucked it under one arm, and headed for the door.

William's voice tickled his ear. "I don't think it's your size, Jamie-boy, which leaves me to wonder what you want with that bit of frippery. Memento of the evening you have forgotten? A spoil of war, perhaps?"

"It is a clue." James stepped gingerly into the hallway and peered down the dank, musty stairwell.

William's chuckle pierced the shadows that swept in from all sides. "Ah, like Cinderella's slipper."

James shook his head, which turned out to be a poor idea. The world spun on a broken axis, and he cursed beneath his breath. He hated feeling weak, out of control. It reminded him of how he had felt as a young man, striking out at and hating everyone and everything. He had worked too hard to overcome that feeling, just to sink back into it after one drunken night.

He focused on feeling his way along the sticky wall until the banister fit into his hand. "No, not like Cinderella. *She* didn't attack the prince the day after the ball. When I find the owner of this corset, I will find the woman who assaulted me." He turned his head back to his brother and offered a grim promise. "And then I will know who to prosecute."

"Oh, aye, that's rich." William laughed. "Let the town know you can't handle one wee lass in your bed." A thick black brow rose in amusement. "And how are you going to find this woman? Are you going to strap the bloody thing on every girl you see until you find the one that fits? Do you need me to hold each one down while you try it on for size?"

James turned away from his brother's taunts, concentrating instead on putting one unsteady foot in front of the other. He knew the value of a good clue. The busk alone was a promising lead. Perhaps it bore an inscription or etching that might hint at the owner's identity. He imagined his bed partner tripping this way only a few hours earlier without her corset. He wondered if she, at least, had a headful of memories to warm her nights for her trouble. It didn't seem fair that he should be left with so little of her, just the feminine garment beneath his arm and the smell of her skin on his shirt.

He reminded himself she had hit him. *With a chamber pot.* If that wasn't a statement of some sort, he was a donkey's arse.

He focused on feeling his way to the inn's front desk. No matter what happened last night, he did not deserve to be assaulted. If history was any guide, she had been an all too willing partner, and he would have done his best to make it memorable for her. But this business about being married, or pretending to . . . it didn't sit well with him. He was a man of the law, dependent on a certain trust among Moraig's citizens for his practice. If he had demonstrated some culpability, or been seen exercising such questionable judgment last night . . . well, it needed to be sorted out, and quickly.

The inn's proprietor stopped them on the threshold to the street. "Ah, Mr. MacKenzie." The man's smile did not reach his eyes. "You weren't trying to sneak out again without covering your damages, were you?"

James breathed out through his nose. "Damages?"

"Oh, aye. You had quite a time in the public room last night, just before you snuck out the first time. Never say you don't recall."

James met William's gaze over the little man's balding pate. William shook his head and lifted a finger to his lips.

Every fiber of James's being told him he was not the only party responsible for the events of last night. But short of admitting he could not remember, he could see no way clear. "I am terribly sorry for any trouble. How much was that again?"

The innkeeper's shoulders relaxed a bit. "Five pounds should cover it."

James gave an incredulous laugh. "Five pounds? That is robbery, man!"

The innkeeper shook his head. "You smashed the entire front row of windows out on the north side. Destroyed a table and a set of four chairs. Knocked out the butcher's front teeth. Had him bleeding all over my public house."

The silence that followed the man's pronouncement roared in James's ear. What the innkeeper was suggesting was impossible. But a faint scratching of his conscience told him *something* had happened. The town's butcher was formidably built, and not a man he would normally invite to brawl, even deep in his cups. "Well, did he deserve it?" was all he could think to say.

"He deserves an apology." The innkeeper crossed his arms over his chest.

James was mollified. If he had created such a public spectacle last night, he needed to invest in some damage control. Between the butcher and the innkeeper, the pair knew everyone in town. "All right," he admitted. "But five pounds seems like a bloody lot of money for a few windows and some furniture."

"The lady bought several rounds for all the patrons," the innkeeper said.

James blinked. "The cost of those drinks is the lady's responsibility, is it not?"

"The lady is not here," the proprietor countered, "and there was a roomful of happy customers last night who can attest you stood up and claimed responsibility for the lady's offer. And then, of course, there is the cost of the room."

"I accompanied the lady to *her* room." James knew it wasn't chivalrous, but something in him balked at the innkeeper's presumption. He had a perfectly good house and a perfectly good bed that he paid rent toward each month. "She did not cover the cost of the room when she departed?" he asked, his throat thick with irritation.

The innkeeper shook his head, the very picture of an affronted businessman.

"Do you happen to know the lady's name?" James wanted a name to attach to his new flash of annoyance.

The innkeeper hesitated. It was clear as the birthmark on the man's right cheek he didn't know the lady's name either. "Er . . . *Mrs.* MacKenzie, wasn't it?"

Behind him, William chuckled. James's fingers tightened to fists. "She is not my wife." At least, he didn't think she was.

The innkeeper cocked his head and his feet spread out mulishly. "'Tis not my business, Mr. MacKenzie, but you do the lady a disservice. If you have misplaced her, 'tis no one's fault but your own. Treat your wife with a bit more respect, and she will be more likely to stay 'round come morning."

"It is not your affair," James ground out. "You know nothing about it."

But the man was not yet done with him. "I suppose, out of all the MacKenzies, it would be you to do this.

Your father, Lord Kilmartie, would never be involved in the likes of this."

"I am not my father." The old familiar beat of guilt began to pound in James's chest. "And she is not my wife," he repeated again, this time through tightly clenched teeth.

"And I did not stumble into town yesterday, sir." The innkeeper's cheeks had gone ruddy. "Last night was an odd state of affairs, I will rightly admit, and I am sorry for it. But I *will* have my five pounds."

James felt near to boiling over. Only William's big hand on his shoulder stayed him. The woman in question had assaulted him before she had sashayed out the door and left him with her bill, and the proprietor was lecturing *him* on respect? If he had been better rested, he would have lodged a more effective argument. Arguing the facts was what he did best, after all. But his brain was still fuzzy, and he reluctantly acknowledged he was tired enough to cut his losses. Anything to escape the stink of the place, and the memory—or lack of memory—of the woman who had brought him so low.

James ran a hand over his jacket. His account ledger was in its usual place, stashed in the left pocket of his coat. He remembered going over his practice's accounts the day before, and intending to make a deposit at the bank, only to arrive—as usual—five minutes past closing. He dipped into his right pocket to find the ivory-inlaid cuff links his mother had given him for Christmas.

But something was missing. He forced his eyes to meet William's. "Have you seen my money purse?"

William let out a low whistle. "She took your purse?"

"That depends," James said slowly. "Did you *see* it in the room?"

They returned to the scene of his downfall, accompanied by the inn's proprietor. Together they searched. Pulled back the bedclothes and looked under the bed. Rummaged through the ruined wardrobe. There wasn't much space in the cramped room, and deucedly few places a full money purse could hide.

"It's not here," James finally admitted.

"Aye, and now that I've seen your room, the bill is now six pounds." The innkeeper swept an arm around the scene.

William dutifully pulled out his own purse and counted out the outrageous sum the innkeeper claimed was due. It made James want to smash something to see his brother hand over money on his behalf.

"I'll pay you back," he choked out.

"No need, Jamie-boy. Only too happy to help." William leaned in close. "I only require your everlasting gratitude, of course."

"You'll have the money," he growled. There was no way he was giving William the satisfaction of bailing him out without repayment. Confusion and resentment fell away to anger as reality set in. That damned missing purse had contained over fifty pounds, the equivalent of a half year's salary given his current slow rate of practice. And she had taken it.

It did not matter if she had the face of a fairy sprite, or the mouth of a courtesan. It did not matter if she had given him a cockstand *and* a headache. There was more at stake here than regaining his memory or his pride.

The purse his evening's escort had absconded with held more than mere money. He had been scraping and saving with only one goal in mind, a goal that now seemed to have been stripped from his reach. There were surely worse things than serving as a solicitor in a little town like Moraig, but in the year he had been practicing here he hadn't found a single one.

He dreamed of establishing a practice in London. But setting up a practice took money, and in Moraig, soliciting didn't pay. Or, at least, it didn't pay *him*. Too often, townsfolk looked at him and saw only the miscreant youth James had once been, and now that he was doling out legal advice, his past proved difficult for some of Moraig's residents to forgive. Worse, the town's currency was little more than eggs and salted pork, and James had little to do other than negotiate the tedious thread of life running through this sleepy village. Sometimes James was tempted to strangle someone, just for the privilege of finally having a real trial to attend.

He *needed* that money, or he was set six months back. Needed it, or he would be stuck in Moraig, fighting his history and being heckled by William for the rest of his life. The flash of resentment he felt now toward the pale, angelic vision that haunted his mind made his earlier irritation seem like mere chafing.

He wasn't dealing with just a heartless wench who had taken him to bed and then awakened with buyer's remorse.

He was dealing with a bloody thief.

And he would see her hang.

Chapter 4

Georgette stared gloomily at the house Randolph had leased for the summer. In his letter some weeks ago inviting her for this visit, her cousin had mentioned neither the house's small size nor its isolation. It lay on the grounds of a larger, more reputable estate. Like many in Scotland, the house sported a traditional thatched roof and small, dank rooms. The fireplace leaked smoke, coating the furniture with gray soot and making the upholstered furniture smell perpetually of winter even though it was newly May.

The most that could be recommended of it was that it made one very much want to spend more time out of doors.

She had been disappointed when she had first seen it and realized her two-week holiday was to be spent brushing shoulders with Randolph in such tight quarters, without benefit of a maid or female companion. The cousin she remembered preferred marble foyers and fine china and a bevy of domestic servants. That he had leased a house best suited for said servants' quarters bespoke either a lapse in the man's financial well-being, or a significant change in his tolerance of such things.

She was no longer sure she knew or understood the

pale, brooding young man beside her. They had once been close, but since he had set off for university some four years ago and she had been married off, they had seen each other very little. As her cousin's carriage jostled up the pitted drive, Georgette acknowledged that perhaps the house *did* fit Randolph's new scholarly image. He was supposed to be spending the summer prowling the surrounding acreage examining seed pods and root systems, not moldering away inside some old Scottish edifice.

"Are you sure you can't remember his name?" Randolph asked again as he reined in the curricle in front of the little stone structure.

Georgette bit her lip to keep from uttering the insult that came to mind. The same bookish instinct that Randolph applied to his study of Scottish flora had been summarily directed toward her since her hasty confession. Even the kitten seemed to object to Randolph's oft-repeated question, twisting and mewling within the confines of her bodice.

No, she didn't know the mysterious Scotsman's name, which meant she didn't know *her* name. "I cannot remember his name any more than I can recall the second and third glass of brandy I had last night," she retorted as she gathered her skirts.

A stooped figure lumbered from the shadows of the stable to assist her from the carriage. The one servant Randolph had seen fit to hire, other than the woman who came to cook every other day, was this grounds-man who also served as groom. He was a local, with weathered hands and the perpetual beard that Scotsmen seemed to prefer. The man lurked in the background and mucked out stalls and brought in the wood, but was helpless against the quarter-inch layer of dust that had accumulated inside the house. As she stepped down onto the springy loam of the yard, Georgette could not help but think, a bit uncharitably, that it was no wonder Randolph seemed so anxious to acquire a wife, with only this groom to ease his bachelor's existence.

"Good morning," she told the man, summoning the courage to put on a smile.

The servant's gaze darted toward Randolph, who was clambering down from his side of the curricle. No doubt he was wondering where they had been all night—not that he was the only one. " 'Tis good to see you safely returned, Lady Thorold."

Georgette winced. Only yesterday, that had been her name. She had been accepting of her title and her future. She had a comfortable inheritance that was hers to control and a new life waiting without the bonds of an unpredictable and often drunk husband. True, she was lonely at times, but widowhood had much to recommend it. She was finally out of mourning and she intended to explore her newfound freedom.

But today she was no longer so certain who she was. The groom's deference aside, she was no longer Lady Thorold. If her suspicions regarding how she had acted last night were correct, she was no longer a lady. Everything had changed. *She* had changed.

And she only wanted to pretend it had never happened.

Instead of correcting the servant's presumption, she asked, "Has anyone come by today? The cook, perhaps?" She cupped a hand around the fabric that held the kitten, still curled up between her breasts. Though her own stomach was not up to the task of breaking her fast, the little thing needed milk. Although, to her recollection, the cook had not brought a bottle of milk during her previous visit. Her cousin was vocally averse to dairy, claiming it affected his bowels in a disagreeable fashion. It had not occurred to her when she had accepted the little burden that such luxuries would be as hard to find at Randolph's home as ladies' maids.

"No, miss." The groom shook his head. " 'Tis Mrs. Pue's day off."

Concern for the kitten tugged at her. It was but a bit of fur and claw, and it would certainly not survive long without sustenance.

The servant looked nervous. "But there is—"

"There is bread and cheese in the larder," Randolph interrupted, coming around to stand too close. He handed the reins to the servant, who, after casting an uncertain glance toward Georgette, began to unhook the traces from the swaybacked gray mare.

"It is a blessing Mrs. Pue is not here to see you looking like this," Randolph went on, pulling her to the side and whispering fiercely. "Why, the woman is a notorious gossip and would spread the tale far and near." His gaze scoured her misshapen neckline. "You look shameful, Georgette. And I think just the bread for you this morning. It is clear you cannot be trusted to have a care for yourself, and I do not want to have to clean up after you when your stomach objects to heavy fare."

His cutting words stung. Georgette forced herself to stand still, to bear the heavy touch of his hand. Randolph scolded her as if he had a right to do so. Her husband had used just that tone, all too frequently. She was never good enough. Never obedient enough. Never desirable enough. Nausea pricked at her like a needle threaded with painful memories. Her husband stumbling home, another woman's scent on his skin.

Her husband trying to touch her, and her pulling away.

The vicious doubts her life as a married woman had conjured had not disappeared with her husband's untimely, drunken death. She had felt inadequate then, a failure as a wife. She felt inadequate now, a failure as a woman. What sort of lady spent a forgotten evening frolicking with a stranger, but could not bring herself to bear a husband's touch? Perhaps that was why her husband drank so much during their short time together. To forget his disappointment in his wife.

Perhaps that was why she drank last night—to forget her cousin's similarities to her dead spouse.

But she was no longer a wife. At least, she was not *Randolph's* wife. He had no right to speak to her as if she was. Georgette drew herself up. "It is my mistake, and my problem. We are not married, and you do not control me." Resentment colored her voice. It felt good to speak so directly after a morning mired in guilt.

Randolph's eyes narrowed, making his nose appear a thin, sharp hook. "I daresay if you had married *me* you would be enjoying the morning a bit more."

Bile, hot and acrid, knocked against the back of her throat. The idea of sharing a bed with her cousin made her knees buckle in revulsion. She could not imagine doing with Randolph what she had apparently done with her mysterious bed partner.

"I did not say my morning was without enjoyment." The words were out of her mouth before she could stop them. But it was the truth. On some level, she *had* enjoyed the view of her naked, brawny Scotsman this morning, more so than she was enjoying the course of the current conversation.

Randolph's eyes bulged behind his spectacles, bringing to mind a myopic frog. "Acting the lightskirt does not become you, cousin." The light pressure on her arm shifted to a forceful push on her elbow. "Go inside while I sort out what to do about you and this marriage you have gotten yourself into."

Georgette stayed planted in place. "There is nothing to sort out." She pulled away from the unwelcome pressure of his fingers. "We shall pretend it did not happen. I cannot remember who the man is, and I do not wish to." The idea of escape beckoned, and she gratefully turned herself over to it. "I shall return to London immediately, and neither of us need speak of this ever again."

Randolph's face turned a mottled shade of red, making his blond hair almost seem to glow in contrast. "You cannot be that naïve," he snapped. "You cannot simply hie yourself back to London and pretend a marriage didn't happen, Georgette. What if you wished to marry again? Would you add bigamy to your crimes?"

Georgette stiffened with shock. She had never heard Randolph say such mean-spirited things, not even as a carelessly cruel child. "What crime?" she protested. "I am a widow, and past mourning. 'Tis no crime to seek an evening's pleasure. And I will not marry again, so I do not see . . ."

"If you do not track him down and annul the thing, the man will have access to your fortune," Randolph interrupted. He canted his pale head and took a menacing step closer. He enunciated slowly, as if she was a dim-witted child. "There is more at stake here than memory, Georgette. You have thrown away your future on a man you do not know."

She chose to ignore the condescension in his tone and

focused on the message. It was the first time Randolph had mentioned her marriage settlement, which would be controlled by a new husband on marriage. She thought of those funds sitting safely in the coffers of the Bank of London. Thought of what a new, living husband could do to them.

And she was stunned to silence.

She had not thought this morning, had simply run. But she could see, reluctantly, that Randolph was right in this. She needed an annulment, or she would risk her future to a man who appeared nothing of the gentleman.

And to procure an annulment, she needed to first find out who her Scotsman was.

"My God," she breathed. "You are right."

"Of course I am right." The smile Randolph offered seemed to grip his face in a painful embrace. "And if you had only taken me up on my offer last night, you would not be in this muddle."

Georgette shuddered against the venom that laced her cousin's words. A niggling thought surfaced, one that refused to be pushed away. Randolph, for all his uttered contrivances about wanting to protect her, seemed a little too focused on the financial difficulties of her impulsive night. She looked around, wondering where the groom had gotten off to. Her cousin's interest bordered on indecent at times, and she wanted a body to step behind if the need arose. She spied the man leading the horse to the stable, within shouting distance if the circumstances called for it. She was reminded again that her decision to stay here, without proper escort, had quite possibly given Randolph inappropriate ideas about her own interest.

She curled her fingers into her palms and dug until it hurt. "How do you propose we find him?"

"There is no 'we' in this. *I* will find him, and you will stay here and resist doing further damage."

"But you do not know his name," she protested. "You do not even know what he looks like. This is my fault, and it is my responsibility to undo it." She worried the gold ring on her finger, the only piece of tangible evidence left from her eventful but ultimately unmemorable evening.

Unless she was pregnant. Her toes clenched in her slippers as she considered such a fate. Dear God, she had not even considered that possible outcome when she had fled the scene this morning. She could not go through such a thing again, could not survive it.

So why did a part of her seize up at the terrifying, tantalizing thought?

As she stood frozen, her silent thoughts locked up tight, Randolph's gaze fell on her hand. "Let me see the ring."

Georgette drew back, startled. "I beg your pardon?"

"The ring." Without waiting for her concurrence, he snatched up her hand and inspected the stamped gold seal, a heavily antlered stag on a shield.

"Do you recognize it?" Georgette choked out.

His fingers tightened around hers, and his mustached upper lip thinned to a razor's edge. "Did the man have a beard, or no?"

"He had a beard," Georgette, answered, confused by the question, unsure how that narrowed the field. What man in Scotland *didn't* sport a ragged, filthy beard? "Why do you ask?"

Randolph flung away her hand without answering. "Saddle the mare immediately," he shouted to the groom, who had just emerged from the little stone stable. "I will ride out from here without the curricle."

Georgette burrowed her hand and the ring in the safety of her skirts. "You are leaving me here?" she accused. "*Alone?*"

"I am securing our future." Randolph pivoted toward the startled groom. "A future which you seem all too willing to toss away."

Georgette reached out a hand to stop him, but she clutched empty air. Her cousin was already striding toward the stables, his ungainly stride and loose-limbed posture the closest thing to a walking slouch. She watched him with a dawning sense of horror. Randolph thought he was securing their joint future, a future that she had repeatedly denied wanting. She thought of a lifetime spent with him and felt suffocated by the same certain sense of repulsion that had forced her objection to his offer—or insistence—of marriage earlier this morning.

In the end, she was left with no answers, and no further chance to protest. Randolph swung up on the aged mare, dug his heels to the beast's flank, and cantered off with the gracelessness of a man far more comfortable in a library than in a saddle. She watched him ride away with rising panic.

The sharp pleasant scent of the surrounding pine forest should have been a balm to almost any hurt, but she could feel nothing but panic. She had a kitten needing milk. A husband she didn't want and a pressing need to find him. And she was stuck here, without a horse, no idea where her cousin was going or when he would be back. Was Randolph trying to help her?

Or punish her?

The groom approached and they stood a long moment, watching Randolph disappear over a ridge. "Did he happen tell you where he was going?" Georgette asked despairingly. Her feet ached and her eyes pricked as if they were laced with sand. The journey from Moraig had taken less than an hour in a curricle, but the distance might as well be the length of London to attempt it on foot.

The big groom shook his head. "No, Mr. Burton did not say." He paused, and cast an apologetic look toward her, spreading his thick, work-roughened hands. "You have a visitor waiting for you, miss. I . . . I placed 'em in your bedroom. I thought it best not to mention it while Mr. Burton was in such a temper. I ken he will not approve of this one."

Georgette's throat threatened to swell closed over the groom's halting explanation. She had a visitor. The sort of visitor of which Randolph would not approve.

The sort of visitor who sent the great, burly servant's color high and his hands twisting at his side.

Whereas moments before she had been facing a long, hard walk back to Moraig, certainty thudded in her chest. She knew—she *knew*—her mystery Scotsman had come for her.

Randolph's threats and barbs fell away to an odd state of reassurance. If she could just speak with the man, she suspected she would find some answers, and of a better sort than those sought by her cousin, who was heading into town and tilting at shadows.

She whirled, her skirts in hand and the kitten bouncing in her bodice, and hurried toward the house. She stumbled into the sudden darkness, the rented cottage's musty interior balanced by the fragrance of dried herbs and sheaths of plant life Randolph hung to dry from the rafters. She tripped up the narrow staircase past portraits of unknown Scotsmen, thinking she was seeing the man whose image was branded on her brain in every one.

She paused on the threshold of her room, her hand on the latch, her heart pounding all the way to her ears. Scarcely ten minutes ago, she had been resolved to never see her evening's partner again. She could not explain her body's reaction now to the thought of doing just that. Green eyes and a strong, beard-framed jaw were burned into her memory, but the man's temperament was an unknown thing. The state in which she had left him had scarcely registered as she had bolted into the house, but now she paused, sucking in mouthfuls of herb-scented air. If he was here, surely he was none the worse for wear for the little incident with the chamber pot.

If he was here, surely he had forgiven her.

She hovered a moment, her hand a hairbreadth from knocking, pondering her choices. But what could she do beyond confront the man?

The door swung open, almost of its own volition, and Georgette stepped inside. Her skin felt flushed, her limbs loose with anticipation.

But instead of the man she expected—nay, *wanted*—to see, she was greeted by the sight of a woman lounging in a copper hip bath. The woman's head was stretched back, rich auburn hair damp and curling, her neck exposed to the ceiling. The unexpected joy that so recently kindled in Georgette's chest fell away to abject discomfiture.

Because the only thing she hated more than her own nudity was that of other people.

And this woman was clearly, unabashedly naked.

Chapter 5

Jᴀᴍᴇꜱ ꜱᴛᴇᴘᴘᴇᴅ ᴏᴜᴛ of the inn, still simmering with anger, only to find himself accosted by brilliant sunshine and happy citizens. Moraig was bustling, a seaside Scottish town fully in the throes of market day. All around him the town swirled, bits of business and pleasure being transacted on every corner.

Normally, James enjoyed a good market morning. It was one of the things he had missed most about Moraig during the ten years he had spent in Glasgow, apprenticing with a curmudgeon of a solicitor. For all its urban bustle, Glasgow had felt sterile to him after Moraig's small-town warmth. Market day was something to look forward to. It offered a chance to greet neighbors, to catch up on gossip, to snatch up a currant bun and hold its sticky sweetness between his teeth with the enthusiasm of the young man he had once been. It was one of the things that had called him home a year ago, when he had considered where to set up his first solo practice.

But the pleasures to be had on market day were meaningless to a man who couldn't even afford to pay his evening's debt. Six pounds was not a bloody lot of cash to someone like William, who was heir to the Kilmartie earldom.

But it was almost a month's salary to James, and money he could ill-afford to waste.

He settled his hat gingerly atop his head, taking care to place it so it covered the injury on his scalp without rubbing to further damage. As a result of its precarious perch, the hat provided precious little shade. He stood a moment, blinking and adjusting to the insistence of the day's sunlight. A sharp tap in his rib cage from William's elbow made his head jerk in annoyance and sparks dance behind his eyes. "What?"

"Nice bit of handiwork." William nodded to their left.

Despite his attempts to remember something of the night, James's recollection remained little more than a string of hazy pictures. But the jagged shards of glass beneath his feet and the row of smashed windows taunting him beneath the wooden Blue Gander sign gave life to his imagination. A disbelieving groan escaped him. He could see a maid with a busy broom in her hand through the ruined opening, and he could hear hammering coming from the depths of the building. The sound echoed inside his skull with fierce retribution.

Someone had enjoyed a rip-roaring good time last night, and according to the proprietor, it had been he.

On either side of them, a dozen townsfolk gawked and whispered. The same stab of guilt he had felt earlier at the mention of his father hit him now. This was no small mistake, to be swept under his mother's Persian rug and left forgotten. This was a fall from grace witnessed by half the town.

He stepped off the paved sidewalk and cursed again the ill-mannered female who had caused all this trouble. If he was going to be forced to pay six pounds for a night of violent debauchery, it seemed unfair that he couldn't fully remember the positive aspects of the evening. A few things lurked in his mind, knocking about like rocks in a tin bucket. His bed partner, whoever she was, had smelled of lemons under the scent of brandy, a sharp, pleasant combination of flavors that teased his senses. Even now, he could separate both fragrances from the collar of his shirt.

The unbidden thought occurred to him that he would have liked to have seen her *in* his shirt, the tails tangling around her knees. Despite the prevailing town opinion, he had never taken a woman to his bed indiscriminately, had always selected his bed partners with care and appreciation. The flashes of memory that lined his scattered thoughts told him she had been very fine, indeed.

He closed his eyes. He had a sense of a pert chin, gray eyes, and a soul-bending laugh that escaped her lips like a sudden breeze. He recalled the feel of her in his arms, vibrating against his chest as she had chuckled over something. His senses had been dulled by her brilliance.

He wondered if that had been before or after she filched his purse.

"Where to, Jamie-boy?" William asked as if they were out for a casual stroll and not stumbling from the scene of a crime. "The church, perhaps?"

James opened his eyes to confront his brother's amusement. "Whatever would I want to go to church for?"

"To seek forgiveness for last night's sins." William chuckled, an obscene sound that made James want to throttle him. His brother knew he hadn't set foot in a church in eleven years, not since that business with the rector, and James wasn't planning on having an epiphany today. He had but one thing on his mind, and that was to track down a woman he couldn't fully remember.

"Or maybe you'll find another woman there in need of marrying," William went on, apparently oblivious to how close he was hovering to a lethal outcome.

"I dinna marry her," James ground out, hating the way his Scottish burr came out. It was the stress of the morning, he knew. Though he fought hard against the telltale cadence, his heritage came sneaking out at the most inopportune times. He shoved it to the hidden place his own forced Cambridge education had drilled into him. "At least, I do not think I did." He enunciated with care, his uncertainty tucked around the improved bit of grammar.

William inclined his head then. "Should we make sure?"

"How do you propose we make sure of that?" James snapped. "I cannot remember shite about last night, nor of this morning either. *You* were not there, and I would bloody well rather dig a hole to Hades before I ask the innkeeper for any more information about what I may or may not have done." He paused for breath and near choked on his annoyance. "The man would probably charge me another six pounds for my trouble, only to tell me I married a man."

William's eyes widened in mock horror. "Was the girl a man, then?"

"Shut up and help me home," James muttered, shaking his head to clear away the thought that surfaced as a result of the absurd conversation. The sprite who featured in the snippets of memory he carried with him had been no man, nor mere girl either. For some reason, he remembered her breasts. Not her name. Not the sound of her voice.

But her breasts . . . ah, they had been glorious. Pale as new milk, with a delicate pattern of veins he had traced with his tongue. Quality breasts, those had been, the fully rounded tease of a woman. He regretted their loss almost as much as he regretted the disappearance of his purse.

Only he was damned well going to find his purse again. Her tits he was going to do his best to forget.

With his mind so inappropriately occupied, James stepped off into the street. The world slanted in a dizzying array of dust and noise, and only William's strong arms saved him from falling face-first into the business of Moraig's main thoroughfare. "Ach, Jamie," his brother muttered, hauling him vertical. "I don't think home is where I should take you, at least not the home I think you mean. You are not well, have taken a serious blow to the skull. Let me take you to Kilmartie Castle."

James recoiled against his brother's well-meant suggestion. Home. At least, his family's home, rather than the dreary little house he kept with Patrick a few miles outside of town. There was no way in hell he was going to Kilmartie Castle. Not with such uncertainty about the events of the previous evening.

Not when he was such a disappointment to the family that waited for him there.

"No." He fit the word between his lips, knowing he had never meant anything so much as this.

"Father might be able to help . . ."

"*No.*" He was relieved to hear his tone was stronger now, brooking no argument. It was his best impression of a solicitor, a "no" that would serve him well when and if he ever made it to London.

James shrugged off his brother's faithful arm and stepped out, more carefully this time, into the clogged artery that was Moraig's Main Street on market day. He dodged children and loose dogs and the odd steaming pile of horse manure. "Near as I can piece together," William called out from behind, "you made quite the spectacle last night. Don't you think Father will hear about your escapades soon enough?"

"Perhaps," James tossed back over his shoulder. "But I intend to have everything set to rights before it comes to that."

And he did. He was as determined to make his own way in this matter as he was determined to succeed in his chosen profession. And he would be beholden to himself and no one else, or by God he would die trying.

He tried very, very hard not to think about the fact that he currently owed William six pounds. He would take care of that injustice as soon as he could. But first, there was the little matter of procuring transportation.

James stopped on the edge of the paving stones at the far side of the street and twisted around in agitation. "Have you seen my horse?" he asked William as his brother caught up with him.

William's brown eyes crinkled at the edges, and concern colored his words. "I don't think you are in any condition to ride."

"And yet, that does not explain where I left Caesar," James snapped.

Together they turned in a circle, scrutinizing every four-legged animal in sight, and even a dog that was gnawing on some prize bit of refuse under a parked cart.

William gave a long, low whistle. "Did she take your horse too?"

For a moment, James gave himself over to the idea, but a clear memory asserted itself over the more tempting spectacle of calling foul. "Er . . . no." He shook his head. "The livery stable. I am quite sure I left him at the livery."

William clapped him between the shoulder blades. "Thank goodness. Didn't know how I was going to explain that one to Father." He laughed. "Wouldn't seem right, you losing the horse you first refused as Father's gift, and then negotiated to buy behind his back. Nearly sent the old man into an apoplectic fit, that one did. Quite the good joke." He came up for air from the chuckle-inducing memory. "Which livery?"

James let his mind massage the question a moment. There were two stables in town, and they were of highly disparate quality. His chestnut stallion was one of the few things of value in his life, and he was usually quite careful with the animal. "Cairn's, I should think."

But Caesar was not at Cairn's, and that left only Morrison's, a disreputable establishment on Bard Street characterized by weather-eaten wood and the distinctive odor of ammonia wafting out of the open stable door. A boy leaning against the wall of the derelict structure snapped to attention as they approached.

"Mr. MacKenzie," he said, "have you come for your horse?"

James looked at the boy skeptically. Despite the young groom's attentive response, this was clearly the sort of place that did not care much about appearances. The boy's shirt was untucked and ripped along the lower edge, and his chin was smeared with dirt or something less palatable. To James's mind, the cleanliness of the staff was a clear reflection of the condition of the stables.

He did not know what had possessed him to board a fine piece of horseflesh overnight at Morrison's Livery, any more than he knew what had possessed him to take to bed with a light-fingered doxy. Caesar had probably been fed moldy hay, or stabled next to a beast stricken with strangles. He would be lucky if the stallion didn't colic over the course of the coming day.

"Er . . . yes. Could you fetch him please?" James tapped an impatient boot in the dirt as the boy hesitated. The groom darted a nervous gaze between James and William. "Mr. Morrison said to have you settle the bill first."

That James apparently owed money here too should not have come as a surprise, but the reminder of what he could not pay stung. He was a man who prided himself on his self-sufficiency, and the thought of how deep in debt last night might have left him made him near break out in hives. "Just fetch my mount," he said, "and I will settle my bill when I make sure he has been well cared for."

The boy took a cautious step toward the depths of a straw-strewn alleyway that ran parallel to the entrance to the stables. "Mr. Morrison will have my hide if you leave without paying for the damages," he objected, his voice cracking under the weight of his competing obligations.

James paused in mid-breath. "What damages? And where are you going?"

The groom's eyes focused somewhere in the vicinity of James's boots, his eagerness suddenly more akin to nervousness. "The mews, out back. Had to tie your horse out there or risk my life."

"Tie him?" James objected. "Risk your life? *Caesar?* The horse is as gentle as a newborn calf. What kind of a groom can't handle a well-trained horse?"

The boy kicked at the dirt, his face as red as a gooseberry. "Your 'gentle' calf of a horse kicked out the back partition to the stables last night and tried to take a piece out of me, to boot." He gestured to his tattered shirt, and suddenly James saw the boy's dishevelment in a new light. "Never seen a horse so ill-tempered," he added. "Was a terror since the moment you dropped it here. Mr. Morrison says it will cost you too."

"How much?" James asked through clenched teeth.

"One pound, four pence." The boy sounded almost frightened to admit to such a fee, as well he should be. Caesar was a famously even-tempered stallion, a thick-boned mount that could take a fence with ease and was the envy of half the town. The idea that such a horse could turn this place on its head and make an adolescent groom cower was ludicrous. James was beginning to suspect the entire bloody town was either conspiring on how to separate him from his savings, or else having a good laugh behind his back. Neither would get him any closer to London.

James shuffled the corset from one arm to the other, and stretched his free hand toward his pocket, searching for the ivory cuff links he had felt there earlier. The groom's eyes narrowed on the corset. "Mr. Morrison dinna say anything about taking trade for it either, and that tiny thing isn't going to fit the Missus Morrison." He flushed to be imparting such delicate information, but plowed on. "She's expecting twins next month, you know."

James raised a brow. As if he would trade the one bloody clue he had.

"You fetch the horse," William broke in. "We'll scrape together the fee, and we'll make an exchange, nice and even-like."

The boy eyed them both, as if he suspected they might disappear on him, then darted down the alley. "What was that all about?" William muttered.

"Damned if I know." James squinted down the lane, half expecting Caesar to emerge as a fire-breathing dragon. "I . . . I will have to borrow the money if I can't barter my cuff links."

William smiled. "Of course." He amiably patted his coat pocket. "And I shall be only too happy to offer my aid. If you can bring yourself to say please, that is."

James worked his jaw around the objectionable word and found he could not say it.

"And in the Queen's English." William waved one finger in front of James's nose. "It does not count if you say it like a Frenchie."

"Please, you son of a—" James pulled up in astonishment as the young groom emerged from the dark alley dragging a saddled horse behind him. The oddity of the morning's exchange fell into place as the boy dodged a near miss of clicking teeth and dancing hooves.

The moment called for something dramatic, but James was at a loss for what a proper reaction should be. Beside him, William started laughing, hearty guffaws that made the groom pink up in ignorant embarrassment and the anger churn red in James's stomach. Of *course* this horse kicked down a stable wall. Of *course*

James had left it here in a state of dim remembrance. It fit perfectly with the ridiculousness of the rest of his evening's activities.

"Take it, sir." The groom was practically begging now, handing over the snorting black horse as one would a lighted fuse.

James reluctantly reached out his hand and closed it over stiff leather reins that felt foreign in his hand. He gave voice to the thought tripping around in his head, though he doubted the question would win him any friends or do him any good.

"What is this?" He gestured toward the horse and earned a flattening of the animal's ears for his trouble. "Is this some sort of joke?" He half-expected to see William bent over in laughter, having concocted this elaborate ruse merely for entertainment value.

The groom's eyes widened in confusion. "It's your horse, sir."

"This is not my horse." As if agreeing with him, the horse reached out and nipped at James's waistcoat, ripping the fabric and taking a bit of skin, to boot. "My horse is chestnut." He rubbed a hand over his newest injury and eyed the beast with irritation. "And *male*."

"Well, it's the horse you left with me last night." The groom's voice wavered.

"It's not my horse, and therefore not my problem." James started to hand back the reins, but the groom's cry of protest halted his progress.

"Never say you aren't going to pay!" The boy sounded frantic now. "If you dinna pay, I'll lose my job. That would be a fine meddle, the town solicitor and Lord Kilmartie's son, to boot, running out on his bill."

The grim reminder of his father's inevitable disappointment and what he stood to lose in this made James's fingers curve inward, itching for release. Respect. He had worked hard to build the town's trust of him, to prove he was more than a rough-and-tumble second son who needed to be saved by his father. He had turned his life for the better, and done it without the help of his influential family. He did not want to toss those gains aside.

He tamped down the urge to strike out at something with a skill born of long practice and necessity. It was not this groom's fault he had misplaced his horse, any more than it was the groom's fault James had forgotten himself last night. He turned to his brother, his decision made. William was already counting out coins from his money purse. When it was all over, the groom skittered back into the filthy darkness of the stable, and James was left holding the reins of the ill-tempered black mare and the ends of his own frayed temper.

He eyed the horse with distaste, wondering what he was going to do with it. Riding it certainly seemed out of the question, at least if he wanted to make it to the end of the street with his neck intact. She seemed none too sound anyway, obviously favoring her right rear leg.

He took a step toward the mare, his hand raised in placation. This was not his horse, but it obviously belonged to someone. She had good conformation despite her foul temperament, with a high crest to her neck and slim legs. The horse's ears, when not pinned back flat against her head, formed two graceful arcs above intelligent eyes.

There were only a handful of Moraig's citizens who could afford a piece of horseflesh so fine. When he found the mare's owner, he would likely be able to add another clue to the puzzle of his evening.

He placed a firm hand on her nose. The mare responded with a squeal and kicked out violently with her forefeet, striking James in the knee with a body-shuddering crack. He pitched backward, knocking his head against wall of the stable. His hat went rolling on its brim across the dust and straw that littered the ground. He lay there a long moment, unsteady and sick and contemplating whether he could afford the cost of a bullet for the intemperate beast.

Probably not. That would just place him further in debt.

William leaned in, concerned. More precisely, two Williams leaned in. "Are you all right?" His brother's voice sounded slurred and distant, but that couldn't be right, not when there were two of him speaking.

"Piss-poor and proper," James groaned, fighting a wave of dizziness. His leg hurt like the very devil, but he forced himself to standing. The earth undulated beneath his feet. He snatched up his battered hat and then lifted a hand gingerly to his skull and probed the memento of his past evening's indiscretion. Fresh warmth coated his fingers. The wound had started to bleed again.

William's mouth stretched into a smile. "If you are done boxing with the beastie, I have to ask. What do you want to do now?"

James reached out a hand to grab the mare's reins, this time taking care to stand to the side. He decided against a steadying hand on the mare's neck, choosing instead to live. "Isn't it obvious?" he grumbled, wiping his blood-covered fingers on his ruined waistcoat. "We need to figure out who in the deuces this horse belongs to."

The horse, like the corset, was a clue. A reticent clue, but a clue nonetheless. He needed to get started on the investigation. Each lost moment was a risk to his future and an opportunity for the woman in question to flee town with his money purse in hand. If this had been a case brought to him by a client, he would have eagerly set foot to pavement, ruthlessly tracking down each beckoning trace of her.

Unfortunately, his body did not agree with his mind. He leaned a hand against the weathered wood of the livery, breathing deeply through his nose. He had never come so close to fainting in his life.

"I think we need to get you to the surgeon." William's voice was colored gray with concern.

James shook his head and pushed himself straight. He renewed his grip on the reins with one hand and his hold on the corset with other. "That's all I need, word of this getting out amidst the town gossips. If I go to see the sawbones, he'll want to know how I got cracked on the head with a chamber pot. Wouldn't be surprised if there's a piece or two of china left in there, given the way my head hurts."

"To your house, then." William's drawn, bushy browns and stern voice brooked no argument. "Let your friend Channing take a look at you."

James snorted, and immediately regretted the expression. He lifted a hand to his head. Its pounding was dwarfed only by the sharp, immediate pain in his shin. "Oh, aye, that's rich. Let's have Patrick, the town veterinarian, take a look at me. I'll be the pride of the MacKenzie clan for that."

"At least he won't spread the tale far and yonder," William argued. He spread his hands in supplication.

"You need help, Jamie. And if you won't take it from me, at least ask it of your friend."

A fresh wave of dizziness pressed in from all sides, and James closed his eyes against the weakness. He felt William's hands slide across his back and reluctantly turned over some of his weight against his big brother's ready shoulder. He had to fight against the urge to push himself away. He didn't want to ask Patrick for help, any more than he wanted to accept William's. But neither did he want to pitch over face-first in the sawdust-strewn entryway to Morrison's Livery, the smell of urine-soaked shavings in his nostrils and the ringing laughter of the townsfolk in his ears.

Though he knew it was shameful, pride had everything to do with it. His pride had been the only thing he had taken with him on his journey to manhood, the one thing he could not shake off when he had fled his father's house eleven years ago and abandoned everything in his life that carried the stamp of the Earl of Kilmartie about it. Once upon a time, his ego had been the instrument of his downfall and very nearly his family's. But that inborn arrogance had also pointed his feet down the road to self-sufficiency. That same pride now screamed at him to move on, to handle this himself.

But luckily, good sense trumped pride, at least in this moment.

"Fine," James muttered, opening his eyes to take in his brother's pinched concern. "To Patrick, then." At the very least, he supposed if he went home he could change his clothes and wash from his skin the smell of the woman he could neither fully remember nor forget. "But remember, I've seen the man work," he warned as they began to take their first tentative steps, dragging the mare behind them. "He's as likely to put a bullet between my eyes as a bandage around my head."

"I'm proud of you for seeing reason," William said, no small degree of amusement edging his voice. "Although, to be honest, I am beginning to think putting you out of your misery might be just the thing."

Chapter 6

"IF YOU'RE GOING to stand there with your mouth hanging open, the least you could do is fetch me a towel." The woman in Georgette's bath spoke as easily as if she had asked for the salt over dinner.

Only that conversation would have surely involved clothing.

Georgette could voice no objection beyond a strangled, whistling sound lodged deep in her throat. Embarrassed heat stained her thoughts, but she could not look away. It was as if her eyes were operated by marionette strings.

She forced her hands to stay relaxed, though her fingertips ached from the strain. Had she been half so brazen last night? If she had, it was no wonder she had ended up in a handsome stranger's bed. "Who are you?" she finally choked out.

The woman's head lolled toward her. Two auburn brows drew up in confusion. "Why, I'm Elsie, miss. Have you taken a bloody great blow to your bean?"

Georgette swallowed a surprised gasp. The chit was naked *and* profane. "Your full name, if you please," she said crisply.

A sigh of annoyance escaped the girl, as hot and damp

as the steam rising from the tub. "Elsie Dalrymple. As if you dinna already know."

Georgette blinked at that. The girl implied no small degree of familiarity, yet Georgette did not recall having ever seen her before. "Why are you here, Miss Dalrymple?"

The girl's lip puckered in amusement. "Well, my, my. Aren't *we* formal this morning. Just plain Elsie was good enough for you last night." She stretched a pale, freckled arm over her head and pulled a washing cloth down its length, as if daring Georgette to remember. "I'm your new maid, you daft ninny."

"My *maid*?" Lack of memory aside, she couldn't imagine hiring this colorful girl for such a delicate task. Most ladies' maids didn't boast a vocabulary that would curl a sailor's rigging. Or call their mistresses ninnies.

Or last very long if they did.

"Hired me last night at the Blue Gander, you did." The girl moved on to wash her other arm. "Plucked me from the jaws of the serving line. Promised to pay me better than the innkeeper." The girl stopped her motions and ran a critical hazel eye over Georgette's stained, misshapen gown. "Either you were lying about being able to afford me, or you are in serious need of a ladies' maid. Which is it then?"

"The latter." It came out as a whisper, so Georgette cleared her throat. She *did* need a maid, at least while she was staying with Randolph. But the girl was yet more evidence of her aberrant night on the town. "If you are my maid," she said, louder now, "why are you bathing in my tub? And asking me to fetch *your* towel?"

The woman dropped the washcloth and shook a forelock full of wet hair from her eyes. The motion sent her bare breasts bouncing and Georgette's eyes stinging. "You told me I needed to clean myself up before we started the job proper. Am I not doing it right?"

Though Georgette tried to control her eye's downward track, tried to prevent *looking*, her gaze swept the bits of the girl's body visible beyond the confines of the hip bath. The embarrassed heat that had pricked at her before exploded to full-bore mortification. "You look quite clean."

In fact, Georgette was quite sure she had never seen such a clean creature.

Elsie stood up, sending water splashing over the sides of the tub and sluicing down delicate limbs. "I suppose you'll be wanting your own bath, then." The fierce flare of the girl's hips drew Georgette's eye, causing her cheeks to burn poker-hot. One bare foot prodded the rug while Elsie's hand fished for the towel folded on a nearby chair. "The water's still warm if you want to have a go."

The disarming thought of sliding into used bathwater—the same water that had just touched Elsie's bare skin—could not compete with the full, shocking sight of the naked woman stepping out of the copper hip bath. Georgette slapped a hand over her eyes, struck by the oddest sense of shame. Not for the girl's nudity, which Elsie wore as proudly as if she was clad in a smart new gown. No, Georgette was ashamed of herself, and the disappointment she sometimes felt in her own body. Wasn't she every bit as young—and beautiful—as the young woman dripping before her?

And yet, Georgette could not recall ever being so comfortable in her skin, or so at ease with someone else watching her.

She wondered if she had stood similarly naked in front of her Scotsman last night, wondered if the man's dancing green eyes had watched appreciatively as she slowly peeled off her clothing. Confusion heated her thoughts. Surely she had not done something so brazen. So uncharacteristic.

So wrong.

Elsie's voice floated between the tight clench of Georgette's fingers. "Or if not a bath, will you be wanting something else? Breakfast, perhaps?"

Georgette cracked her fingers open a fraction and risked a peek. The girl was wrapped in a towel now. She dropped her hand cautiously, ready to clap it back in place at the first threat of additional nudity. "I am not up for breakfast just yet."

"A good thing, that is," Elsie agreed. "Because I already ate the wee bit of food I found in the larder. And I would really recommend the bath first, miss." Her nose twisted in concern. "You're a ripe one this morning. Do you want me to help you undress?"

Georgette shrank against the idea of a stranger stripping her bare. Her usual ladies' maid in London was a woman she had known since childhood. "No, thank you. Your help will not be necessary."

The dripping woman's cheeks colored pink. "Have you changed your mind then?" When Georgette did not immediately respond, the girl dropped the towel and snatched up a well-worn chemise from the floor, pulling it on with hard, jerky movements. "Well, ain't that the way of it. I finally find myself a mistress that looks to be a little fun, and come morning light she wants to see nothing but the backside of me."

Something akin to a giggle tickled at the back of

Georgette's throat. "To be fair," she pointed out, handing Elsie the old patched dress she spied lying in a rumpled heap near the door, "I've seen more than the backside of you."

It was startling to be having this conversation. No one *ever* talked to her like this. She would have never hired a girl like Elsie in London, where a ladies' maid was as much a symbol of your status as the matched bays in your stables. But in Scotland, where everything seemed turned on its ear, it somehow seemed fitting to have a foulmouthed hoyden laying out her gowns. And judging by the threadbare nature of the girl's clothing, there was no denying Elsie needed a better means of income.

But Georgette wasn't staying here long enough to truly *need* a ladies' maid. As soon as she found the mystery Scotsman and procured the annulment, she was bound for London. She already had a ladies' maid waiting for her there, one she would have brought with her if the woman's mother hadn't just died.

"I . . . I don't think this is a good idea." Georgette lifted her shoulders in apology. "You are a bit . . . *different* than my usual choice in a maid."

Elsie's brows pulled down in an expert impression of a pout as she worked the buttons of her bodice. "Well, I guess I don't fit your specifics for a ladies' maid, not that I know what they are. Tell me, miss. Do I need to be taller?" Her lips followed the downward arc of her brows. Her voice took on a hysterical ring. "Prettier?"

"Covered," Georgette mouthed, breathing a sigh of relief as the last button slid home beneath Elsie's busy fingers. Now that the girl was respectably clad, she could think. "You are pretty enough," she offered. And

Elsie *was* pretty, if a bit frayed around the edges. She had dark reddish-brown curls and a nose scattered with freckles, strategically placed to attract the eye but not overwhelm the canvas.

"Suppose it doesn't matter," Elsie sniffed. "Can't do much about my looks, can I? But I'm handy with a needle and have muscles to fetch and carry your bathwater. I don't mind a little hard work. What is wrong with me?"

"It isn't you," Georgette said carefully, realizing it was true. "It is me." Her lips pursed, amusement now soothing her initial discomfort. There was no denying the girl needed a chance to improve herself. And if Georgette didn't provide it, who would? If nothing else, Elsie would provide a loud, opinionated shield against Randolph when the man returned from town. Yes, there were definite advantages to keeping this girl on.

If she would only promise to keep her clothes on.

"I'm a frightful snob." Georgette paused. "And I'm only here for a few days, after which time you'll need to find a new post. I will probably need to beg you to stay."

Elsie's brows winged up. "You want me to stay?"

"Do *you* want to stay?"

Elsie placed her hands on hips now hidden by the wrinkled skirt. Her face broke into a smile. "Well now, that depends. I prefer my patrons a bit cleaner, if you ken what I mean. Let's get you cleaned up."

Elsie stepped forward, her fingers stretching toward Georgette's gray silk gown. Georgette stayed her with a firm hand. "I can manage this part."

The maid stepped back. Georgette carefully slipped the buttons from their anchors. She lifted the alarmingly listless kitten from its perch between her breasts and handed it to the maid. "Would you happen to know someplace nearby where we could find some milk?" she asked hopefully.

Elsie's eyes widened in surprise. Her nose gave a twitch, and then another, until finally her entire body was racked with a brutal sneeze. "What is this?" she gasped once her body stopped shuddering.

"A kitten." Georgette slipped the wrinkled silk from her shoulders and clasped it against her breasts. The motion brought to mind the shame she had felt this morning putting the gown on, and the appreciative glow in the Scotsman's eyes when he had seen her in it. *At least he didn't see me naked.* Well, not that she remembered. Given her natural state upon waking, she had to presume he had seen her in the buff at some point in the evening.

"I can see it's a bloody kitten." Elsie's voice snapped through her heated thoughts. The maid leaned in close. "What is it doing here?" she hissed.

The maid's contempt and language surprised Georgette. Vehement tone aside, what kind of person used the words "bloody" and "kitten" in the same breath?

"After my morning in Moraig, it seemed best." She gripped the gown over the front of her body, wondering if Elsie would think it odd if she turned away to finish undressing. She slid the fabric lower, mortification curling around her fingers. "I almost got trampled by a cart, and the front of my dress seemed the safest place to keep the animal from suffering a similar fate."

"Not the bit with your dress, although I'll admit it's an odd place to stash a kitten." Elsie flapped her free hand in consternation and clutched the ball of tabby fur with the other. "What is the wild beast doing in your *house*?"

"Well, it's not precisely a wild beast," Georgette offered weakly. "Or my house." She dropped her dress and scrambled into the tub as quickly as she could, hoping her rapid progress would conceal her regrettably necessary lack of clothing. Her uncoordinated efforts sent water sloshing over the sides, but the water offered a grateful bit of cover. She sank down to her neck, wishing the maid had someplace else to go, and someone else to watch.

Apparently oblivious to the embarrassment tripping about Georgette's breast, Elsie threw one hand up in disgust. "I specifically asked last night if you had any cats before I agreed to take this position. Swell my eyes and nose up something awful, they do." She sniffed, and Georgette could see the girl's hazel eyes were indeed watering profusely. Those bleary eyes narrowed, and she leaned closer. "You'll have to get rid of it if you want me to stay."

Georgette sighed. She had carried the tiny bundle from Moraig, lodged like a wish against her chest. But the need for a human buffer between her and Randolph was all too real. Moreover, it was obvious she could not care for the kitten, not here in a house better suited for a bachelor than a nursing pet. She knew which she needed to choose, but it would hurt to give up the little bit of fur. She had grown quite attached to it over the course of the last hour.

Of course, it was the one thing she remembered vividly out of the last sixteen.

Elsie pointed toward the water. "And look what it's done to *you*, miss."

Georgette looked down. Through the murky water, along the inner edge of one partially bared breast, she could see a reddish mark. She stared at her marred skin. She did not remember feeling any pain during the time the kitten had been nestled there.

Elsie hefted the kitten to her other hand and leaned in for a closer look at the mark, her nose already twitching again. "Well, whatever else its sins, I don't think this wee bit of fur did that." She sniffed once, paused, sneezed again. "And that mark wasn't made by a corset, because you weren't wearing one." Humor edged Elsie's sneeze-altered tone as she acknowledged Georgette's shocking lack of undergarments had been noticed.

"I . . ." Georgette fell silent, shifting uncomfortably beneath her wet, transparent blanket. What on earth could she say to that? *I left my corset in a strange room with a strange man this morning. Could you please pass the soap?*

Elsie peered down at Georgette, her eyes scrunched in amusement. "That, my lady, looks very much like a love bite. Probably from that great, lovely blighter you married last night."

Georgette froze, all worry of nudity forgotten. She latched on to that bit of information. The maid knew something about her disremembered night. Hope hammered in her chest. Perhaps she now had a more articulate clue than the simple signet ring that still lay on her finger. "Do you know the man?"

Elsie sighed dreamily, her eyes lifting to the herb-hung ceiling. "Oh, aye, right enough. *All* the ladies in town know him. And if James MacKenzie's reputation is well earned, I would imagine you had a right fine time acquiring it."

Chapter 7

"MACKENZIE." GEORGETTE FIT the name around her lips. It triggered no memory, no hint of recognition, but it *did* incite a spark of warmth, fluttering in her abdomen. She found herself insanely curious about Mr. MacKenzie, now that she had a knowledgeable, breathing body to press for details. She wondered what kind of man he was. Kind or hard? Generous or tight-fisted?

Faithful or indiscreet?

The thought flew unbidden from the depths of her subconscious. She shook her head, sending water rippling against the sides of the bath. She had been only twenty-two years old when she had married the first time, and had not thought to ask such an indelicate question then. Her husband had turned out to be of the faithless variety. But it did not matter if this James MacKenzie was a man who honored his vows or was the biggest philanderer in Moraig.

It was not a question she needed to ask of a man she planned to leave.

"Do you know anything of what I did last night?" Georgette asked, pushing her curiosity about the bearded Scotsman to a quieter place.

"Oh, aye, miss." Elsie picked up a washcloth with her

free hand, the kitten still balanced precariously in the other. She reached over the edge of the bath. "You hired yourself a maid."

Georgette snatched the cloth from her. "I can take care of this part myself." The promise of learning more about what might have happened last night warred with her prudish aversions. She pointed to an upholstered chair that until recently had been occupied by Elsie's towel, scarcely able to believe she was not only going to invite the maid to stay and provide an audience, but insist upon it. "Sit, please. And tell me what else I may have done."

Elsie perched on the chair and arranged her skirts. She placed the kitten in her lap and wrinkled her nose, seemed to focus a second on averting another sneeze. When the moment passed, the maid laughed. "Can't remember, eh? I'm not surprised, to tell you the truth. You came banging into the rear entrance of the Blue Gander last night, close to eight o'clock." She leaned forward. "Looked three sheets to the wind, if you ken what I mean, and I thought to myself as I was cleaning up the tankards, she looks like a handful of fun."

Georgette looked up from where she was lathering the cake of soap between her hands. Surely she could not have heard that right. "You thought I looked *fun*?"

Elsie nodded. "Ladies, you see, hardly ever come in the back door of the Gander. That's an exit usually reserved for patrons looking for a quick poke in the alley."

"A poke?" Georgette asked in mortification.

Elsie's cheeks colored prettily. "Sorry, miss. I forget sometimes you are a lady."

Georgette's own face heated as she went to work cleaning one filthy foot. Apparently, so did she. While she scrubbed, she thought. She was still unable to piece together how she had come to be at the Gander when she was supposed to have been at the church with Randolph. "Was I alone?" she asked

"Oh no, you weren't alone."

Georgette forced her horrified eyes to meet Elsie's. Had Randolph *taken* her to the Blue Gander? "I wasn't?"

"Not for long, anyway. The entire table was mighty interested in the pretty young lady who had dropped in their laps." The maid wrinkled her nose against another sneeze before adding, "I believe you may have *sat* in one or two of their laps. And you talked to me, of course. Never did see a lady who wanted to talk to the serving girl, but you were quite interested in a heartfelt chat. By the time MacKenzie came in, the whole place was roaring with laughter and I was your new maid."

Georgette squeezed her eyes shut. It was mortifying to learn these details from the bemused servant. It was every bit as bad as she had feared. She tried to move her hands, to get on with her bath, but was riveted in a watery prison, listening to every last hardscrabble detail of her night gone wrong.

"Of course, once you clapped eyes on MacKenzie, it was obvious to all of us you were bound for the altar. Why, from the time you sat in his lap until the time he hoisted you onto a table and presented you to the entire room as the future Mrs. MacKenzie, couldn't have been more than an hour or two."

"I was on the table?" Georgette asked, sinking lower into the water. Who *was* this wild, uninhibited creature Elsie remembered with such glee? She gave her feet a hard scrub, wondering if she could rub hard enough to strip the stain of last night's antics as cleanly from her soul as it apparently was from her memory. "You said future wife." Georgette hung a moment on that bit of the conversation, hoping she had heard the maid correctly. "So we weren't married after all?"

Elsie inclined her head. "Not then. But the magistrate took care of that, right enough. The man stood up and offered to make it official. Whole bloody place served as your witnesses." She offered Georgette a delighted smile. "Don't often get to attend a wedding at the Gander. Why, you even let us tar and feather your feet. Fetched the feathers myself, I did, a whole pile of them from the kitchen."

Georgette blinked, piecing together forgotten bits of her morning. That explained the mess of feathers she had stumbled over in the room this morning, and the black, sticky mess that she could not quite get off the soles of her feet.

It did not, however, explain what had been tripping around her head when she had made the crucial, ill-formed decision to marry Mr. MacKenzie. The description painted by the maid was of a fun, confident woman. The kind of woman who did not care what Society thought, or what bed her husband had stumbled from. The kind of woman Georgette had long wished she could be, but had never been.

What about the events of last night—and this man, in particular—had brought that woman out in her?

"What kind of man is Mr. MacKenzie?" she found herself asking, though she had promised herself she wouldn't.

Elsie wiggled in her seat. "Oh, he's a right fine one. Handsome devil, and with a wicked tongue. Has those green eyes that don't precisely undress a woman, but make you want to right enough." She sighed. "Shame you can't remember. That recollection's sure to be one worth storing away for a cold winter's night."

Georgette realized then the maid had misunderstood her. She didn't want a physical description of the man. She had enough of that from her morning's experience. She knew the man was sinfully attractive, had felt that quickening response in her own body as those green eyes had swept her appreciatively. She did not need to hear from Elsie the man had a way of making women act like love-struck adolescents.

No, she wanted to know what made James MacKenzie's heart race and his palms sweat, not the color of his eyes.

"Was he also, how did you say it, three sheets to the wind?" Georgette pressed. If they had both been incapacitated, perhaps that would play better into her plan to demand an annulment.

"Well," Elsie mused, "MacKenzie looked none too fresh himself, but he's a strapping big man, so of course he holds his liquor better than most."

"A big man," Georgette mouthed, wondering just how big a man he was. It had been difficult to tell when he had been lying in bed. His shirttails had reached her calves this morning, true enough. An unbidden thought rose, refused to be pushed back into shadows. *Was he big in other places too?* She squeezed her hands to fists in the water, imagined touching him intimately last night. The dissipating heat from the bathwater ill-compared with the warmth that suffused her body from the inside out.

"It sounds as if I quite enjoyed myself." She swallowed, forcing herself to rinse the soap from her limbs. The lemon verbena scent tickled her nostrils, but she ignored it for more important things. Like trying not to think about what manner of intimacy she might have engaged in last night.

And like resisting the urge to find the man and make a proper memory.

Elsie laughed again. "Oh, aye. You had a right fine time. Of course, that was before the fight. You dinna enjoy that awful much."

"I got into a fight?"

"No, MacKenzie did. Over you."

"Over *me*?" Incredulous, Georgette dropped the cloth. She was not a woman men fought over.

"Well, to be fair, half the blighters in the place wanted to kiss the new Mrs. MacKenzie. And your husband has a reputation for not wanting to share. Once he took care of that nonsense and knocked them all over the place, he gave you a great bloody kiss, swept you in his arms, and the pair of you stumbled out the door."

"The rear door?" Georgette whispered in mortification. Surely she wouldn't have. Surely she had been more circumspect. Then again, according to Elsie, she had gotten married on a table in a public barroom. A tup up against the wall in the alley behind the Gander was not the physical impossibility it should be.

Elsie stood up and placed the kitten on the seat of the chair, then held the towel out for her mistress. Georgette dutifully rose and let the maid wrap it around her. "You left through the front door, miss," Elsie soothed, as if she could sense her distress. "And that was the last I saw of you."

Georgette fell silent as Elsie set about dressing her,

lost in her thoughts. She suffered through the maid's in-experienced fumbling over the snarled nest of her hair. Stepped into a clean gray merino walking dress, al-though without benefit of the corset she had so thought-lessly left behind at the Blue Gander. And through it all, she tried to sort out how she would find James Mac-Kenzie and undo this thing.

"You want to undo it?" Elsie's voice rang uncomfort-ably close to her ear. Georgette winced. She had not re-alized she had voiced that last part aloud.

"I . . . I was not thinking clearly last night." Georgette fought the urge to wring her hands against Elsie's incred-ulous stare. "I don't *want* to be married," she added. It was not just an afterthought.

It was the entire thought.

"But, miss . . ." Elsie's eyes grew wider. "*Everyone* wants to be married to MacKenzie. He's . . . he's . . ."

"Not for me," Georgette said firmly. The issue of the man's right to control her finances aside, she didn't know what kind of man Mr. MacKenzie was. Elsie's innocent words might have been meant to titillate, but they spoke all too eloquently of the man's randy nature and his rep-utation about town as a ladies' man. No matter how the man made her feel when he looked at her, she did not want to suffer through another marriage to a man who cared not where he trimmed his wick.

And then there was the little matter of Randolph, rushing about town, out for vengeance, and no doubt imagining himself the great hero. Why, he would prob-ably challenge MacKenzie to a duel without a moment's thought as to the consequences.

And that was why she needed to get back to Moraig as soon as possible.

Elsie knelt to lace up her mistress's heeled boots. "Well, it's a fine muddle you've gotten yourself into. Tied up to the most eligible man in town and desperate to see it undone." She blew an errant wisp of auburn hair out of her face. "I suppose you, being a lady, think you're too good for the likes of him."

Georgette stared at her new maid in surprise. Aside from those first shocked moments upon waking this morning, the difference in stations between herself and the Scotsman had not even crossed her mind. "That really isn't it at all," she protested. "I am scarcely out of mourning, and finally in control of my life." She drew in a breath. "I don't want to toss that away on a careless, drunken mistake!"

Elsie looked up at her. Sympathy skirted her gaze. "I reckon I can understand that, miss. There's no sense getting worked up." She patted Georgette's ankle awkwardly. "I suppose you'll be wanting to get to Moraig then. Do you have a more sensible pair of shoes?"

Georgette stilled. Why was the maid concerned about her shoes? "How did you get here, Elsie?"

"Came on a boat from Ireland," Elsie said, rocking back on her heels and wiping an uncouth arm across her brow. "Nigh on five years ago." She ran a critical eye over the front of Georgette's demure, high-necked bodice. "You mentioned you were out of mourning. If you're going to meet with Mr. MacKenzie, I would recommend something a bit brighter."

Georgette prayed for patience. "I do not have anything brighter. I am newly out of half mourning. And I mean here. How did you get *here*, from Moraig. On a horse?" she added hopefully.

"Oh no, I walked, miss. 'Tis only four miles."

Four miles. It was an impossible distance.

The maid's question about shoes made more sense now. Georgette had never walked four miles in her pampered adult life, and she owned not a single pair of shoes suitable for the purpose. Though it felt good to have on somewhat sensible shoes after a night apparently spent tripping about town in drunken slippers, the heeled boots Elsie had just laced were not precisely made for walking. They were of fine kid leather and embossed with tiny, trailing vines, and boasted a two-inch heel that threatened the safety of ankles everywhere. They had cost Georgette a month's pin money at a shop on Regent Street, and were intended to carry their mistress from London town house to coach to shopping and back again.

On a rocky trail, they would fall apart halfway through the journey.

That Elsie could walk such a distance and think nothing of it told Georgette she herself was ill-equipped for life in general, and life in Scotland in particular. Inadequacy pushed at her from all sides. What sort of a woman did that make her?

And what sort of a woman did she want to be?

As they made their way out of the room and down the dark, portrait-laden stairwell, Elsie asked, "If you aren't in mourning, why are you dressing as if you still are?"

Georgette chewed on that a moment. She couldn't answer, because there was no good answer. She should have put away her gray and lavender gowns a month ago, preparing to step out in the midst of a gay London Season. And instead, she had fled. To Scotland. Ostensibly to live a little, but how could she explain she had not yet even elected to live through her choice of wardrobe?

A resounding knock scattered her thoughts as she reached the bottom of the stairs. She and Elsie froze, staring at the front door as if Satan himself hovered behind it.

"Who do you think that is?" she asked, her heart in her throat. MacKenzie? The groom? *Randolph?* Of course, Randolph wouldn't knock at the door to his own house, and the groom, if he didn't use his usual entrance in the scullery, would probably do no more than scratch deferentially at the door.

That left Mr. MacKenzie. And that left Georgette in a state of warring emotions.

She lifted one shaking hand to her hair, checking that her blond hair had been properly contained, grateful for having had the temerity to go ahead and suffer through a bath in dirty water. It would not do to greet her new husband in a state of disarray.

She wanted him to regret the loss when she demanded an annulment.

"Answer it," she urged, pushing at Elsie.

"Oh no, miss." The maid resisted, pulling back. "I'm the upstairs maid." A smug tilt fixed on her lips. "I don't answer downstairs doors. Never know who might be lurking behind them."

"Oh, for heaven's sake," Georgette snapped. She strode toward the door, which echoed again with their unseen guest's impatience. She struggled one-handed with the latch, yanked hard. It fell open in a rush.

Before her stood a red-haired young man, holding his cap in one hand and the rope to a snarling dog in the other. He had the tall, gangly body of a newly minted man, but the sparse stubble on his chin suggested he was still on the south side of twenty. The black and white beast lunged at the kitten in Georgette's hand with a desperation she had seen only in hungry street children in London, fighting over a currant bun. She lurched back, clutching the kitten to her breast, her heart skidding against the confines of her chest.

"May I help you?" she managed to get out.

The visitor broke into a broad smile. "I've brought it, just like you asked."

Georgette eyed the odd pair, smiling young man and snarling dog, and wondered if she had any hope at all of escaping the beast should the owner lose his grip on that precious rope.

Elsie materialized at her shoulder. "Well, if it isn't Joseph Rothven, come for a social call." She smiled at him, and the boy's cheeks went pink at the attention. "What did you bring us? Oh, I do hope it's your mother's gooseberry scones. There isn't a bite to eat in this bloody house."

"I . . . I brought Lady Thorold's dog," he stammered. His cheeks went redder than the scant hair on his face. "I mean, I brought her one of my father's dogs."

The maid leaned forward, and her uncoordinated movements to see the dog better had the unfortunate effect of pushing her mistress and the kitten closer to the snarling, snapping canine.

Georgette met the youth's eyes in speechless dismay. He stood there, a hopeful, swooning expression on his face. "Why would you think I needed a dog?" she asked, her voice faint. As if she needed a vicious dog on top of the randy husband, the listless kitten, and the harridan of a domestic servant she had already acquired in the space of only two hours.

His brow scrunched up in confusion. "That was

part of the bargain we struck, wasn't it? You mentioned you could use a big dog for protection, staying way out here with your cousin. Said you needed something that wasn't afraid to bite."

"I did?" She searched her memory. As was the rule for matters related to what had happened last night, her mind was alarmingly blank. And yet, his words echoed truth. She *had* thought the isolation of Randolph's house unsettling, enough to have hired and promptly forgotten hiring Elsie. That she may have also sought a dog for protection was not that far of a stretch.

"When did this transaction take place?" Georgette's temple started to throb with the ridiculousness of it all. She couldn't leave a great snapping dog alone with a three-week-old kitten. Gooseberry tarts stood a better chance of emerging unscathed in this house.

"While you were showing me what to do, in the alley behind the Blue Gander." Joseph's cheeks went positively scarlet. "I can't take payment for him, not after how patient you were with me. You didn't laugh, even though I didn't know what I was doing."

Georgette's mind whirled like dandelion fluff in the wind. Only the bits in her mind were more like shards of glass. And the wind was more like fierce summer storm, hammering her senses mercilessly.

What this young man was implying was sordid. Impossibly vile. Had she really corrupted this fresh-faced youth last night, in the notorious alley behind the Blue Gander, no less? Shame and a desperate sense of denial kicked at her, as violent as the objection that formed mutely on her lips. She couldn't *remember*.

But that did not lessen the magnitude of what she appeared to have done.

Surely she was mistaken. But what if she wasn't? Her acute embarrassment over the forgotten parts of her night, and her fear of the details she might still learn, made Georgette lock up tight the questions that wanted to tumble out of her. Her breathing didn't just slow down then, her lungs pinched shut.

"Oh my God," she moaned, eyeing the young man and the dog. What was she going to do? Apologize to young Mr. Rothven? Apologize to his *parents*? And the dog . . . the dog she had no idea about. It probably wasn't mean. After all, the boy still had all his limbs intact, and he didn't seem afraid of the animal in the slightest. But she couldn't let the creature run loose with that uncertainty. No, she would have to lock it in the room Randolph used for his study.

Elsie's affronted voice broke through the train of Georgette's thoughts. "If you were looking for lessons, Joseph," she admonished the lad, "why didn't you come to me last night?"

"I . . ." His gaze darted between the two women. "I mean . . . Lady Thorold seemed like she would know about these things. She's a London widow, you know." He leaned in closer, his eyes going wide. "She's *worldly*."

Elsie rolled her eyes. "Aye, the whole town knows. It's not like she kept it much of a great bloody secret, cavorting about Moraig as she did."

Joseph shuffled his feet. "Well, she offered to help me. Saw me trying to figure things out all by myself in the alley outside the Gander."

Beads of sweat had formed on his brow during the halted explanation, and Georgette watched in sick fascination as Elsie reached out a hand and brushed the drops away. "Why, if it's an experienced partner you were looking for, Joseph, next time come to me." Elsie cast a shrewd glance back at her mistress. "I know my way around the Gander's alley better than any uptight London lady."

He swallowed hard. "I appreciate that, Miss Elsie. Now that I've tried it with Lady Thorold, I ken I'll want to try it with other women too." His eyes widened hopefully. "Maybe we could have a go later tonight?"

Elsie giggled, an amused, inappropriate sound. She offered him a saucy wink. "Well, sure then."

Georgette concentrated on breathing through her nose, unable to believe the audacity of her new maid to not only proposition a near-innocent young man, but to disparage her mistress's capabilities in the process. "How do you propose to see him later tonight if we are stuck here with no means of conveyance?" she asked, her voice cracking under the strain of the morning's surprises.

Elsie rolled her eyes. "If you weren't so prone to hysterics, you'd have already seen your answer." The maid's chin gestured toward the open door. "Today's your lucky day."

Georgette looked out, past the flushed-faced Mr. Rothven, past the dog that had finally stopped lunging against the rope but was still eyeing the kitten with a feral gleam in its eye. The sun was shining brilliantly, and the day was the sort a cloud would never think of ruining. She normally lived for days like this, loved the lazy promise in them.

But right now she could think of nothing beyond the immediate question of how to deal with the newest shock of the morning. "How?" she choked out. "How, precisely, is this my lucky day?"

"Well," Elsie said, already moving toward the door, "It appears Joseph has brought your new pet in his father's potato cart. And that, my forgetful mistress, is our ticket back to Moraig."

Chapter 8

A THREE-LEGGED DOG GREETED James and William as they walked into the courtyard of the cottage James called home. The dog, whose name was Gemmy, barked and lurched around in unsteady excitement. The familiar sight of the shaggy yellow terrier and the small stone house where James had rested his clear head every night for the past year could not dispel the knowledge of where he apparently laid his drunken head last night.

He tried in vain to block out the circumstances of the morning as he looked around the front garden for a place to tie the black mare. Preferably someplace out of striking range.

Patrick's dog needed every available limb he had left.

"Down, Gemmy!" James commanded. The dog dutifully dropped to all threes and wiggled in the dirt, whining his enthusiasm rather than expending it in further movement. James looped the mare's reins over the post of a makeshift pen that had been constructed near the corner of the yard. Patrick's newest orphaned lamb paced on the other side of the rails, bleating for its bottle.

"Like your dinner that fresh, do you?" William joked, jerking a thumb toward the pen.

"We only eat the ones Patrick loses," James told him,

wondering again why he was still tolerating his brother's nettlesome presence.

"Which means to say we don't eat very much." Patrick emerged from the front door, wiping his hands on a rag and blinking into the near-noon sunshine. Straw clung to his light brown hair, which was a step up from the sorts of questionable things one could sometimes find there. His usual quick smile fell into place as he looked James up and down. "So you survived your night."

William's chuckle echoed in James's left ear. "In a manner of speaking," his brother said. "Parts of him weren't so lucky. You might want to take a look."

Patrick snorted. "If you are speaking of his parts below the waist, they probably died happy, and I'm none too interested in seeing the aftereffects. The woman he left the Gander with last night would have made an eighty-year-old eunuch tumble into bed." Patrick paused on the edge of laughter, his amusement trailing off as he took in the mare. "Why is that horse tied to the fence post?" His gaze swung back to James. "And where is Caesar? Never say you traded this knacker-bound beast for your fine-tempered stallion."

"That," William broke in, "is the question of the morning. Well, one of them, anyway." He reached up and snatched the hat off James's head. "What to do about this great bloody mess is another."

Patrick's eyes widened. A low whistle escaped his lips. Before James could lodge a reasonable objection, before he could even wrap his head around what was happening, Patrick grabbed him under the right arm, and William hoisted him by the left. They dragged as much as helped him into the house.

The foyer smelled of farm animals, and James's stomach settled halfway on its side at the scent. When Patrick had unexpectedly turned up in Moraig six months ago and offered to help pay the rent, James had eagerly accepted, no questions asked. True, it was sometimes a struggle to live among the sea of misfit pets and animals needing nursing. Mornings found him awake with the damned dog stretched next to him instead of a female companion. Their kitchen had been taken over by the needs of Patrick's work, and was now little more than a makeshift clinic and sparring ring, better suited for a barnyard or back alley than polite company.

Not that polite company came to call very often. There was only his mother, who came once a month or so and sat primly in a cast-off chair, drinking tea from a chipped china cup and pretending not to notice Gemmy had better manners than her own son.

But there were benefits to sharing the space with Patrick. Such as having only half the rent due each month, and rekindling his acquaintance with the friend he hadn't seen since they had left Cambridge eleven years ago. Although it was a little hard to appreciate that sentiment when that friend had a death grip on his arm.

They stumbled into the kitchen. William shoved aside the sawdust-filled bag that James used for exercise and sparring, and kicked a chair closer to the sunlight-filled window before pushing him down in it.

"Sit," his brother commanded, as if he were Gemmy.

Hell, as if he were lower than Gemmy. A protest rose to James's lips, but before he could give voice to it, Patrick moved in, squinting down at him like a commanding officer. For a moment James was tempted to bare his teeth and give the veterinarian a better look in his mouth.

"I was concerned when you did not come home last night." Patrick pushed the lids of one of James's eyes apart and stared at it, his upper lip curled in concentration. He trailed a finger slowly in front of him. "I'm glad William was able to find you. Follow my finger, please."

James followed the bobbing finger, and when it came close enough, he grabbed it and twisted. "Would have preferred it if you set Gemmy on me," he growled. "Why in the bloody hell did you send my brother after me, anyway?"

Patrick dropped his hand, apparently satisfied James could see well enough if he could swipe at him so precisely. He grinned. "The rent's due. I needed your share."

James winced. Ah, the rent. That had been tangled up in his money purse too. His morning's debt was accumulating faster than ice in winter.

"And the dog would not have enjoyed it half so much." William sniggered. He pulled out his money purse and shook it, making the coins inside rattle as viciously as the thoughts in James's head. "I'm serving as Jamie's banker today. It's nice to have him beholden, after so many years of him shunning all offers of help."

James glared at William before shifting his gaze to his friend. "Can you put my brother to work shoveling the sheep pen?" he asked. "Two hours into the morning and I'm already sick of the sight of him."

Patrick crossed his arms. "Sick of the sight of your own brother." He clucked his tongue with mock sympathy. "Is *that* why you look so terrible? And here I thought it was that great gaping wound on your head. Which requires sutures, in case you were wondering."

"I'll just step outside," William offered, his feet already threading their way toward the kitchen door. "I'd hate to see my own brother reduced to tears. Begging, perhaps. Aye, that would be nice, though I doubt we shall live to see that." His deep-throated giggle followed him through the doorway and down the hall.

James heaved a sigh of relief he didn't know he had been holding. "It's been maddening having him around this morning. I can't think when he's hovering over me like a mother hen, clucking and squawking and scratching about."

Patrick cocked his head. "Someday," he said slowly, "you are going to learn how fortunate you are to have a brother to annoy you. Family is a blessing, MacKenzie, not a curse."

James snorted. "Spoken like a man who has never lived in the shadow of the Earl of Kilmartie. What the hell do you know of curses?"

Patrick leaned back, a frown snagging low on his thin face. "Enough to know yours is not as bad as some."

A pulse leaped below his friend's right eye, and not for the first time, it occurred to James he knew very little of Patrick's history. They had been roommates at university, commiserating about their lot in life as useless second sons with an all-too-frequent pint. It was only natural their friendship had continued when Patrick had mysteriously shown up in Moraig six months ago, a lean, hunted look on his ribbed frame. Money was tight, and sharing a domestic space had made sense, at least until Patrick had started plying his trade and collecting every cast-off animal in town. More importantly, their casual bantering burned the edge off each other's loneliness.

But that friendship did not make him privy to Patrick's inner thoughts. He had no idea what made Patrick so closed off to his past, or what had happened to the man since his easier-going Cambridge days.

"Look." James sighed, loath to keep poking at his friend's implacable secrecy. "Can you stitch me up, or do I need to take myself to the sawbones on Kirtland Street?"

As James had suspected, the prospect of trying out his veterinary skills on a living, breathing human was too great a temptation for Patrick to pass up. Like any dependable friend, the man expressed a proper amount of sympathy over the blood-crusted head wound as he began to irrigate the injury with clean water.

And as predictably as the turn of the minute hand on a stopwatch, Patrick abandoned all concern and convulsed in laughter when James haltingly explained how the injury had been acquired.

"So this bit of damage was done with a *chamber pot*?" Patrick choked out. An acrid bit of astringent wafted down to James's nose, stinging almost as much as the cloth his friend pressed against the wound. "And here I thought your pretend wife seemed so nice."

"*Pretend?*" James winced as his friend's fingers probed at the tender flesh of his scalp. "You mean I didn't marry her?"

Patrick held up a needle and examined the point. "I only know what you told me at the Blue Gander. You told me you were protecting her from someone who wanted to hurt her, by pretending to be married. Looked to me like you were having a right fine time doing it too. The way I hear it, you always were one to feel sorry for a lady in distress," he said, trying to work a length of thread through the needle's eye. "Now look at where it's gotten you."

James fidgeted in his chair, fingering the corset in his lap. It was the first time his friend had ever mentioned James's past, or hinted he was aware of the rumors that trailed James across time and space. Yes, he was ever one to help a pretty face, and once again, look at where it had gotten him: about to be sacrificed to the surgical skills of the town veterinarian, and missing half a year's savings.

His fingers tightened on the fine cotton fabric of the corset. He knew that if he lifted it to his nose it would smell of brandy and lemons, because he still imagined he could catch those scents from his shirt. He wished he could forget her, whoever she was, wished he could simply relegate the evening to that bulging coffer of things best forgotten about his past.

But his pride, as much as his financial circumstances, demanded otherwise.

Patrick muttered something unintelligible as he missed the first attempt to thread the needle. As he waited, James liberated the busk from the center of the corset that still sat in his lap, and turned it over in his hand, searching for some hint of who the woman was. No name had been engraved on it, just a delicate etching of flowers that trailed down the center of the thing. He peered closer, and just made out something along the lower edge.

G. T.

Were they her initials? Or those of a lover?

He swallowed hard at the thought, and acknowledged he was no closer to finding her than he had been on waking. The thought of failure—the thought of *losing* her—pulled at him as surely as the needle Patrick finally set to his scalp. He tried to think of something, anything, but the pass and pull of the needle.

Unfortunately, his mind wanted to think of her. Perhaps it was because he was sitting still, paying penance to Patrick's medical skills. Or perhaps the fog of forgetfulness that had dogged him since waking was finally lifting. Whatever the reason, he realized he could remember more.

She had been an enthusiastic, if not entirely skilled, flirt. After a quarter hour spent watching her work the crowd at the Gander, he had become increasingly inebriated by both the woman in his sights and the ale in his tankard. She had shown such *joy* in her untutored efforts, it was a pleasure to simply watch her. She had unfurled like a new butterfly, testing her wings, finding them functional. She looked like someone who had spent her entire life in darkness, only to awaken to find sunlight streaming through her window.

And then, her flirtations with every other man in the room had no longer mattered, because that shaft of sunlight became focused squarely on him.

He realized with relief he would recognize her now if he saw her on Moraig's streets, something he had not been sure he could do an hour ago. His memory on waking had been little more than a few still, snatched images, so indistinct as to be meaningless. But he remembered more now.

He remembered *movement*. She had not been still a moment out of the entire night. Her hair had been so blond as to appear almost white. She had been full of life, pulsing with energy and excitement, and waves of that memorable hair had spilled out of her pins as if they too could not bear to be contained. Her mouth had been wide and frequently laughing, and he remembered tossing back the ale the barmaid kept pouring into his tankard and thinking, *This is a girl I could marry.*

Not that he remembered much about the marrying part.

Or the *not*-marrying part, for that matter. He was still a shade confused on the issue. He recalled joking with her, wanting to soothe the panic that had sprung into her eyes at some imagined slight or insult from someone in the pub. He had poured his own ale into her empty glass, and then offered to marry her and spend the rest of his life refilling her cup.

At least he was no longer confused about *why* he had gotten caught up in this mess, because now, of all things, he remembered the kiss. She had thrown herself into his arms, there atop the old scarred table in the public room of the Blue Gander, and pressed her lips against his in front of a cheering, jeering crowd. He remembered being all but knocked over by the unexpectedness of it, her breath surprising and sweet and filling his senses. He remembered the feel of her lithe body surging against his chest. Remembered her own gasp of surprise against his lips, as if she too was shocked by the intensity of it.

James swallowed hard against the prison of that memory. "I need to find her," he muttered.

"I don't blame you," Patrick agreed far too easily, bending over James's head. "I wouldn't mind having a go with her myself. She was a right pretty piece of . . ."

Before he could even think, James snaked a fist out and grabbed his friend's necktie, pulling Patrick's face down within inches of his own. "That's my pretend wife you are disparaging, so I'll thank you to think twice."

Patrick carefully disengaged himself from his friend's grip and gave him a cocky grin for his trouble. "Same reaction as last night. Just checking to see if you were still arse over elbow for the lady. I suppose I should count myself fortunate. You knocked out MacRory's two front teeth last night for far less an indiscretion."

James blinked against a swirl of confusion as Patrick set in again on his scalp. He knew he had busted the butcher's teeth last night—the innkeeper had told him as much. He even remembered doing it now, recalled the satisfying crack of his fist, a woman's high-pitched scream, and the violence of shattered glass and splintered wood. And of course, there had been the inevitable rush of guilt as MacRory had spit out a mouthful of blood.

But no one had yet told him why he had done it. Had he brawled with the butcher last night, over the girl? "Why did I hit him?" James asked.

Patrick shrugged, which was in hindsight a reaction best avoided when one was putting a needle to skin. "Hell if I know. He said something about the girl, I suppose. One minute you're laughing, and the next you're swinging. Never seen you like that, truth be told."

James winced as his skin twitched under Patrick's painful ministrations. His thoughts were a jumble inside his head. His purported reaction last night made no sense. He had spent his adult life carefully controlling those impulses, ensuring a veneer of respectability that would stand fast, no matter how thin a shield it actually was. After the failures of his youth, he had sworn never again to be brought to violence, and certainly never again over a woman.

Only he had apparently abandoned all that effort last

night, and all for one false female. She was a thief, had probably plotted to steal his purse from the moment she first sat upon his lap and felt its promising bulge through his coat pocket. If *he* wanted to see her brought to justice, what did it matter what Patrick thought of her?

"I suppose it doesn't matter." James gave his thoughts of her a good hard shove and returned his attention to the fact he had almost hit his best friend. The pain in his head had numbed to a dull ache, but the bite of each pass of the needle made his eyes pull shut. "I do not know where she is, anyway."

"Well, the first place *I* would look if I had misplaced my wife and my horse in the same night would be David Cameron's house," Patrick said, leaning in close to inspect one damnably sure stitch after another.

James squinted up at his friend. Patrick was already in dangerous territory, ribbing him about the girl and poking him with the unremitting needle. But mentioning the woman he sought and the man he despised in the same breath was tempting violence. "Why would I want to visit Cameron?" he asked carefully, his nails digging crescent moons into the upholstered seat beneath him.

"Because that great black beast you have tied up to the fence post outside is his mare. Treated her for founder, just last month. Lame as Gemmy, that mare is. She'll make a decent broodmare, but will be useless as a riding animal. If you traded that horse for Caesar, you've been swindled, my friend."

James's head buzzed in alarm. Not because he thought he might have done something so stupid as to trade Caesar. It was more the mention of David Cameron, Moraig's magistrate.

James knew Patrick still counted the man as a friend,

a side effect of the time the three had shared at Cambridge. They were all second sons, thrust into the requirements of receiving a proper education but denied the benefits that came with any rightful claim to a title. Surrounded by young men who were wealthier and more assured of their lot in life, the three had come together to form a sort of club.

But despite this history, and the fact that both he and Cameron hailed from Moraig, James had long since ceased to think of David in a friendly manner. In fact, he tried very hard not to think of him at all, although his position as the town solicitor and Cameron's role as the town magistrate made some degree of professional communication necessary.

He could not avoid thinking of him now, however. A memory returned from the previous evening, of pulling the girl up on the table and standing beside her as the room spun around them. It was not real. At least, it was not *supposed* to be real. He remembered staring down at her, her hands reed-slender in his own, as Cameron—equally as deep in his cups as anyone else in the place—had performed the mock ceremony with the dramatic flair of a born thespian, and then grandly pronounced them drunkard and wife.

He had no memory of why he had agreed to such a farce. It was outside the bounds of decency, and it made a mockery of marriage and love and things James generally viewed as sacred. It made no sense for him to have risked his reputation in such a way. He could only imagine the girl had asked it of him, and that he had done it for reasons separate from the way she made his body stand at attention.

But David Cameron . . . he was a wild card in this.

The man of whom they spoke was a surprisingly decent magistrate, fair and direct in his dealings. But outside of the job, he still acted exactly like the spoiled second son he had always been.

"About Cameron . . ." James swallowed. "Do you think . . . I mean, could he have . . . performed a legitimate ceremony last night?"

He held his breath as he waited for Patrick to answer. Damned if *that* wouldn't muck things up, even worse than they already were. The ceremony had sounded real enough to his ale-buzzed ears. It would be just the kind of sick humor Cameron had specialized in so long ago at Cambridge, before life had thrust them in opposite directions. David might be Moraig's newest magistrate, but James doubted the man's new professional geniality extended to the point of forgoing such a delicious joke, or a chance to exact such an ironic measure of revenge.

Patrick squinted down at him. "I was there for only the last bit of it. If you've a mind to find out, you'll need to ask Cameron himself." His friend ducked down and snapped the last bit of thread with his teeth. "All finished."

James reached out an unsteady hand and balanced himself against the sawdust bag that hung temptingly from a rafter. Normally, when he felt this coiled up, he used it to release his pent-up energy, working his muscles into compliance and his mind into submission. But given the way his head was pounding, he suspected it would be several days before he felt well enough to use the sparring bag again. One more thing to add to his growing list of reasons to be annoyed with the girl.

Patrick sighed as James pushed himself upright. "If you were one of my four-legged patients, I'd recommend a bath and a few days' rest before you go traipsing all over town."

"I've seen what you do to your four-legged patients." James headed toward the hallway on unsteady feet. "And if poor Gemmy is any indication, I prefer to keep my limbs and my balls intact."

A bath, unspeakably tempting as it was, would take time James did not have. No, he would have to make do with a quick wash in his room, using the sliver of plain, brown soap that awaited him there. He would sacrifice the thirty seconds it would take to make use of his toothpowder and put on a clean shirt, if indeed one even awaited him in his near-empty chest of drawers.

But the few days' rest Patrick suggested was out of the question. Every minute he let slip past without pursuing the few clues available to him was another minute she could use to cover her tracks. He had no choice. As soon as he could manage to stumble his way out the door, he was off to Cameron's.

And God help the man—or brother—who tried to stop him.

Chapter 9

Arriving in town on the back of a potato cart that smelled of moist earth and rotting vegetables was more tolerable than Georgette had first imagined.

It helped that Elsie Dalrymple was a fountain of local lore, distracting Georgette from the indignity of their conveyance by pointing out the distant loch shimmering in early afternoon sunlight and the thin blue band where fresh water met the sea. As the wagon rocked over the rutted road and Georgette cradled the kitten protectively against her chest, Elsie spun fanciful tales about Kilmartie Castle, which sat high on a bluff over the loch. And as they drew closer to town and began to pass curious residents, Elsie diverted Georgette's embarrassment by elaborating on the history of Moraig itself and its role as a smuggling port twenty years ago.

By the time they pulled to a stop outside the Blue Gander, Georgette felt as if she could have grown up here, so complete was her knowledge of the town.

Of course, if she *had* grown up in Moraig, it would not matter that her memory from the previous evening showed no signs of returning. She would know precisely the sort of man Mr. James MacKenzie was, and what made him so irresistible that she had agreed to marry him after a courtship the length of a heartbeat.

She no longer felt panicked over what she had done. She felt resolved. There was no time to waste in tracking him down, no reason to delay the inevitable. She needed an annulment.

But first she needed to find him.

Elsie tumbled out of the cart first, shaking out her skirts and ignoring Georgette's expectant look. Georgette cleared her throat. "A ladies' maid helps her mistress down if there is no footman about."

Elsie dissolved into giggles. "Oh, that's rich, miss. Are we pretending the potato cart is a coach now?"

Georgette had to admit, it *did* seem a little silly. She slid from the back of the wagon, her reticule and kitten uncomfortably in one hand. Small steps, she reminded herself. It took time to train a proper servant.

"I enjoyed seeing you again, Joseph." Elsie smiled at the young man who had served as their coachman. "Perhaps I'll see even *more* of you later tonight."

The boy flushed red. Georgette grabbed Elsie by the elbow and pulled her out of earshot as the cart began to move off. "A ladies' maid does not say such things," she hissed.

Elsie lifted a hand to one hip. "Why not?"

"It's . . . it's just not done." Georgette shifted the kitten from one hand to the other, trying to remember *why* it was not done.

Elsie's eyes trailed back the cart, which was already threading its way into Main Street traffic. "I suppose you think I should not associate with the likes of Joseph Rothven anymore," she sniffed. "Well, I don't see why being a ladies' maid should turn me into a nob. And he was good enough for *you* last night."

"No." Georgette cleared the embarrassment from her throat. "I mean, *no*, you are free to associate with whomever you want. Servants just need to be more careful about what they say in public. Your comportment reflects upon your employer."

"Well, that doesn't sound like much fun," Elsie muttered, but any further inappropriate words she may have planned were captured in a sneeze that shook the maid's whole body.

Georgette sighed. It was the third such reflexive sneeze in the past hour. Either Elsie was catching a summer cold—which seemed unlikely, given the unseasonably warm weather—or it was yet another reminder that in addition to finding Mr. MacKenzie, they also needed to locate the butcher and return the kitten.

She looked around, taking note of her surroundings and searching the crowd for either a large, blood-spattered butcher or a man with a brown beard and eyes the color of absinthe. To their right, a man climbed up a ladder to string colored paper lanterns along the Blue Gander's broken front facade. His height and beard looked about right for Mr. MacKenzie, but when he finished his task and turned around to face her, she could see his face was too thin, his eyes too blue.

Disappointment settled over her. Moraig seemed larger than it had this morning, possibly a town of several thousand people. How was she supposed to find MacKenzie when everywhere she looked there were brawny Scotsmen with beards? If she had to go about staring into every resident's eyes, it was going to be a long afternoon, indeed.

"Are they preparing for some sort of celebration?" Georgette asked, nodding toward the paper lanterns.

" 'Tis Bealltainn, miss."

"What is Bealltainn?" The word sounded foreign on Georgette's lips, but carried a hint of the local dialect her ears were coming to recognize.

"The May festival." Elsie offered Georgette an impish smile. "There will be dancing tonight, and a bonfire. Lots of dark corners, and opportunities for stolen kisses."

Georgette grimaced. Bealltainn sounded like just the sort of activity she usually avoided.

Then again, so was the evening crowd at the Blue Gander.

She pulled Elsie south along Main Street, heading in the direction she had plunged that morning. The smells and sounds she remembered from the dawn's dash to freedom had shifted, and instead of frying dough and market voices raised in trade, the unmistakable scent of roasting meat and the sound of hammers filled the air. Preparations for Bealltainn appeared in full swing, which made it all the more imperative she find Mac-Kenzie and the butcher and escape before the impending revelry made it an impossible task.

"Tell me more about Mr. MacKenzie," she directed Elsie as they walked, the kitten bundled tight against her chest.

The maid offered her mistress a knowing gaze, her hazel eyes shining in amusement. "I thought you were anxious to be done with the man."

"I am."

She was. But the curiosity Georgette felt about him was like an electric current in her veins. She hummed with the need to know more. "In order to find him as quickly as possible, it would help if I knew more about him. Where he goes. What he's like."

The maid shrugged. "What else is there to tell? The man is handsome as sin, and there will be throngs of women grateful you don't want him." She grinned. "When I think about how he tossed the butcher through the window . . . well, what I wouldn't give to wake up to *that* one in my bed."

"The butcher?" Georgette asked, trying to follow the maid's erratic train of thought.

"MacKenzie." Elsie's lips stretched wider. "Once you're done with him, of course."

A flash of jealousy turned Georgette's stomach, end over end. She clutched the kitten tighter, confused by her body's unexpected reaction. What did it matter if Elsie sighed like a love-struck schoolgirl in need of a kiss whenever she mentioned MacKenzie's name?

Georgette didn't need his kiss—she needed to be *rid* of him.

"Treats women well, that one does," Elsie continued, oblivious to her mistress's unanticipated turmoil. "Never seemed close to settling down, though, until you showed up." She leaned in closer. "Of course, there's the rumors."

Georgette pursed her lips. She could well imagine the rumors that would trail a man of Mr. MacKenzie's obvious . . . virility.

Elsie looked right, then left. "Some kind of tragedy. In his youth," she whispered.

"That doesn't sound so sordid," Georgette whispered back, though she really had no idea why they were speaking in such low, hushed tones.

Elsie scanned the people on either side of them before stepping closer to whisper behind a cupped hand. "It was apparently quite the town scandal some years ago. A girl got herself with child, and claimed someone else was the father. MacKenzie claimed it was his."

Georgette stilled, trying to imagine such a terrible thing. "What happened?"

"That was before I came to Moraig. But the way I hear it, the girl pitched herself over a bridge soon after, and MacKenzie went a little mad, fighting any scrapper who cared to take a swing at him. Gave him a bit of a reputation. But I don't see the problem. Sometimes a body needs to use their fists."

"Not in London," Georgette said, weak at the thought. She couldn't imagine ever facing a scenario in which she could strike someone.

"Well, perhaps you need to get out more, miss."

Silence descended. Really, what was there to say after such a personal, tragic bit of gossip?

They walked on. Georgette thought about the laughing rogue who had beckoned her back to bed this morning, tried to imagine him as a hurt young man taking out his frustrations on anyone close enough to suffer his fists. Her heart squeezed for him.

"He's the son of the Earl of Kilmartie," Elsie offered next.

"The son of an *earl*?" Georgette exclaimed. She had trouble reconciling the hard musculature she had ogled this morning with the soft, pampered life of a peer. Why, she had thought the man was a footman! Shouldn't they be referring to him as *Lord* MacKenzie? Her cheeks burned in surprise and mortification before her mind leaped to a new destination. "Will we find him at the castle, then?"

Elsie shook her head. "He's not the heir. Lives in

town. And the earl doesn't come anywhere near the Blue Gander. But MacKenzie's different. You'd hardly know they were kin. Seems more like the common folk, with his skulking about and that great, shaggy beard."

That description of the beard seemed in keeping with Georgette's memory, at least. "Should we try his house in town then?" she pressed, unwilling to let even a single opportunity to find him slip by.

"I don't know." Elsie pursed her lips and glanced up at the sun, which hovered just overhead. "This time of day, I think he'd be working."

Frustration pulled at Georgette with a thousand tiny fingers. Sorting this out with Elsie was like conversing with a soothsayer, each new twist to the conversation revealing hidden depths. She sighed. Clearly the girl had not told her everything she knew about MacKenzie. "What is his profession?" she asked, wondering if it might not be easier just to torture the information out of her new maid.

"He's the town solicitor," Elsie said with an air of distraction. She turned her head and smiled invitingly at a gentleman who passed by to their left. It wasn't MacKenzie—this man's beard was longer and speckled with gray, but he leered at Elsie in a way that very much brought to mind the way MacKenzie had looked at her this morning.

Georgette gave herself a hard mental shake. She was seeing the man in every shadow, but inching far too slowly toward seeing him in the flesh. If he was a solicitor, he wasn't a gentleman, at least not in the sense she was used to. And it was still difficult to reconcile the muscled physique in her memory with such a bookish profession. But this, finally, was a clue worth following.

"Why didn't you mention this before?" she demanded. "Presumably he has an office we could visit."

"Aye, he lets an office in north Moraig. Serves his clients ginger water and cakes, even the guilty ones." Elsie pulled her attention away from the retreating gentleman and skirted an awkward pause. An uncharacteristic blush stained her cheeks. "I mean . . . so I've heard."

"Elsie." Georgette stopped dead in her tracks. "What aren't you telling me?" A fearful suspicion became tangled in her mind. "Have you interacted with Mr. MacKenzie in a manner more significant than serving him a pint of ale?"

Elsie shrugged in that odd, one-shouldered affectation she so favored. "Once or twice. In my old position, of course."

"Your position? You mean, at the Blue Gander?"

"Before that." Elsie jutted her chin out, but Georgette could hear the hesitance in her voice. "I used to work . . . *behind* the Gander."

Georgette's hand fell away in shock. "You are a prostitute?" she asked, her throat going dry. Her feet were frozen, but her thoughts were anything but still.

Had Elsie done *that*? With the man who was currently—if temporarily—Georgette's husband?

"Was." Elsie shifted her balance from foot to foot. "I *was* a prostitute. And not a prostitute, really. I just stepped out with the occasional man who caught my eye."

"In the alley," Georgette pointed out. "That's not precisely a traditional place for courting."

"There's no need to look at me like that," Elsie said, peevish now. "You knew about it last night, when you offered me the position. And it is not as bad as you think. It was a right fine life, until MacKenzie intervened."

Anger flashed through Georgette. She did not want to judge Elsie for her choices, no more than she judged herself for falling prey to her first ill-designed marriage. If the maid had chosen to do those things, there was no doubt in Georgette's mind she had done so willingly, or at least tolerably. But the man in this sordid story . . . it was entirely too tempting to judge him.

Even if he did serve his clients cakes and ginger water.

"Did Mr. MacKenzie have need of your . . . services?" Georgette's voice roughened with distaste. "Or abuse you in some way?"

Elsie's eyes widened. "Oh no, miss, you have it all wrong."

"He tried to prosecute you, then?"

"No, nothing like that." Elsie's face twisted. "He *helped* me, last spring when the town rector charged me with public indecency. Stood up with me at my court hearing, and didn't charge me a ha'penny either. MacKenzie looks out for those of us who find themselves on the wrong side of things. But he said he couldn't protect me if I kept at it, and helped get me the job serving pints at the Blue Gander instead."

The relief that stole over Georgette at learning of MacKenzie's good deed disturbed her almost as much as the earlier concern that he might have been someone worth hating. She shook herself from the thought. It would not do to develop any kind of attachment to the man, or to feel solidarity with his methods.

One did not feed or pet the creature one planned to set free.

"I am not ashamed of what I was," Elsie went on,

eyeing yet another passing gentleman with a feral gleam of interest. "I *enjoy* men. And they enjoyed paying me for a romp."

That made Georgette blink. She had no comprehension of what made the servant's color run so high, or caused her to use the word "enjoy" and "men" in the same breath. Coupling was a quick, fumbling act, performed as nothing more than a conjugal duty. To be sure, she had dreamed of more. It seemed there should be more to it. It seemed there should be more to *her*.

She felt again that quickened step to her blood, the awareness of self that had so surprised her this morning when she had faced the audacity of Mr. MacKenzie's bare chest. Perhaps there *was* more to her.

Pity she couldn't explore it further.

The kitten stirred against the fabric of her walking dress, mewing its irritation at waking to find a wool-clad human holding it instead of its mother. Georgette tucked the kitten up against her chin as she sorted out what to do next. It occurred to her she might need to change up her priorities. The little thing's life would be in jeopardy if she didn't provide for it soon. She scanned the street for a tea shop or café where they might request a bit of warmed milk. "We should probably try to find this kitten something to eat," she told Elsie.

"I wouldn't mind a spot of food myself." Elsie patted her hip suggestively. "Need to keep my figure up in case this ladies' maid position doesn't suit. But I thought you wanted to find MacKenzie right quick."

"I do." Georgette took a deep breath. The need to locate her mysterious Scotsman had thickened into something indistinct, complicated by the surprising turn in the conversation with Elsie. It seemed she was dealing with more than a rogue in her bed—the man she sought had layers she had not anticipated.

She wanted to find him with new urgency now, and not only to demand an annulment. She wanted to soften her memory of the man as a rakehell with the heroic image Elsie had painted of him. She wanted to offer an apology for her unladylike behavior this morning, courtesy of the chamber pot. And even if it was inappropriate, even if it was *dangerous*, she wanted to experience that awful stirring in her stomach at the sight of him, just once more before returning to a staid life in London.

"And as soon as we eat," Georgette said, her heart already tripping in anticipation, "you must show me exactly where Mr. MacKenzie's office is."

Chapter 10

DAVID CAMERON WAS as hard at work as James had ever seen him.

Which was to say Moraig's magistrate was bent over a manger in his father's stables, arse to the rafters, surrounded by a puddle of skirts and enjoying his afternoon a little too much.

For a moment—a disturbing, anger-driven sliver of time—jealousy roared through James's limbs. He imagined he would find both his horse and his pretend wife here, used to ill-form by his former friend. It would not be the first time Cameron had taken something from James, only to discard it when he grew bored.

He almost hauled the man upright and called him out. But then James caught sight of falling-down brown hair and a white servant's cap, and realized the woman in question was not the blond-haired thief who now occupied a place front and center in his memory.

The anger leached away, leaving him drained and shaking. Dear God, if the thought of finding the woman he sought under this man threatened to send him into a flying fit of rage, it was no wonder he had acted so impulsively last night.

But of course, this was not just any man. This was

David Cameron. And the insult would have been too great to ignore.

The smell of straw and leather hammered his senses as he considered what do to with the indelicate situation he and William had just blundered their way into. The black mare pulled hard against the reins, as if instructing him to walk away. Beside him, William shuffled his own impatience. "Should we do something?" his brother asked, his voice a low whisper. "Save her, perhaps?"

A woman's gasp of pleasure reached James's ears. "No. I don't think she objects." He took a step backward, intending to withdraw to the brighter sunshine outside and wait for the pair to be finished. Even though they hadn't been friends for years, James recalled the man's proclivities from their days at Cambridge.

This was Cameron. Surely it wouldn't take very long.

"Well, *I* object." The grim line of William's jaw conveyed his censure as clearly as his words. "He's tupping the wench in broad daylight. It doesn't matter if she is willing. Any woman worth the trouble of wooing is worth a proper bed. The baron would have his head."

At the mention of Cameron's father, James paused, one foot in retreat. That, at least, was something he knew and remembered all too well. Living in your father's house carried a price. Made you constantly question what you were doing, how you conducted yourself, whom you spent time with. Whom you loved.

It was part of the reason James had left Moraig for Glasgow eleven years ago, burying himself in an apprenticeship with a tyrant of a solicitor. If nothing else, it was a choice he had made for himself. Cameron had escaped Moraig a few months before James, using his father's money to purchase a commission in the army. But Cameron had discarded more than the dust of Moraig when he left, and therein laid the rub.

They had both returned to Moraig in the past year, each by his own circuitous path, each for his own reasons. James was the prodigal second son, determined to shrug off his past and change the prevailing opinion of the townsfolk through hard work and self-reliance. Cameron was playing at the heroic second son, with a chest full of damned medals he apparently used to get servants to lift their skirts.

Patrick Channing was the quiet spine between James's and David's more raucous pages. With his history of friendship with both James and David, Patrick had unwittingly disturbed the rigid peace that had just started to spring roots in Moraig.

Not that Cameron couldn't do a perfectly good job of disrupting that peace himself.

James lifted a finger to his lips and shook his head, motioning to William to back up. He pulled on the reins, trying to turn the horse around, but the mare chose that moment to nicker to some unseen inhabitant of the cavernous barn. A shrill neigh answered her back. The horse's ears swiveled forward, and she began to dance at the edge of her lead, scattering sawdust and shaking the boards beneath her feet.

With his injured head and still-throbbing shin, it was all James could do just to hang on to the horse. Stealth, at this point in the game, was out of the question.

The woman beneath David Cameron gave a squeak of surprise. James saw her shove at Cameron's broad chest. "Please, Mr. Cameron. I . . . I need to get back to the house."

The girl was definitely a servant, to show such deference, even in the middle of a torrid embrace. Probably his mother's parlor maid and forbidden fruit, if the girl's pale cheeks and worry-filled eyes were any indication.

Cameron twisted his head from his awkward position on the straw-filled manger. The man's dark blond curls stuck out in disarray, a testament to the maid's busy fingers. His lazy eyes fixed on James as the girl gained her feet and struggled with the buttons of her bodice. "Do not worry your pretty head over it, Meg."

Cameron might as well have taken a hand to her, for the look on the girl's face. She stilled. "My . . . my name is Maggie."

Cameron at least had the good sense to look chagrined. "Er . . . Maggie. Yes, well, he won't tell. He's good that way, always has been. Lips sewn tight as stitching. Isn't that right, MacKenzie?"

James curled his fingers into a fist and considered how best to respond. "Aye," he finally said, struggling to ignore the hidden meaning in Cameron's taunts. "I won't tell."

The maid patted a shaking hand over her hair, tucking errant wisps back under her cap. "I . . . I am sorry," she whispered. "I should not have done this."

"No," James agreed. "You shouldn't have. But the fault is not only yours. *He* should know better."

His taunt earned a glower from the blond giant who was gaining his feet. "Why don't you head back to the house, Maggie." Cameron's voice was a low rumble—a warning to James, not the girl.

Not that the poor chit could tell the difference.

With one last confused look at the man she had just been kissing, the maid lifted her skirts and darted away toward the big stone manor up on the hill. Her feet fairly flew over the manicured lawn, and David Cameron watched her go a long, studied moment. "Satisfied, MacKenzie?"

"More so than you, by the looks of things." James eyed his former friend in distaste. Cameron was covered in hay, and without his coat and hat he resembled little more than a common groom. James had never understood why, but women were as drawn to the man's looks as to his promised wealth. It had always been that way, even when they had been friends an age ago. It was as if women couldn't see past the man's handsome face and his father's heavy purse to see the person beneath.

It had sometimes made James want to bust Cameron's nose, just to lessen the golden, shining perfection of him.

Funny how time had not lessened the desire.

"Still up to your same tricks, I see." James patted the black mare's neck in lieu of using his hands for a more satisfying purpose.

"And you still have frightful taste in horseflesh," came Cameron's bold taunt as he worked the buttons of his trousers to respectability. "What in the devil are you doing with the beast I sold to the butcher yesterday?"

James's mind cartwheeled in response to the question he had not anticipated. Damn David Cameron, would *nothing* go right today? If the horse he had just dragged through the streets of Moraig had recently been sold to the butcher, James was unlikely to find his stallion grazing contentedly in Cameron's back paddock.

And that meant Caesar, who was descended from a sire who had won the Grand National and was arguably the finest mount in Inverness-shire, might be in danger of the fate intended for the black mare.

Panic skidded against the walls of his chest, but James forced himself to stay calm. "The mare deserves a chance to heal." He cursed this ill-fated quest that seemed to take on a new degree of urgency with each bloody clue he uncovered. "Channing says she might still be useful as a broodmare, and she's got fine conformation. It's just like you to presume something is lost without taking the time to make a meager effort, or measure its real worth."

"And you were always too quick to pick up my pieces," the man snapped, snatching up the reins to his horse.

James did not immediately relinquish his hold on the mare. His gaze arrowed in on the flush that now darkened Cameron's face, but he gave the bulk of his attention to the line of questioning simmering in his head. "I'll offer you a trade: the mare for some answers." He eased his hand away from the reins. "I'd like a word with you about last night, and the woman I was with at the Blue Gander."

"Which woman?" Cameron asked, brushing off the bits of hay clinging to his shirt before settling a hand on the mare's nose. "The tavern wench, Elsie Dalrymple?" He grinned through his anger, displaying the straight, white teeth of a predator. "Or the lovely Mrs. MacKenzie?"

William stiffened beside him. Though his big brother's constant shadow was something James had cursed more than once since waking, a wave of gratitude rolled through him knowing William was here, now, ready to stand by him if need be. He stayed his brother's forward momentum with a wave of his hand. He didn't need his honor defended. He needed answers.

And ruining Cameron's long, straight nose would not get him there.

"Do you know her given name?" James asked.

Cameron's eyes narrowed, squinting through a shaft of sunlight that found its way through the open stable doors. "I can't think why you would even have need to ask that." He started to turn away with the mare in hand, then halted, his brow pulled down in thought. "Unless you are having trouble remembering. Didn't think you were that drunk, MacKenzie, although Lord knows *I* saw the deep end of a bottle last night." Cameron's smile broadened, all teeth and no laughter. "What an interesting twist that would be to all of this."

James ignored the man's taunts. "Was it a real ceremony?"

"Well, that depends. She was a real enough woman, and you said real enough words."

"Just answer the bloody question," James growled. "Before I give in to the urge to take myself up to the house and ask how your little afternoon diversion is faring." He paused, and then leaned in. "And the first person I will ask will be your father."

Cameron laughed then, his big body shaking with it. "Threatening me won't help matters, and well you know it. But no, to answer the question, it was not a real ceremony. 'Twas nothing but the fun of the moment. You and your bride signed no register, exchanged no ring. I may not like you, but even I would not sink so low as to marry a man without his consent."

"You know as well as I do that Scots law does not require such things," James pointed out. "It requires only a witness, followed by consummation or cohabitation and repute."

Cameron's face darkened at the challenge. "And I already told you, I cannot be considered your bloody witness. I knew the thing was nothing but a farce. You've nothing to worry about, MacKenzie."

Relief darted through James. His profession relied as much on reading people as on uncovering the facts of a case. His instincts told him David Cameron was telling the truth. But having the truth was not the same as having a full explanation. "Why did you even play at marrying us then, if you hate me so much?"

"I did not do it for you." Cameron's smile faltered, showing the cracks beneath. "I did it for her."

There were only two women James recalled being at the Gander last night. His blood started to thump in his ears. "You did it for Elsie Dalrymple?"

"I did it for Georgette."

"Georgette?" James felt like the most stupid man alive, but he could do no more than echo the name pricking his ears.

"Lady Thorold," Cameron clarified. "Still can't believe a lady of that quality would be interested in you when she could have had me, but there's no accounting for taste."

James's world tilted off-kilter, moving in a long, slow slide that started in his chest and ended somewhere on the straw-strewn stable floor. Georgette Thorold. It matched the initials he had seen on the busk, suggesting she had at least told the truth about her name. He had something to call her now, vowels and consonants to accompany the lively picture he carried in his mind.

And apparently, so did David Cameron.

"She told you she was a lady?" James tried to summon a laugh, only there wasn't much funny in how this was all unfolding. Ladies guarded their reputations. They did not swill ale from stranger's cups. They did not sit in men's laps and laugh with wide-open mouths.

And they did not engage in mock wedding ceremonies with men they had known all of an hour.

"A lady far too good for the likes of you," Cameron all but snarled, pulling the mare then into an empty stall and going to work on the girth.

William leaned over the wall of the adjacent stall, the deep bass of his voice making the black mare dance in agitation. "Are you saying a Cameron is better than a MacKenzie? Because being indiscriminate with your prick doesn't make you the better man, and I've a fist I'm willing to sacrifice to prove it."

"It would take the both of you." Cameron pulled the saddle from the mare's back and dumped it in an unceremonious heap on the stall floor. "I can hold my own against any MacKenzie."

James positioned himself in front of William. No sense letting his brother hit Cameron before he got the answers he needed. "What would a lady be doing unchaperoned in the public room of the Blue Gander?"

"Who the hell knows?" Cameron slipped the bridle from the horse's ears, taking care to hold the bit as he extracted it from the mare's mouth. "But she was quality, all right, from the tip of her pert little nose to the trim ankle she flashed everyone as she climbed up on the table. Perhaps she was looking for companionship. Perhaps she came to the Gander looking for a little sport, and decided to slum it with you."

Cameron licked his lips as he came out of the stall, as if regretting not having been able to taste the woman they were discussing. He slung the bridle over the stall door. "She's not the kind of lady you tell no, MacKenzie. When she asked me to perform a sham wedding, I was happy to oblige. And if I had been lucky enough to have her fasten those pretty gray eyes on me, I would damned sure remember every blessed second."

"If you were so enamored of her, you should have told her," James pointed out. "But then again, why would you? Fighting for what you want has never been your strong suit."

The sharp intake of breath Cameron took as he bolted the door on the horse he had just unsaddled spoke volumes. "She didn't want me," he ground out. "The lady had eyes only for you."

The confirmation that the woman in question had selected James last night over the other pickings in the room should have made him all the more suspicious that it had been an orchestrated event, carefully calculated to relieve him of a heavy purse. Instead, it heightened the unexpected possessiveness James felt toward her. "That couldn't have been easy for you, given that every woman in a room is usually fawning over you."

Cameron's eyes probed at him, hawklike over the straight arrow of his nose. "Aye, I admit it doesn't make sense. So it doesn't matter how pretty she was. She is clearly addled in the brain."

James reacted poorly to the suggestion that the woman in his mind's eye was something less than fully right in the head. His body's objection was visceral, a quickening of his blood, a tightening of his fists. The woman he was beginning to remember had not been addled. She had been quick-witted, full of humor and life. Every man in the pub had wanted her, including David Cameron.

"Of course," Cameron went on, as if he hadn't just slandered her, "if you don't want her, I might be persuaded to give it another go. A lady of that quality doesn't surface in Moraig every day."

A sharp curl of jealousy centered in James's stomach. "It matters not whether you want her. You should have more of a care with whom you associate. The woman is no lady."

Cameron's incredulous laugh echoed off the stable rafters, sending horses rustling in hidden stalls. "Are you forgetting I spoke with her first? You may not remember much about her, but *I* do. She claimed a distant kinship to the Bonhams, and said she was the widow of the late Viscount Benjamin Thorold. I'm not in the market for a wife, but if I were, it would be a better match than I could make with any of the country misses around here."

The suggestion that Cameron knew the woman better than James grated like steel wool on soap. He had spent the night with her, while Cameron had done no more than moon over her. And yet, the man spoke with the calm assurance of someone who knew such things.

Someone who *remembered*.

"Appearances can be deceiving," James muttered. He, of all people, knew that pedigree did not make the gentleman. It stood to reason it did not make a lady either.

Cameron sobered and looked at James with a speculative gleam in his eye. "Are you saying you don't believe she's a real lady?

"I'm saying she's a bloody thief. Took my money purse and the fifty pounds I had inside. And if she had any notion of your worth over mine, I suspect it would be *you* in this situation this morning, missing your horse and lacking your life's savings."

That, finally, seemed to shut David Cameron's mouth. James had expected laughter at the confession, but instead the man stood a long, silent minute. Beside them, William shuffled in the straw, breaking the tension as cleanly as a knife through butter.

Cameron ran a hand through his tousled hair. It was a gesture James knew well, a look he had seen over the judicial bench and actually respected.

David Cameron had just shrugged off the insolent air he usually wore and put on his magistrate's hat. "I suppose that explains why you are here," he said speculatively. "What do you need from me?"

What *did* James need? He needed to find the woman who had stripped away the town's respect he had been working so hard to earn. And, God help him, he wanted to punish her for leaving him this morning as much as for stealing his purse.

He had been chasing nothing but the shadow of the mystery woman's skirts across Moraig. But now that he had a name, he was chasing a person, not just a memory. He would catch her, eventually, and when he did he intended to be armed to the teeth.

"A summons should do nicely." James was more sure of this next step than any he had entertained so far.

"MacKenzie," Cameron said, shaking his head. "Are you sure you want to do that? You don't know with certainty she took your purse."

"Hence the summons." James crossed his arms and tried to look like the imperious solicitor he was supposed to be. "She is lucky I don't charge her with theft outright."

"You don't *need* to charge her with anything," Cameron countered. "Your father is one of the wealthiest men in the county. Why in the devil are you doing this, and all for a piddling fifty pounds?"

James grimaced. Accepting William's charity today had been damning enough; his pride would never withstand such a blow as to admit a weakness to his father. Fifty pounds might not seem like a lot of money to David Cameron, but it was everything James had in the world.

"Just do it," he growled. "And be sure to make it out to Lady Georgette Thorold."

Chapter 11

No sooner had Georgette mentioned the need to feed the kitten than her own hapless stomach grumbled as loud as the Bealltainn hammers working steadily up and down Main Street.

She wasn't just hungry, Georgette realized. She was ravenous. She literally could not remember the last thing she had eaten. And while perhaps not as tragic as forgetting whom she had married, it demanded equal attention.

Her gaze settled on a bright red awning a half a block away, and she pointed toward it with her free hand. "Shall we try over there?" The tea shop that had caught her eye was busy, with a dozen or so patrons sitting outside at wrought-iron tables. It looked like an utterly pleasant place for a luncheon, particularly after the disgrace of their ride into town.

The maid, however, did not seem as impressed as Georgette's rumbling stomach.

"Oh no, miss. I can't eat there." Elsie shook her head. "We should try the back kitchen at the Gander. They know me well enough, and I'm sure they could make us up something quick."

Georgette's face burned hot at the thought of sitting

down to a meal in the same establishment where she had achieved infamy the night before. "Definitely not the Gander. What is wrong with the tea shop?"

Elsie rubbed a hand over her faded cotton skirt. "I can't afford to eat there."

"You are not expected to pay for your own meals, Elsie."

The maid's thin shoulders refused to relax. "I would rather just wait outside."

Georgette reminded herself to go slowly. After all, the girl was just learning her duties. "If you are to excel at this new role, you must act the part. A ladies' maid is expected to accompany her mistress into shops." Why was Elsie making this so difficult? Georgette was leaving for London as soon as her circumstances allowed, and the maid needed to learn these skills quickly in order to find another position.

Elsie lifted her chin. Sunshine glinted off her auburn hair as clearly as the stubbornness glinting in her eyes. "People here know me, and they will judge you for it. You are a lady, miss. I am not fit company to sit at a table with you."

"That didn't bother you two hours ago when you were soaking in my tub," Georgette pointed out. Exasperation edged into the hunger, making her cross. "I thought you were looking to improve your situation."

"I was!" Elsie exclaimed. "I mean, I am. But I didn't think this through." She looked up at the sun and shaded her eyes. "I don't have a hat," she grumbled. "How can I be someone better if I don't even have a hat?"

That was when Georgette realized the maid's problem was more complicated than a lack of funds, or want of a smart new bonnet. Sympathy struck with the efficiency of the hammers ringing in her ears. She knew what it was like to be measured by strangers' eyes and come up short. The London Season, with its glittering balls and women so impossibly beautiful it made her eyes ache, had been a snake's nest of just such self-doubt. In some ways, the stranglehold of mourning, with its rigid requirements for clothing and comportment, had been a relief.

It was easier to be a widow. One dressed in black and stayed indoors.

"We don't need a hat to sit down for tea," Georgette assured her, aiming for urgency over honesty. It was an outdoor café, and ladies did not walk about bareheaded out of doors. Why, in London, the lowest of scullery maids would not dare such a thing! But she was hungry, and each moment's delay served as a reminder that she didn't know when she had least eaten.

"It's not just the hat," Elsie protested. "You're dressed like a proper lady. You are wearing gloves, and know which fork to use. I don't know *any* of that."

Georgette looked down at her gloved hands, one clutching the kitten, the other spread against her gray woolen frock. Her former husband had not deserved a year of mourning, much less the two Georgette had dutifully delivered. And yet here she was, dressed in gray, the brim of her bonnet the perfect length to hide her face, not a frill or flounce anywhere in sight. Though it had felt comfortable when she put it on, the outfit now seemed wholly inappropriate.

"We can order finger sandwiches," she told Elsie, as much to convince herself as the maid. "I'll forgo a fork on your behalf."

"You don't understand." Elsie threw up her hands in exasperation. "You could shove a bloody finger sandwich in your mouth sideways and you'd still be a lady. And I could learn to use a fork proper-like and still always be thought of as the girl from the Gander. And I don't mind that, truly I don't. But I don't want folks to think ill of you because of me."

Georgette stifled the urge to smile. The girl was worried about *her* reputation? It was a little late for that, and not because of anything Elsie had done.

"Being a lady is not the wondrous state of being you seem to consider it," she told the maid, her heart thumping its agreement as she realized it was true. "You think people don't talk and whisper, just because I am a lady? Let me tell you, they whisper *more*. And I think you should stop using that title to describe me, given the way I behaved last night. I'm no different than you. No better, no worse."

This was no kind sentiment, intended to soothe Elsie's fears. When she had taken the girl on, Georgette had thought this arrangement would provide a chance for Elsie to better her lot in life, and to learn something about being a ladies' maid.

It was uncomfortable to realize she seemed farther along in learning something about herself.

Was she still a lady? And did she really care if she wasn't?

Georgette stood in the bright Highland sunshine and thought about Elsie's words and the absent Mr. MacKenzie. *He* had not cared last night whether she acted with decorum. He had apparently liked her well enough to wed her, despite the fact that Elsie's recounting of events suggested she had acted more the tavern wench than the lady.

She wished she could remember how she had felt in

his arms, remembered what it was like, for once in her life, to be wanted by a man who made no demands on her to say something different, or wear something different, or *be* someone different. She wished she could recall what it felt like to fall asleep next to him, satisfied and happy and dreaming of tomorrow.

But the memory remained as elusive as the man.

And so Georgette settled for the next best rebellion. She reached up with her free hand and untied the ribbons to the plain gray bonnet she had donned this morning. She slid the somber bit of fabric from her head and dropped it to the dusty street. Her scalp tingled in exhilaration, the strip of skin revealed by her severe part reveling in the sunlight.

"Now I don't have a hat either." She offered the maid a conspiratorial smile. "I don't think anyone will care if we dine together in disarray. And if they do, *I* don't care. Shall we try it?"

Elsie stooped and snatched up the bonnet, dusting it off. "You shouldn't do that, miss," she admonished. "People will think I don't take proper care of you, and then how will I find a new position?" A smile touched her lips. "And your nose will turn pink in this terrible sun. You wouldn't want the other ladies to talk."

Georgette laughed and stretched her face skyward. She had the palest sort of English coloring, with hair closer to the color of bleached linen than spun gold. Men did not tend to write sonnets about ghostlike countenances, and she had always considered herself somewhat ugly for it. But something told her that James MacKenzie, with his unfashionable beard and his hard, sculpted muscles, did not care a farthing whether her skin was tanned or not.

"I don't care much for deadly dull bonnets," Georgette admitted, realizing that a month ago something so incongruous would have never been permitted to fall from her lips. She caught Elsie's eye. "Or people who judge you for what you are wearing or the company you keep."

The maid's eyes grew round. Not that Georgette blamed her. These were thoughts she was supposed to keep bottled away like last year's preserves, alongside her opinions about brandy and husbands.

And then a smile edged out from Elsie's earlier frown. She settled the discarded bonnet over her own head, tying the ribbons with firm, deft fingers. "Well, bully for you, miss." She lifted an auburn brow. "But *I'm* not going to let you toss away a perfectly good hat like yesterday's rubbish," she said before marching toward the tea shop.

Surprise caught Georgette's mouth open. She watched, incredulous, as the newly bonneted maid approached a table and sat down with a smirk.

Georgette walked slowly toward the table where Elsie was already pretending to read an upside-down menu. No matter her assurances to the maid they would be welcomed here, her walking dress was smudged with earth from the floor of the potato cart, and her uncovered hair had already started to loosen from its chignon. She had on gloves, at least, which assured she was partway to respectability.

But even as she embraced that comforting thought, the kitten squirmed in her hand. An unmistakable warmth seeped through the kidskin. Dimly, Georgette registered what had just occurred. The creature had relieved itself.

On her.

This could not be happening. She could do without a hat or fork, and manage a half hour's conversation with a prostitute-turned-abigail, but she could *not* sit down for tea with a urine-soaked glove.

Only she could. And unbelievably, she did.

Elsie exploded in laughter when she saw what had happened, and then waved her hands in refusal when Georgette tried to get her to hold the moist animal. Smiling herself, Georgette placed the kitten on the table, stripped off the soiled glove, and then picked the animal up again in her bare, cupped hand. The touch of soft fur on skin was startling. It felt small and wet in her hand, but it felt alive.

And she realized that she did, as well. Elsie's pealing amusement, the resolve to not care whether she was properly attired, the good smells coming from the shop's open door, all coalesced into a single, unexpected thought: she was enjoying herself. More than she had in months, perhaps more than she had in years.

They placed their order, and the tearoom attendant immediately brought warmed milk in a china cup. At first, the kitten seemed capable of little more than nosing at the spoon. Georgette grew worried that perhaps she had waited too long, that the kitten would be too weak to survive. She dipped the edge of her handkerchief into the cup and tried offering it the soaked bit of cloth, finally placing the edge directly in its mouth.

The kitten made a small, contented sound and began sucking at the cloth, protesting with claws and mews when Georgette pulled the handkerchief back to remoisten it with milk.

"You look like you were born to do that," Elsie said,

awe warming her voice. "I've never seen a lady do anything like that before."

The continued insistence she was a lady made Georgette's chest flutter in discomfort. "Haven't we already discussed this? A lady is permitted to love babies and animals as much as the next person."

"If that were true, there would not be such a fearsome demand for wet nurses." Elsie cocked her head, a puzzled slant to her brow. "You were married before."

"Yes." Georgette concentrated on the little mouth working at the edge of her handkerchief. She could see it coming, and yet could not steer clear.

"Were there no children?"

The familiar pang of disappointment had not lessened in the two years since the unfolding of her own personal tragedy. Georgette made no move to explain, settling instead for a swift shake of her head. It was too painful, still too fresh, to explain that she had lost a baby, the one thing in which she had placed her hopes, two months after her husband's fatal, drunken tumble down a flight of stairs. If she tried, she would have to skim over the shock of the bloodied sheets and the weeks of depression that followed. And if she skimmed, Elsie would not understand.

It was better to simply shake her head. She *wished* she could have a child.

But not enough to risk another husband.

The kitten stopped nursing the cloth and gradually fell asleep in her cupped palm, sated by the bit of milk. Georgette called for soap and water to wash her soiled hand, and then sat there, enjoying the living, breathing feel of the sleeping animal in her lap, but the feeling was arrested as she caught sight of someone she recognized.

Unfortunately, it was not her big-boned Scotsman. Neither was it her cousin Randolph. Instead, she saw the man her cousin had pointed out on the street that morning as Reverend Ramsey. Georgette tried to ignore the prickling awareness that ran the length of her spine as he stared at their table. She accepted her plate of salmon and watercress sandwiches from the attendant, even though her first instinct was to gather her things and leave.

But then a shadow fell across their table, and the man became impossible to avoid.

"Good afternoon, Lady Thorold," he said.

She put on a smile, noticing from the corner of her eye how the man's approach caused Elsie to slide down in her chair. "Reverend Ramsey." She offered him her still-gloved hand. "We have not been properly introduced, but my cousin has mentioned you. It appears he has spoken to you about me, as well."

The gentleman took her hand, as propriety dictated, but there was nothing of warmth in the gesture. Reverend Ramsey's starched white collar was an obscene contrast to his dark disapproval. "Does Mr. Burton know the company you keep?" he asked as he released her hand.

Georgette curved her fingers into a fist. An admirable conversationalist, the rector was not. Her mind raced along every available path and arrived at one sure conclusion: he must be referring to the situation last night. It was not a surprise, really. To hear Elsie tell the tale, half the town had been in attendance at the Blue Gander last night and served as witnesses. It was sure rumors were flying through Moraig faster than the afternoon coach.

But then the man's eyes pulled to Elsie. The maid stared back, one auburn brow cocked belligerently.

"Do you refer to Miss Dalrymple?" Georgette asked in confusion. "She is my ladies' maid."

"Maid?" The man's face reddened through Elsie's uncharacteristic silence. "Is that what she's calling herself now?"

Georgette looked between the pair, wondering how to handle the situation. Her early lessons in decorum had never addressed how to defuse a brewing altercation between a former prostitute and a man of God. Was this the man who had charged Elsie with public indecency?

Reverend Ramsey settled the issue for her as he turned his back on the maid. "Where is Mr. Burton?" he asked bluntly. "I presumed there had been a change of plans when you did not arrive at the church last night, but when I saw you together on the street this morning, I assumed you were simply delayed."

Her cousin's earlier insistence that the rector would form his own conclusions about what he had seen this morning still rang in her ears. Georgette swallowed. "I would like a chance to explain, Reverend, about what you may have seen. I was delayed last night. And Randolph found me. But—"

"You do not need to provide the details," he interrupted with an impatient wave of his hand. "You were with your betrothed this morning. It is improper, of course, but not unmendable. Of course, I would not advise delaying the wedding further. People will start to talk."

"I . . . I beg your pardon?" Georgette asked, appalled as much by the insinuation that she was engaged to her cousin as by the man's stark delivery of the news.

"I must presume you still plan to marry Mr. Burton," he said.

Georgette risked a glance at Elsie. The maid was doing an admirable job of ignoring the conversation and displaying dutiful appreciation for the sandwiches in front of her. Georgette no longer felt quite so hungry herself. "Did you say *still* marry?" she asked, squinting back up at the man.

"Mr. Burton told me last week you both wanted a quick ceremony with minimal fuss." His eyes raked over her, resting on the dirty dress, her uncovered hair, the single glove. "Given appearances, I would not waste a single moment."

He offered a curt nod to Georgette's stunned silence, and then turned and walked away.

"What in the criminy was that all about?" Elsie asked, already halfway through her first sandwich.

"I was wondering that myself." Georgette sat as still as the water in her glass, not knowing what the odd, aching emotion in her throat was.

No, that wasn't quite true.

She was angry. Randolph had scheduled their wedding. And he had done it last week, before she had come to visit, before he had even asked for her hand.

And he had handed her that first brandy last night with the assurance of a man who knew what he was about. She could not remember what happened after that, but she could suspect. Randolph had intended to marry her last night, whether she agreed or not. Brandy, consumed by someone with so little experience with spirits, could have only helped his cause.

"What are you going to do?" Elsie asked, chewing with her mouth open. "You can't marry two men."

"No, I can't." Georgette considered for a moment the insane urge to correct the maid's atrocious eating habits. In the end, she picked up her sandwich and abandoned the idea. She had little enough time to accomplish all the things on her list today without reforming Elsie's table manners too. "But you see, I have no intention of being married to either one of them."

"Sounds like you might need to inform your cousin of that fact." Elsie licked a smear of sauce from one side of her sandwich.

Though the maid only stated the obvious, truer words had never been spoken. And that meant Georgette's list had a new, necessary addition:

Teach Elsie the fundamentals of being a ladies' maid.

Search for Mr. MacKenzie.

Return the kitten to the butcher.

And find her cousin and give him the dressing-down he so clearly deserved.

Chapter 12

JAMES PUSHED INTO the butcher's shop on Main Street with his stomach halfway to his feet. He dreaded what he might find, and yet he owed it to his horse and his sanity to find out.

William followed close behind, an unshakable shadow apparently determined to make sure James didn't take out the rest of MacRory's teeth. It was laughable, really. If Caesar had already been sacrificed to the butcher's knife, it wasn't MacRory's teeth his brother needed to worry about.

William would need to hold him back from full-blown murder.

James had not a single idea what he had done with his horse, or how he had lost him. Over the course of the last hour, he had begun to remember even more about his evening, starting with every dimple possessed by the delectable Lady Thorold. James had counted them last night, in that ramshackle room above the Blue Gander. There had been two lovely divots of a size to hold kisses resting on her back, just above the flare of her hips. The dimples of her cheeks had prompted him to work hard to elicit the smile that brought them into full relief. He remembered the indentation he had discovered, quite by accident, resting behind her left knee.

Yes, he remembered Georgette Thorold now, every bewitching inch of her.

But he could not remember trading Caesar to the town butcher.

No matter how hard he tried, the gleaming counters inside MacRory's shop brought no sense of recall, no flash of memory. The fresh copper smell of meat did not seem familiar, and the view from MacRory's shop to Main Street outside was equally unknown.

He wanted to presume he hadn't done it. There was no way he would have traded Caesar to the butcher, not when he had worked so hard to possess the animal. James had wanted the stallion since his father had first sent the animal to his house, two weeks after he had returned to Moraig. The Earl of Kilmartie had offered the horse as a gift, but James had refused the man's generosity. His pride was flying high, and his anger at his father's meddling was still too great, even after being gone so many years.

But one look was all it had taken. James had wanted the horse with a passion, scraping for months to come up with enough money and then negotiating the deal to purchase the stallion behind his father's back. He couldn't afford such a fine horse, but somehow he had done it, even though his finances were better saved for other things.

The horse had represented his future and his pride. And James had just lost them, all to one drunken night.

Furious with himself, he paced the confines of the little shop. "MacRory!" he shouted. "We need a word with you!"

Instead of a toothless butcher, a tabby cat the size of a toddler emerged from some hidden corner of the butcher shop. Its enormous yellow eyes stared at the visitors as if in accusation for disturbing its sleep. After a twitching moment, it ambled past them through the front door to the sunlit street outside and then sat down and began to clean itself.

"Where in the deuces is he?" James slapped his fist down on the countertop with a force that made the front windows rattle.

William glanced out a window along the far wall of the shop. A low whistle escaped him "You might want to take a look out back."

James stalked over to the window, which looked out on an alley behind the shop. The view here was far different from the pristine white counters where most of Moraig purchased their cuts of meat. Out back, he could see barrels of offal and buzzing flies, and everywhere he looked there was dried blood and bits of hair. His stomach churned like a spinning top, threatening to purge itself from the visual violence.

If Caesar *had* been here, there was no evidence he still lived.

William peered out at a split carcass that was hanging from a chain across the narrow alley. "Does that look equine in origin?" he asked, squinting at the shape of it.

"Bovine." James closed his eyes to the red muscle and white cartilage outlined in the shape of ribs. He willed it to be true. *Please God, let it be true.*

A shadow fell across them, and James whirled to find the butcher's rotund shape outlined in the door frame.

"MacRory," he said slowly.

"MacKenzie." The butcher stepped inside his shop, moving from backlit sun to shadows, each footfall more menacing than the last. His mouth parted, revealing the red-rimmed space his front teeth had so recently occupied. The sight brought a spasm of guilt to James's chest.

He had knocked out MacRory's teeth last night. He had forgotten that part in his concern over Caesar. He supposed an apology was in order. Instead, he swallowed the bile that rose in his throat, and forced himself to ask the question he had come for. "My horse has gone missing. Do you know anything about him?"

MacRory's eyes narrowed. He made a great show of scratching his whiskered chin. "Well now, I see a lot of horses. Which one was yours again?"

Was. The man had said "was."

Worry for Caesar surged through him. "He's a chestnut stallion with a white blaze, socks on his hind feet. Stands just over seventeen hands." James risked a peek out the nausea-inducing window again. "A bit too-fine boned to make a good steak," he added.

"I don't sell horse meat." The butcher sounded offended. "And I don't like customers looking out in the alley behind my shop. 'Tis bad for business."

James returned his gaze to the glowering butcher. He supposed he could see the logic in that. He wasn't sure he could bring himself to touch a nice cut of beef again after witnessing the carnage that lay just beyond the plate glass.

"I'm here because David Cameron sold you a black mare. He's got no cause to lie about it. So if you don't deal in horses . . ."

The butcher interrupted him with a snort. "I didn't say I don't deal in them, just that I don't carve them up."

James took in the man's soiled apron, the dirt and less mentionable filth that lay beneath MacRory's fingernails like a storefront sign. He raised a brow. The man was a butcher. There were not a lot of other options here.

MacRory flushed under the scrutiny. "I admit I purchased a black mare from Cameron. But I bought her with an eye toward her value as a broodmare, not as dog meat." He leaned in, his lips curving upward beneath his disgusting beard. "Don't tell the magistrate that, though. He gave me the mare at a bang-up price."

"Well, how did I end up with her if you bought her?" James asked in irritation. It seemed he was no closer to finding Caesar than he had been on storming in here, and while he was happy not to find his horse in pieces, he still had no idea where the stallion was.

The butcher shrugged. "How the devil should I know?" He grinned then, the atrocity of his ruined mouth front and center. "I didn't keep her more than a day. Sold her right quick, and at a profit to boot."

James grabbed on to the one meager clue. "Who bought the mare?" If he could find the end buyer, intuition told him he would also find Caesar. Although how these damnable pieces of the puzzle all fit together was becoming impossible to imagine, much less sort out.

MacRory shuffled his feet a moment, hands fluttering about his hips. "Can't rightly remember. If it wasn't you, guess it could have been Hillston, down on the south side of town. Or maybe McDougal. I do a fair bit of this sort of thing, though I'll thank you not to spread it around. It's hard to keep it all straight."

James struggled against his mounting impatience. Each new clue, each lead, just seemed to lead him further into a quagmire of confusion. Caesar was still missing. Lady Thorold was still hiding. And apparently, the butcher was a discriminating connoisseur of horseflesh, but not horse meat. He stared at his brother, thinking hard. What should they do next?

Head off and ask every horse trader in Moraig if they had seen Caesar?

Or, now that he at least knew the horse wasn't bound for someone's dinner table, did he return his focus to the more pressing issue of finding the woman he had married last night?

William, for his part, appeared to have something different in mind. He cleared his throat, and tossed a narrow-eyed glance toward James. "My brother has something he wants to tell you."

"I do?"

"Yes." William nodded toward the butcher. "Go on with it." When James did no more than stand there stupidly, he jerked his chin encouragingly, spreading his hands palms-up in a universal symbol of apology.

James slumped in defeat. Damned if his brother wasn't right. Damned if his brother wasn't *always* right.

"I'm sorry about your teeth," James offered, knowing it was true, knowing that an apology was the only thing that might convince MacRory not to spread and expand upon the tale about what had happened last night. "I was not thinking clearly, and, well . . . suffice it to say, I wish it hadn't happened."

The butcher's bushy brows shot up. "Oh, I'd say you were thinking plenty clear. And I don't blame you a bit. Why, if I had just gotten married and you tried to kiss *my* pretty new wife, I'd have aimed a bit lower than your teeth."

James was startled. "You tried to kiss her?" His mind

flew faster, wrapped wider around the memory the man's words conjured. The butcher lifting the blond-haired sprite up in a big bear hug, her squeak of protest, and then his fists, swinging of their own accord.

The butcher's cheeks turned ruddy at the question. "Well, she was a right sweet thing, and it *is* a tradition. Kiss the bride and all."

James managed to grind out, "She's not my bride." And she wasn't. His own memory disowned it, and Cameron had confirmed it.

So why did part of him still squeeze tight at the thought?

MacRory perked up at that. "She's not? Well, that's a fine bit of luck then." He licked his lips, and his eyes took on a predatory gleam. "Does that mean she's still available?"

All thoughts of apology promptly became tangled up in James's ears. It occurred to him it would be only a little more trouble to aim for the man's back molars. His fists were halfway to attention when William grabbed his shoulders and shuffled him out of the shop, calling out a chorus of "thank-yous" and "sorrys" behind them.

His brother gave him a hard shove, sending James stumbling out onto the busy street. "You just got through saying you were sorry to the man, and there you go, about to do it again! MacRory is only having a bit of sport with you." William poked James in the shoulder with a self-righteous finger. "This woman has you tied up in knots. You have to decide: either you want her or you don't. This flipping back and forth is going to make you cross-eyed and annoy everyone who is trying to help you."

James took a deep breath. He didn't need his brother's reminder to realize he was acting like a fool. What was it about this girl that simultaneously aroused his anger and his protective instincts? His fists resisted his commands to unfurl, and he concentrated on loosening his fingers in slow, deliberate steps. He had become adept at controlling his unruly temper with the sawdust-filled bag he kept in his kitchen, spent hours each day throwing punches until his lungs burned and his knuckles cracked and bled.

But there was no sawdust effigy here. There was only William, with his crooked nose and congenial smile and damnably right words. William, and a gathering crowd of curious onlookers.

James's hands dropped to his waist. His brother was right. He had forgotten what was important, neglected to consider that no matter what damage he had done last night, he still had a responsibility to Moraig's citizens—and to himself—to conduct his affairs with dignity. Knocking out more of MacRory's teeth or picking a fight with his well-meaning sibling was not going to help the town's residents trust his legal advice. And neither would milling about the streets like a love-struck swain, searching for his missing paramour in every hole and crevice.

Just as he was taking the deep breath necessary to restore himself to calm, he was nearly bowled over by someone who darted from the crowd, moving like the wind. He felt the impact of the knife rather than the pain of it, a blow to his chest that snagged a second on muscle and bone before sliding southward. He shoved hard against his attacker, caught the slightest glimpse of white-blond hair and a slim build before the figure was off and running, trouser-clad legs stirring up clouds of dust on Moraig's dry streets.

And then his assailant was gone.

James lifted an incredulous hand to his chest. His fingers came away sticky with blood.

William's strangled gasp came louder, closer, and then, finally, James felt the grasp of his brother's fingers on his arm. "That bastard stabbed you!" William exclaimed. "Can you stand?"

"Aye. It did not go deep." His legs, oddly enough, felt steady beneath him. He edged his fingers around the periphery of the wound. Although it bled, it was reassuringly shallow. "'Tis a scratch," he clarified. "I would not even tolerate one of Patrick's sorry bandages on it."

His gaze fell to the street. A knife lay there, coated with his blood. He bent down and picked it up, turning it over in his hand. No, not a knife . . . some sort of instrument. It was curved and had a folding blade, but that was where the similarity ended. A sharp implement would have been cleaner, quicker.

Deadlier.

"Bloody hell, that's the second time someone tried to kill you today," William growled, shaking his head at the discovery. "First the girl tries to kill you with a chamber pot, and now this."

James wiped the blade on his coat and nodded grimly as he slipped it into his pocket. The pain, momentarily delayed, became a slicing want in need of attention, but he ignored it as he turned over the facts in his mind. Yes, it *was* the second time he had been attacked today.

And only the second time in his life, as well.

"Do you think this could be related to the business

with Lady Thorold?" William asked, his voice a hard rumble.

His brother's palpable anger made James feel better for some reason. He nodded again and lifted his eyes to the crowd, searching. *There.* Moving north, past the milliner's shop. A towheaded figure wove its way in between the crowd. The figure was dressed like a man. That much he had ascertained during the attack. But wearing trousers did not make one male, any more than wearing a dress made one a lady.

The figure who had careened into him had been bone-thin, with a pale shock of hair barely visible under a cap. James's earlier anger returned tenfold then, burning an empty hole inside him. Had she just tried to kill him? His feet had already started moving before he figured out what came next.

What had William said in the moments before he was attacked? He needed to decide what he wanted. This little incident had just helped him make up his mind.

He *did* want her.

He wanted to see her pay.

Chapter 13

IT TOOK NEARLY the entire rest of the meal for Georgette to shake off the unsettled feeling that plagued her following the conversation with Reverend Ramsey. Her sandwich tasted like sawdust, the tea like warm river water. Her mind felt as numb as her taste buds.

How had she not seen what her cousin was plotting, what he was capable of? She had thought Randolph's invitation for a summer visit innocent, an altruistic extension of the fondness they had once shared for each other. It was not the first time she had been wrong about a man.

But that did not make it any easier to digest.

It was disconcerting to realize how narrowly she had escaped her cousin's plans. Had James MacKenzie helped her in that? Had she turned to him for assistance last night at the Blue Gander, and found him the better man?

There was only one way to discover the truth.

Georgette pushed back from the tea shop's wrought-iron table, determined to hunt down both men and find some answers. As she gathered her reticule and tucked the kitten up in one hand, a startled shout from the opposite side of the street claimed her attention. She looked up to see some sort of a scuffle taking place in front of a shop across the way. The gathering crowd blocked her view, but she could hear loud voices and pounding feet.

Two figures broke free, running north. Georgette watched them go with an odd, fluttering sensation, just below her rib cage. One had a beard, the other did not. Beyond that, she could not make out any discernible features across the distance that separated them. She could not see whether one of them had straight, white teeth. She could not see either man's eyes, be they green or blue or even hazel.

But something about both of them seemed familiar.

"Elsie," she mused, nudging the maid with her elbow in a manner that could never be called ladylike. "Are either of those men . . ."

But the maid was not looking in the direction of the men, who were rapidly falling from view. Her gaze was directed squarely at the remaining crowd. "Oh, I do love a fight!" Elsie said, moving toward the melee, instead of away from it as any sensible girl would do.

"Elsie . . ." When the maid did not slow, Georgette reached deeper. "Elsie!"

The maid turned, hands on her hips. "I'm not deaf, miss. There's no need to shout."

"Those men." Georgette pointed in the direction they had gone. "Do you know them?"

Elsie followed her mistress's finger, but the men in question had been swallowed by the afternoon crowd, leaving only ordinary townsfolk milling about. "I've known a few of them," came Elsie's amused response. "Why? Are you looking for an introduction? Here I thought you wanted to be done with men."

"I thought one of them looked familiar."

"Like MacKenzie?"

Georgette nodded.

The maid looked again. "Well, I don't see him now." Elsie shifted from foot to foot, clearly anxious to keep moving. "You are probably just seeing him in every shadow, looking for him as we are."

Georgette sighed and stared down at the kitten, which was still sleeping in her left hand. "Perhaps." She realized, after so many false starts, she would be crushed if they didn't find him today. Not because she needed to procure an annulment, although that was still a part of it. There was no sense pretending that was the only reason, not anymore.

She wanted to see him because she couldn't stop thinking about him. She felt sure now this mess was in some way tied up with Randolph's shocking behavior last night. Had she married MacKenzie for the protection of his name? The bits and pieces of the man being revealed to her suggested he was just the kind of man to help someone in need.

No, she no longer felt ashamed when she thought of how she might have behaved with James MacKenzie the previous evening. She was more ashamed of how she knew she had treated him this morning. He had wanted her, and she had cracked him over the head with a chamber pot.

"We'll find him, miss." Elsie took a step away, toward the crowd.

"Of course we will," Georgette agreed. "As soon as you show me where his office is."

"Oh no," Elsie protested, pulling up short. "Surely that can wait five minutes." She tilted her chin toward the disturbance across the street. "We're missing all the fun."

"*Fun?*" Georgette eyed the crowd, which had begun to disperse but was still a jumble of voices and jostling elbows. "That does not look like fun to me."

Elsie huffed. "It's but a bit of noise. Didn't bother you overmuch last night at the Gander." She lifted an agitated hand toward the thinning crowd. "Look. We're missing it. Have a little backbone, will you?"

But Georgette scarcely heard the maid's retort. Instead, she stared at a bit of brown and black fur that caught her eye through the dispersing mob. Her mouth fell open, scarcely able to believe it. A cat that looked remarkably like the tiny kitten in her hand was sitting outside a shop across the street, directly under a weathered wooden sign marking the establishment as a butcher's shop.

Georgette dimly registered the maid's surprised shout of caution as she crossed the street and dodged a trio of fast-moving carriages, the kitten clutched tightly to her chest. She did not stop until she gained the sidewalk and lowered her bundle to the ground, straight into the welcoming tongue of its mother.

"Oh," she breathed as the mother cat began to dutifully clean her missing charge. The thing seemed to come alive under the scrape of its dam's tongue, mewling and moving.

Elsie came up behind her, grumbling about mistresses that changed their minds and didn't let anyone know what was going on, but Georgette ignored her. She crouched there on the paving stones, frozen by the privilege of witnessing the reunion and trying to ignore the ache in her gut that it brought.

"That's a pretty scene."

A disembodied voice floated down to her, and Georgette glanced up to see the man she recognized as the butcher standing in the doorway. He was wearing the same stained apron from this morning, and was just as toothless as he had been several hours ago.

She stood up from her crouch. The strain of the morning and her body's emotional response to the tender homecoming made her feel jumpy. "No thanks to you," she retorted, poking the man in the apron-covered chest with a bare, angry finger. Now that she knew the kitten was safe, the earlier worry dissipated, leaving only irritation in its place. "What were you thinking, taking such a young animal away from its mother?" She turned herself over to the tirade that had been simmering inside her ever since she first awakened this morning. "Why would you do such a thing? Why would you think I would *want* such a burden?"

The large, bloodstained man shuffled his feet, his hands spread in surprise. "But it was a gift, miss. You earned it."

The reminder that this man thought she had somehow earned the kitten brought a spasm of dismay in her stomach. "You keep saying that," she snapped, poking him with her finger again. "But there is clearly some mistake."

The butcher's face scrunched in confusion. "You saved my life, miss."

Georgette's eyes widened and the spasm in her stomach subsided to more of a minor cramp. "I did?"

Elsie broke in. "What did you think MacRory was talking about?"

Georgette looked between the two, trying to remember but falling short. "I thought . . . I thought he was referring to something else." She shook her head. "Whatever you think I did . . ."

"I choked on my teeth," the butcher said. "MacKenzie's fist shoved them clean down my throat. Thought I was done in, sure enough. Whole room thought it was a great bloody farce, nobody taking me seriously. And then you stepped up, quick as you please, and looped your arms around me and squeezed. *Hard.*" He peered down at her. "You've a mite of strength in you, for being such a little thing."

Georgette did not know what to say to that.

"And then his teeth popped out, right there onto the table, and the whole place cheered," Elsie finished with a sharp intake of air, and then sneezed.

"God bless you," Georgette said automatically, still trying to wrap her head around the retelling of such an improbable event.

"Thank you." Elsie sniffed once, and then leaned in close to MacRory, whispering loudly behind a cupped hand. "She can't remember a bloody thing that went on last night. Can't hold her drink."

Georgette sighed, though she did so in relief. Whether she had saved the man's life was not up for debate: they thought she had. The cramp in her stomach eased into nothing. She had not done something unmentionable with the butcher. She had helped him, though she had absolutely no recollection of doing it.

Thank heaven for *something* going right last night.

"Don't you want it, miss?" MacRory blinked at her. "The kitten, I mean. Like I said, you earned it."

This time, Georgette chose her words with greater care. "It was a lovely gift, truly. I was honored to receive it. But the kitten is too young to be away from its mother. Perhaps in a few weeks' time . . ." She trailed off. It was a promise she couldn't make. She wouldn't be in Moraig in a few days' time, much less a few weeks.

But she had already said too much, if the butcher's gaping smile was any indication. "That's brilliant, miss. I'll save it for you, until it's weaned. I've a feeling this one will make a good mouser, and will take right good care of you."

"Thank you," she said reluctantly, knowing it would cost too much to explain why she was already planning her escape. "It would be nice to be cared for."

MacRory offered her a grin. "You could marry me, and I'd care for you the rest of your days," he said cheerily. "Not like that blighter who just left."

Georgette sucked in a breath, her heart near knocking out of her chest as she registered the importance of the man's words. "What blighter? Who just left?" When the butcher took too long to answer, she stomped her foot. "*Who just left?*"

"You dinna see MacKenzie?" MacRory lifted his big shoulders, spreading his palms wide. "You practically tripped over him. He was just here, talking about *you.*"

The suggestion that James MacKenzie was talking about her made the fine hairs on Georgette's arms stand at attention. He had been standing here, in this shop, mere seconds ago.

And she had been on his mind.

"No," she said, casting a frantic gaze down the street. "I did not see him." Her thoughts followed the path her eyes took. The man she had seen running away had looked familiar, and now she knew why. She was but minutes behind him.

And that meant there was no time to waste.

She grabbed up her skirts, grateful that her hands were finally free of the bundle of fur she had been carrying about like a fifth limb. "He went north," she gasped to Elsie, already moving in the direction he had been heading.

The maid dutifully fell into step alongside her. "His offices are on the north side of town," she said, keeping pace. "He might be heading there."

Georgette nodded, her heart in a close race with her feet. She could think of nothing beyond her desire to see him, to explain her behavior of the previous night and apologize for hurting him this morning. The thought of what she had to do after that pulled at her, but did not slow her feet. She couldn't risk losing MacKenzie again, not when he was so close.

Not when her future depended on it.

"Remember what I said!" MacRory called after them, his big voice echoing down the street. "I've a two-room apartment above the shop. And you could have all the beef you want!"

Georgette choked back the hysterical laugh that rose in her throat at the thought of being married to the butcher. Not that it wasn't a kind offer, and not that MacRory didn't appear to be a lovely man, now that she realized she had done no more than save him last night.

But what girl needed the headache? Being married to one Scotsman was more than enough.

Two would do her in.

Chapter 14

He was gaining on her.

James's lungs labored for air and his arms pumped in time with his burning legs. His head hurt like the devil, and the knee Cameron's horse had kicked halfway to Sunday throbbed with every jolt of his feet on the road. And then, of course, there was his new wound, which might be less serious than the paper cut he had given himself yesterday but felt as if there might still be a metal blade dancing a Highland jig inside his skin.

But the wool-capped head that bobbed and weaved among the gathering Bealltainn crowd was an unholy incentive to keep going.

He lost his hat by the time they rounded Frankston Street, and he lost William a scant three blocks later. Either his drive to catch the girl was greater than his brother's, or the long hours logged in front of his saw-dust punching bag made him better able to handle the demands of the pursuit. Whatever the reason, five minutes into the chase James realized he was alone.

A quick glance around told him he had stumbled into a less reputable part of Moraig now. The colorful paper lanterns that had been put up on Main Street in promise of the Bealltainn celebration had fallen away to reveal fetid alleys reeking of refuse. The residents of this part of town had a hollow-cheeked appearance, their sallow complexions a testament to poor diet and poorer prospects.

He knew these streets well. His practice brought him in touch with *all* of Moraig's residents, and he did not shy away from those who could not afford to pay. If anything, he veered toward them. It was part of the reason he struggled so hard to secure a decent income.

And part of the reason I need to catch this thief now, while I have the chance.

He put on a fresh burst of speed, though his body objected with a shaking groan. The person he was chasing seemed to be powered by wind as much as fear, and was clearly not burdened by the same injuries as James.

It occurred to him, as the figure nimbly ducked beneath a laundry-laden rope that had been stretched across the street, that the person he chased not only seemed more agile than he remembered, but taller too. Perhaps only a few inches shorter than he. Not that he trusted his memory. It was still a fragmented mess, and the strain of the chase was surely scattering his thoughts even more.

Up ahead, the person he was pursuing ducked down a side street. By the time James burst out onto Main Street again, his attacker had disappeared completely into the swelling mob of shoppers.

He leaned over and braced himself against his knees, gulping in fistfuls of air and trying to ease the pain in his chest. Everywhere he looked there were people. People he knew. People he didn't.

Damned Bealltainn, and its May Day crowds. The process of sorting out a blond-headed stranger among them proved impossible. The night's pending celebration was an annual event, and it drew in every self-respecting Scotsman within a fifty-mile radius. By nightfall, the streets would be even more distorted with merrymakers and costumed revelry.

James straightened, wincing against the effort and his muscles' screamed protest. He had lost her. Lost his horse, his money purse, and his goddamned self-respect right along with her.

James turned back toward the center of town and walked a slow half block before he spied his brother jogging toward him. William's face was red, his chest heaving. Although there was little good to be found in the last ten minutes, the visible demonstration that he was better than his brother at *something* made him feel a little better.

"You should get more exercise," James told him as William came to a labored stop in front of him. His own lungs still burned, but at least he was no longer short of breath.

"And *you* shouldn't be running like that," William told him. "What would you have done if you caught her, hurt as you are? Are you trying to get yourself killed?" Between breaths, William's dark eyes probed at him like knowing fingers.

"On the contrary." He ticked his list off on his fingers. "I am trying to locate my horse, catch the girl, and wring her devious neck."

William shook his head. "Go home, Jamie-boy." His voice was tinged with concern, belying the lightness of his words. "You're exhausted. You need sleep. And you need to be examined by a doctor."

"No." By James's reckoning, working on *his* list

would make him feel a lot better than succumbing to his brother's well-meant suggestions. "If I didn't need a doctor this morning, I sure as hell don't need one now. And I won't rest until I find her."

"That only proves my point," William snorted, waving his hands in exasperation. "You're not thinking straight. Knife wounds are nothing to ignore, and you aren't acting like yourself, running all over, chasing some piece of skirt through the gutters. I wouldn't be surprised if there's a trail of blood following you. Let me take you home."

James shook his head against the thought. *Home.* He really didn't have a home, didn't belong anywhere. There was nothing tempting about the thought of returning to his lonely rented house and his sliver of brown soap, with only Patrick for company. He did not want to be put to bed like an infant, only to wake up to Gemmy's soulful eyes and the steady thump of the dog's tail instead of the gentle touch of a woman.

He was tired of living that way. It was not just that he was injured and in need of tending. He had been injured before, and had never entertained such maudlin thoughts.

It was because he was lonely. The thought was startling in its simplicity. William's company today, and the warm memory of the girl he had held in his arms last night, made him want . . . something. Perhaps last night, he had even done this irrational thing, had pretended to marry the girl, because it filled a void in his life he hadn't known had been there. He had not given much thought to marrying before, but now, having gone through the motions, it had him thinking.

Of course, the woman in question was beyond inappropriate. She was as likely to slit his throat as wake him with kisses.

"I don't want to go home." James sighed. "I want to keep looking for her."

"Well, it is clear that she doesn't want to be found," William pointed out. "If you won't let Patrick Channing look at you, let me take you home to Kilmartie Castle. Father will know what to do."

"God, no. That is not my home." *Not anymore.*

His big brother was one of the most genial people James had ever known, full of riddles and ribald teasing. But anger flashed in his eyes at James's staunch refusal to even entertain the idea. "For Christ's sake, Jamie. Ask for some help, for once in your life. Father is not your enemy."

"What in the hell do you know about it?" James challenged. "Your path was laid clear from the time Father took the title. My path keeps changing beneath my feet, and more times than not he is the cause!"

"He did not have a damned thing to do with this latest mess."

"Only because I have not permitted him to." James had blamed his father for his life's direction for so long that it came as naturally as breathing. The fact that he had fallen into this latest trouble purely on his own was hard to acknowledge.

"Father can help with this. He has connections, and he can—"

"No." *Never again.*

William shook his head, sadness overtaking the earlier anger. "I can tell you won't listen to reason, and so I am not going to waste my breath. Just hear this: you are not the boy you once were, Jamie. I'm proud of the man you have become. Hell, half the time I'm jealous of you. Father is proud of you too. But if you keep dwelling on the past, you're going to make a muck out of your future."

"You don't know what the hell you're talking about." James was so stunned at William's admission, so lost at the mention of his past, he could scarcely get the words out.

William threw up his hands in defeat. "I am going home." He pivoted and stalked away. "But watch your back," he snarled out, behind his shoulder. "I'm tired of cleaning up your messes."

James refused to give in to the urge to call him back, to apologize. The old anger tumbled inside him, wild as the heather, as he watched his brother walk away. He felt twenty-one again, trying to do the right thing and having fingers pointed at him instead. And his father's doubt, and subsequent attempt to fix things, had been the worst part of it.

James shook himself out of his morose thoughts. William was wrong. Dwelling on his past was a necessary part of his future. He had been paying for old sins one lonely day at a time for as long as he could remember. He had come back to Moraig as penance, determined to show his father and the entire town he was a reformed man.

And this woman threatened to topple all his efforts to change.

He glanced up, once, measuring the angle of the sun. It seemed early yet. He consulted his pocket watch. Two o'clock. The day was far from over. His mind settled on his next step.

He carried the summons in one coat pocket, but this

latest attack made him see things differently. Assault with intent to kill was a serious crime. If he could prove it, he could do more than demand simple recompense.

He could have the chit transported.

James started to smile, imagining his options, imagining her face when she realized she was caught. First, he needed to consult his legal tomes, and find out if he could charge the woman with more than theft.

He turned north again. No, he was not going home. He was going to work.

Chapter 15

THE LAW OFFICES of James MacKenzie, Esquire, were located on a nearly deserted street on the north side of Moraig, an easy walk from the bustle and noise of the swelling Main Street crowd. The practice was housed in a wood-plank building flanked on one side by a saddlery and on the other by a tailor's shop. All three businesses were closed up tight.

Georgette knew this because she watched, aghast, as Elsie rattled the knob of each one and boomed out a hearty hullo.

"A ladies' maid does not say 'hullo' like a newspaper crier," Georgette told her. She covered her eyes with one bare hand, letting the skin of her fingers absorb some portion of the intense afternoon sun. In retrospect, the loss of her bonnet now seemed a poor idea.

"Well, what should I say instead?" Elsie asked.

"You should say 'good afternoon' or 'excuse me.'" Georgette dropped her hand and fixed the maid with a stern gaze. Elsie's nose looked perfectly fine, shaded as it was by the generous brim of Georgette's old bonnet. "You need to try a little harder if you want to do this."

Elsie wrinkled her perfectly pale nose, and probably would have stuck out her tongue if she had been a decade younger. "Being a ladies' maid isn't as much fun as I thought it would be."

"It's a paid position. It's not supposed to be fun."

"Well, working behind the Gander was fun," Elsie pouted. "A little hullo usually did the trick, especially if I swung my hips and followed it with a wink, like this." She closed one eye dramatically. "I suppose a ladies' maid doesn't wink either."

Georgette shook her head. "Particularly not at the man of the house." She swallowed the amusement the image built. It was impossible to stay irritated with someone as exuberant as Elsie, no matter that her manners were better suited to a barmaid than a trusted domestic servant.

"Well, if the lady of the house winked a bit more, the man of the house probably wouldn't be chasing the maid's skirts," Elsie pointed out, her voice far more innocent than her words.

The maid's logic was irrefutable. Georgette had never once winked at her former husband, and he had definitely chased a maid or two. Perhaps if things didn't work out as a ladies' maid, Elsie had a career in philosophy ahead of her.

"You try it," Elsie urged. She winked again. "It isn't hard."

Georgette pursed her lips. Almost of its own volition, one eye fluttered closed. "Like this?"

"Aye, that's a start," Elsie said, craning her neck. "If you're looking to scare him off."

"Then I'd best stop, before Mr. MacKenzie shows up." Georgette chuckled, and opened her eye. The man was still nowhere in sight. In point of fact, *no one* was in sight. There was an odd feeling of isolation to the otherwise mercantile street, as if it had been stripped of inhabitants and left to decay.

"Where is everyone?" Georgette asked as Elsie rattled the locked door of MacKenzie's office again. "Does no one *work* in Moraig?" She knew she sounded frustrated, but she felt so close to finding him. The shock of finding his practice locked up as tight as a bank vault was unexpected.

Elsie peeked into one window. "Actually, Mr. Mac-Kenzie is known for working *too* hard," she said. "He only comes into the Gander a few times a week, usually for a meal rather than a pint, and more often than not he has a stack of papers with him."

Georgette tucked that bit of information away in the back of her mind. So the man she had married didn't spend his every free moment carousing at the Gander. She wasn't sure how she felt about that.

"I can't see a thing," Elsie muttered, her face pressed full-on up against the glass.

"Come away from there," Georgette chided. "It's not polite to peer into windows."

Elsie turned back with a thoughtful expression on her face. "I suppose you're going to tell me a ladies' maid doesn't do that either. Well, you know what I think? It's not polite to chase after a man, but I can respect you for doing it. I thought you wanted to find him. Polite isn't going to get you there."

Georgette shrugged off the maid's far too perceptive observation. Instead, she sat down on a nearby wooden bench and fanned herself with her hand, determined to wait for him and answer the questions burning in her mind. It was just her luck to have married a fledgling, work-bound solicitor. Not a common sort of man, but not a peer of the realm either. The thought did not bother her nearly as much as it would have a month ago. And perhaps his legal skills would come in handy when she pressed for an annulment.

Unless he used them against her.

"Why aren't we hunting him down?" Elsie asked, plopping down beside her with a breathy sigh.

"Because we're out of leads." Georgette met Elsie's perplexed hazel gaze. "Logic argues that if we just wait here, we'll come across him soon enough."

"I don't know, miss." Elsie looked up at the still-bright sun skeptically. "It's already afternoon, and the Bealltainn celebration starts tonight."

"So?" Georgette knew she sounded snappish, but she was tired. And hot. And becoming increasingly frustrated over how *hard* it was to find one missing husband.

"So, the celebration will last till tomorrow night," Elsie said, a peevish note creeping into her tone. "Why do you think all the businesses are closed up, and so many people are in the center of town? MacKenzie may not come here till Monday."

Georgette's earlier hope of a quick, easy solution splintered at Elsie's matter-of-fact explanation. "I . . . I don't have until Monday."

"And I don't have all day. There's dancing tonight." Elsie offered Georgette an unapologetic smile. "I never miss dancing."

"Damn," Georgette muttered, low on her breath. The uncharacteristic act of cursing brought a warmth to her cheeks, but she had to admit it felt good to voice a strong opinion. She fit her lips around one of Elsie's favorite expressions. "Bloody hell." The mere utterance of the forbidden phrase sent her heart pounding.

"Indeed," Elsie agreed, nodding her head in approval. "That's the spirit, miss. Tell it like it is."

Georgette searched for a new expression and came up blank. Clearly, her new vocabulary needed some work. She threw her hands up. "Well, that's it. We're out of options."

The maid stared at the locked office door. "You know, if we're in that much of a hurry, we'd have a better chance of finding him if we went to his house."

"Do you know where he lives?" Georgette sat up straighter. She did not want to imagine how Elsie might have come by such knowledge. She did *not* care about MacKenzie's past associations, did not care if he was the biggest rake north of Hadrian's Wall. It was a topic she was determined to steer clear of.

"No." The maid shook her head, bringing a pinch of relief to Georgette's tight lungs. "But I bet there's something in that office, some bit of paper or other thing that might give us a clue." The maid stood up and began to examine the lock on the door with undisguised interest. "I think I could get us in."

Georgette's stomach twisted its objection. Dear God, Elsie couldn't be serious. What she was suggesting was wrong. *Illegal.* But Elsie was already sliding a hairpin from beneath her borrowed gray bonnet. It was as plain as the freckles on the maid's face that she was going to pick the lock.

Georgette stood up, intending to push her away from the sordid task. "Stop that," she hissed, darting a glance to either side. "That's breaking and entering. And he's a *solicitor.*"

"Not breaking," Elsie scoffed, straightening from her examination of the lock mechanism. "Just entering."

She handed Georgette the hairpin. "It's a skill every ladies' maid should teach their mistress. You know you want to find him, miss. This is your chance."

"I don't know . . ." Georgette swallowed, her throat a tight mess of unspoken objections. The hairpin felt as heavy as a pistol in her hands, cocked and ready to use.

Elsie snorted. "Where is the fearless lady that waltzed into the Blue Gander last night? If you need to find him, you need to be brave enough to take a chance."

Georgette was frozen with indecision. On the one hand, the woman she was supposed to be would never do something like this.

On the other hand, she was halfway to proving she was someone else.

She *wanted* to be that brave. The new Georgette was not quite sure who she was. But she wanted to get a sense of the man she had married, and she found she might be willing to break the law to do it. She leaned over and pensively slid the pin into the lock, her breath a block of ice inside her. Lo and behold, lightning did not streak from the sky and strike her dead. She twisted the pin gently, and to her surprise, the earth did not crack open and swallow her up.

Her lungs began to thaw. Being brave, apparently, was not so different from the usual way of things.

Emboldened, she turned herself over to the task in earnest. "Keep an eye out," she whispered to Elsie, who leaned in to watch.

"There's no one here, miss. Now, turn it to the left and lift up a little. Hold it, then jiggle it, just so."

"Elsie," Georgette admonished. "Let me do it."

"I *am* letting you do it," the maid retorted. "If I had been doing it we'd be in already."

"Oh, for heaven's sake," Georgette muttered. She stilled, hopeful as she felt the hairpin catch on something and hold fast. But the lock didn't turn, and the pin no longer jiggled. She tugged, but it didn't budge.

Georgette looked up at Elsie. "It is stuck." She pulled against it again, but it remained lodged in some unseen crevice.

Elsie stooped to pick something off the ground. When the maid stood back up, Georgette's eyes widened, her fingers frozen on the cool metal hairpin still held tight by the lock mechanism. Elsie offered her a cheeky grin and then without further ceremony tossed the rock through the window.

It made a sharp, splintering sound, followed by bits of glass raining down like an afterthought.

"*Now* it's breaking," Elsie said happily.

Impossibly, the door swung inward. "And now you have some explaining to do," came the deep baritone voice that haunted Georgette's mind.

Chapter 16

GEORGETTE STRAIGHTENED TO the sight of the man who owned the window they had just smashed. Her heart slapped against her ribs. Dear God, it scarcely seemed possible.

He had been inside the entire time.

Elsie, the heartless wretch, stood off to the side, wringing her hands. As if she was not to blame. As if she was as appalled by her mistress's behavior as he was. Georgette made a mental to note to inform the girl that a ladies' maid *always* took the blame for her mistress in questionable legal matters.

James MacKenzie took a step toward her, and her next ill-advised thought was one of worry. Well, that wasn't quite true. First there was the raw, shimmering awareness of him. This morning when she had first seen him, he had been abed. Her memory of him was of a man waking with a rakish grin, teasing her back to some forgotten, forbidden pleasure.

This afternoon he was all too awake, and his eyes conveyed nothing of pleasure.

He was impossibly tall. His uncovered head skimmed the painted sign over his doorway, and his tousled brown hair stood at odd angles, as if his hand had raked through it only seconds before. His beard, so wild and incompatible with the boyish charm he had shown this morning, now seemed a perfect accompaniment to his hard eyes. Her stomach turned over once in acknowledgment of how utterly, inappropriately handsome he was.

Worry, then, was her second ill-advised thought.

She eyed the disheveled, bloody man glowering down at her. She had been so focused on finding him and exorcising him from her life that she had forgotten about the chamber pot. He was still every bit as handsome as he had been this morning. But new to the image was the row of ragged stitches that marched across his scalp and the blood-soaked jacket on his broad shoulders.

"Oh," she breathed. "I am so, so sorry. I have hurt you."

"Indeed." His eyes, so green they glittered like ice on new grass, narrowed.

Georgette took a deep breath. He was a difficult man to read, his expression stern and unrevealing. Was he glad to see her? Angry? Indifferent?

There was no point denying it. That last bit would sting, no matter that she knew she did not deserve his interest.

According to Elsie, who was still standing white-faced beside her, Georgette had led him on a merry chase last night. *She* was to blame for the outcome, and so she never should have struck him. And while she could not quite imagine staying and crawling back into bed beside this man, as he had asked her to this morning, she should have at least waited until he dressed and talked to him about what had happened.

Instead, she had given in to fear.

"I am happy to see you," she whispered, glancing up at him through her lashes. She knew it was probably too late for such a soft sentiment, no matter that it was the truth. She *was* happy to see him. She only wished he looked a bit more . . . inviting.

He reached out a lazy hand. For a moment, she thought he might take her arm, or smooth back the lock of hair that had come free from her pins and was waving like a flag of truce about her right cheek. "I wish I could say the same thing about you," he said.

Instead of touching her, he reached down. "In fact," he said, yanking the stuck hairpin out of the lock and holding it up in front of her face, "the only thing that will give me greater pleasure than never seeing you again is seeing you brought to justice."

And that was when Georgette realized this meeting was not going to go at all as she had imagined.

JAMES HAD WONDERED what it would feel like when he found her. All day long, through the frustration of each dead-end clue, through the pain of his mounting list of injuries, through the unexpected disappointment of William's desertion, he had wondered. Now he knew.

He felt numb.

The woman he had been searching for down every dirty alley between here and Main Street was finally in front of him, guilt etched on her face. Her auburn-haired companion hovered nearby—Miss Dalrymple, unless his eyes were playing tricks on him.

Pity. He had thought the prostitute–turned–tavern–wench who normally poured his glass at the Blue Gander had more sensible associations.

"You may leave us now, Miss Dalrymple," he growled. "This is not your concern."

"But . . . I am her ladies' maid, sir," the auburn-haired girl stammered.

"How fortuitous," James replied, not even missing a beat. "She is no lady, and therefore has no need of a maid."

When the girl did no more than shift wordlessly from foot to foot, he added, a bit more kindly, "When have you ever known me to hurt someone, or be deliberately cruel? I promise you, your mistress will not be harmed. Go on and leave us."

Still, she hesitated.

"*Now!*" James barked it out as he would a courtroom objection.

Miss Dalrymple showed a sudden spark of obedience he would have never thought possible. She lifted her skirts and ran down the road at a pace that would have put Caesar to shame, had his mount been anywhere close.

Unfortunately, his mount *wasn't* close. There was only the blond-haired woman standing before him. They were alone.

And he had never been more aware of another living thing.

His quarry stared at him with wide eyes, so brilliantly gray they made the waters of Loch Moraig seem colorless in comparison. She looked nothing like a lady, with her hair coming down and her head bare to the afternoon sun. He took a step toward her and she took a complementary step back, as if they were birds engaged in a ridiculous courtship ritual. Only he didn't want to court her.

He wanted to throttle her.

He forced himself to stand still. Though her feet stopped moving, the rest of her did not. Her hands fluttered about like moths trapped in a glass jar, and her gaze darted from side to side. It occurred to him she might have an accomplice, someone lurking nearby with another large rock, this time aimed at his head instead of his window.

He turned a half step so he could see his target and the street. "Looking for someone?" he asked.

"Truth be told, I've been looking for *you*." She gifted him with a smile so bright it stung his eyes, though her voice shook around the edges.

James didn't believe that for a second, not even as he registered the cultured vowel sounds that suggested she probably *was* well-bred. "I did not fall off the cart yesterday," he told her, enjoying the way his sarcasm made her wince. "You'll have to try better than that."

Her eyes widened. "It's true!" she protested. "That is why I am here." She worried her lower lip with her teeth, a gesture that tempted him to taste it, even though he knew she could bite.

Anger thumped in his chest. "You were breaking *into* my offices," he pointed out, "not waiting for me on the bench outside."

"I . . . I thought I might find something inside that would lead me to you."

James wound up his disbelief and let it fly like an arrow from a bow. "Were you looking for more money? Something of additional value? Because I assure you, if you think I am wealthy, you are more stupid than you look."

She answered with a squeak. *A squeak.* The woman

he remembered from last night would have had a witty comeback, would have taken his verbal bet and raised him fourfold. This woman squeaked like a mouse. Not quite the brilliant conversationalist of his dreams.

"There seems to be a mistake," she finally said, her hands spreading before her. "I am not what you think."

He answered with a sweep of his eyes. The girl was the same, and yet she was not. Same unusual hair color, and the same pert nose, albeit pinker than he remembered. She possessed the same too-wide mouth, and he, for his troubles, experienced a familiar swelling of attraction in the vicinity of his cock as he stared at her. One elusive dimple flashed like a lighthouse beacon, calling him home.

But she was different too. She seemed more awkward today. Uncomfortable in her skin. Then again, she had just been caught red-handed, throwing a rock through his window.

Nothing comfortable about that.

"I know your name is Georgette Thorold," he told her. "And that you claim to be the widow of a viscount."

He watched her draw an impatient breath, watched as the lovely breasts he remembered far too well strained against their dull gray prison. Standing so close, her lush mouth within easy reach and her citrus-ginger scent wreaking havoc on his senses, was nothing short of torture. As he tried to keep his eyes from wandering too far afield from her face, it occurred to him that, unlike the person he had just been chasing through the seedier parts of Moraig, she was not wearing trousers.

It occurred to him he might like to *see* her in trousers.

James gave his head a violent shake, the predictable pain honing his scattered thoughts back to the task before him. It did not matter if the thought of her curves outlined by men's clothing struck him as violently as the black mare's hooves.

Someone had tried to kill him.

And she was the most likely suspect.

"But it matters not what you claim to be," he told her, his voice hard as steel. "Every word out of your mouth is suspect."

She grew pale, if such a thing was even possible for someone of her unique coloring. She opened her mouth, closed it again. James watched her soundless lips work in reluctant fascination. "Was there something else you wanted to say?" he taunted. "Another meaningless apology, perhaps?"

Because I won't believe that one either.

Her hands knotted and unknotted, and then her lips started to work. "It . . . it has come to my attention," she sputtered, delivering the obviously rehearsed speech with a definite quaver to her voice, "that we . . . I mean, *I* may have engaged in some unfortunate conduct last night. I regret it, truly, and I am sure you will agree that the best thing to do is to pursue an annulment. Miss Dalrymple tells me you have some skill in legal matters, Mr. MacKenzie, so it seems as if it should be a simple—"

"My friends call me James," he interrupted, taking back the upper hand she was attempting to verbally wrestle from him.

She licked her lips. "James, then . . ."

He raised an imperious brow. "*You* will call me Mr. MacKenzie."

Her face colored violently, and a flash of something—was it anger?—widened her eyes. "I will call you whatever I please," she retorted, lifting her chin.

James felt an answering tug in his chest. "You'll have to do better than the stammering speech you've delivered so far," he told her.

"Rogue," she spit out, displaying a hint of the flirtatious temper he remembered from the night before. "Scoundrel is a good name, and fitting, don't you think?" Her gaze swung southward for a scant moment, lingering a hair too long in the vicinity of his abdomen before finding his eyes again. "*Husband*." She drew a deep breath, as if for courage. "That last one is the most annoying, I will admit."

James suffocated an irrational urge to acknowledge her spirit with an answering grin. When she finally—*finally*—stood up to him instead of stuttering out an apology, she was glorious. Good God, was it any wonder he had behaved so impulsively last night? He was not tempted just to throw caution to the wind in response to her smile.

He was tempted to wrap caution around a rock and toss it through his other bloody window.

Instead of telling her that, he wrangled his thoughts into a neat, orderly pile, willing himself to remember why he was here, and what she was. "It matters not what you call me," he said. "It only matters what I call you."

She looked up at him, her forehead creased in confusion. "And what do you call me?"

In the harsh afternoon light, last evening's regrettable actions seemed very far away. James stuffed the instinct to soothe her worried brow into his empty coat pocket, the same pocket where his money purse was supposed to be. Did she think she could bat those pale eyelashes at him and turn his insides to jelly, the way she had last night?

He wouldn't permit it. Not anymore.

"I call you a criminal." James handed over the summons with a flourish. "Consider yourself served, Lady Thorold."

Chapter 17

DREAD, COLDER EVEN than James MacKenzie's damnable green eyes, lurched through Georgette's stomach.

He thought she was a criminal. Not a lady. Not even a lightskirt, which was a title she arguably deserved. A *criminal*.

She was going to kill Elsie when next she saw her.

To be fair, she *had* been breaking into MacKenzie's office, but she had only meant to pick the lock and have a peek at his desk. For him to so misread her intent and serve her with a summons . . . the very thought of it made her chest squeeze in anger.

She reached out a hand and snatched the proffered papers from him. The name he had growled at her was there, written in a firm, bold script by someone with excellent penmanship. She peered up at him. It occurred to her, as she craned her neck to meet his eyes, that it was a long way up. What sort of genie was this man, that he could produce an official-looking document like this on such short notice?

"Mr. MacKenzie—" she started, only to be cut off by his feral snarl.

"Do not say anything," he said, taking a step closer.

"Mr. MacKenzie," she said again, refusing to cower.

She was still appalled by the way he had all but invited her to use his given name, only to cut off her attempts to have a nice, decent conversation. "I insist on the opportunity to speak. You have clearly misunderstood the situation, and—"

He lifted a finger to her mouth.

She inhaled sharply, stunned to silence by the contact of his work-roughened skin on her sensitive lower lip. All too soon he pulled his finger away, no longer touching her, but not leaving her in peace either. He had smelled like plain brown soap. That was all. No brandy. No woman's perfume hinting at an earlier assignation.

Just soap.

She glared at him. "You cannot stop me from speaking my mind."

"No," he agreed, taking a half step back. "But you may wish to withhold your words until you can find yourself an attorney." An angry pulse jumped beside his right eye, and she could see his hands clenching and unclenching.

Georgette's mind felt fuzzy, as if she was surfacing for air after being too long under. Why did she need an attorney? She was still focused on the way he had smelled. His fragrance was far, far different from her former husband's. And her body reacted far, far differently to him. But despite her body's approval, her mind was disappointed. He was different from how she had imagined him. Harder, somehow. Less inclined to listen. She supposed it was because she had built up an image of someone heroic, thanks to Elsie's prattling. Someone worth knowing.

This was not that man.

She licked her lips nervously. "That seems an odd bit of advice. *You* are an attorney."

"True," he said. "But I am not *your* attorney. If I was, I would advise you to hold your tongue. You need to protect yourself against those who might exploit your inexperience with such matters."

Georgette raised a brow. "The same way you exploited my inexperience last night?"

His eyes narrowed before dipping to roam over her body. Belatedly, she realized her careless words had all but invited him to do so. "While I admit my memory is not fully returned, you did not strike me as being inexperienced last night, Lady Thorold."

Georgette's cheeks burned under his scrutiny. But something gave her pause . . . he had suggested his own memory was suspect. Through all of this, she had presumed that he, at least, would remember enough to help her undo the marriage. She had imagined he would *want* an annulment, once she helped him see reason.

But he had not yet acknowledged they had even gotten married. What game did he play?

Georgette breathed in. "You misread the situation, sir. I wasn't breaking into your office to *steal* anything."

"You are correct." His smile grew firmer, more dangerous. The points of his teeth were clearly visible.

Georgette blinked. "I am?"

He leaned forward, and for some reason she could focus only on the wicked slant of his lips. "You have already stolen my money purse, and quite possibly my horse. I have nothing left of value. So unless you are a thief with a penchant for books, you would have left my office empty-handed."

His words brought the reality of her situation into

sharper focus. This made more sense. The prepared summons. His harsh tone. He thought she had stolen his money purse? And his horse—where on earth would she have put a beast of that size, what with the kitten and the snarling dog she had been gifted?

"Why would you think that?" she asked. "What *proof* do you have?"

"Why wouldn't I think that?" came his damnable answer. He tapped his scalp. The stitches stared back at her in accusation. "I awakened this morning to a nasty head injury, courtesy of a woman I could scarcely remember. Spent the day sorting out reports and clues about who you may or may not be, and what we may or may not have done last night. My horse, which is probably worth more than both of us put together, is gone, maybe dead. My purse is missing, and you are the only one who knew I even had it." He leaned in, closer still, and she could see the rich gold flecks rimming his green irises. "It does not take someone of overwhelming intellect to see it all points back to you."

MacKenzie's admission that he did not fully remember last night either sent Georgette's head spinning. "You have made a mistake," she told him, fear eating up any eloquence she might have reached for.

"The mistake is yours," he said, shaking his head now as if he was disappointed in her response. He reached out a hand, and this time he *did* tuck her errant coil of hair behind one ear. She shivered like a horse, trapped beneath its master's touch. "Only a stupid thief chooses a target with such lack of care."

Georgette drew herself up. "That is the second time you have called me stupid, sir." Her mind flew to a logical argument, one she had yet to make though she had noticed it immediately upon examining the papers he had thrust at her. "Yet *I* am not the one who issued a useless summons."

His hand flashed out again. This time, instead of a gentle touch, he wrapped his fingers around her arm. She was held fast, and there was no one around to hear her scream should it come to that.

"Why do you think it is useless?" Uncertainty graveled the texture of his voice.

Georgette lifted her chin. "Because it is made out to Georgette Thorold." His fingers tightened on her arm, but there was no stopping her now. She was willing to own up to the errors she made last night, but stealing his purse had not been among her sins.

"And in case you don't remember, *my* name is now Mrs. James MacKenzie."

DAMN HER, SHE was close to right. James struggled with his annoyance, even as he grudgingly acknowledged the sharp mind at work behind those soft gray eyes. If they *had* been married, the summons would be useless.

But they were not married. David Cameron had assured him of it, and his own recollection supported their vows as nothing more than a joke. That meant she was trying to exploit his memory loss, not realizing he was already beyond the fumbling forgetfulness to which he had first awakened.

It was easier to remember his primary goal now, with her protestations of innocence and her false, injured air. The thing inside him that had been leaning toward her only moments before shifted violently to the left.

"So you are a liar, in addition to being a thief." He

locked up his office and began to walk down the street, pulling her with him. The soles of her boots slapped against the loose gravel, and the sound scraped at his ears.

"No!" she cried. "Please, you have to listen to me. You have to *believe* me."

Her soft, panting sounds of distress made James's fingers loosen on her arm. "I will only listen if you walk," he warned her. He did not like dragging an unwilling woman down the street. It wasn't just that the sight would raise eyebrows once they made it out onto Main Street.

It was because the act made him feel the opposite of powerful.

She nodded, her anger a swath of red across her cheeks and décolletage. James released her cautiously, ready to give chase if she showed any inclination to run.

He no longer believed this was the person who attacked him. This issue of clothing aside, she was about six inches too short and about ten times too curvaceous. That didn't mean she hadn't somehow influenced the earlier assault, of course, just that he didn't have enough evidence to charge her with more than theft. He held out a hand, motioning her to walk on down the empty street, as if they were nothing more than friends out for an afternoon stroll. As if he hadn't seen her naked last night.

As if she hadn't cracked him over the head with a chamber pot.

She lifted her chin but did not move her feet. "Why did you just accuse me of lying?"

"Why did *you* claim we were married?" he responded, pushing her elbow in the direction he wanted. He could hear the shouts and whistles building from the crowd on Main Street. The Bealltainn festivities would be starting in an hour, maybe two. There was not much time to get her before the magistrate but he was determined to try.

"Because Elsie told me we were," she said. "Because *you* told me we were, this morning at the inn." She planted her feet and twisted a ring on her finger. "And because of this."

He noted she did not say anything about remembering. He glanced down, and his lungs ceased working. She had his ring on her finger. Correction: she had the Kilmartie ring on her finger. It winked up at him, the outline of the stag embossed in gold.

Goddamn it. He didn't even wear the blasted thing. Refused to wear it, in fact. He had taken it off when he shed his financial and emotional ties to his family, nigh on eleven years ago. But despite the finality of the act, he had never quite relinquished the need to carry it around in his pocket.

How had she come by it? Cameron's words came back to him. *You and your bride signed no register, exchanged no ring.*

The evidence suggested otherwise.

He dragged a hand through his hair, wincing as his fingers skirted the row of sutures. "I don't *think* we are married." He blew out a too-hot breath, more unsure of himself than ever. "The ring does introduce some doubt."

Of course, she could have stolen that too. He wished his memory was sharper. Several pertinent events of the previous evening were still a jumble. Such as what happened to his horse. And why the hell he had risked his reputation doing such a stupid thing.

"I can't remember *anything* that happened last night," she admitted. "I only know what I have been able to piece together this morning, from Elsie and Mr. MacRory . . ." She trailed off, her hands spread in a silent plea. "I have been trying to track you down, to sort it out. I just hadn't expected that you might not be able to remember either."

He concentrated on centering his breathing, square in the middle of his chest. It was necessary, because his lower body was taking far too much interest in the delectable little thief standing before him. All through the long, maddening hunt for her, he had envisioned her as a cunning seductress. Instead, she seemed far more vulnerable than he had imagined.

His instincts, honed from years of professional practice, told him she was telling the truth.

"You can explain all this to the magistrate," he said, motioning her to move on. But despite his harsh words—the words he had been planning to deliver for the past five hours—he could not even convince himself.

"The magistrate?" she gasped, putting her hands behind her back. "Surely there is no need."

"There is every need." He had a few questions for David Cameron himself. Such as how the girl was wearing his ring when Cameron swore the ceremony had not been real. "And you'd best not lie to him, or he can charge you with perjury, in addition to your other crimes."

"I am not lying!" she exclaimed, and then looked up and down the street, as if searching for someone to corroborate her story. There was only the two of them and the swelling noise from the center of town. "If your purse is missing, either someone else took it or you haven't looked hard enough. I have no need to steal, from you or anyone else." She sounded offended by the notion.

James found himself in a very unpleasant place. She'd made him doubt himself. When he had imagined this moment, he had thought he would feel vindicated. But his resolve to hold her accountable, to seek his revenge, was beginning to falter.

"Fifty pounds," he said reluctantly. "That is how much was in my purse." He could scarcely believe what he was about to do. "If you can replace the missing money, I will consider withdrawing the charges. If not . . ." He spread his palms upward. "Moraig has a very nice gaol. No windows. Infested with mice."

Her mouth opened. Guilt surged through him. It *was* a lot of money. And an unchivalrous threat.

And then she started laughing.

Anger and embarrassment collided in the hollow of James's chest. "What is so amusing? You are facing serious charges, and although I cannot help but question my sanity, I just gave you the means to extricate yourself."

"You think I need to lift a purse with a paltry fifty pounds in it?" she gasped, her whole body shaking with some kind of sick humor. "Let me make this easy for you," she said, wiping her eyes with the back of one hand. "I'll give you a hundred. *Two hundred.* Consider it payment for any inconvenience I have caused you."

"I don't believe you have a hundred," James said slowly. He felt as if she had kicked his feet out from under him, there on the dirt and gravel street.

"Two hundred," she repeated stubbornly. "On one condition. You will grant me an annulment. And then you will never bother me again."

What kind of fresh torment was this? Not only did the woman not wish to be married to him, she was offering to pay him off? The entire notion of her proposal rubbed

James so far wrong he struggled for air. "Are you trying to blackmail me?" he asked, incredulous. Memories of the past, of another woman, and another bribe, closed in. He kicked them away with a stern, mental foot. "Because if you are, you mistake the kind of man I am."

"It would be a gift. Payment for services rendered. Whatever you wish to call it."

Gift, his arse. Although . . . the services-rendered part was arguable. He had a dim memory of one service in particular he had performed for her last night, involving a glass of brandy, his eager mouth, and those luscious breasts.

"I do not accept bribes, Lady Thorold," he told her, swallowing hard. "And I cannot grant you an annulment." He turned toward the noise coming off of Main Street.

"Why not?"

The panic tinting her words halted his progress. He cast her a sidelong glance. "Because we are not married."

She stepped in front of him. He could scarcely believe she was now the one blocking his way. "Are you quite sure?" she asked, her voice ringing in challenge.

That, of course, was the problem. He kept *saying* they weren't married. The events he could remember did not support it. But there were too many murky pieces for him to be sure.

Her finger made contact with his chest, an angry point through which he could feel her entire body quivering. "You stand before me, spouting ideas, theories about what might have happened to your damned money purse, and whether we are or aren't married, when it's as plain as the stitches on your head you don't remember any more than I do!"

Her shouting made James stop. More to the point, her shouting made him think.

She was right. It was not like him to leap to such conclusions without giving the matter due thought, or offering her due process. "If you didn't take it," he asked slowly, "where is my money purse?"

"It's probably still sitting on the bedside table at the Gander, for all you remember."

James considered the room in which he had awakened this morning, in all its patent disarray. The nightstand he could remember, and he was quite sure the purse had not been there. But were there places he hadn't thought to look? He had looked in the wardrobe, but not beneath it. And he recalled a cabinet now, beneath the washstand. He had not looked there either. Uncertainty burrowed under his collar.

He eyed the angry woman standing ramrod-straight before him. He didn't trust her. She had tricked him into *something* last night. And yet he found himself wavering on the edge of offering her a chance at redemption.

"The Blue Gander," he told her, giving up the struggle to be right. He almost hoped he wasn't. "I will give you five minutes to search the room. And then, if my money purse is still not found, you'll need to argue your case before the magistrate. I don't want your promise of two hundred pounds, and I won't listen to any more excuses. Fair enough?"

Her gray eyes narrowed on him. "What about the gaol?"

He shrugged. "I was not being fully honest about Moraig's lockup. It may have a bed. And a window." He hesitated. This next bit was his one advantage here, but he found himself wanting to be honest. "The summons is actually for a civil matter, not a criminal charge. As you have pointed out, the evidence I have is mainly circumstantial."

She shifted her balance, a wary bird seeking flight. "It feels a bit like a trap."

James sighed. "Lady Thorold, I promise you. I have no intention of trapping you. If you are responsible for the loss of my purse, you claim you will replace the money. If you are innocent, I am more than willing to hear any evidence you have supporting that as well."

She tilted her head and considered him a long moment. James could almost see the careful measure of trust blooming in her gray eyes. He was solidly caught in that gaze, just as he had been last night when she had stared up at him over their false vows. Only this time, instead of being drunk and lascivious, he was stone-cold sober and sympathetic.

Damn, but this woman affected him in unexpected ways.

She nodded. He hadn't even realized he was holding his breath until his lungs began laboring again. Instead of grabbing her arm or pushing her elbow, he warily clasped her hand.

This he remembered. It felt small but warm. He remembered he had liked her hands, last night.

He pulled her in the direction of Main Street, his fingers threading over hers. Tried to ignore the way his touch made her flinch. He was not supposed to care whether she liked him or not. And yet, part of him hoped they would indeed find his purse in the little room above the Blue Gander.

And part of him was afraid of what he would need to do if they did not.

Chapter 18

FOR TWO LONG blocks, Georgette was pulled along by Mr. MacKenzie's grip on her hand. And all the way, she simmered. In irritation at the way he had presumed her a thief. In anger at the ultimatum he had given her. And worst of all, in awareness of the way his hand fit over hers. By the time they rounded Main Street and began to dodge the crowd, her mind was numb from all of it.

It confused her, that hand. It secured her to his side as tightly as a nail to a board, and yet churned up feelings that were dangerous to examine. He was not the heroic man she had imagined, come to rescue her from a forced elopement. Neither could she see signs of the disheveled rake who had invited her back to his bed this morning. The flesh-and-blood man was sharp-eyed and hard. His purposeful stride and firm hand made her stomach flip in nervousness rather than attraction. All through the gathering Bealltainn mob, past shops and storefronts that were by now becoming familiar, she told herself that.

And *still* she had difficulty believing it.

The sight of the Blue Gander, with its boarded-up windows and colorful paper lanterns, made her sag in relief. He released her hand, though only to open the door and stand back. Her freed limb tingled in new self-awareness. She clasped her hands together and stepped inside, studiously ignoring the way MacKenzie's hand hovered near her elbow, offering but not demanding aid. "Mannered" was the word that came to mind. Some-one had drilled a bit of good English decorum into this bearded Scotsman. She wondered who had taken the time. A mother, perhaps? More likely a lover. She hoped the woman had received more than threats and accusa-tions for her trouble.

Inside, the building was blessedly cooler than the four o'clock heat of the street. The place smelled of week-old ale, no doubt spilled from someone's mug and left to molder in dark corners. The pervasive scent was overlaid with roasted chicken, wafting from the back kitchen. Georgette recalled Elsie had mentioned MacKenzie took his meals here, on occasion. As if on cue, she caught the telltale rumble of his stomach. She wondered if he had missed breakfast today looking for her. Not that it mattered. It was not like she was feeling inclined to buy the man a plate of food, not after the difficulty he was causing her.

They approached the front desk nearly side by side, and that was when they ran into the first bit of trouble. She had half expected a dramatic intervention from Elsie somewhere along the route, but the girl was nowhere to be seen. Neither did they encounter a problem in the form of her cousin Randolph, whom she hadn't seen once since he had left this morning on the gray mare.

No, trouble was found in the form of the innkeeper, who crossed his arms and raised a bushy eyebrow at her request to have a little peek at the room.

"Absolutely not." The man shook his head. "I just got the room set to rights. Took a pair of maids all morning too. Tar on the bedsheets, brandy soaked into the floorboards . . . I can't afford to let you up there again, not after how you left it the last time. Why, the pair of you should be ashamed of yourselves, carrying on that way in a respectable establishment."

A snort of disbelief erupted from MacKenzie's lips, no doubt due to the description of the Gander as a reputable place. "Did either of the maids happen to find my missing purse?" he inquired acidly.

The innkeeper shook his head. "Not that they reported. But I wouldn't blame them for keeping it if they had, with the disaster you left them to tidy up."

Georgette chewed on her lip, wondering if her stiff shadow of a Scotsman had already started counting down her five minutes. "How much?" she asked, worry pinching her throat. No doubt the proprietor would demand something extortionate, but it would be a small price to pay to ensure her freedom.

The innkeeper's eyes narrowed. "I reckon I could let you up there if you pay for the night."

"The *night*?" MacKenzie burst out. "But we only want it for five minutes!"

The innkeeper leaned in toward Georgette and clucked his tongue. "That quick in bed, is he? My sympathies, miss. Most Scotsmen can do a bit better." He flicked a glance toward James. "No doubt he'll improve as the marriage matures."

A flush crept onto her neck, stinging and high and unwelcome. Clearly, the man thought her the kind of lady who engaged in such talk after her antics of last night. And clearly, he too thought they were married.

A strangled growl came just behind her left ear. She silenced MacKenzie with a backward thrust of her elbow, smiled grimly as she heard the breath whoosh out of him. "How much?" she asked, already loosening the strings of her reticule.

The innkeeper lifted a gnarled finger and scratched at his chin. "One pound."

"That's thievery!" MacKenzie protested.

She considered elbowing him again, just for the pleasure of it. The bit of contact had reminded her he was human, and she sensed she would do well to keep thinking of him in such mundane terms. Instead of giving in to the impulse, however, she counted out the coins and placed them in the innkeeper's greedy palm.

"Are you sure that isn't *my* money you're giving him?" MacKenzie demanded.

"Quite." Georgette jerked the strings of the reticule closed. She waved the proffered key his way, then swept a hand toward the dark stairwell that rose up from the inn's entryway. "And I'm about to prove it. After you, Mr. MacKenzie."

"'Tis James," he said, setting one boot to the stairs. "My name is James." He cocked his head over his shoulder, grinning down at her. "Unless the purse is still missing in five minutes, that is, and then I suppose we'll be back to Mr. MacKenzie."

She followed behind him. "I expect as far as names go, Mr. MacKenzie would be the more appropriate address for the man who would haul me before the magistrate." The reacknowledged threat made the blood pound in her ears.

"I told you, if you can return missing money, there will be no need for me to pursue the charge."

"Yes, well, you'll forgive me if I harbor an innate mistrust of the man who all but dragged me here." Georgette stomped up three steps in rapid succession, then paused at the first landing. Her hands settled on her hips. "How do I even know you speak truthfully about the amount of money that was in that purse? Perhaps you have really lost five pounds, and are looking for me to pad your bank account."

He paused in mid-step, but did not look back. "If we find it, you'll have no need to wonder, now will you?"

They ascended the remainder of the stairwell in stiff silence. They went up two, maybe three more flights. This morning's headlong flight had been so rushed she had scarcely noticed whether she had been upright, much less how many steps it had taken to move from above to below. Mr. MacKenzie—or James, as it were—seemed to know the way. He climbed with steady feet, turned left at the top, and set the key in the lock of the third door on the right. The door swung open, and then they were there, back where she had left him.

Back where everything had started.

It looked different. Clean, for one thing. She remembered rumpled sheets and feathers and broken glass. The scrubbing the floor had received in the interim eight hours had done the room some good. The bed was neatly made with a clean white counterpane. A new chamber pot sat at the ready. She noted its location, handle-out, at the foot of the bed.

Just in case, of course.

"Your five minutes starts now," he told her, pulling a watch from his pocket and pointing toward the center of the room.

Relieved to hear the discussion with the innkeeper

had not detracted from her allotted time, but irritated she was still expected to prove her innocence, she stalked to the nearest bit of furniture. She pulled out the washstand drawers with a series of hard jerks. Nothing there but clean folded towels. A peek inside the chipped china pitcher told her it too was free of missing money purses. She straightened and eyed other parts of the room where a wallet could hide.

He stood watching from the open doorway, one lazy shoulder against the frame. Amusement creased his brow. "They did a good job cleaning up your mess, I see."

His words brought a fierce wave of heat to Georgette's cheeks. *Her* mess, he called it. It was the height of arrogance. There had been two soused souls wreaking havoc here last night.

"*I* don't recall making the mess," she told him, dropping to her knees to peer under the fringed coverlet. She had a peculiar memory of doing almost the same thing this morning, when she had been searching for her slippers. This time she found nothing of importance beyond a feather or two the maids had missed.

"Well, I remember." His words floated down to her. "You smashed a bottle of good French brandy on the floor." From her prone position, she watched his boots as they moved toward her. "Right about here." One dusty toe circled a spot the size of a bedside rug, about a foot from where she crouched. "I picked two or three pieces of glass from my foot when I got home this morning."

Georgette gained her feet and wiped her hands on her skirts. Being here, with him, in this room, and *not* remembering what they had done on the bed sent her stomach churning. "I suppose I should applaud my ingenuity in simultaneously destroying such a vile drink and giving you something to remember me by." She raised an irritated brow. "And I thought you couldn't remember what happened last night."

"Now, I didn't say that exactly. Parts of it are there, sharp as a pocket knife." His eyes met hers, brilliant green. He rubbed a hand across the back of his neck and offered her a smile, the very portrait of a rake bent on seduction. "For example, I remember kissing you, even if I don't remember properly marrying you."

Her heart began a new, awkward rhythm in her chest. *This* man she remembered, from bed this morning. "How lovely for you, given that I don't remember any of it."

"I reckon my recollection of events would be even better," he drawled, "if you hadn't introduced me to the chamber pot this morning."

She rolled her eyes. Of all things, why couldn't the chamber pot be the part both of them forgot? "I already apologized for that."

"For what it's worth, I believe you," he said. And then he walked away.

She blinked, staring at the spot where he had just been standing. He believed her, but which part? The bit about her not being a thief? Or was it just her apology he believed?

She turned in time to see him approach the one piece of furniture in the room that had not been fully put to rights. The wardrobe was a monstrosity, dominating one entire wall. Its ornately carved door still hung sideways off its frame. It was empty inside, but instead of rummaging there, James crouched and peered into the two-inch space that yawned beneath it. His nicely shaped bum waved in salute.

Georgette's mouth went as dry as cotton batting, and for a moment she could not even summon the presence of mind to blink. Dear God, she was ogling the man's posterior. Here she had been trying to teach Elsie to be a lady and she was behaving no better. She forced herself to swallow and looked instead at the taunting row of stitches running across his scalp. Yes, that was better. Look at the damage she had done, rather than the man's more tempting parts.

A hot scald of attraction washed over her and she shifted her eyes to neutral territory. The stained wallpaper made a nice study. It was not too much of a stretch to imagine why she had acted so irrationally last night. Not with a body like that tempting her to misbehave.

He pushed up and shook his head. "Can't see a thing under there." He paced the length of the piece once, and then put a shoulder against one side and gave it a hard shove. Though Georgette estimated the thing had to weigh close to three hundred pounds, it scooted an impressive inch or so. He waved her over. "Help me move this."

She approached warily, particularly given the inappropriate direction of her recent thoughts. James MacKenzie was as confusing as he was concerning. She had thought he would simply stand there while her five minutes clocked down, wanting to see her fail. Instead, he was rolling up his sleeves and putting a sturdy shoulder to the furniture.

She positioned herself where he indicated and pushed when he asked her to push. The wardrobe slid in slow degrees across the floor, revealing a swath of wood planking that more closely resembled the floor she remembered from this morning. A thick layer of dust and feathers lay there, accusingly, along with some shards of glass and a button that looked suspiciously like the one from the bodice of the dress she had been wearing earlier.

"Christ," he muttered, staring at the floor. "I was really hoping it would be there."

The admission struck her as odd. What did it really matter to him, after all? She had offered to replace the missing purse, with money to spare. His intensity of effort seemed more directed toward the matter of finding the thing than securing the money. *She* was the one who stood to lose in this, with his threats about going to see the magistrate. And between the bed, the washstand, and the wardrobe, she had to admit there were not many places in this small, rented room a money purse could hide.

Had she taken it? Perhaps last night, when she had apparently given no thought to propriety or the coming morning? She honestly couldn't say. Georgette slumped against the wardrobe, defeated by her doubts. The door fell the rest of the way off its hinges, hitting the floor with an outrageous clatter.

MacKenzie's upper lip curved into smile. "The proprietor's probably going to make you pay for that."

She wished he would continue to frown at her. It was easier to retain her annoyance with him when he kept that mouth properly leashed. "I think we've paid the man enough, don't you?" She blew an angry wisp of hair from her eyes. "Do you even remember how we broke the wardrobe door last night?"

His gaze fell on the piece of wood in its sad, horizontal position. He nudged it with his boot, his eyes a narrow study. For a moment Georgette was struck with the notion that this was how the man must look in court, all serious intelligence and speculation. He cocked his head in the direction of the bed.

"I already looked there," Georgette told him, but he began moving toward it anyway. "I'll not be the one who replaces the bedding," she protested as he stripped away blankets and sheets and threw them onto the floor. "And the maids would have surely found it when they made the bed if you had left it on top of the mattress."

"I'm not interested in the top of it," he told her, flipping the entire mattress sideways off the bed.

And there, caught between the wood of the footboard and the last bed slat, was a bulging leather purse.

Chapter 19

GEORGETTE HAD BEEN mentally preparing herself for the looming visit to the magistrate, formulating her arguments for what might have happened to the missing money. And instead he had found it. James MacKenzie, for all his threats and barbed insinuations, had freed her.

For some reason, she started laughing. Her relief demanded release in some form, and crying seemed the less appropriate response, under the circumstances. He joined her after a moment, and the sound echoed about the room. They sounded good together, laughing. It occurred to her they even sounded good together arguing.

She wiped her damp eyes with the back of her hand. "How did you know to look there?" she gasped.

"I remembered how we broke the wardrobe door. You had pulled the mattress off the bed and you were jumping on it, trying to reach your corset. You knocked against the door during one unfortunate leap."

Her cheeks flamed hot. "Why would I have needed to *reach* my corset?"

He grinned at her, and her stomach did that unfortunate twisting thing again. "It was on the drapery rod."

She swept her gaze from the tip of his boots all the way to the brown curls atop his bare head. He was quite the tallest man she had ever seen. "I find it hard to believe I needed the help of a mattress to lift me in reach of the drapery rod when you could have just plucked it down for me."

His face dissolved into a brilliant smile. It touched every part of his features, transforming his bearded visage from something potentially wild into the kindest of vistas. "Oh, I did not say I was trying to *help* you. I was enjoying the view of your bonny, bouncing breasts far too much, as you danced about on the mattress."

Georgette's ears tingled around the edges. She had imagined doing things with him, but the notion of jumping on a mattress had not been among her imagined activities. "So you have your purse," she said, anxious to change the subject from bonny breasts and the like. She paused, then tried out the new name she had earned the privilege of using. "*James.*"

He slipped the leather wallet into his front coat pocket. His eyes slid across the top of her bodice. "Aye, and I have your corset too. At my house." He cleared his throat. "I suppose I should return that."

The thought of him returning such a personal item after he had touched it seemed more wrong than whatever he might have touched in the process of removing it. "That won't be necessary, thank you." She eyed his bulging coat. "You should really keep your money purse in the inside pocket of your coat, you know. Anyone who has been to London knows you risk pickpockets to have it sitting there, just so. Why, there isn't even a flap, or a button on that pocket. It could fall out if you so much as bent over."

"Having not been to London, I will have to take your word for it." He had the grace to look chagrined. "So not only did you not take it, you are dispensing advice on how not to fall victim to thieves." He shook his head. "I am sorry I accused you of stealing it."

It felt good to have him admit it, after all the turmoil of the last hour or so. "You can make it up to me by granting me an annulment," she told him.

His brow lifted. "Lady Thorold, we are not married. As we have already discussed at length."

This, then, was the missing piece of the night, and still a point of contention. "If I am to call you James, you should call me Georgette. And Elsie *saw* us get married. Even the innkeeper, odious man that he is, thinks we are married."

He shook his head. "I told you. I am remembering more now. There was a ceremony that appears to have confused some of the bystanders, but it was a sham, a lark carried out in the public room for the benefit of a good laugh."

She blinked at him. "I do not understand."

"It wasn't *real*, Georgette. So you do not need to worry."

"THAT DOESN'T EVEN make sense," she retorted, her fingers curling into fists at her side. "Who *pretends* to be married?"

"Someone deep in their cups," James admitted. He had certainly fallen into that category last night. And he regretted it. Not because of what he had done, or whom he had done it with. Now that his memory was more settled, he could be a little proud of how he conducted himself in that regard. It had been damned hard not to take advantage of all she had offered him.

But he could not help but feel poorly because it so

obviously agitated her today. "We don't often do things with the right degree of forethought in those situations," he added kindly.

She met his gaze with a glare that might have set fire to paper, had he been so careless as to wave the ill-considered summons about again. "I do not drink," she told him. When he raised a brow, she started pacing, a lit fuse in full skirts. "Neither do I kiss strange men, nor sit upon their laps, nor *pretend* to get married."

James watched her stalk her absent memories with growing sympathy. She was right. It didn't make sense. But with the familiarity of the room and the sight of her to guide him, his memory had become close to flush in the past few minutes. There were still pieces missing, such as what they had done in the time between when they had left the Gander and returned to this little room. And of course, what in the devil he had done with his horse. But he finally remembered some essential bits. The money purse and the mattress were part of it, but most importantly, he remembered *why* they had done it.

"Miss Dalrymple told you I was a solicitor, which was how you came to be sitting on my lap," he told her. She slowed her maddening tempo, her head tilting toward him, and he was encouraged to keep on. "You said someone was trying to marry you against your will. Whispered it my ear, and asked my legal opinion on the matter."

Her feet ceased moving. "And your opinion was I should pretend to marry you?"

He chuckled at that. She had a wicked tongue. He remembered that now too. "I explained your best recourse was to wed someone else, someone who could protect you. And *you* said you wouldn't be repeating the lamentable experience of marriage anytime soon."

That memory sobered him a little. He recalled the darkening of her eyes as she had described her first bastard of a husband. It had tugged at him then, and it tugged at him now.

He spread his palms upward in a mute apology. "I offered to show you how easy it could be to marry the right man. Pretending to do it wasn't the brightest thing we could have done, but I was drunk, you were beautiful, and the magistrate was all too willing to perform. But going through the motions doesn't make it real. There has to be intent."

Her gaze bored into him. "Do you trust your memory, truly?"

He canted his head a quarter angle. "It seems clear enough to me now. And I have it on good authority from a reliable witness it was not real. The magistrate who orchestrated the spectacle, for one."

Her tongue darted out to moisten pink lips. "So we *aren't* married?" she asked, her voice hesitant and yet hopeful.

"No." He added an emphatic shake of his head. "Not by my reckoning."

"But we did . . . *things* last night. Outside of marriage." Bright spots of color rose on her cheeks.

There were a whole range of possibilities to be inferred from that. Yes, things had been done. Things he was tempted to do again. But he was trying to reassure her, not upset her.

He took a step toward her, and when she did not back away he moved closer still. He tipped her chin up with a determined finger. He could feel her taut skin twitch beneath his finger. Her lips drew his eye like a bright, flashing stone, tumbling in water. "Things," he chuckled. "That is one way of describing it."

Her eyes narrowed. "I'll have you know, I do not normally do *things* either . . ."

Her mouth drew him closer still, and then almost without thought, he was silencing her objections with his lips. It was not a planned seduction, or an attempt to change her mind. He simply wanted to quiet the private revulsion he heard in her voice.

She went still beneath him. He paused, hovering on the edge of temptation, waiting to see what she would do. Her lips parted beneath his and he felt the tentative touch of her tongue. That was the moment when he could have stepped back and done the gentlemanly thing. Instead, he gave himself over to the sort of kiss she offered back.

He kissed her properly, just to see if his memory was correct, just to see if the woman he had known last night still breathed inside the proper, buttoned-up miss he found himself with today. He gathered her close and surged into her mouth, as if he could swallow her objections and challenge her self-doubts. Her hands came up and fisted in his coat lapels. Her chest pressed upward, a charity that could not be refused. He lifted his palm to her breast as he kissed her, smoothed a finger over the fabric that hid her body from view. Today there was no corset to impede his discovery, no whalebone obstruction to grapple with.

His memory was more torturous than helpful. He recalled that when he had finally unwrapped her last night, her nipples had been a mouthwatering splash of color against impossibly pale skin. But now they were covered, strangers tucked away out of sight. He wanted to meet them again.

One button of her bodice fell to his fingers, then another, creating just enough space to slide one hand in. His fingers inched over the edge of her chemise and his anticipation was finally rewarded, skin on skin. She quivered under his hand, as if experiencing his touch for the first time. He was reminded that in *her* thoughts, she was, and he found himself grateful for the gift of her memory loss.

He circled her nipple with a deft finger, and her resultant gasp of pleasure sent his self-control into dangerously thin territory. Oh God, the feel of her without a corset was just sublime. Her body pressed inward, a wall of fabric teasing against his straining erection. The faint, screaming objections of propriety fell away at that touch. It was all exquisite promise and denied release. He felt the flutter of her hands, fairylike against his chest, tangling in his jacket.

His coat was halfway off his shoulders when the sound of his money purse hitting the floor jerked him back to present circumstances.

Goddamn it. He broke off the kiss, breathless from the shock of reality's intrusion. Coins and five pound notes lay scattered about their feet, a testament to the fact they had both nearly lost their heads. She was as close to sitting in his lap as a standing woman could be. He could almost hear her pulse, hammering in his own ears.

He put his hand gently against her, pushing her back a safer distance. He had just kissed a woman who made it very clear she did not want anything to do with him. He pulled his coat back across his shoulders, seating it properly with a violent shake. Could he sink any lower, or prove himself any more of a fool?

"I am sorry." He winced as his words came out torn and ragged. "I should not have done that."

Her hand rose to her lips. She blinked, her eyes a bewildered shade of blue. "*We* should not have done that," she corrected.

James knelt and applied his attention to the matter of his scattered savings. It was necessary to keep from focusing on the accusation he feared he would soon see in those lovely eyes, edging out the lingering pleasure bit by bit. What had he been thinking? There was no logical argument that could be made in his defense. Last night she had been a willing participant. Hell, one *minute* ago she had been a willing participant.

But she was also not interested in making their arrangement permanent. Had offered him two hundred pounds for the pleasure of *not* having him.

Had just agreed it was a mistake.

She did not want him, no matter that he had just made her flush pink with pleasure.

A memory twisted, of another time and another girl. Elizabeth Ramsey, the minister's daughter. It had been so long ago it lay inside him with scarred, wrinkled edges, but the wound was still raw at its center. Elizabeth had not wanted him either, had toyed with him and then gone on to choose David Cameron as her lover, until her circumstances and Cameron's unexpected departure had demanded James play the hero.

But Georgette was not Elizabeth. She had clearly enjoyed his kiss, but she was not asking him to play the hero. In fact, she was demanding he not.

Which left him with nothing to do but clean up his mess.

He gathered up the five pound notes and stuffed them in the half-empty wallet, then reached for the coins that had scattered within arm's reach. She had been correct about the matter of his front pocket, it seemed. But what an ungraceful way to learn the lesson.

She knelt down, displacing the air around him and treating him to a spectacular view down her gaping bodice. James tried to avert his eyes, truly he did, but his body disagreed with his instincts, because the rounded tops of her breasts looked every bit as glorious as they had felt beneath his fingers. She cleared her throat, amusement feathering the edges of the sound.

He raised his eyes, only to be confronted with the sight of Georgette waving something in front of his face.

"What is this?" she asked.

James took the scrap of paper from her. "It is a receipt. For money paid to the blacksmith." His memory prodded him, demanding completion.

"I can see that." Her voice seemed muffled to his ears. "Do you think that is where you might have misplaced your horse?"

Hell and damnation. What had they done? James shoved the receipt into his purse, alongside the rest of the coins. He was sick with the possibilities. She did not appear to hate him, not yet, but the day was not over. "It stands to reason we should investigate the possibility." He stood and helped her to her feet. "You'd best come with me."

Her lips parted in surprise. "Surely you don't need me. I had hoped to be on the next coach, now that this matter about our marriage is resolved."

She was leaving. Of *course* she was leaving. What was there to keep her here, except the investigation of the last remaining bits of his memory loss? "There is no coach tonight," he told her. "The town closes the street to carriage and horse traffic, after they start the bonfire. And I expect there are questions you'll want to ask the smithy."

"I . . . I don't understand."

James sighed. "What we did in the time between when we were seen leaving the Gander and when we returned to take this room is still unresolved." His gaze fell to the ring she twisted nervously on her finger. *His* ring. The ring that still demanded some sort of explanation.

"And unfortunately," he admitted, dreading the words but knowing they were all too true, "the usual place to get married in Scotland is the blacksmith's shop."

Chapter 20

The smell of heated coal announced their arrival at the blacksmith's shop a block in advance. As they moved closer, the smell of burning hooves introduced itself too. James had wondered if they would be too late, given it was approaching five o'clock on Bealltainn Eve, but the sound of a hammer ringing on steel assured him the man was still bent over his day's tasks.

Pity. He was not looking forward to this interview, and would have been quite willing to delay it until morning. For the first time all day, he had a pretty good notion of what to expect *before* he asked the questions. His memory had settled with the discovery of the receipt in his purse, and he was quite sure he remembered all of it. All that was left to do now was to check the evidence and sort out which pieces could be undone.

Georgette's gentle grip on his arm told him she still hoped for an easy resolution. He let her think that. She would be shattered soon enough.

The blacksmith grinned at them over the top of his leather apron as James approached the shop with an uplifted hand. "Oho, MacKenzie," the man called out. "Not like you to be so late. Was expecting you back for your horse hours ago."

James covered Georgette's tightening fingers with his own and squeezed. "I had an unavoidable delay."

The man released the bellows and came around the edge of the forge, wiping his hands on his apron. "Well, I replaced the missing shoe first thing this morning, and he should be as good as new. He's tied up out back, and wanting some oats over the bit of hay I tossed out for him."

James nodded. Yes, so far his memory was proving correct. They had slipped out of the Gander after his fight with MacRory, and he had been drunk enough he had forgotten to pay for the physical damage wrought in the pub. He had kissed Georgette good-bye, fully intending to let her go. But she had difficulty walking, no doubt due to the feathers still attached to her feet. Moreover she had been frightened of the nameless, faceless man she claimed had threatened her. And so James had put her up on Caesar, intending to transport her to safety of his own house. Halfway down Main Street, the horse had thrown a shoe, right in front of the bloody blacksmith's shop.

"Thank you for the loan of the mare last night," James told him. "Although you should know, the beast came up lame before we made it four blocks. I don't think the horse will be much use as a riding animal in the future," he added. "David Cameron has the mare now, and I expect he'll want to keep her." He grinned then, one good thing coming out of this mess. "You'll need to contact him about what he owes you."

"I reckon I know where to find him." The blacksmith glanced between James and Georgette and grinned. "Congratulations, again. I was right proud you picked me for it."

"What, exactly, did we pick you for?" Georgette asked beside him, her voice as thick as the smoke coming off the forge.

"Why, the nuptials. You were the third couple I married this week, although I suspect the others won't last a fortnight before they start at each other's throats. You two seem different. Happier, I suppose."

James heard the whistled intake of air in Georgette's throat. Her hand dropped from his arm. He felt the loss of contact like a fist to his abdomen. "Did . . . did we actually get married?" she stuttered.

Not that James blamed her. They had both done a lot of swinging back and forth on this particular issue today. She didn't remember, but he did. They had banged on the blacksmith's door and the man had come, bleary-eyed in his nightshirt, and presumed they were there to elope. It had been *her* decision, not his. But he had not objected.

In fact, he recalled being all too willing.

Georgette's stunned reaction seemed to confuse the blacksmith. He picked up a rumpled sheaf of papers from a nearby shelf, flipped through several pages, and presented it to them. "He gave you a ring. Signed my register and everything."

James took the bundled pages and scanned them quickly. Both their names were there, his in a barely legible scrawl, hers in a neat, feminine script. The date appeared correct, as did the spelling of his name. "Not that a signature on the register is absolutely required under Scots law," he murmured, the solicitor in him already sifting through possibilities. "But it does serve as an unfortunate piece of evidence."

Georgette whirled on him. "You told me we weren't

married." Her finger pushed into his chest in relentless condemnation. "I refuse to believe that this farce of a ceremony could be any more legitimate than the fun you had over the public table at the Blue Gander! Why, the man isn't even a registered official!"

Beside him, he could see the blacksmith's eyes grow wide, no doubt in response to such a visible display of their purported "happiness." James covered her accusing finger with his own hand and pushed her arm down gently. "It doesn't take a man of the cloth or the law, Georgette. It takes only a solid citizen witness, claiming intent. The smithy is clearly that. He officiates half the marriages in Moraig." James knew from personal experience. One of the most depressing parts about being the town solicitor was dealing with the desperate requests of people who regretted their irregular marriages. It was one of the reasons England had passed Hardwicke's Marriage Act. It prevented foolhardy mistakes such as this.

But this was Scotland, not England. And James was not yet convinced this was a mistake.

"So we *are* married." Her voice dropped to a harsh whisper.

The blacksmith broke in. "Well, you started the process." He squirmed a bit, an odd sight for man of his size and profession. "Was it . . . I mean, did you . . . *finish* it?"

"I am sure I don't know what you mean." Her voice sounded hollow.

"He means did we consummate it," James explained.

"'Tis none of his business!" she exclaimed.

But it was. It was an entirely legitimate question. And because of it, the issue of whether they were married was still a matter of legal interpretation.

"Thank you," James told the bemused blacksmith by way of ending the awkward conversation. This was a discussion best continued in private. He eyed the woman shifting beside him. Her color was high now, her lips a flushed shade of red. She was unspeakably beautiful, spitting mad, and looking to make someone pay. If they had they been married properly, with a posting of the banns, the issue of consummation would not be a point of concern.

But they had not embarked on a regular marriage. They had eloped. That made things more difficult, but also offered a possible way out.

Georgette had made it very clear she did not want this outcome, no matter that she had seemed close to tupping *him* a half hour ago. It struck him as unfortunate that there could be no exploration of the promise in this marriage. But with the way she had stiffened at the blacksmith's congratulatory remarks, and the way she had colored up now at the discussion of consummation, he more than had his answer.

If she wanted it undone, he would do his best to give her that, his pride and feelings be damned.

GEORGETTE WAITED AS James slipped around the side of the shop and came back leading a saddled horse. It was a fine-looking animal, all rangy chestnut limbs and springy steps. No wonder he had been so anxious to find it, and angry with her when he thought she had something to do with the stallion's disappearance.

He stopped in front of her, lines of strain visible around the edges of his mouth where beard overtook skin. Georgette wanted to put her hand on his lips and ease some of the worry she saw branded there, but instead she lifted a hand to the horse's nose. It was like stroking crushed velvet. The horse pushed impatiently against her hand, demanding more attention.

Unlike the man.

She dropped her hand and surveyed the horse's owner. James MacKenzie had shown her a good deal of decency today. If she had trapped him into a marriage he didn't want, she was going to be damned twice over.

"So are we or aren't we?" she asked him, her voice low enough so the smithy couldn't hear. Her mind seemed squeezed from four sides. She had gone from thinking she was married, to believing she wasn't, and back again in the space of less than an hour. It was enough to make a woman want a glass of brandy.

He picked up her hand. He had a habit of doing that, she noticed. Touching her, when it didn't need to be done. She wasn't sure how she felt about it. In London, such an action would be considered vulgar, particularly lacking gloves as they both were. The feeling of skin on skin was shockingly improper. But the way he did it, so easy, made it seem more a meeting of minds than an attempt to seduce her, or worse, shackle her to him.

"It is not that simple," he told her as they began to walk, his big fingers working circles over hers. "By Scots law, we are nearly there. We are lacking only consummation, or cohabitation with repute."

Georgette swiveled her head to meet his profile. Surprise did not begin to describe the sentiment scuttling through her. "We did not . . . ?"

"No." He did not look at her, kept moving forward. But his voice sounded firm on that point. She was reminded that he, at least, had his memory restored.

A curious sense of disbelief prodded at her. "But we spent the night together. We *did* things."

"Things." The corner of his mouth quirked upward. "Yes, well, that was not one of the 'things' we did."

She stopped short and pulled her hand out of his. "You tossed my corset on a drapery rod and watched me jump on a mattress!" *Unclothed*, her mind screamed, though she could not bring herself to give voice to that part. "We were both undressed when I awoke. It seems a stretch to believe that did not happen."

"I'll not say we didn't want to, Georgette, or that it was easy." He took a half step to face her, one hand still firm on the reins. "It was just that I thought it would be better to wait until morning, when you could no longer claim a clouded judgment." He reached out his free hand and tucked an errant strand of hair behind her ear. "I wanted you to remember it, *wife*. In bone-shaking detail."

She stood a long, frozen moment, caught between the desire to lean into his touch and the need to shrug it off. James MacKenzie made her want those things they had been verbally dancing around, things she had never stopped to think about during her first marriage.

But such thoughts were treasonous, no matter how his unexpected display of tenderness made her knees wobble. Her first husband had not been above the occasional pretty phrase, or the blatant lie. She had not known *his* true nature either, not until she married him and discovered his penchant to spend her dowry on things like jewelry for his luxury-minded mistresses.

Unlike her cousin Randolph, the man gazing down at her now had not once hinted that he wished to marry her because of the money she had received through her wedding settlement. He had no knowledge of such circumstances, had appeared shocked to his toes by her earlier suggestion to pay him two hundred pounds to be done with it all.

But she must not forget what was at stake here. Her future, her financial independence, the *rest of her life* were in the hands of a man she barely knew, and would remain so unless she fixed this now.

Enjoying James MacKenzie's caress was an extravagance she could ill afford.

She pulled away from his lingering fingers. "So can it be annulled?" she asked. "According to *English* law?"

His hand fell away. "The annulment of a marriage under English law is exceedingly difficult. Lack of consummation itself is not usually adequate grounds. You would have to prove I was impotent."

Georgette raised a brow. "*Are* you?" No man of her admittedly limited experience would have willingly spent the night with a naked woman and emerged saying he hadn't touched her.

He snorted. "Certainly not." His gaze turned hot and suggestive. "And I would be more than happy to prove it to you."

She felt a blush creep onto her face. "Well, that cannot be the only way to an annulment. If it is, there are a horde of impotent men striding about Britain."

That brought a chuckle out of him, and her body warmed to the sound. "One can file for an annulment on the basis of fraud as well," he admitted. "But we both signed our legal names on the register, and I don't believe either of us promised the other anything that we are incapable of delivering." He paused. "You can claim one spouse or the other is incompetent. You don't strike me as the hysterical sort, so I don't think it's a viable option."

"Why, thank you," she huffed. "Although we were both apparently quite drunk . . ."

"Intoxication is not the same as mental incompetence." His hand shuffled on the reins. "One of us would have to be locked away in order to prove that claim."

Georgette pondered the few options he had presented. There *had* to be a way. "Elsie said you were an excellent lawyer. Can't you do something?"

"There are people who are not above lying to meet the qualifications for an annulment." His lips hardened, and the tone of his voice matched. "But you should not count me among that crowd."

She looked at him in surprise. "I would never expect you to compromise your principles on this matter. I just want to know what we can do within the bounds of legal authority."

His shoulders loosened, ever so slightly. "We might be able to argue the union was never legal under Scots law. That would require a presentation of facts before Edinburgh Commissary Court, but I am afraid the evidence may not be in our favor. Proving we did not consummate the marriage may be difficult, given your lack of memory and no proof of your virginity." He paused. "There's no chance of that, is there?"

Her face lit with embarrassment. She shook her head mutely. She had been married to a dissolute peer who demanded his marital rights on a regular, if unfortunate, basis. She certainly could not claim she was untouched.

His eyes seemed an open, desperate question. "Would being married to me really be such a bad thing?"

"I—" She stopped, not knowing how to answer.

Her fear of losing control of her life inched higher, and sneered down at her inexplicable attraction for this man. "I don't want to be married at all," she told him. "Whether or not it is to you is not the point."

He stepped closer. "You said something about that last night. That you did not like marriage."

Georgette could not remember what she had told him, but there was no denying his words parroted her own thoughts. "I did not find marriage to be a pleasurable institution," she told him primly. "My first husband was . . . a disappointment."

"You did not seem to mind *my* kiss."

She swallowed, and her chin inched up a notch. "You pointed out I was not in my right head last night."

"I was talking about the kiss this afternoon." His eyes lowered to her mouth. Heat flamed through her, the same heat that had exploded when he had kissed her so expertly but an hour ago. Her lips tingled, as if they had been trained to want his touch.

She licked them uncertainly. "We do not need to be married to kiss." Her heart pumped far too loudly in her ears.

"I am glad to hear you say that," he told her, his mouth slanting down toward hers. "Because I want nothing more than to kiss you again."

Chapter 21

"No."

James stopped cold, even before she put a hand between them, her fingers pressing into his chest in warning. The word that fell from her lips, deceptively soft, was the nearest thing to a knife for severing his body's enthusiastic charge.

"We shall not repeat that mistake," she told him, the flicker of her eyes belying her composure. "It is not wise to keep . . . *exploring* such paths when I have no intention of finishing the route."

James jerked back. He had been halfway to her mouth, despite the fact there were probably half a dozen of Moraig's curious citizens within a stone's throw of seeing them. He noticed she did not say she lacked the *ability* to explore the road he had been about to take them down. She was reminding him this was her choice, and it did not matter if he was inclined to see where this might lead.

He could not fault her thinking. If they were seen kissing on a public street, they would have even fewer options to extricate themselves. And if she let him have a kiss, he was going to want more, given the way his body announced its own intentions every time he stepped near her.

James could not even justify his own wants here. A marriage like this, to someone he barely knew, would do little to build a case for his father's approval. Worse, he was scraping and saving every penny, trying to finance his future. He couldn't *afford* a wife, especially not one whose fine clothes and manners suggested her tastes ran toward expensive trinkets. She was doing him a favor, really, by rejecting him.

Curious how his arguments sounded the weakest sort of defense, even to his practiced ears.

He stepped back a half foot, renewing his grip on Caesar's reins. "You might consider drawing me a map, Georgette." His chest felt thick with regret. "I get bloody lost every time I look at you."

She did not answer. Instead, her head jerked somewhere to the right, and after a moment's confusion, he saw what had claimed her attention. Through the sounds of Bealltainn celebrations up and down Main Street, he sensed someone was bearing down on them. Caesar sawed on the bit and danced at the person's approach, and James placed a calming hand on the horse's neck.

He did not recognize the man who emerged from the smoke of the town's bonfire, which had just been lit to much clapping and whistles. It was not William, or David Cameron, or any other number of Moraig's townsfolk who might object to their proximity to each other.

And so, James did not step away from her. If anything, he stepped closer.

The man stalked toward them, his face an angry mask. As he drew closer, James could see he was young, probably in his twenties, with hair of a similar color to

Georgette's. With his striped waistcoat and polished boots, he appeared to be a gentleman, although the image was somewhat farcical given that the glasses on his nose were twisted at an off angle and a blood-soaked bandage was tied around one hand.

Georgette's hand touched her throat once, hovering over the little space where sound was formed. "I . . ." She breathed in deeply, as if for courage. "James, this is Mr. Burton." Her voice sounded very small.

"Her cousin," the man spat out. "I have been looking for her everywhere, and then when I do finally find her, it is in clearly questionable company." Burton took a menacing step closer, and James could see the resemblance now. Beyond the fact they both had pale yellow hair, their eyes were the same unsettling shade of gray.

James shifted uneasily. She had not mentioned having family close by. A warning began to rattle about in his head.

"I am disappointed in you, Georgette," Burton went on, his words a caustic blur. "You are well and truly ruined now, when if you had simply done as I instructed we could have cleaned this up quietly."

James honed in on the man's spoken words. The man was no gentleman, not to speak to her in such a way. This was a discussion meant for private ears, not a spittle-drenched accusation on a crowded street. He wanted to smash his fist into Burton's thin nose. And moreover, he wanted to nudge Georgette, to see what she had done with the woman who had rejected him so unswervingly just moments before. Why was she standing there, dumb and mute, that wicked tongue so silent? It was not lost on him that he once had spoken that way to her himself, when he thought she had been a thief. She had shown far more spirit then. But she had *known* she was not a thief.

Did she truly believe she was ruined, or that she deserved this fop's scorn?

She had claimed a man was threatening her, and here one was, in the flesh. The pieces of evidence began rubbing up against each other, blending into an irrefutable pattern. Was this the man who had tried to force her to marry him? The thought crawled down his throat and sat inside him, threatening to explode.

"You did not let the lady finish." James's muscles were already coiling up, ready for use. "My name is James MacKenzie. Her *husband*."

Burton's attention shifted to him then. "One picks up a lot of information, following people about and keeping to the shadows. Seems to me the lady still thinks that is a matter of debate."

The suggestion that the man had been following— nay, *stalking*—them sent James's blood boiling. "That is a private matter."

"*Private?*" Burton shook his head. "I think not. This is nothing that simple. She had an agreement with me, sir, made before she met you. A betrothal. You do not have a claim here."

"The lady is mine," James replied firmly. Georgette's stated intentions rattled about in his head, but he ignored them for the moment. This man was a more immediate threat than her desire to end the marriage, and he would not leave Georgette to deal with this man alone. "We are married," he growled to Burton. "Doubt it at your own peril."

"James," Georgette hissed at him. "It may not be for long."

Now, *now* she found her voice? No doubt she intended to remind him he did not need to fight on her behalf. James focused on the fact that he needed to disarm this threat permanently, before he no longer had a right to help her.

"So, you see how she changes her mind," Burton sneered. "She cannot be trusted." He waved his bandaged hand around like a weapon. "She left a vicious dog to attack me in my own house. There's no telling what she'll do to you. Why, look at the bloody gash on your head. I hear she's already tried to kill you once."

Memory prodded at James, fully intact and demanding attention. Someone *had* tried to kill him today, and not just with a chamber pot. He hesitated, turning over the events of the afternoon in his mind. Did he trust her fully? She had proven she wasn't a thief, and Caesar was safely in hand. But who was to say she wasn't plotting something more nefarious, possibly in conjunction with the man in front of them?

But as quickly as the uncertainty flashed in his mind, it was extinguished by the grim fear he saw on her face. Either she was the most accomplished actress to ever grace Moraig's dusty streets, or this man made her uneasy. There was no time to juggle doubt. He must rely on his instincts, muddled as they were.

And his instincts told him she was in danger.

He took up her hand and addressed Georgette's cousin as he would a courtroom adversary, all bristling threat and bald facts. "If I ever hear you speak to my wife that way again, Mr. Burton, you will find yourself in the infirmary with more than a bandaged hand for your trouble."

A bark of incredulous laughter escaped the man.

"I've heard about you, MacKenzie. The whole town talks about you, behind your back. You are nothing but a wastrel second son, a disgrace to your father."

James lost control of his feet then. He leaped forward, his body vibrating with suppressed violence. Georgette's hand jerked in his, a warning not to hurt her cousin. That she thought him capable of it was telling. He *was* capable of it, had proved it in his past. He drew a deep breath and fought for the presence of mind to remain civil. He wanted to kill the man, of course. But he did not want Georgette to see that side of him.

His hesitance seemed to embolden Burton. The man tugged at his waistcoat, like a great, preening fowl who had escaped the butcher's knife. "Perhaps I no longer want her as a wife. Perhaps there's a better way." His eyes narrowed. "Seems like the two of you may not be in agreement on this little matter of whether or not you are married. When I tell your family what you've done, they'll pay to keep this quiet."

The threat snapped the last of James's restraint. He jerked away from Georgette's grip and rounded on the man. Burton showed some meager slice of intelligence then, taking two steps back in rapid succession, his feet scraping on dirt and stone.

Faster than a rabbit, and before James could even lift a fist, the man was gone, dashing off into the Bealltainn crowd.

And James was left with his fists curled and a lifetime of frustration held barely in check.

GEORGETTE COULD SCARCELY believe the man who had just confronted them was the same man who had invited her here on holiday.

It was as if he had become someone else entirely.

"Pray do not listen to my cousin," she told James wearily. "He . . . he wanted to marry me, and I told him I would not. It has made him come unhinged, I think."

"Unhinged. That is one way to describe it."

Georgette winced. Because of her, James had just been threatened. How had she thought Randolph was someone she could trust, someone who was looking out for her best interests? The isolation of the estate he had chosen for his summer residency seemed more ominous now. Had he plotted this, even as she had mourned the death of her first husband?

"Last night, you mentioned someone was trying to force you to marry against your will." He regarded her as he might a courtroom dilemma, hard eyes and flexing fingers. "Is it safe to presume that person is your cousin, or must we sniff out the handful of other fiancés you have lurking about?"

She gave him a sharp glance. "Randolph Burton is not, and has *never* been my fiancé. I believe he meant to force the issue last night. I must have escaped, somehow."

His expression softened. "I suppose that fits. You were frightened of *someone* last night. Do you have any idea why he would try to do such a thing?"

Georgette shook her head. No matter how she tried, she could not conjure that piece of the puzzle. Randolph's motives escaped her. She could guess at a financial cause, perhaps. He did not strike her as harboring a mad passion for her, not when he spoke to her so.

"He has threatened to go to my family," James said, his voice hard.

"We must explain our circumstances to them. There will be no need for—"

" 'Tis not so simple, Georgette." His words were issued quietly, but they fell with barbed points. "My father will believe him over me."

She sucked in a breath. That anyone would believe a ranting near-lunatic like Randolph over someone as steady as this man before her seemed the height of absurdity. She reached out a hand and placed it on his arm. It felt like the trunk of a tree beneath her fingers, rough bark and solid strength. He had been about to tear her cousin's limbs apart. A glad little hitch settled in her chest. In her entire life, she had never been treated as if she was someone worth fighting for.

This man did. And she did not even belong to him. Or at least, she would not for long.

"Randolph is nothing but a poor scholar, bent on securing his future through theft or force," she told him. "Surely your family will see that and turn him away from an audience."

"I doubt Mr. Burton will present anything close to such an incoherent argument when he speaks with my father," James responded. "You said he was a scholar. Of which sort?"

"Botany. Plants and such. I should have known he wasn't stable from the moment I arrived." She could pinch herself now, for being so naïve and staying there without a female escort. "He walks about brandishing his pruning shears as if they were a weapon, muttering Latin names to himself."

James released a long, drawn-out breath. "That is the very sort of thing that may *gain* your cousin an audience." He looked away from her, toward the bonfire. "Instability, after all, is the mark of an excellent scholar."

Georgette followed his gaze. She could see the glow

of the town fire as it gained strength, a block or so away. A shower of sparks rose toward the evening sun like a phoenix, and she waited for him to be ready, to explain the jumble of confused thoughts in her head.

"My father was once a scholar, of early Roman culture." James shifted beside her, one foot to another. "He studied at Edinburgh as a young man, and we lived near Moraig, excavating Caledonian artifacts for the British Museum."

"Is your father unstable?" Georgette asked in confusion.

He offered her a sad smile. "No, my father was not an excellent scholar. Merely a middling one, but it made him happy, and it provided for our family. The title was not supposed to fall to him, it came only through a quirk of fate. Happened when I was eighteen or so. The moment he became earl, my father's expectations for me changed, and I have given him nothing but disappointment." He shook his head. "He has paid to silence my naysayers on more than one occasion. He will presume this is yet another thing he must fix."

Georgette stewed over that a moment. She recalled the past tragedy Elsie had hinted at this afternoon. "Was this . . . *is* this about the rector's daughter?"

His face twisted in surprise. "How do you know about that?" His hand lifted. "Never mind. The people in this town have a fearsome memory."

She slid her hand down his newly tensed arm, realizing she had fallen into James's own pattern of touching. It seemed natural, somehow. "Elsie mentioned something about it, that you claimed her child was yours."

He laughed, the sound humorless. "I told her father

it was mine, at any rate. She was terrified of the man, and all too willing to let me shoulder the blame. I was twenty-one, fresh out of Cambridge. I was head over heels for her, thinking I had a chance to win her heart by proving myself dependable. Most likely the child was Cameron's."

"Who is Cameron?" she asked, confused.

"David Cameron. The magistrate. Or at least he is the magistrate now. Then he was my friend."

Anger rushed in. For James, for the nameless, faceless girl. "But . . . why did he not step up? Why did he let you do such a thing?"

"His father had bought him a commission in the army, and he'd been sent down to Brighton for training. She took her own life, before any sense came of it all. Before Cameron could be notified, before I could even tell my own family what I had done, or tried to do. I learned later the rector had stormed into my father's study demanding money to take her away and pretend it had never happened. My father paid him off, without even speaking to me first." His voice hitched around this last bit of it. "And . . . she took her own life because she thought I held no more worth for her than that."

Georgette sat, stunned to silence as she realized James blamed himself for the girl's death. She watched his fists clench and then unfurl, slowly, as if invisible fingers were straightening them. But apparently, he was not yet through.

"So I confronted her father, after the funeral. Broke his jaw. Damned near broke his neck." He swallowed. "My father bailed me out, this time from the gaol. He paid the rector's medical expenses and no small amount of restitution. And never, not once, did he ask for my side of the story. It is one of the reasons I left to study law. I had been tried and convicted in the eyes of my father and the town, without ever setting foot in a proper courtroom."

"But why would the town think badly of you?" Georgette asked, heartsick to hear his halting explanation. "You were trying to help her."

"It was mostly because I let my fists get away from me. I hit the *rector*, Georgette, a man they feared and respected. But he is no man of God, at least not a God I would wish to know. I could see why his daughter might have taken her own life, rather than live, pregnant and unwed, in the shadow of a tyrant like that."

The pain in his voice came nigh onto splintering her. She wanted to soothe it, erase the mistakes of his past that sounded as if they might not have been mistakes at all.

She recalled Elsie's words. "Sometimes," she told him, "a body needs to use their fists. That sounds like one of those times to me."

"I am not convinced there is ever a right time," he muttered, looking at his feet.

Georgette pressed her lips tightly together. It was not her place to criticize, but she could not be silent on this. "If someone had fought for me like that," she told him, "or had *ever* loved me enough to make the sacrifice you offered this girl, you can rest assured I would never do something so selfish as end my life, or take that of my unborn child's."

His head jerked up, widened eyes meeting her own. She had shocked him. *Good*. She would shock him yet again.

She stepped closer, rose to the tips of her toes. Looped her hands around his neck and pulled him down to meet her lips. She closed her eyes and kissed him, no matter that she had just told him she would not, no matter that they were on a public street, with the smell of wood smoke and the sounds of Bealltainn swirling around them.

He groaned into her mouth and wrapped his arms around her in an exhilarating show of strength. Their first kiss, or at least the first she could remember, had been negotiated around an afternoon of flirtatious banter that had her blood humming. But *this* kiss, this was something different.

He had just stripped his conscience bare and laid his troubles at her feet. He was vulnerable, achingly so.

And she wanted to dive in and not come up for air.

He accepted her invitation—nay, her demand—and stroked the inside of her mouth in a rhythm that was pure promise. His beard scraped against her cheeks, a rough, happy hurt that made her wonder what his face would feel like rubbed on other, more susceptible parts of her body. She clung to him, wanting more of this kiss, wanting more of *him*. With his deft, knowing mouth, he broke apart the resistance she held inside her, piece by piece. He left her wondering why she had never considered that a marriage could be more than the sum of her past experiences.

He pulled back first, breathing hard, his eyes painfully unreadable. Did he find her bold? Or merely imprudent, after her earlier refusal of just such a gesture?

Someone catcalled to them, "Kiss her again, MacKenzie!" A series of hollered agreements and whistles followed.

Georgette looked around in a daze, realized that the

Bealltainn crowd had broken away from the bonfire and spread further through town. Around them were other couples, many embracing. Her heart fell two feet. It was still bright daylight, and someone had seen them, recognized them. Why had she not been more circumspect?

His knowing voice tickled her ear. "Relax those stern shoulders," he whispered. "Kissing is a bit of the Bealltainn tradition. If we do not call further attention to ourselves, no one will think anything of it."

Heart still pounding, she glanced toward his horse, waiting placidly beside them. The animal appeared far less fazed by the Bealltainn madness than she. It was only six o'clock or so, and the celebration promised to go long into the night.

Something James had told her earlier came back then. The town closed to all but foot traffic after the bonfire started. That meant Randolph would have to walk some ways to reach the old gray mare he had ridden into town. And that meant they had a window of opportunity here.

"Can your horse run any better than it walks?" she asked, hope elbowing its way through the embarrassment that still constricted her chest in the aftermath of their kiss.

James's brows pulled down in confusion. "Why?"

"We have a chance to warn your father about my cousin's threats," she told him. "Randolph will need to negotiate the crowd to find his horse, and you already have yours."

He tensed. "I've not spoken to my father in eleven years," he told her. "He'll not be open to hearing from me now."

Georgette stepped toward the horse, more sure than

ever of this course. "Eleven years ago, your father acted without all the information he needed to make a proper decision. Would you force him to do so again?" She turned away from him and moved into place, lifting her hands onto the saddle. "Give me a leg up," she commanded.

"You would come with me?" He sounded incredulous.

Georgette rolled her eyes skyward. For a Cambridge-educated solicitor, he could be incredibly dense. "I'm not staying here alone, navigating my way through Bealltainn. I want to help you. And perhaps your father will be more apt to listen if I can explain my history with Randolph, and how this all came to pass."

She held her breath, facing the saddle, waiting to see what he would do. His hands skimmed her ankle, the grip tighter as he came to some sort of decision. She felt the sheer strength of him as he boosted her high into the air. She landed awkwardly, but quickly scooted forward, making a space for him to swing up behind her. She looked down at him, waiting for him to follow.

He looked perplexed. Had no one ever helped the man before? "And I *want* to come with you," she told him. "There is that."

His face settled into grim acceptance. He put his foot in the stirrup and swung up behind her and then he was there, a solid wall of warmth pressed against her back. She closed her eyes and bit her tongue to keep from saying the rest. *Though God knows I may regret it tomorrow.*

Chapter 22

A HALF HOUR OF balancing Georgette on his lap convinced James he was bound for hell.

Or, indeed, that he had already arrived.

He had set Caesar to a canter as soon as they broke free from Moraig's busy streets, the need to reach his family before Burton a shrill demand. While the gait was faster and more comfortable than the horse's body-jarring trot, it had the misfortune of rocking her against him in a very vulnerable place. He had no doubt she could feel every inch of his interest, pressing through her skirts. To become aroused on the back of a horse—particularly one who was being pushed at such a mad pace—was no easy process.

Apparently, it was a skill he could master.

By the time he reined in the exhausted, froth-flecked stallion in front of Kilmartie Castle, his member was hard with want and his knees were weak with longing.

He dismounted and took a necessary second to adjust the front of his coat over the evidence of his frustrating trip. Distance from this woman could only help matters. But when he lifted Georgette down, he could not prevent his eyes from settling on the stockings that spilled from beneath her rucked-up skirts, nor hurry his fingers that wanted to linger at her waist. He had held this woman in his arms last night. After such a ride, and such a day, he wanted only to do it again. The kiss she had offered outside the blacksmith's shop, for no apparent reason other than comfort, had proven the most emotionally jarring experience of his life.

Then again, he was on the cusp of facing his father, after eleven years of sullen silence. "Emotionally jarring" was about to be redefined.

He dropped his hands and forced himself to step away from her. A groom emerged from whatever mysterious place grooms lurked when they did not have a horse in hand, and James handed the sweat-soaked stallion over to him. "Walk him for at least ten minutes, please. He's carried two riders from town and is winded."

The groom nodded. "Of course, sir."

"But do not unsaddle him," James warned. "We won't be staying long."

The groom set off with Caesar, and he watched them go with no small amount of misgiving. No doubt the animal would emerge from the Kilmartie stables better groomed and better mannered than going in. His father would demand nothing less.

James lifted his eyes toward the stone turrets lining each wing of the manor. "Kilmartie Castle," he told Georgette, splaying a reluctant hand in the direction of the front door. The place had been built four centuries ago, but new wings had been added in the last fifty years, giving the place an undecided appearance, as if it could not quite determine what it wanted to be. The house, if you could even call a draughty old castle that, sat on a high bluff overlooking the loch, a rough stone sentinel that shouted out for attention.

James had ignored it successfully for over a decade.

His chest contracted painfully. He was about to march inside now and demand an audience with the very man who had driven him away. He consulted his pocket watch, stalling the inevitable.

There was no chance Burton could have beaten them here, not with Caesar's ground-eating stride. "Seven o'clock," he told her. "At this hour, my family is probably dressing for dinner."

"But we are not staying?" Her voice sounded childishly hopeful.

"No." His stomach objected to the refusal. He had not eaten all day, and that bodily need now nosed its way in front of his other competing demands.

He usually took his evening meal at the Gander by six o' clock, and more often than not was fast asleep by nightfall, which came close to nine at this time of year. Through most of his childhood, his days had followed a similar pattern. But when his father had become the earl, boisterous family meals around a scarred kitchen table had disappeared. James and William had been expected to present themselves for dinner at eight o'clock sharp, properly scrubbed and dressed, manners displayed like the museum specimens his father no longer collected.

His collar tightened at the memory of cold soup and stilted conversation. No matter how hungry he was, he could not imagine staying long enough to endure such a spectacle.

Georgette seemed not to notice his unease. She had turned to stare at the vista that spread out in front of the manor. "It's like looking on someone's dream," she said, her voice hushed.

"Whether a pleasant interlude or a nightmare depends on a person's perspective," he replied.

She offered him a curious look. "'Tis a house and a view fit for royalty."

He answered with a tilt of his head. The damned vista took his own breath away, seeing it for the first time in eleven years. He could scarcely imagine what a stranger felt.

Presumably the place had once offered an excellent outlook of the loch in order to warn of approaching danger, but now it offered simply a view to end all views. Beyond the loch, where the cool mountain water met the warmer brackish tide, the ocean sparkled in the promise of the coming sunset, still an hour or two away. On a warm evening, like today, the air carried the sting of salt off the distant waves. On the west side of the estate, just visible on the horizon, were high cliffs where James had spent one pleasant summer learning to balance himself on the edge, toes gripping the crumbling rock, and then hurl himself away to plunge into the surf.

When he shifted his gaze back to Georgette, he realized she now stood watching him instead of the view, her lips pursed in studied silence. Perhaps she had not imagined he came from castle stock. He looked nothing like a gentleman, after all. He had no idea of this woman's circumstances, where or how she lived. She was the widow of a viscount, but peers came in all shapes and sizes and bank accounts. Did this castle, with its ostentatious view, seem to her the worst kind of excess, as it once had to him?

He had hated it when his family had first come here, and had refused to answer when the servants had addressed him as Lord James. He had been eighteen years old, chafing under his father's stern new rules. Nothing seemed to fit. He had been raised to go barefoot in the summer, only to awaken one morning to find himself stuffed into tailor-made boots. That had been a dark time, and he had welcomed being shipped off to Cambridge, partly as a way to rebel, and partly as a way to escape.

"I suppose we need to go in," he mused, lost in the swirl of memories.

She nodded and gathered her skirts. When he still hesitated, she cocked her head. "Is something the matter, James?" Her face colored. "Or would you prefer me to call you Mr. MacKenzie when we seek our audience with your family? It would be more in keeping with our plans, I suppose."

He let out a breath. She could not know how she looked at this moment, hair escaping, dirt from the blacksmith's shop smudged high on one cheek. Her dress bore ill traces of having galloped four miles on a sweating horse. But none of that mattered, because she was here with him, prepared to face down his demons in her quest to make this right.

"James," he told her. "I want you to call me James. I see no reason to pretend we have no association, no feeling of affection in the process."

Her eyes widened at his ill-considered confession. It was the truth, even if it was an incredible thing to admit after knowing her for less than a full day. His heart lightened a little. No matter what waited beyond that door, no matter the tomblike, echoing silence he knew would envelop them upon stepping into the earl's domain, she had come with him.

Had insisted upon it.

"Thank you," he told her. "For coming." The words were simple enough, but they conveyed what he felt, to the letter.

She smiled at him, a windswept vision. "You may thank me after we speak with your family. And rest assured, I shall require more than words." She reached out her hand and took his up. A jolt of awareness surged through him at the uninitiated contact. "Shall we?"

He braced himself. Strode up the stairs.

Knocked on the door and tumbled into madness.

The foyer into which the doorman admitted them rang with shrieked laughter and pounding feet. Overhead, high on a banister James had never once had the pleasure of sliding down, a child in some sort of red uniform leaned over, brandishing a wooden rifle. "Death to Napoleon!" the boy shouted.

A blur of white muslin and bare feet flashed by, no doubt the escaping "general" dodging enemy fire. The child squealed, the sound ringing with laughter. James felt the noise every bit as sharply as if he had a taken a bullet to his chest.

Christ above, whose house had he stumbled into?

"James!" A feminine voice burst from the right hallway, and then collided into him in a tangle of arms and skirts and rosewater essence.

"Mother," he choked out, bowled over by the cacophony. He loosened his grip on Georgette's hand and dazedly kissed mother's cheek. "Who . . . *what* are all these children?"

"Your cousin sent his children for the summer, and we are glad for the company. Of course, if you would call on us here once in a while, instead of leaving the visiting to fall squarely on my shoulders, you would have known that." His mother gave him the merest hint of a reproachful smile, then drew a sharp breath as her gaze moved upward. "Oh, Jamie," she breathed. "What on earth has happened to you? Do I need to fetch a doctor?"

He shook his head. "Patrick Channing has seen to my head, and the other is little more than a scratch. It looks much worse than it is." He swallowed his reluctance as if it was a spoonful of horrid boiled pudding. "Is Father about? I . . . I need to speak with him. Immediately."

"He's probably napping. The children wore him out. They insisted on going fishing this morning. I'll go find him."

James's mouth dropped open. The image of his father, fishing with children, was so incongruous with the image he held like a miniature portrait in his mind that he could not quite bring himself to speak.

"Shall I fetch William too?" His mother's voice wriggled through his thoughts.

"Er . . . no." James hesitated. "Not yet." He owed his brother an apology, true enough. But first he needed to sort things out with his father.

His mother's hands fluttered nervously and finally settled at her side. "It is good to see you here." She smiled at him, her cheeks coloring with emotion. "Your father will be so pleased."

The little general darted by again. James could see now the boy was about five or six years old, and moreover, that he was a MacKenzie, with green eyes of a color to rival his own. The redcoat on the banister was harder to see, but showed every promise of growing into his uniform, with time and good meals. That the house he remembered as quieter than hell itself could ring with such sounds of family seemed impossible, and yet, even as he grappled for logic, the boy let out a war whoop and slid down to land in a puddle at his feet.

"You can wait in his study, it you would like." His mother stepped over the boy, who lay groaning in glee on the floor, a hand clasped to his pretend injury. She motioned for James to follow. "And I'll see if I can't find an old coat of William's to replace that torn, bloodied one."

That shook him from his reverie. "I don't want a coat." His voice turned out gruffer than he intended. He didn't want anything from this house, or this family, but his quarrel was not with his mother. He softened his tone. "I am fine, Mother. Truly."

He stepped forward, meaning to make his way to his father's study, but pulled up short as his movement took him from the woman standing patiently behind him. His mother's eyes settled with surprise on Georgette. She waited, no doubt for some hint of the manners she had once drilled into his eighteen-year-old head. He drew a breath. He had forgotten to introduce his … Well, what was she? Georgette wasn't his wife, or anything easily explained. He settled for the obvious.

"Mother, I would like to introduce you to Lady Georgette Thorold. From London, and presently staying in Moraig." He glanced at the woman who had pushed him here, the woman who made his blood jump to attention even now, with circumstances as they were. "Lady Thorold, this is my mother, the Lady Kilmartie."

Georgette gave his mother a nod, and her lips curved upward. The sight bounced around in his chest. He glanced to his mother and realized her lips had settled into a matching smile.

A *delighted* smile.

His mother nudged aside his surprised silence and stepped around him, holding her hands out to Georgette. "Welcome. I cannot tell you how happy I am to meet you."

SHE HAD NOT expected children.

Everywhere she looked, they were skittering about, shouting, knocking into things. The two little ruffians bore a strong familial resemblance to the man before her, leaving no doubt of their distant heritage. Georgette had never seen eyes that color outside of Scotland.

But more than that, it occurred to her they looked as James must once have, with picked-at scabs along their arms from old mosquito bites and noticeable gaps in their bright, eager smiles. This was what she was poised to give up if she pursued the dissolution of this marriage. Children of her own, children that looked like this. She was not so naïve as to imagine she would be brave enough to make a match with someone else.

Her heart settled sideways and refused to be righted.

She wasn't convinced she *could* have children, or that she deserved them. Two years of marriage had produced only the one hopeful seed. The loss of it sat knifelike in her memory. She had loved the promise that unborn child had brought to her life, even if it originally had been conceived through nothing more than jaw-gritting duty. She had felt all the more guilty when she had proven too insufficient a wife and widow to merely hold on to it.

Georgette turned her head about, looking for James. She found only Lady Kilmartie, watching her with a bemused expression. "He's gone into the earl's study," his mother said. "A man's domain. I don't recommend the experience."

Georgette read between the unspoken lines. *He does not want you there.*

"I . . . had not realized he left." Georgette shifted uncomfortably.

"Have you eaten?" his mother asked.

Georgette eyed the woman who waited patiently for her response. The countess looked nothing like James. Her gray hair bore evidence of having once been a sunny yellow, and her eyes were soft blue instead of a penetrating green. But she carried the same hint of warmth in the lines around her eyes, a suggestion that she would be quick to smile or laugh, though she was doing neither at this moment.

"I had something to eat near noon, thank you," Georgette answered slowly. "James has not." She fought the flush that threatened to submerge her skin at the use of his given name in front of his mother. No doubt Lady Kilmartie would think her the most forward kind of woman.

No doubt she would be right.

She was not what Georgette would want for her own son, a lady who forgot herself and behaved so shamefully after only a glass or two of brandy. His mother was a countess. Surely she would think he deserved better, once the shameful circumstances of their meeting came to light. He *did* deserve better. But still, a hot curl of jealousy flamed inside her at the thought.

Lady Kilmartie smiled and beckoned with one hand. "We can't leave you standing here waiting. James has not spoken to his father for eleven years, and it is certain he will prefer discretion for some of what must be said. This will likely take a while."

Georgette grimaced. "James mentioned how long it had been."

His mother shook her head. "Fools, the both of them. Alike as two men could ever be, stubborn to their last breath. 'Tis a wonder he's come at all, and I suspect that has as much to do with you as anything."

Georgette could not disagree. It was definitely her doing that had brought James to this point. Only it was not the motivation this kind, gracious woman suspected. Guilt was setting in, with claws as sharp as a raptor's. The conversation James was getting ready to have with his father was her fault, and would never have been necessary if she had not been so stupid as to take that first glass of ill-advised brandy last night.

"Let's stop by the kitchen," Lady Kilmartie went on, oblivious to Georgette's churning thoughts. "Before I go to fetch his father."

Georgette took a step in the indicated direction, relieved to have the situation so quietly discharged. A thought occurred to her, one spurred by the rumble she had caught from James's stomach as they stood outside. "Might we send a plate into the study?" she asked.

His mother smiled approvingly. "Indeed, I think we should insist upon it. James never did remember to eat, was always too busy to stop and take the time. It will be one of your sorest trials as his wife, I can assure you of that."

"I . . ." The flush that had started on Georgette's neck some minutes ago deepened into a full-body rush of embarrassment. "You mistake matters. I am not your son's wife, Lady Kilmartie."

The woman's light brows drew down, perplexed. "Forgive my presumption . . . I saw his ring on your finger, and I thought that is what he had come to tell us."

Georgette fought the urge to shrink against the polished marble floor of the foyer. She worried the damning bit of jewelry on her finger. She was without a ready answer here, had not imagined the woman would be so astute. She wasn't sure why she was still wearing the ring. She should have given it back to James the second he found her outside his offices.

"It is more that I shall not be his wife shortly," she clarified. "It was a mistake." She thought back to James's explanation they would need to present the facts of the marriage before some commission in order to ascertain if it was legal or not. "One we are both planning to see undone," she added.

His mother's lips parted. "I see. And the affection you hold for each other does not sway that thinking?"

Georgette blinked against the question. There was no accusation in Lady Kilmartie's voice, just a far too observant inquiry. She could not deny an unexpected affection for the man who would not be her husband.

Indeed, she felt more strongly toward James after a day's acquaintance than she had ever *hoped* to feel for her first husband, even after two years of marriage. But her desire for some measure of independence after such a poor first experience would not be swayed. "I . . . I honestly am not sure if affection is enough," she admitted.

Marriage should not be something a body undertook so lightly. How a man treated his wife was one consideration, and whether his family would accept her, although those things seemed pointed in a hopeful direction. There was also the matter of a man's financial acumen to ponder. James's performance in that matter was questionable, given that he had become so overset at the threatened loss of a mere fifty pounds. Georgette had learned the hard way that having a man who was undependable in the matter of making and keeping money was a hard burden to bear.

Then, of course, there was the smallish matter of whether a man might keep a mistress in addition to a wife. Georgette had learned that the hard way too.

At her reluctant silence, Lady Kilmartie laughed, looping her arm through hers. "Good for you." Her face dissolved into the smile promised by the fine lines that framed her eyes. "I knew I liked you, from the moment I saw my son's hands linger after he pulled you off the horse and you stood up straight instead of falling at his feet." She leaned in with a conspiratorial air. "I was watching from the drawing room window as you rode up. Anyone can see he cares for you, but I am happy you are not going to make this easy for him."

Georgette's mind squirmed in protest. She wrangled her words into something precise. "You do not understand, Lady Kilmartie. I am not going to make this *anything* for him."

His mother waved a hand in dismissal. " 'Tis far too late for that, dear. The pieces of a pairing are there, you simply need to fit them together. My son is a hard man to understand, contrary to the extreme. Like as not he would toss the gift of your love away if you presented it tied up in a neat little package." The older woman pursed her lips. "Both of you need to work for it, to see if it's right. Only then will it show some promise of growing into a marriage worth pursuing."

Georgette's throat swelled shut, as much in astonishment as worry. His mother spoke of love. It was preposterous. Love was a quality that grew in time between two people, nurtured by fond feelings and shared life experiences. Her mother had explained upon her come-out, in no uncertain terms, that such a sentiment only came with hard work and kind intentions, following a smart match. Georgette had tried her best to find it with her first husband, but night after night, month after month, her heart had remained locked up tight. She had thought there might be something wrong with him, a deficiency of spirit or regard. She had done everything she knew to win his favor, and he had become increasingly critical of her every move.

And then one afternoon she had seen him walking in Hyde Park with his red-haired mistress. The woman was animated and colorful and everything Georgette was not. Her husband's head had been bent low over his mistress's, his face lit with a delighted smile. That was when she had realized the faithless man was capable of love.

He simply didn't love *her*.

The situation in which she currently floundered was different. Despite the stirring of attraction she felt, Georgette had known James for only four hours. The vows they exchanged last night could not count toward a shared experience, given that it was without a guiding memory on her part. Love was not a possibility.

Was it?

There was nothing she could say in response to his mother's presumption, even had she possessed the physical ability to speak. So she numbly accompanied Lady Kilmartie into a warm-smelling kitchen, trailed by the two little soldiers who emerged with a fine display of manners at the last minute. She sat down at a table and regarded their curious, open stares, and conveyed the proper amount of approval at the exaggerated size of the fish they had caught that morning. She pretended not to notice when James's mother hurried off to collect her husband.

And all the while, in a hidden corner of her mind, she wondered what on earth she was going to do about this marriage.

Chapter 23

JAMES SAT ON a chair in his father's study and waited.

He supposed, if he were to be honest, the green damask upholstery might be considered comfortable. He ran a hand over the curve of the seat, sinking the tips of his fingers into the luxurious weight of the fabric. Unlike most chairs, it had been built of a size to easily accommodate the frame of a MacKenzie male. James had no such chairs in his bachelor's house. Instead, he squeezed himself into whatever decrepit piece of furniture he and Patrick collected as castoffs from neighbors and prayed the joints would hold.

It was probably William's chair, used when his brother sat at their father's desk and applied his thick head to the study of ledgers and bills and invitations and such. The life of an earl-in-training demanded a chair that fit, he supposed. He did not begrudge his brother the demands of the job, but he did feel a twinge of jealously over the chair.

Despite the promise of the solid seat, James hovered near the edge. His mind and muscles refused to settle. He had been left waiting for many a client, and many a magistrate as well. Waiting was part of the life of a solicitor.

It was a part at which he had never excelled.

He rose to his feet with a strangled snarl and began to pace. Six steps to the east wall, six steps to the west. He mentally sorted through what he was going to say. He needed to plan and present the most logical side of the argument. Old worries and resentments needed to be pushed aside. It was either that or succumb to frozen silence.

James paused, fiddling with a paperweight resting on the edge of his father's desk. He turned it over in his hand. An old stone tool of some sort. It reminded him of his childhood, of the hours he had spent digging in archaeology sites with his father. He cast his gaze farther. On the other side of the desk lay an old hammer, and on the outer edge of one bookshelf lay pieces of metal that looked to have come from a horse's bridle. He turned in a circle. Artifacts lay here. Papers lay there, with notes scribbled in his father's tight, familiar hand.

A knock on the door sent his heart leaping, but it was only an aproned maid, bringing him a plate of food.

"Lady Kilmartie asked me to bring you this, and to tell you Lady Thorold bade you to eat," the servant explained, setting the china dish on his father's desk and then taking her leave.

James eyed the roasted pheasant and new potatoes with an urgency removed from anything natural. Georgette had asked for him to have a meal. A flutter of appreciation bloomed in his stomach as the smell of sage and thyme reached his nose. His stomach growled its enthusiasm for the idea, and reprimanded him for its neglect.

Had he really forgotten to eat all day? And moreover,

had the kitchen really produced such a meal on such short notice? The facts were irrefutable. His family must have already eaten, to produce a plate so quickly.

Before seven o'clock in the bloody evening.

His chest tightened. Eleven years had changed things. The house he remembered as sterile and cold was bursting with warmth and the shouts of children. The lifetime of work his father had abandoned for a title had crept back in. And James was here, burning with news and things that must be said, demanding the audience he should have over a decade ago.

His father caught him perched on the edge of William's chair, gulping down the last of the peas. James shoved the plate away like a ten-year-old caught filching pies from the kitchen window, and wiped his fingers hastily on the too-clean seat of his chair.

He stood. Swallowed. Offered his father his still-greasy hand.

"Sir." As far as greetings went, he knew it sounded pitiful. But as the first word spoken to the man after so many years of silence, it was an olive branch of an oak tree's proportions.

"Jamie." His father sidestepped the proffered hand and went instead for an awkward embrace. James lifted his hands to the man's shoulders in stunned silence. It was a brief gesture, lasting no more than a second or two.

But it stung, that contact. Sharp as needles raking his skin.

His father recoiled and motioned for him to take back his seat. As he turned away, the earl rubbed a quick hand across his eyes. To James, the significance of that stolen gesture hit him like a hammer on glass. He sat down and wordlessly regarded the man who had sired him, the man whose shouts and disappointments he had been prepared to bear.

His father looked . . . old. James had not seen him since that day, eleven years prior, when he had confronted the man over what he had done and received nothing close to an answer. His eyes took in the new gray hair around his father's formerly dark temples, and the way his clean-shaven jowls folded into wrinkles. The intervening years had stripped James of more than just his father's company.

He had neglected to consider his father's advancing age.

"It's been a while," James acknowledged, canting his head in a show of respect. It was not what he had planned to say. The words he had been rehearsing while he paced the confines of the room were all tangled up inside him.

"Eleven years, two months, and thirteen days." His father leaned back in his chair and tented his fingers on the desk in front of him.

Time might have taken the man's dark hair, but it had not, it seemed, stripped his father's memory. Ever the industrious scholar, he never forgot a fact.

Nor, it seemed, a slight.

"And for over a year of that time, I have been in town." James welcomed the steel that crept into his voice, replacing the maudlin sentiments that had briefly threatened to derail him. "I have been living scarcely four miles away. You could have come anytime you wanted."

"You have not invited me." His father regarded him

with brooding eyes that belied his age. His voice seemed textured with varying shades of pain.

"The Earl of Kilmartie does not need an invitation to come to town," James pointed out, refusing to be swayed. "William comes to see me, with awful regularity, and Mother calls at least once a month."

His father's mouth drew down. "Yes, she has told me about taking tea in your odd excuse for a kitchen, ducking the sawdust bag you keep hanging from the rafters. Do you think I bloody well don't know it has been a year? You made it very clear you did not want to see me."

James gaped at his very proper father's angry lapse into obscenities. "When? When did I ever tell you that?"

"When you refused me."

James clenched his hands in surprise. "When did I ever refuse to see you?"

His father's eyes snapped, a sharp shade of green that was all too familiar. "The horse. You refused my gift of the horse. And then you tossed the gesture back in my face."

" 'Twas not a gift, but a test," James protested. "Do not look at me as if it was not. If you had come bearing Caesar yourself, it might have softened my response. But you sent a groom, Father. You couldn't bring yourself to come down from your great, echoing castle and acknowledge the shameful way your youngest son had chosen to live."

"Is that what you think?" A muscle jumped along his father's clenched jaw. It was like looking in a large, angry, gray-haired mirror. "That I am *ashamed* of you? Jamie, I have been many things with you. Exasperated. Confused by your decisions. Saddened by your neglect.

But I have *never* been ashamed of you, not of who you are or what you have made of yourself."

James sat in stunned silence. The chair might have collapsed beneath him and deposited him on the floor, so off-kilter did his father's words make him feel. All this time, all those years, he had thought himself a failure in his father's eyes.

"What about the matter with the rector?" he asked, his voice a hoarse whisper.

"I knew what pushed you there." His father leaned back. "Your actions were justified." His mouth settled in a grim line. "Wholly."

"You never explained that to me." A wave of emotion, strong as the surf pounding the rocks not a mile west from where they sat, threatened to knock James over. "You paid for his silence. His daughter's death was on his hands as a result, and on ours as well. Your actions told the world you thought I was guilty. They told *me* you thought I was guilty, that I was unfit to be your son."

"That is unfair, Jamie. I was trying to help you."

James drew a deep breath, his brain dimly registering the fact his father had called him Jamie. William and his mother had continued to use his boyhood name, all these years. But he had become "James" to his father two months after his eighteenth birthday, the minute the man was made earl.

It made no sense. *None* of this made sense.

"Help me?" James choked out. "How did you help me? Every decision I made when I lived here, every step I took, which bloody university I attended, it was all subject to your deepest scrutiny. I was not permitted a single choice of my own. The matter with the rector was not the only piece of it. It was simply the tipping point that forced me to leave."

The earl looked away. His gaze lingered over the artifacts littering his desk. His voice, when it came, was carefully measured. "It may be hard for you to understand, but I was a new peer, thrust into a situation I had not been brought up for and did not want."

James leaned forward, his hands seeking purchase beside him and finding only slippery damask. He had never known his father had not wanted to be earl.

"I believed, at the time, I had to give up who *I* was in the process," his father went on. "And though I hated to do it, I thought it kinder to prepare you for the possibility of the title too, to protect you from the shock it was to me."

"But I was not the heir," James pointed out, his words flung like pebbles against a wall.

"Neither was I." His father spread his hands in a silent plea. "I was happier as a scholar, living a simple life in town with your mother and my boys. And yet, here I am."

James shifted, his hands planting themselves more firmly on the chair seat. "Why did you not tell me this eleven years ago?"

His father's eyes lifted, watery with regret. "Would you have listened if I had?"

"You did not give me the chance to find out."

His father spread his palms out flat on the desk and drew a deep breath. "I suppose I deserve that. I let you down, Jamie. I was ill-equipped to handle the responsibilities of the peerage *and* fatherhood, and I did some things very poorly. I am sorry now that I took out my frustrations on you and William. I have learned, over the years, that I can be true to myself and still be an earl. I realize this is coming too late, but I am sorry for any hurt I have caused you."

Stunned did not begin to describe the feeling that slammed into James's chest. His father had offered him an apology. James had not known what to expect when he rode here bent for hell, but an apology had not been among his list of demands.

His father's shoulders hunched, tight as a fist. "I have long been sick over what happened to the girl you cared enough to offer for. It was a terrible tragedy. But you must believe me, at the time, I thought the only good thing that had come out of that terrible new life I had been tossed into was having the ability to assist you financially. When I paid the amount demanded by her father, I thought I was helping. Truly."

James turned that over in his head. With his father's explanation, things about his past were already reordering themselves in a different light. Would he really have done anything differently, had their positions been reversed? And would he have had the maturity to listen and understand had they embarked on this conversation eleven years ago?

He wasn't sure. He knew only that he was glad for the chance to do this now.

"Thank you," James told him, his throat tight. He leaned back fully in his seat, testing the structural integrity of both the chair's frame and this fragile new truce. "I will have your promise you will not put another penny toward fixing my mistakes. I am a proud man, Father. I suspect I come by that lamentable trait honestly." His mouth quirked upward. "I do not deny that I have made errors in judgment, or that I will make them still. But I would ask that you let me be the man I choose to be."

His father's shoulders softened. "Does that include the mistake of letting eleven years go by without speaking?"

James nodded, relief dancing in his chest. "I do not think we could put a price on that, even if we tried. I am sorry I let it come to that. Do I have your promise, then?"

"Aye." His father nodded.

James exhaled, leaning forward again. "I am glad to hear that. Because I have something important to tell you."

JAMES SET HIS hand on the door with a heart lighter than it had been in years. It was going to be all right. His father had listened to the explanation of what had happened last night and the description of a possible threat from Georgette's cousin. He had shown some amusement, but no obvious judgment, when he learned of his son's drunken folly. He had expressed surprise to learn Burton's name, telling James that he had leased the old hunting cottage on the east side of the estate to the man just last month.

And then the earl had asked James what he wanted him to do.

To be not only accepted but *consulted* on the matter was something James would have laid money on as a physical impossibility only a quarter hour ago. He asked for nothing. Or rather, he asked that his father *do* nothing. And incredibly, his father had agreed.

It was an unspeakable relief. There would be no blackmail attempt, no exchange of money. Should

Burton show up here demanding an audience, his father indicated he would not receive him. Georgette's insistence that they come here and tell his family now seemed the most sensible thing imaginable, though it had been one of the most difficult things he had ever done.

James's mother scrambled backward from the door when he opened it, her cheeks pink with guilt. James fought a smile. One should not acknowledge eavesdropping with good humor. Still, after the difficulties two of the men in her life had caused her, he supposed she had every right to wonder about the conversation behind that big, locked door.

"Did you hear anything of interest?" he teased as he stepped out into the hall, pulling the door shut behind him.

His mother's lips pursed. "No, the door is too solid for my tastes." Her hands clasped and unclasped in front of her. "How do things stand between you?"

James grinned. He couldn't help it. It started in his mouth, but rapidly consumed his entire face. "I think you can expect me to make an appearance for dinner, on occasion," he told her, enjoying the way the news made her face light with happiness. "Father asked me to find you, so he could speak with you. I suspect he thought I might have to travel a bit farther than the doorway, though."

His mother answered with a sheepish smile of her own. "I expect your father knew exactly where I would be, and what I would be doing." She cleared her throat, and her gaze turned thoughtful. "Lady Thorold waits for you in the kitchen. Or should I call her Mrs. Mac-Kenzie?"

James almost tripped over his feet, though he was

standing stock-still. "How . . . how did you know?" Surely Georgette, with her protestations over the permanency of the thing, had not confided in such a virtual stranger and perpetual busybody as his mother?

"I saw your ring on her finger." His mother clucked in disapproval. "Really, a lady deserves a finer piece of jewelry than a man's signet ring, Jamie. What were you thinking?"

He shifted uneasily. "Well, truth be told, neither of us was thinking."

His mother cocked her head, her eyes searching his. "She explained something of that. She told me you were both planning to undo it. Is that true?"

James nodded, his stomach turning hollow. So Georgette had told his mother she did not want to be married. Somehow, when it had been a conversation between just the two of them, it seemed still negotiable. To bring others into the scheme made Georgette's regrettable change of heart seem more real.

"Does your father know?"

"He does now." James lifted his gaze to the floral-patterned wallpaper lining the hallway. He feared looking in his mother's eyes, lest she catch a glimpse of the uncertainty he was sure radiated from him. "How is Georgette?"

"She's fine," his mother assured him. If his mother disapproved of his use of the woman's given name, the tone of her voice gave no sign. "Being entertained by the boys and their tall tales, last I saw her."

James shifted his gaze to his mother's. "I abandoned her in the foyer. I was anxious over how the interview might go, but I should have been kinder in explaining that to her."

"She understood." His mother's eyes softened. "I like her, Jamie, and I can see you do too." She fished a hand in a hidden pocket of her skirts and it emerged, palm out, holding a small, feminine-looking ring. "I do not know if your minds are made up or not, but I would urge you not to react too hastily."

James picked up the delicate bit of gold with interlocking knots carved on the surface. "I do not understand."

" 'Tis a fede ring," she told him. "It belonged to your grandmother. The intertwined knots represent a strong bond. Fitting, I think. A marriage is something you should reflect carefully on before tossing it away like ashes in a grate." There, finally, was the slightest bit of reproof echoing in her voice.

His mother was parroting the thoughts in his own mind, but unfortunately they did not reflect the thoughts of his fair bride. He struggled against a rising sense of irritation. "That is the problem, Mother. We did not think carefully before doing this. We've known each other only a few hours. You and Father courted a year before you married. 'Tis impossible to know if this is right or not, and we risk making the mistake permanent if we engage in a delay."

His mother inclined her head. "The length of time you take to come to the vows is not what matters."

"There is also the little matter that I may have accused her of thievery," he added. "She did not think much of me then, I can tell you."

That brought a chuckle out of her. "There are days when I feel like I could wrap my hands around your father's neck as soon as kiss him, over a matter as trivial as what sort of meat I should have Cook serve for dinner.

There are always frustrations. And it may have taken a year, but I also knew how I felt about your father within seconds of our first meeting. If you like her, you should give her a chance. And if you give her a chance, you should give her a real ring."

James fingered the gold band with unsteady fingers. He had not expected such an ally. "You want me to give your mother's ring to a woman I have known for all of a day?"

Her eyes shimmered with mischief. "You know how long it took your father to come up to scratch when we were courting, but have I ever told you the story of how *my* parents met?"

At the confused shake of his head, she went on. "They met on board a ship, crossing the Northern Channel when they left Ireland for Scotland. They walked on strangers, and walked off husband and wife. And they were married, quite happily, for forty-three more years."

James cupped the ring tightly in his hand. "Just because they loved each other enough to withstand such a risk does not mean it is the sensible thing to do in my case." His protest seemed shallow. "She's practically a stranger," he added. "She could be off for London tomorrow."

And she does not want me.

His mother laid a hand on the door through which he had just exited. "There is a history in that ring worth considering, Jamie. I don't know if this girl is the right one for you. I only ask that you think hard on it."

James slid the ring into his pocket, his ears pounding with the same hopeful rhythm of his heart. "I will consider it," he told her. But the words were meaningless if they were only one-sided. Thinking on it was not what was needed here.

Convincing Georgette to reconsider the legitimacy— nay, the necessity—of their vows would take something more than a skilled negotiator.

It might take a miracle.

Chapter 24

THE CLOCK IN the hallway was striking the eight o'clock hour when James walked by. The long, distinctive chimes felt like a series of punctuation marks in his head.

Georgette had indicated a desire to be off for London, as soon as she was able. The thought sat like hot coals in his stomach. He knew he was attracted to her, but he felt there was something more lurking beneath the surface of it all. And while he was not sure what his feelings meant, he knew his emotions would not be better defined by distance. Time was slipping by, time he might use to change her mind, time he might use to get to know her better. The tiny ring felt like a solid gold bar, weighing down his trouser pocket. Did he dare take the chance?

Did he dare not?

He did not find her in the kitchen, although he did find a lovely apple pastry there, hot from the oven. He nibbled on a generous share of it as he continued to look. She was neither in the drawing room nor in the library, though the places he scanned brought the familiarity of his father's house back like a returning tide. His lungs grew tighter with each missed opportunity. Finally, he stood still and cocked his head, listening for some hint of her.

The front windows in the library had been opened to catch the breeze. Through one of them, he heard faint shouts and shrieks of laughter, coming from outside. His feet followed his heart out the front door.

He found her in the hedgerow maze, playing tag with his cousin's children. He stood a moment in the late evening sunshine and watched Georgette bob in and out of the chest-height greenery, reaching for the boys with a shout here, a twist there. She was fighting a losing battle, playing such a game with children whose heads did not yet extend above the bushes, but she kept at it gamely, laughing at her own ineptitude.

Night was but an hour or so away, and the sun's light had wound down from a bright, startling thing to something gentle. Georgette's hair had tumbled all the way down, her hairpins a casualty of the game.

James's chest pinched in envy. *He* wanted to be the one to make her look happy.

He could imagine her this way, mothering her own children without thought to care or propriety. James had told his mother this girl was a stranger but that was not precisely true. The proper side Georgette had shown him today was something he was still sorting out. But this woman, the one laughing into the wind, this woman he *knew*. His body leaned toward her, even from a hundred yards distant.

He shoved his hands in his trouser pockets and moved toward the maze. His fingers found the fede ring as he walked. He worried the bumps and ridges along its outer edge, turning over his concerns in his mind as the ring tumbled in his hand. Georgette had given him a gift, the strength and purpose to reunite with a father he had lost due to his own stubbornness.

How did one repay a kindness like that?

Fifty yards away, she saw him. He judged the exact moment she became aware of his approach. The angle of her body shifted from carefree to careful. He regretted the loss of freedom on her behalf. Why did she feel the need to be so staid, so proper, that she could not enjoy a game of tag with children? As he came closer still and entered the maze, she lifted her hands to work at her hair.

Ten yards out, his jealousy of the boys shifted closer to a heartfelt thanks. By God, she was beautiful like this, her chest rising and falling from her exertions, her cheeks flushed pink. Her hair scattered over her shoulders, a swinging curtain of ivory muslin brought to life by her animated smile.

He stopped in front of her. Shadows cast by the manicured hedgerows were starting to lengthen around them, and the breeze had cooled to close to tolerable, but the air near her shimmered with absolute heat.

The boys protested their loss of a playmate. Loudly.

James tossed them a grin. "You do not have to stop on my account. I enjoyed watching the game." He leaned in closer to Georgette, whispering wickedly into one ear. "Or rather, I enjoyed watching *you*."

Her hands tangled nervously in the snarled mess of her hair. "I look a fright, and well you know it." She inched away from him. "Your family will believe I am deranged."

"Delightfully so." He watched her try to compose herself, the very picture of a woman flushed with pleasure. He had seen her look much that way last night, after . . . well, the thought of what he had been doing to make her flush that way made his stomach jump in three directions. His gaze pulled to the boys, who were watching him with matching petulant expressions. They were a problem worth a moment's consideration.

Clearly, he had come to spoil their fun. And he, horrid man that he was, could not wait to do so.

"When I looked in the kitchen, the cook was just pulling a tart from the oven," he told them, remembering what had ruled his actions when he had been their age. They pitched themselves toward the front of the maze and ran toward the house with excited shouts, the game forgotten. After all, what game had ever withstood the call of baked apples and cinnamon?

He could think of one. His body tightened in agreement, honing in on the sight of the woman who inspired such thinking.

The subject of his wayward thoughts was trying valiantly to twist her hair into a knot. "Your cousin's sons are charming," she told him through the battle to secure her hair. It slithered loose the moment she lifted her hands from it. "If ruled a bit strongly by their stomachs."

"They do seem possessed of an exuberant appetite," James remarked, enjoying the view. Her struggle for dominion over her coiffure was pure entertainment.

He was betting on the hair.

"If you hand me the pins, I will help you put it up," he told her, though he was reluctant to put his hands to such a regrettable purpose.

She lifted her chin toward the house. "I am afraid they came loose somewhere over there, and are well and truly lost." She grinned over her hands' busy efforts. "How did things go with your father?"

"Better than expected," he murmured, distracted by the way her movements made her chest push against her bodice. "There will be no further concern from your cousin. You might . . . ah . . . try looping it that way." He motioned weakly with his hands.

" 'Tis hopeless." She sighed. "My hair has always been one of my greatest struggles. The individual strands are too thin to stay solidly in my pins, but as a whole it is too thick to tame." She made a face and dropped both hands in defeat, letting the pale strands fall where they would. "And the color is most unfortunate. Even gray would be an improvement."

Such an invitation proved impossible to resist. James reached out and lifted a handful of her hair, sliding the strands between the pad of his thumb and forefinger. His memory pricked at him, the sharp point of a knife. He remembered being fascinated by it when she had taken it down in the little room above the Gander. She had revealed it slowly, removing one agonizing pin at a time. She had let it fall across his bare chest, the cruelest of sensual devices.

They had rubbed on well together last night. Literally. They might have started in the opposite manner from most couples, but perhaps there was something to be recommended in acknowledging the physical tug of attraction before turning themselves over to the maelstrom of emotion in which he now found himself tossed. There was something between them, something thick and solid and possibly lasting. Something beyond the beauty of her hair or the pleasure of her smile.

The fede ring felt like heated iron in his pocket, nudging him in the direction of his thoughts. He could scarcely believe he was considering this. He was a man who plotted his arguments with slow purpose, who planned his future with agonizing care. But the thought of giving up on this moment, this *chance*, seemed a lamentable folly. He bent down on one knee, intending to beg for her hand.

Only he neglected to consider his injuries in this hastily constructed plan to win her favor. The knee he chose to kneel on was on the leg the black mare had kicked earlier in the day. His weight refused to stay balanced in face of the lightning-crack jolt of pain that shot through him as his knee hit the ground. He pitched over, the air whooshing from his lungs. He came to rest flat on his back, staring up at the orange-tinged sky.

Georgette dropped to the ground beside him in an instant, her face drawn in worried creases. The tall hedgerows cast her in deep shadows, and for a moment he felt as if the air had been sucked clean from his chest. She had looked much the same way last night, leaning over him in their room at the Gander . . . just before she had put that tempting mouth on him.

Only then she had been wearing far less clothing.

She framed his face with her hands, and her hair fell, soft and fragrant, to tease at his nose. She pushed it back with an impatient hand. "Are you all right? Should I fetch someone from the house?"

He answered with a breathless nod.

"I *should* fetch someone?"

He shook his head this time, his gaze centering on the lush lower lip she was worrying with her teeth.

Her eyes, which had been wide with concern, narrowed suspiciously. "Is this some trick to get me to kiss you again?"

He almost laughed. Such a prim look she was giving

him, and such stern words in accompaniment. The rebuke in her voice was a direct contrast to the invitation presented by her lips and their circumstances. They were lying on the grass pathway of the hedgerow maze, in absolute privacy. Anyone who might attempt to find them could be heard long before they made it this far, and no one could see them from the windows of the house.

Kissing was the least of what he wanted her to do.

He wanted to roll her farther into the shadows. He wanted to unpeel her dress from those stern shoulders and mold each rounded curve into pliant submission using only his tongue and lips. That she looked so stern over the thought of a little kiss disturbed him. She had offered him more than a simple kiss five minutes into their meeting last night.

She doesn't remember, his conscience prodded.

I could show her.

"Am I finding success with my unorthodox methods?" he asked, pressing his hands into the grass in an effort not to reach for her.

She rocked back on her heels, her lips compressing to tight bands. "This is not wise, James. What sort of game do we play here?"

How quickly she shifted between the two women she carried inside her. One was quiet and proper, as easy to startle as the deer that ran free on his father's estate. The other woman was confident and bold, an uninhibited caricature of her other self. But which one did he need to appeal to, in order to have her consider the offer sitting on the tip of his tongue?

"I don't know," he told her, settling his head back onto the soft spring of grass. Hope sat like a rock on his chest. "I do not intentionally play with your feelings. I only know I am reluctant to see it end."

He waited for her reaction, his breath caught up tight. The trouble with honesty was it could frighten her off. He was frightened of his own thoughts, now that he had admitted to himself he wanted to make this real.

Her lips parted in surprise. A smoky gray challenge flashed in her eyes. She leaned over him, and this time he felt the full body contact like a kick to his heart. "That hardly seems fair, sir. I have you at a disadvantage."

"Indeed." His voice came out as a whisper, but it was all he could manage with her breasts pressing down on him in such a way. "And you should surely take it."

GEORGETTE'S HEART KNOCKED about in her chest like an unruly colt.

He wanted her to kiss him.

He was asking her—nay, he was daring her—to take the chance she denied herself. He had all but invited her to explore his mouth with her own.

And dear God she wanted to. More than she had ever wanted anything in her life.

The waning sun and long shadows bathed his skin in shades of orange and gold, bringing out the red of his beard. He looked rough and hopeful, his green eyes beckoning her. Her head was lowering before she could even begin to rein in her body's agreement.

She told herself she should be in better control of her actions. She told herself she should pick up her skirts and run out of this far too private maze back to her safe life and her easy future and her certain independence.

Unfortunately, she told herself those things too quietly. Because the moment her mouth touched his, she stopped thinking about the noise of her objections and forgot everything but the feel of him beneath her lips.

He tasted like cinnamon and apples. The rogue must have taken a bite of the treat he had promised the boys. She moved her tongue over his lips, tasting not only the sweet goodness, but the precarious heat of him. She had never kissed a man like this, leaning over the top of him, her bare feet pushing against grass. The danger of it, the sheer *difference* of it, sent a thrill humming through her.

A dim part of her brain bade her to go slowly. They were out of doors, for heaven's sake, lying in the dirt and grass like eager young lovers, heedless of the danger or the repercussions. But logical objections took second place to her body's demands. She had gone twenty-six years without giving herself over to self-indulgence.

She refused to go another second.

She lifted her hands to his face and curled her fingers around his beard. She kissed him hard, silencing all her mind's doubts with the slide of her tongue and the welcoming heat of his body. The memory of how he had touched her this afternoon in the room at the inn sent her reservations scattering. She wanted him to touch her again, to lift his hand to her breast and pluck at her heart. But he remained still beneath her, content to let her guide their progress.

She lifted her own trembling hand to her bodice and showed him what she wanted. Slipped her buttons free from their moorings and reveled in the ragged sound of his lungs, laboring in time with her moving fingers. She slid one shoulder of her gown down, then the other.

Finally he moved, helping to push her chemise down with eager, rowdy fingers that knocked against her own tentative ones.

And then he stilled. For a long moment, Georgette wondered if she was not what he had imagined. Was not what he wanted. But then, finally, he reached out a hand and gently cupped her bare breast, rubbing the calloused pad of one thumb across her aching nipple.

"Do you ken how beautiful you are?" he asked, his eyes dragging up to meet hers, his words thick with appreciation.

And then his mouth followed the direction of his hands, his tongue was on her breast, and she came undone. Sensation she had never imagined snaked through her, connecting parts of her body that had never seemed remotely related before. Her insides throbbed, taut on a string, and he was the masterful musician who would play the instrument she had become. A cry bubbled up in the back of her throat. She pressed a hand against her mouth, unwilling to make even the slightest noise that might bring outside attention to what they were doing.

Noise that might encourage him to stop.

His lips left her breast and came up to claim hers. His tongue danced circles on her lips, explored the space of her mouth with sure intent. She pressed the length of her body against him, imagining what it would feel like to be completely skin on skin. Through her skirts she could feel the jut of his body, hard and promising. This was no tentative interest on behalf of a disinterested partner, no prelude to a dutiful bedding from a reluctant spouse. The heat of his mouth and the thrust of his member against her thigh told her he *wanted* her. And the knowledge did not frighten her.

Quite the opposite. When he touched her like this, she could almost imagine him doing so for the rest of her life.

Her fingers curled convulsively into his hair and she pulled his mouth closer to hers, desperate to close the hairbreadth distance that yawned between them.

And then he groaned.

Not in pleasure, though it was a sound that came close. No, the noise came from his chest and it was distinctly soaked in pain.

She drew back, confused. "What is the matter?"

"My head." He squeezed his eyes shut. "You need to be careful."

She moved her gaze to her fingers, which were gripping his hair a scant inch from the row of stitches on his head. She released him with a gasp. "Oh!" One hand coming to cover her mouth. "I am so sorry," she cried.

"'Tis nothing." He opened his eyes and gave her a weak smile. "Just a little injury someone gave me this morning."

"That is not funny." She fumbled to reseat her buttons, hurrying to put herself to rights so she could see about putting *him* to rights. Her passion doused, Georgette took a good, long look at the wound she had just been mauling. The stitches were still intact, thank goodness. A more effective antidote to desire had never been invented. "I hurt you this morning. I should not be allowed anywhere near you, for your own safety." She put a hand on his chest to push herself up, but froze as he groaned again.

"Have a care there too," he croaked.

She dropped her eyes to his coat, where old, dried blood stained the fabric. She had presumed, somehow, that the blood had been related to his head injury. But now she could see the fabric was ripped.

She pushed the coat aside and probed the tear, ignoring his hiss of pain. "Did I do that too?" she asked, her voice small. Shame suffused her every pore. She had treated him dreadfully.

"No. I was attacked in town this afternoon."

"What?" Georgette pulled back, studying the lines of strain around his eyes. "*Where?*" His words made little sense. According to Elsie, most in town thought James MacKenzie a hero among men, a shining example of maleness that all of Moraig emulated. Who hated him enough to do such a thing?

He struggled to a sitting position, rubbing his head as he leaned forward. "Outside of the butcher's shop. I have not given it much thought since I found you. I thought you had stabbed me, for a time."

"Someone *stabbed* you?" she gasped. "And you thought it was *me*?"

He nodded, then reached a hand in his coat pocket and pulled something out. "With this, in fact." He turned the tool over in his hand, his brows pulled down in a frown. "But as soon as I found you, I realized it could not have been you. The clothing differences aside, the person who attacked me was taller." He gave her a wolfish grin, his appreciation obvious even through his pain. "And far less attractive."

Fear had grabbed hold of Georgette and it shook her now, fiercely. It was perhaps the only thing in the world that could make her ignore such suggestive teasing. "But you thought it was me," she said slowly. "Because your attacker resembled me in some way."

He looked at her more sharply. The playfulness in his eyes burned away, leaving only suspicion. "Aye. The same hair color. How did you know that?"

Georgette bit her lip. The relief she had felt earlier on

learning that things had gone well between James and his father settled into a sharper, stronger emotion. "Because that is my cousin Randolph's pruning knife." She pointed to the pearl-inlaid handle, which she had recognized instantly. "And if he was bold enough to attack you on a public street, I fear for your family's safety."

Chapter 25

JAMES'S FAMILY MUSTERED quickly in the library with a map of the estate unrolled on the table in front of them. The comfortable smell of leather book bindings and yellowed pages did little to offset the fear Georgette felt. She had not even stopped to put on her boots, instead picking them up and carrying them with her to stand barefooted on the carpet.

Georgette had been quickly introduced to both the Earl of Kilmartie, who was warm and welcoming, and James's glowering brother, who had shown her only a stiff sort of courtesy. A palpable distrust hung from the man, like a heavy woolen cloak. Not that she blamed him. They would not be here, staring at a map and sorting out her cousin's next possible move, if it hadn't been for her.

She was surprised to hear James's father explain he had rented the little stone cottage to Randolph. If her cousin had been audacious enough to attack an earl's son in broad daylight, they might all be in jeopardy, especially now that the earl knew of Randolph's plan to blackmail him. And her cousin had already wounded James, just this afternoon. The thought of anyone else hurt on her account sent her pulse pounding. She had credited Randolph with only a grandiose narcissism.

That he might be violent had regrettably not crossed her mind.

"The hunter's cottage is here." The earl pointed to a spot a few inches from where the castle was marked on the map.

"Why, that is scarcely a mile away!" Lady Kilmartie gasped, leaning in for a closer look.

Georgette glanced over as well. The little house had seemed so isolated, it was a surprise to see how close it actually sat to Kilmartie Castle. She had been living scarcely a stone's throw from James's family since arriving in Scotland.

His father looked up from the map, his face grim. "When I rented the place to Mr. Burton last month, he seemed an amiable enough young man. Reminded me of myself at that age, so focused on scientific explorations he barely had time for polite conversation."

"Did you ever force an unwilling woman to marry you?" James asked.

"I should say not." His father's voice rang in surprise. "How could you even ask such a thing?"

"Because it proves he is *nothing* like you." James's gaze darted toward her. She squirmed as three other pairs of eyes followed suit. "Do you want to tell them, Georgette?"

She did not want to speak. Talking about it highlighted how naïve she had been to trust her cousin. How *stupid* she had been. But being silent would not help matters either.

"He tried to force me into marriage last night, after I

refused him," she admitted, her tongue thick with fear. She pressed backward, relying on the wood-paneled wall for support. "Your son's involvement in this affair is due in no small part to his attempt to keep me from harm at my cousin's hand."

James's eyes swept the room before coming to rest on his father. "I do not know what Burton may yet be capable of. Do we have legal means to see him evicted?"

"He paid for two weeks up front." Kilmartie rolled up the map. "But he is late on the remainder of his rent. Should be a simple matter to have a footman escort him off the property."

James picked up the map and began to tap it against one palm. "I dare not trust the job to a footman. Burton seems out of his head at times. One or more of us will have to do it."

"Are you sure he is mad?" James's broad-shouldered brother pushed off his own perch along the opposite wall and shot a suspicious glance in Georgette's direction. "An inability to pay his debts does suggest some motive." He raised a challenging brow that only she could see. "And he might have accomplices."

James was staring at her, his forehead wrinkled in thought. "Has your cousin been having financial difficulties of late?"

Once again, she was startled by his attempt to draw her into the volley of conversation. She pressed her bare toes into the carpet. It was so much easier to prop herself up against the wall while others more capable than she discussed their strategies.

She drew a breath and considered what she had seen of Randolph in the days since she had arrived. She had been suspicious of his interest in marrying her for the financial security she would bring to the match, but that was not proof. "He did not say anything about his income," she mused. "But I admit to being surprised by his modest choice of summer lodging."

Lady Kilmartie broke in. "Perhaps he preferred a rustic holiday."

"Randolph? *Rustic?*" Georgette shook her head and motioned toward James's coat pocket, her confidence in her ability to contribute to the cause strengthening. "The man prefers nothing of the sort. Might I see his pruning knife for a moment?"

James placed the knife on the table where the map had just been stretched out. They all stared at it. She swallowed, thinking of how close it had come to doing James serious injury. The tool might have been too dull to properly do the job Randolph intended, but the scratch it had inflicted was centered over James's heart. There was no doubting the man's aim.

James's brother bent over to examine it. " 'Tis a man's folding knife, simple in design."

" 'Tis a bit more than simple." Georgette stepped forward and reached out a hand. "See here?" She brushed a finger over the thing. "The handle is inlaid with ivory and intricately carved, when a simple wooden piece would do. It is a ridiculous extravagance in a tool used to trim weeds, but all too characteristic of my cousin's tastes. He is a poor scholar, but with the preferences of a peer."

Kilmartie broke in, his mouth turned down. "He negotiated the summer's rent for a pittance. When I think that I let him that house, so close to us . . ." He ended with a shake of his head. "It put my family in danger. I should have written to the references he offered."

Georgette absorbed the regret in his voice and magnified it tenfold in her own head. She had done this to them. And she was helpless to make it right.

"When I saw him this evening, his clothing certainly suggested a penchant for expensive tastes." James's dry voice cut through her thoughts of guilt. "His coat was cut in the latest London fashion, and he was wearing Hessians to troop around Moraig's dusty streets. Not even William is stupid enough for that."

"You noticed his clothing but did not recognize him as the man who attacked you?" Georgette asked, surprised at both his power of observation and his lack of perception.

He offered Georgette a sheepish shrug. "I did not get a good look at the man's face this afternoon, and I decided within minutes of our first meeting you could not have been the same person. As to his clothing, one notices these things when one is contemplating bloodying an adversary's nose. I was more concerned about what he might do to you than what he may have done to me."

Georgette released the breath she was holding at his admission. His words did little to ease her remorse at having forced this situation on him.

"Seems to me you're a little *too* concerned about her," his brother pointed out. "If her cousin's circumstances do not support the lifestyle toward which he leans, perhaps this *is* simply about the money." His gaze flickered toward Georgette. "And perhaps he did not act alone."

Nausea churned in her stomach. The brother's unspoken accusation hung in the air, waiting to be plucked and picked apart. But James simply shook his head. "If money is the motive, perhaps he is not merely mad. Perhaps he is desperate." His eyes met hers from across the table, his jaw hardening. "And desperate men are the most dangerous sort. I need to fetch the magistrate."

"I'll go with you," his brother said.

"No." James shook his head. "I will do it. Mother and Father need you here for protection, and there are Georgette and the boys to consider too. I would ask that you stay here and make sure no harm comes to any of them."

His brother scowled, looking none too pleased to be relegated to the role of nanny. On this, at least, they were of an accord. The idea of being left behind under the protection of a man who so obviously distrusted her opened Georgette's mouth before she thought better of it.

"I want to go with you. To Moraig." Her body tensed, already anticipating the rejection but refusing to accept it without a fight.

"'Tis too dangerous." James set the rolled-up map forcefully down on the table. "I'll not see you hurt."

"And I'll not see *you* hurt, nor your family!" Her voice came out a shrill jumble, but the words demanded release. "Not on my account."

James pulled her to the side, his fingers a rough pleasure on her arm. Sympathy scoured his features. "I understand, truly I do. But I want you to stay here where I know you will be safe." He glanced toward his brother. "William will make sure Burton causes you no harm."

The fearsome William canted his head in her direction. His gaze was so heavy as to feel like a hand pushing her backward. "Aye. You certainly bear watching. You've caused enough trouble here, and 'tis dangerous work that awaits him." He spared a sour look for his brother. "Work *I* should be doing."

Her heart twisted at the betrayal of being passed

off so easily. She crossed her arms, glaring at the man who would leave her behind with his large, mistrustful brother while he rode off to town. She knew she was being stubborn. Possibly irrational. But the long, hard day and the discovery of not only Randolph's perfidy, but quite possibly his plot to do James harm, snapped what thin thread of sense she had left. Her mind grasped for a narrow foothold. "The magistrate will need my testimony in order to issue a summons for Randolph," she told James. "You need me with you."

"I *need* you to stay here, Georgette." Exasperation crept into his tone. "You are wasting precious time."

"Then stop arguing with me and listen to reason," she challenged, sitting down on a nearby chair and pulling up her skirts. She picked up a stocking, which had been wadded unceremoniously into one boot, and began to pull it on over her foot.

His eyes narrowed dangerously, all pretense at placating her gone. "There is no reason to be found in this conversation. I don't *want* you with me. I've enough to worry about with adding watching you to my burden."

Georgette's hands stilled, her objections splintering inside her.

There was a familiarity to his words and this path he would force her down that tasted of past disappointments. He would leave her here, a bystander to her life, and deny her any choice in the matter. He didn't want her. She was nothing but a burden.

A bright, sharp pain pierced her heart. She had thought . . . she had thought James was different. That was what came of thinking.

More often than not, one found herself wrong.

"I'll not stay here and be trouble for your family,"

she repeated. It did not matter that one of the people she was trying to protect harbored suspicions of her innocence, or that the other two were staring at her with sharp-eyed surprise. If she stayed here with them, she was nothing but a burden. James had said as much himself. "I'm leaving, with or without you," she warned, yanking the stocking the rest of the way up her calf.

Dimly, the distance of four miles and her inappropriate shoes clattered about in her head. But she was already pointed in this direction, like an arrow that had found its target. She wanted to punish him for such careless regard. "If not to Moraig, then to London," she told him.

His eyes flashed, green fire that threatened to singe anything within arm's length. "By God, if I have to lock you in here to keep that pretty neck of yours safe," he growled, "so help me I will."

"You'll have to have a strong key," she shot back. "Because I refuse to sit here and be your biddable wife." She glared up at him, her hands already working on unrolling her other stocking.

He glared back. And then he stooped and picked up her boots.

For a moment, she actually thought he might help her put them on. Instead, he tucked them up under his arm, turned on his heel, and left. His family followed him out, his mother casting a last, worried look over her shoulder.

Georgette remained frozen on the chair, her stockings halfway on. She gathered her fractured protest into a ball she could hurl after him. He had taken her shoes. Her *shoes*, damn the man.

"I don't trust her." His brother's voice echoed from the outer hallway.

"I don't either," came James's heart-shattering reply.

And that was the last thing she heard before the key scraped in the lock.

HE HATED DOING it. God knew he hated treating her so, but the woman was proving a headstrong handful. At least James now knew to which part of her personality he needed to make his appeal for a real marriage.

Apparently, the wild, impulsive side of Georgette could quite overrule the proper, logical lady.

As he had left, he heard her banging on the library door, calling him any manner of names, threatening his manhood. She had shown him the full force of her temper and it had been magnificent. He almost chuckled at the thought. For a moment he regretted he could not be there to enjoy the spoils of such a glorious transformation.

Instead, he was bound for Moraig, on a mission he found more urgent with every indrawn breath. Burton had tried to murder him today. There was no telling what he might do to Georgette and his family.

He sent up a silent prayer of thanks to William's solid strength as he swung up on Caesar. He only hoped that by the time he returned with the magistrate, Georgette would have come to see that what he did was for the best.

He put his heels to the stallion's flanks and gave him his head, letting the horse run. Shadows danced beneath Caesar's hooves as they ate up the distance between Kilmartie Castle and town. To his left, the loch blazed red and orange, catching the last colors of the sky. The sun was threatening a rapid descent, streaming through the trees like a mirrored light and blinding him to the road ahead. And all the while, he prayed for speed.

He was almost to Moraig when he felt the first change in the horse's rhythmic gait, an unmistakable slowing. He heard the whistling of laboring lungs, and knew he was pushing the stallion too hard. He should have taken a different mount to fetch the magistrate. Caesar had worked hard for him today, cantering first to Kilmartie with two riders, and then returning that same way a scant two hours later at a full gallop.

The urgency of the mission pushed at James, prodding with firm insistency, but he reluctantly pulled Caesar to a trot. The stallion jerked his mouth against the bit, as if to chastise his master for the decision to slow their pace, but James held him in check.

He leaned low over the horse's sweat-soaked neck, whispering words of encouragement. "Easy, boy. We've time yet."

As they jogged the remaining stretch of road, James caught the unmistakable smell of wood smoke. In the distance, a half mile or so east, he could see the glow of the bonfire on Main Street, an unholy halo welcoming the coming night and the building festivities. It occurred to him he might have trouble finding David Cameron, and that when he did, the man might already be drunk. Cameron would surely be drawn to the depravities to be found among Bealltainn's fervor.

Just as he was considering where to first begin his search for the magistrate, James felt the impact of the unseen missile, sharp against his jaw. He hit the ground a full second before the matching crack of a rifle hit his ears.

He rolled over and stared up at the treetops, unsure of what had happened. Caesar came up and pushed against him with his nose. James's ears felt stuffed full of sand, his head murky. The noise he had heard and its significance registered, even as his consciousness dimmed. Someone had shot at him.

And then blood was pouring everywhere, and he wondered if he would make it to Moraig at all.

Chapter 26

GEORGETTE DID NOT spend her breath on tears, or platitudes, or apologies. Crying over her predicament or begging forgiveness of the empty air would not help matters.

James was gone. She had seen him ride off through the library window, bent over his horse's mane and riding for Moraig as if his life depended on it. Regret was not something that would fix this breach of trust, and so she did not take the time wondering what she might have done differently. Neither did she waste her energy sitting on her hands, nor reading one of the many books lining the shelves, nor doing any of the things she might have done even a month ago.

Instead, she studied the map.

Her eye fell on the hunting lodge the earl had pointed out. A mile away, Lady Kilmartie had said. James had locked her in a first floor room with an open window and underestimated her tenacity.

Foolish mistakes, those.

She curled her toes into the carpet, testing the weariness of her limbs. She had already walked several miles today, traipsing up and down Moraig's streets in search of the man. She was facing a mile to reach her trunk in

Randolph's house, where a spare pair of boots waited. It was another four miles to town. Through the library window, she could see the sun was falling out of the sky, darkness certain in a half hour or less, but it did not dissuade her. Only this morning, she had doubted whether she was the kind of woman who could attempt to walk any respectable distance on her own.

How satisfying to know that not only was she the sort of woman who could, she was the sort who would insist upon it.

It was almost dark by the time she reached the little stone house. Her feet were sore and cut from stumbling over sharp rocks, and the hem of her dress was an absolute mess, but she had done it. The difficult, hazard-strewn walk had at least one positive outcome. It had cooled her anger, and now she felt only a smug sort of pride. No doubt James would be angry with her when he found her gone. She almost wished she could be there to witness it. Georgette's conscience pushed in from wherever it had been hiding and reminded her that this mission carried some foolhardy elements. No one knew where she was. She was alone, without a weapon, and approaching a madman's house in the dark. The rhythm of the few days she had spent here told her the grounds-man retreated to his own house come nightfall, somewhere off the estate. She stood still and watched the house, noted the dark windows and lack of smoke from the chimney. All good signs, but still she approached the front door cautiously, ready to bolt should the circumstances demand it.

She was through underestimating Randolph, or herself. She would no longer be that girl who was surprised when her bogeyman appeared.

She paused in the foyer and stood a moment, listening. There was no hint of light anywhere in the house. She could hear a cricket chirping in some distant corner. Above that noise was a quiet groaning, as if the evening wind was playing tricks amid the dark rafters.

She felt her way up the stairs and lit the taper on her bedside table. The little bedroom came into candlelit focus, and the bunched herbs hanging from the rafters sent dramatic shadows spinning along the walls and the floor. Her clothing from this morning lay in a heap where Elsie had tossed it, and the still-full hip bath sat in one corner, a pool of cold water soaking the floorboards beneath it. She made a mental note to tell Elsie that a proper ladies' maid would have never left the room in such disarray.

Her breath caught as she realized her departure on the morrow would prevent her from seeing through the worthy cause of transforming Elsie into a dependable domestic servant. Guilt nudged at her, a stern rebuke. Perhaps, after she arrived in London, she could write to Lady Kilmartie about the woman taking on a new maid. Of course, given Elsie's carnal interest in the countess's younger son, she might need to preface the suggestion with a warning.

It took but a moment for Georgette to pull her spare pair of boots from her trunk and lace them up. Then she was off, crouching along the stairwell wall with the candle in hand. She kept one ear cocked for danger as she tried unsuccessfully to shove a host of unwelcome thoughts from her head. It was not only Elsie she would leave unsettled when she boarded the morning coach. There was Mr. MacRory and the promised home for his kitten. The welcoming smile of Lady Kilmartie, and the woman's hopes that Georgette might be the right match for her son.

And of course, there was James himself. She was leaving him in the most cowardly way possible, sneaking away in the dark while he was off battling her demons. She really ought to be ashamed of herself. She *really* ought to return to Kilmartie Castle. Her lips pursed in amusement as she imagined marching up to the front door and pulling on the knocker. Wouldn't *that* surprise the glowering William?

As she reached the foyer, the groaning of the rafters seemed louder. Indeed, the groaning seemed to come not from the rafters at all, but from behind the closed doorway to Randolph's study. Another unbidden thought flew in like a startled thrush, bound for cover. What if the groom, who had been so kind to her these past few days, had never made it home? Or worse, what if Elsie had come back here and Randolph had hurt her in some way?

She unlocked the door with shaking fingers and opened it a few inches on objecting hinges. The candle, lifted high, revealed the source of the noise.

The black and white dog Joseph Rothven had delivered this morning lay on a rug in front of the hearth. Her immediate sense of relief at not finding a human body to deal with was underscored by worry over what Randolph might have done to the poor animal. She inched into the room and picked up a poker from the hearth, gently prodding at the once fearsome canine with the tip. Randolph had claimed the beast had bitten him, but it showed no signs of stirring now.

Georgette knelt down and placed the candle beside her. Gingerly, she lifted a hand to the dog's chest, half expecting the animal to explode in a flurry of teeth and claws. It did not move, although the fur felt thankfully warm beneath her fingers. It did not respond to either a whistle or a stern shake. She lifted the animal's head and opened one eye. The pupils were dilated and the sharp smell of herbs clung to its muzzle.

Georgette raised a startled hand to her mouth as the scent registered in some locked away part of her brain. She had no memory of last night following the first glass of brandy, but that scent, *that* she remembered. She recalled the taste of it, firm and bitter on her lips as she had nibbled those terrible ginger cookies Randolph had served her. In an instant, she linked the dog's prostrate condition to her own amnesic night.

Randolph had not merely encouraged her acquiescence with a glass or two of brandy. He had drugged her, with his intimate knowledge of herbs.

As if she had summoned him with her discovery, the door to the study swung open on hinges that badly needed oiling. She rose slowly, her hand white-knuckled on the iron fireplace poker. She should have been frightened to see Randolph looking so, hat missing and a hunting rifle in hand.

Instead, she was seething with anger.

Randolph regarded her for a pensive moment before he set down the rifle. He began to work at his necktie with long, aristocratic fingers, as if this was nothing more than an expected domestic scene and he was come home from a long day's work.

The Adam's apple above his collar jumped as his fingers loosened the first two buttons of his shirt. "I see you have come to your senses and returned to me, cousin. I would not have taken such drastic measures had I known how easily your affections could be turned."

"More drastic than trying to kill James with your pruning knife this afternoon?" she choked out.

"Ah yes. The purported husband." Randolph took a menacing step toward her. "Your impulsive night mucked things up for a time, but you need not worry about MacKenzie anymore. I have taken care of him."

Dread slithered through her, cold as ice. "What do you mean?"

"He is removed from the picture." Randolph took another step in her direction, and Georgette's pulse kicked up a notch.

She renewed her sweating grip on the poker and raised it in warning. "Stay away," she told him, her voice a taut string.

He stopped. "There's no need to threaten me, Georgette. Why, look at yourself. You stand here on the verge of hysteria. My studies have given me a certain expertise in this area, and I know several herbal remedies that will help with that. Calming draughts that will help you sleep."

Calming draughts indeed. As if *that* would help her out of this predicament. Why, oh why had she left Kilmartie Castle without so much as leaving a note?

"And what will you do if I *don't* calm down? Set the dog on me?" she choked out. "That isn't really possible, is it? What did you give it? You've practically killed the thing."

Randolph paused. An almost reverent expression crossed his face. "A combination of plant extracts. Henbane, for one. And a concentrated dose of wormwood oil. Makes dumb creatures calm and placid. He'll wake in a few hours." His face twisted. "I only regret I had to resort to a less scholarly means of disposing of your husband. Bullets are so . . . *messy*."

His words punched a hole right through her. "What did you do?" she whispered.

"I have killed him." Randolph advanced another step. "Shot him on the road to Moraig. And so now you are free to marry me after all."

Georgette's chest felt hollow and her eyes pricked with tears. All the while, her mind raced furiously. She refused to believe it. James was strong, the strongest, most dependable man she had ever known. Surely he could not be felled by a pathetic slip of a man like her cousin. Randolph had already proven himself a liar about the events of last night.

She prayed he was lying about this too.

"Your herbal concoction didn't affect me in quite the same way as the dog, did it?" She brandished the poker higher. "Then again, I'm not exactly the dumb creature you thought me to be. Certainly not dumb enough to be tricked into marrying you."

That drew him up short. His hands reached for her, beseeching. "How could you think such a thing? I care for you, and only want to protect you. I would never . . ."

"I spoke with Reverend Ramsey today."

His head jerked backward. "What?"

"I know what you planned. You invited me here with this plot in mind, so do not stand there and pretend you only want to protect me. You *drugged* me in an attempt to force me to marry you." She lowered the poker and fixed him with a glare that focused all her hatred on his guilt-ridden features. "The Kilmarties have been informed of what you attempted to do. If you know what is good for you, you will leave now, while you have the chance."

"I'm not leaving without you," he growled. "You may have escaped me last night outside the church, but you will not be so lucky this time."

"Why?" she asked, raising the iron poker again. "Why do this? To me, to yourself?" The cousin she remembered from childhood was well and truly gone, lost somewhere in this monster. She ached for the loss of the boy she knew, but also for the painful question of her own role in all this. Had she led him to believe she wanted this, or wanted him in some way?

His acerbic laugh echoed against the oak-timbered ceiling. " 'Tis simple. I need money, Georgette, or I will not be able to complete my studies. Do you know how expensive university is? You are the means to an end. A very *wealthy* end."

The air, thick with the scents of the herbs he labored over so meticulously, seemed close to suffocating her. She felt nothing but nausea to hear the final pieces of her missing night. She had come remarkably close to losing everything, and all at the hands of a man who had either gone mad or was dipping a bit too regularly into the herbs he studied.

She shook her head, wondering if he was so far out of his head that he might not hear what she was about to say. "Hear me now, Randolph. I will never marry you. *Ever.* Not even if all my money depended on it, not even if I was so poor I needed to lift my skirts to find my next meal."

Randolph's mouth opened. His thin lips contorted in rage. "You would probably like that, whore that you are. After all, you have spread your legs for the town solicitor, a man without an ounce of refinement or culture." Spittle flew from his mouth and his expression turned hard and ugly. "Look at you, and what you've sunk to. You don't *deserve* me."

He flew at her then, but Georgette was through being surprised by this man.

She stepped neatly to the side. Her boots, so inappropriate for walking, proved strangely well suited for kicking an unbalanced man's legs out from under him. She knocked him once in the head with the side of the fireplace poker, putting all she had into the blow she felt echo all the way through the joints of her shoulders.

As he moaned on the floor, she put the poker to his throat, pressing into the pale strip of flesh exposed there. "James MacKenzie is a better man than you will ever be," she hissed. "I made my choice last night, and I will thank God every day for the rest of my days that it was not you."

She was rewarded with a wheezing sound deep in her cousin's narrow chest. She leaned in close, enunciating clearly so there could be no mistake.

"Because of you, I have forgotten the most glorious night of my life. And if you have taken my future from me as well, I will bloody well hunt you down and kill you."

Chapter 27

ʜᴇ ᴍᴜsᴛ ʜᴀᴠᴇ blacked out, because when James next opened his eyes, the sky above him was dark gray, that narrow strip of time between sunset and full night. Stars had come out to mock him.

He lifted a hand to his jaw and probed it gingerly, slipping over the moisture that coated him there. The feeling of so much blood worried James more than the pain. There was strangely little of hurt involved in the process of being shot, but a copious amount of the warm, sticky fluid he was coming to regard as precious.

He hauled his battered body back up on Caesar, then leaned low over the horse's neck, giving the animal his head. He didn't know where he should go. He only knew it was folly to stay here, exposed to another shot, his life's blood leaking out into the dust.

Caesar, thank God, did what any sensible horse would do.

He took his master home.

James collapsed in a heap in the courtyard outside his house. He shouted for Patrick and shoved Gemmy away. The little dog would not be dissuaded, scouring James's face with an eager, rough tongue that hurt almost as much as his injured jaw.

Shortly, a light bobbed over his head. Patrick leaned in with a lantern held high, his long face drawn with concern. "Jesus, MacKenzie. You're bleeding all over the friggin' place."

"Someone took a shot at me," James moaned.

"I'd say the man has good aim." Patrick brought the lantern in for a closer look. "Looks like it grazed you. Facial wounds bleed like the devil. I've a feeling this one looks worse than it is, if you're still walking and talking. Still, you might try pacing yourself. One serious injury a day is plenty." He shook his head. "Perhaps now you'll listen to me when I tell you to take yourself to bed."

Bed sounded like the most forbidden of fruit, but the urgency of his mission sent a bolt of fear scuttling through James. He had been so befuddled in the aftermath of the shooting he had briefly forgotten why he had been tearing so recklessly for Moraig.

The fact someone had just tried to kill him—*again*—confirmed the danger Burton posed more effectively than any courtroom confession. Georgette was in grave danger, and he had a mission to complete.

He swiped a hand across his aching jaw and lumbered to his feet. He trusted Patrick's judgment. If his wound looked worse than it was, he was wasting time here. He turned back to the saddle.

Patrick's hand on his shoulder pinned his feet to the ground. "You are in no condition to ride, friend."

"I don't have a choice!" James exploded, whirling on the man as his world tilted sideways. "Georgette is in danger, and every second I waste is a second I don't have!"

Patrick's eyes squinted in confusion. "Who, pray tell, is Georgette?"

"My wife." James meant it. He felt it, deep in his bones. She was his.

She only needed to realize it.

"Ah." Patrick's eyes narrowed further. "So you found the mysterious Mrs. MacKenzie. I take it your morning's labors were fruitful then. Where is she now?"

"Kilmartie Castle," he choked out. "William is protecting her from her cousin and . . ."

"Then you have time for me to at least examine you," Patrick interrupted gently. "I can't tell from looking at it if the bullet is lodged somewhere in that thick skull of yours, or if it has severed something important."

James heaved out a sour breath. His limbs screamed at him to be put to better use finding the magistrate. But his head leaned toward something more rational. Finding Cameron in the midst of Bealltainn would be no easy task. Perhaps a moment's steady thought while Patrick cleaned up the bullet wound would be time not wasted. He could use the time to sort out a plan and map out his route for Cameron's likely haunts.

Patrick added, "If you care for this woman, you should spare a minute to make sure you can return yourself to her intact. If William is guarding her, you can be sure she is safe."

Damned if Patrick wasn't the calm, annoying voice of reason. James nodded reluctantly. His friend lifted James beneath the arms and propped him against one shoulder. "I'm going to need to shave off some facial hair, to get a better look at the injury," Patrick said. "Do you want me to merely trim the one spot, or the whole beard?"

James stumbled once and then righted himself. It was a prospect almost as worrying as his concern over

Georgette. He had worn his beard for eleven years, ever since the rift with his father. Childish, in some ways, but given how much he physically resembled his father, it had served as a daily reminder he was his own man.

"Do it," he said. "The entire beard. I find I've grown tired of the thing."

"About bloody time," Patrick muttered, hefting James's weight more firmly on his shoulder and groaning under the strain. "Weigh as much as an ox, the lot of you. You're a Kilmartie, sure enough. It's time you started acting like one."

GEORGETTE BURST OUT of the cottage into darkness, her heart pounding a dent in her chest. With Randolph secured by a length of twine she had found around a bundle of kindling, she now faced the decision that had been percolating in her head for the last five minutes.

It was a full mile back to Kilmartie Castle. Then would come the half hour of explanations it would take to convince James's scowling, suspicious brother she was telling the truth.

And all the while, James could be lying somewhere, injured.

She choked on a sob. Worry for him, and what she might have lost, cemented her decision. She climbed on top of the gray mare Randolph had left tied to a tree and kicked the reluctant animal into a canter toward town.

She made it three miles without finding his body broken on the road, but her luck ran out as the lights of Moraig came into view. She almost trampled a dark object lying in the middle of the moonlit path, and she had to pull up the winded mare and circle back.

She dismounted, and her heart caught up in a tight

knot as she recognized James's money purse, the one she had warned him could tumble far too easily from his coat pocket. He had passed by here, then. Picking up the purse, she knelt in the dark road and panned a hand around the spot. It was dark and moist, as if something had recently soaked into the dust.

Something sharp and smelling of copper. *Blood.*

Her stomach churned in despair, pushing a wave of bile high into her throat. She clapped a hand to her mouth. Vomiting would not help either of them.

"James!" she screamed, but was answered by nothing but gentle forest noises and her own strained breathing. She looked around wildly. There was no sign of the man or the horse. Whatever had happened to him had been swallowed by the night.

The remaining evidence of trauma, however, was irrefutable.

Terror made her vault back onto the horse and put her heels mercilessly against the mare's flank.

Another half mile and she found herself blocked by the Bealltainn crush. She could see now why they closed the street to horse and carriage traffic. Even had they permitted horses beyond the wooden barriers that had been put up across the street, it would be impossible to navigate one through such a mob. She swung off the horse before it even came to a walk and then released the gray mare with a slap to her rump. The mare trotted off into the darkness. With any luck, it would make its way to a kinder owner than Randolph had proven to be.

She dove into the crowd, shouldering her way through while looking for a familiar face or landmark, someone she could beg for help. The competing smells of smoke and unwashed bodies pressed in at her, and her panic kicked up as she realized how difficult this was going to be.

She needed to find someone she knew, but the crowd was nothing but a mass of strangers who turned away when she tapped on their shoulders, or else leered at her with ale-laced breath. Beyond the wall of bodies, the bonfire was a fearsome thing, at least fifteen feet tall and billowing smoke. The sound of stringed instruments warming up somewhere near the center of the Main Street crowd grated in her ears. That the townsfolk were here, swallowed by gaiety while James had been shot not a mile away, seemed the cruelest of ironies.

Twenty hard-fought feet into the crowd, she finally spied someone she knew. Joseph Rothven was standing along the edge of a wooden dance floor, tapping his foot to the music. She recognized his lanky build and hunched shoulders, so characteristic of a young man who had attained his full height but not figured out what to do about it. He was staring up at several couples who were already dancing to the mismatched strains of instruments not yet fully tuned.

She plunged toward him and grabbed on to his coat sleeve. "Mr. Rothven," she panted, trying to catch her breath, which seemed to have been set free along with the horse. "I . . . I need your help."

He turned to her, his face momentarily confused before sinking into a delighted smile. "Lady Thorold! Have you come to give me another lesson?" He looked around, scanning the congestion of Main Street. "We'll need to find an alley for privacy."

Georgette braced her hands on her knees, filling her lungs with great gulps of smoke-filled air. The reminder of what she had purportedly done with this young man did little to calm her screaming nerves. "I . . . I need to find the magistrate," she gasped over the low roar of the bonfire and the nightmarish band. "Can you tell me where to find him?"

Joseph nodded. "Aye, he's in the Gander. Saw him there not ten minutes ago, when I stopped by to say hello to Miss Dalrymple." He grinned, his teeth flashing in the light of the fire. "Are you sure you don't have five minutes to show me again? There's one bit that still confuses me, and I don't want to disappoint Miss Dalrymple later tonight when I have a go with her."

But Georgette was already spinning away, propelled by fear and a distinct sense of nausea. She didn't want to know what she had done with this boy, didn't want to think about anything but finding the magistrate and demanding he muster a group of sturdy men to scour the woods for any sign of James.

But her feet slowed. That was a cowardly sentiment. Whatever else she may have done last night, she had at least been bold enough to seize the moment and own her truth. She tilted her head back in the young man's direction. "Mr. Rothven," she whispered. "What, exactly, did I show you how to do last night?"

"Waltz," he shouted back, a grin on his face. He motioned with open eagerness to the wooden dance floor. "You taught me how to waltz."

Her shoulders collapsed, weak with relief. "I don't think you'll need another lesson," she told him. Her former life might have left her ill-prepared to teach a young man the physical pleasures of intimacy, but it had certainly equipped her to instruct a gangly youth how to dance.

She elbowed her way toward the Blue Gander. The establishment rose above the crowd like a watchful tower. Her lack of memories from last night slowed her feet as the individual letters of the sign came into clearer focus.

She had sworn she would not go back. This was no quick visit like this afternoon, when she had been leaning on James for strength and courage. She would be entering the public room this time, the very site where she had conducted herself in a regrettable fashion last night.

She drew a deep breath, her feet inching forward. She had hog-tied her cousin, not half an hour ago. If she could do that, she could certainly brave the public room at the Gander.

Chapter 28

THE CROWD THINNED toward the edges of the street, giving her courage and a straight, clear shot. And so she ran the last fifteen yards to the Gander, taking the steps two at a time before bursting through the doors in a clatter of heels. She tossed her unbound hair from her eyes and skidded to a stop in the ale- and whiskey-soaked air of the place.

A stool scraped across the floor in the sudden, settling silence. Twenty pairs of eyes turned to take her in. Several heads dipped in recognition, as if it was just another night at the Gander to have her come bursting through the doors.

"A round for the prettiest lady in Moraig!" one man shouted, raising his cup.

"A round for the *only* lady in Moraig who ever set foot inside the Gander!" shouted another.

An approving chorus followed. Pewter tankards pounded on tables, and whistles filled the air. Georgette hovered uncertainly, one foot across the threshold of the barroom.

They thought she was a lady?

"She's without her husband, lads. I suppose that

means there's a chance for the rest of us tonight," came a disembodied voice from across the room.

"Come and sit on my lap, like the good lass you were last night." A portly older gentleman patted the front of his trousers with frightening familiarity.

"I . . . ah, no thank you." She took a solid step into the room. Just as she had feared, the men all stared at her. Her boots seemed to drag, toes-down, along the floor.

And then she realized they were staring in appreciation, not condemnation.

They smiled at her. Nodded their heads in encouragement. And not one of them regarded her with what she would call disgust, or even disrespect.

For the first time since hearing about her escapades of the previous evening, she wished she could remember. What would it have been like to command this masculine crowd? They hung tonight on her every word and gesture, and she had done no more than walk through the door. She became more sure of herself with each step. The self-induced embarrassment was still there, but it had been shoved into a distant corner. There were more important things to address here, and what she had done last night to enthrall this crowd was not among them.

She put her hands on her hips and met their spellbound gazes squarely. "I'm here for a different purpose tonight, gentlemen." She turned in a circle. "Can someone please tell me where might I find the magistrate?"

"Right here." A gentleman rose up from a lone corner table.

Georgette had the fleeting impression of smartly cut clothing and dark blond curls, but her eyes quickly focused on his face. His aristocratic features seemed wildly out of place amid the rugged beards that defined the pub's other clientele. Worse, his eyes seemed to scour her with open appreciation.

"Stand up gents," he drawled, not taking his eyes off her. "There's a lady in our presence."

Chairs and stools scraped from across the room. Man after man leaped to his feet, and caps were swept off heads in alarming succession, but she moved past them to stop in front of magistrate. "I desperately need your help, Mr. Cameron."

He offered her a wolfish smile. "I am always willing to help a lady in need." His gaze dropped to her bodice. "As I was all too willing to demonstrate last night."

"I don't want to talk about last night."

"I'm not surprised." One brow rose in question. "I doubt MacKenzie gave you as much enjoyment as I would have."

Georgette slapped a hand down on the table, anger and desperation humming in her limbs. "I need your help to find my *husband*, Mr. Cameron."

An uneasy expression replaced his earlier leer. "Sit down and explain yourself."

She sat down. All around her came the sounds of the men sitting again, and the gradual resumption of their conversations. Cameron, obvious gentleman that he was, sat down last. He regarded her with a sideways grin. If James had been here, she was quite sure the man would have had a fist planted in his face by now. But James was not here.

Which was precisely the reason she was.

"My husband is missing." Worry made her words shake like a leaf in the wind. "And he . . . he may be injured."

Cameron leaned back in his chair. "Your husband, is he? That does not match my memory of the events of last night."

"We were married later, by the blacksmith. And regardless of what role you may have played in the events here last night, I need your help again. Tonight."

Cameron spread his hands in apology. "If this is about the summons, Lady Thorold, I am truly sorry. Normally, I would not be bothered to help the man. But MacKenzie insisted upon it, and he had enough evidence—"

"This is not about the summons, nor the marriage, nor any rift between you and James," she interrupted. "He's been shot, and I am desperately worried for his safety."

A terrible sound gouged at her ears, and the cold sensation of ale splashing onto her stockings and skirts sent Georgette twisting in her seat. Elsie stood to one side. She wore an old stained apron that no ladies' maid would have ever been permitted to don, not even when performing the most mundane of chores. One hand was cupped over her mouth. The tray she had been carrying listed sideways on the floor amid now-empty tankards that had not yet come to rest.

"He . . . he's been *shot*?" the maid exclaimed, her voice muffled by fingers.

"I don't know." Georgette's gaze returned to Cameron's sudden hawk-eyed interest. "I . . . I don't know what to believe. I saw . . ." Her voice hitched.

"What did you see?" Cameron's voice probed at her, cold and demanding.

"Blood." She swallowed. "A lot of it. On the road between Kilmartie Castle and Moraig, about a mile east."

"No body?"

She shook her head. The tears came then, tears she had been holding back. Her whole body began to shake. Dear God, if James had been killed because of her, she could not live with the guilt. She was more than half in love with the man. To think what she might have lost felt like a casket being closed over her while she still breathed.

"No horse?" Cameron pressed.

"No sign of that either," she choked out.

Cameron stroked his chin. "So he may have been able to ride to safety. You did not pass him on the road?"

"No. And I traveled the route he would have taken had he headed back to Kilmartie Castle."

"We should check there, though." Cameron was already pushing his chair back. "He may have taken a different route, if he feared for his safety." He picked up his hat and his gloves. "I'll find him, do not doubt it." His jaw hardened. "I owe him that, at the very least."

"Wait . . ." It was all well and good for Mr. Cameron to dash off to check for James at Kilmartie Castle, but James's brother was already suspicious of her role in this. Would William believe the message?

Or would he think it was a devious trick?

"Let me write them a note." She motioned to Elsie. "I need a pencil and a piece of paper, as fast as you can, please."

The maid produced both from somewhere and Georgette wrote down a quick explanation, praying it would not be needed. With any luck, James would be at Kilmartie Castle, alive and mad as a wet cat at her absence. She prayed it was so.

The alternative was too dreadful to contemplate.

As Cameron departed with her hastily scribbled missive in hand, Georgette collapsed head-down on the table. She felt dull inside, a penny gone to tarnish. What was she going to do? She had spent two years mourning a dead husband who did not deserve two weeks of her time.

What sort of penance would she owe a husband she not only loved, but who had quite possibly been killed because of her?

Elsie put a steady hand on her shoulder. "Mr. Cameron will find him."

Georgette lifted her head and offered the maid a grim smile through her tears. "He's my only hope right now." She exhaled, long and shuddering, and then reached out and squeezed Elsie's hand. "Why aren't you outside, dancing with Mr. Rothven?"

The maid's face clouded. "I . . . I need a job, miss. And I wasn't sure if I still had one with you, after I broke Mr. MacKenzie's window and then left you in such a state."

Georgette would have laughed, had her heart not been so sore. "'Tis all right," she told the sorrowful maid. "Mr. MacKenzie and I have come to an understanding. You have a position with me." *For as long as I remain in Scotland.*

She did not know where that last thought came from. The thought of returning to London, after all that had happened, sent her head spinning in reverse. If James was hurt, even if it was no more than a scrape, she would stay here until he recovered.

Her memory kicked at her. She was being dreadfully naïve. The amount of blood she had seen was consistent with nothing so small as a scrape.

And if he had been killed . . . The thought of never seeing him again, of never exploring where his searing kisses might lead, was too devastating to contemplate.

"You should go and enjoy Bealltainn," she whispered to Elsie. "It only comes once a year, and the band is starting up."

Elsie's face softened with want. "Are you sure, miss? What will you do?"

"I'll stay here and wait for word from Mr. Cameron." She would wait forever, if she had to.

A blur of movement caught her eye. The man Georgette recognized as the innkeeper stalked toward them. "See now, Miss Dalrymple, I need my pencil back. And the dishes need washing and there's four or five men waving their cups about over there. Move a bit faster, if you will."

Elsie untied her apron strings and tossed the filthy, wadded-up bit of fabric on the floor. "I've better ways to occupy my time, thank you very much. And a better job waiting for me, come morning."

She gave Georgette a saucy wink and then she sauntered toward the door.

The innkeeper stared after her. "That girl is bound for trouble," he murmured, low under his breath.

"Didn't you know?" Georgette watched the door close on Elsie's eager steps. "A lady never forgoes the pleasure of dancing."

The innkeeper eyed her uncertainly. Not that she blamed him. She sounded hysterical, even to herself.

"I suppose you've come for the key," he huffed.

Georgette brushed the back of her hand across the tears that still wet her cheeks. "I beg your pardon?"

"The key," he repeated. "For the room."

Georgette stared at him. Heavens. She *had* paid for a room. Suddenly, a quiet place to escape the noisy public room and the roaring noise of her fears seemed just the thing.

"Yes, please." She pushed her chair back and forced her feet to move. They rejected the idea, but she insisted on their obedience. "But please, should anyone come asking for me, send them straight up. I . . . I am waiting for news."

Please, God, let it be good news.

"Of course, miss." The proprietor's shifting eyes told her exactly what he thought of such a proposition. After last night, she couldn't blame him.

She accepted the key and made her way up to the room. She sat on the edge of the bed and concentrated on just breathing. When she had been downstairs, with the clamor of glassware and the chuckles rolling like church bells from the mouths of nearby patrons, the idea of silence had seemed unspeakably appealing. But now that she was here, the suffocating absence of sound inside the room, and the faint, merry sounds of Bealltainn coming from outside the window, merely pointed out how alone she was.

Worry lined her stomach like lead in a bucket. She was quite sure there was no way she could sleep, not with the uncertainty of the outcome.

No, sleep would not come tonight.

She would just close her eyes and wait.

Chapter 29

JAMES SQUIRMED IN frustration beneath Patrick's hands. It was the second time today he had sat for the man's suturing skills, and if he never saw another needle, it would be too soon. The wound itself might not hurt, but the damned needle was causing a dozen new injuries and seemed to find, with unerring accuracy, every ready nerve beneath his skin.

"Easy now, almost done," Patrick said, as if sensing his patient was about to turn unruly. Such intuition was no doubt a useful skill for a veterinarian to have.

In a roommate, however, it was most annoying.

In fact, the very idea of a roommate made James want to gnash his teeth in frustration. He had indulged in a good, long look around the kitchen as Patrick shaved his beard a bit too enthusiastically. Everywhere he looked, evidence of his lonely bachelor's life taunted him. The punching bag, with a hole in one end spilling sawdust onto the floor. The unused copper pans above the equally pristine iron stove. Upstairs, he knew his sheets would smell of nothing but his own loneliness and perhaps a good whiff of terrier.

He wanted to return to Georgette and sleep with her head on his shoulder, and wake up in bedclothes that smelled of her.

The reminder of what he still needed to do to keep her safe pricked as surely as Patrick's torment of a needle. His friend finally stepped back, regarding James with an authoritative air. "I suppose you would not listen if I told you to go lie down."

James rose with a groan. "Not even Gemmy listens when you say that." He hissed between his teeth, testing his ability to stand and finding it questionable. "I cannot stay. You know that."

"Aye." Patrick nodded. "I suppose I do. How about I come with you then?"

James eyed his friend. His first instinct, of course, was to tell him no. But he was finding himself considering a lot of things today he would never have imagined. He nodded slowly. "I would appreciate that."

Patrick stepped over to the washbasin and washed his hands. "How are you feeling? I have something I could give you for pain, but it's meant for horses, and I can't vouch for what it might do to you."

James ran a hand along his injured cheek, where the bullet had grazed his skin. On either side of the stitches, the skin there felt exposed and raw where Patrick had shaved him. A mental image of his tanned forehead contrasting with the pale white skin the beard had recently covered made him wince. "Hang how I feel. I must look ridiculous."

Patrick dried his hands and then hefted one of the unused copper pots from its anchor on the wall. He spun it around and held the gleaming copper surface a few inches from James's face. "'Tis not too bad. I've a feeling your bride will not mind."

James peered at his copper-tinted image. He looked like . . . well, truth be told, he looked like hell. The row of stitches along his jaw could not be missed, and a smear of blood still stained the hair around his ears.

But more importantly, he looked like his father. When he had grown the beard eleven years ago, he had been a twenty-one-year-old youth, with rounded edges and an earnest look in his eyes. He had wanted something to hide behind, something to distinguish himself from his family.

Now he was a man, with the hard, angular planes and the beginnings of the weary, careworn lines he had glimpsed across his father's desk this evening.

He rubbed his hand across the uninjured side of his face. "She'll likely not recognize me." He scarcely recognized himself, but there was something settling about seeing his face for the first time in over a decade. He *was* a Kilmartie.

And there was no shame in that.

"Kiss her, then." Patrick shrugged. "That will set her mind to rights, soon enough."

James could not help the chuckle that built in his chest. Kiss her, indeed. That was something he planned to do, every day for the rest of his life.

They headed toward the door together, but James pulled up short at the sight of Georgette's corset. It was lying on the kitchen sideboard atop a cluttered pile of his books and papers. He had forgotten about that. He liked the way it looked there, a bit of feminine frippery amid his things. He tucked it up under his arm and admitted to himself he wanted to make a life with her, not just a marriage.

But first he needed to make sure she was safe.

He stepped outside, Patrick on his heels, only to see William and Cameron riding toward him through darkness. Their horses were winded, their faces grim. They pulled to a halt in front of him.

James glared up at his brother. The man had clearly located the magistrate, but that did little to settle the anger that surged through James.

William had left Georgette. Alone and unprotected.

James might have just garnered his father's favor after eleven years of estrangement, but that did not matter in the face of this betrayal. He was bloody well going to kill his brother.

"What in the hell are you doing here?" James demanded.

"Thanking God you are alive." William's face dissolving into a shite-eating grin. "But good God, man, what happened to your beard?"

"Burton tried to kill me again, and you've left Georgette unprotected. Is the first thing you have to say to me really something about a bloody beard?"

William swore as his horse half reared. He struggled to bring his mount under control. When he finally had the animal settled again, he regarded James with a solemn expression, all trace of humor vanished. "I did not leave her, Jamie. She left *you*."

"What?" James asked, incredulous.

"She's gone missing. Out the window."

"But . . . I took her shoes!" James could well believe she would climb out the window. She had proven remarkably tenacious in the brief time he had known her. But walk about without shoes? In the dark?

With Burton possibly stalking her?

His breath near froze in his lungs.

"Apparently, that did not stop her." William's voice was a terrible rumble. "I thought she was locked in the library, safe where you'd left her, but when I peeked in to check on her, she was gone. I rode here to tell you and intercepted Cameron along the way."

David Cameron cleared his throat and handed something down to him. James closed his hand over the folded piece of paper with fingers gone cold.

"She found me at the Gander and gave me this for your family," Cameron told him. "I was given the impression she was worried about you, but after speaking with William and hearing his concerns about the situation, I confess I am no longer so sure."

Cameron's words stubbornly pushed their way through the tangled web of James's thoughts. He motioned for Patrick's lantern, and his stomach churned in nervous anticipation.

He unfolded the note. Read it.

William, your brother has been shot on the road from Kilmartie to Moraig. I cannot find him, and beg your assistance with the magistrate in mounting a search.

James crumpled it in his hand. His stomach no longer felt empty. In fact, it felt boiling full. A rabid sense of betrayal snaked its way inside him and set up shop. "She knew I was shot," he croaked. His heart did cartwheels in his chest, turning over and over and stealing what breath he had left.

How did she know he was shot if she had no role in it?

"Aye." William nodded grimly. "She knew you were shot. She just didn't know you survived."

IT PROVED EASY enough to find her. They returned to the Gander to ask around, and the innkeeper sent James straight up. Perhaps it was the prospect of thwarting four very large, very determined men, one of whom had caused a great deal of physical damage to the property last night. Or perhaps the Gander's proprietor held no respect for a lady who had four different men asking after her. Whatever the reason, James was waved toward the stairs without so much as a blink from the man.

The other three men followed close on his heels, the pounding of their boots an ill match to the purposeful rhythm in his head. James pushed them back with a stern hand. "I'm not inviting an audience, gentleman. I will do this alone."

William's eyes widened at the rebuff. "That is daft, Jamie. She already tried to kill you once, though her aim could use some honing. Would you march in and bare your chest so she has a clear target at your fool of a heart?"

James shook his head. "I can handle myself, now that I know not to trust her."

"You can handle yourself against a man, sure enough." Cameron's voice poked at him like a stick. "All of Moraig knows that. But having a woman draw a knife on you is different, especially when it is a woman you care about."

James drew in a sharp breath. He had not realized his feelings for Georgette were so bloody obvious. But emotions were irrelevant here. All that mattered was the truth, and his interrogation techniques would not be improved by onlookers. He squared his shoulders against their dissent. "I'm going alone, whether or not you approve."

William looked ready to strangle him. Patrick, damn his eyes, just looked sympathetic. Oh, he understood their objections. He would have lodged the same argument himself had their positions been reversed. But none of them had any idea of the depth of feeling that had passed between him and Georgette in the space of only twenty-four hours. Her perfidy was something he *had* to address in private.

"Ten minutes," James offered as a concession to the worry lining his brother's eyes. "Come up in ten minutes if you don't hear from me by then."

After a long, tense moment, William nodded. "Just make sure it's not a body we'll be coming up to collect."

James took the rest of the stairs two at a time. He opened the door with a silent hand. The chit had not even thought to turn the key in the lock. A dangerous mistake, that. Anyone could come in and find her the way he was doing, stretched out on the bed with only her silken hair for a blanket.

She slept, lost in some deep and twitching state of slumber. He contemplated shaking her awake, decided against a jarring hand on her shoulder. The gentlemanly side of him objected to jerking such a peaceful body from her dreams. Far kinder to do it with words.

Not that he was feeling very kindly toward her at the moment.

She had left a lamp burning low on the bedside table, and he reached over to turn the wick up. An object that looked suspiciously like his money purse snagged his attention for a half second before he set the corset down beside it. Evidence that she was involved in some way, and a possible motive as well. Had she really shot him for so paltry a sum?

His gaze returned to Georgette. She had not taken the time to pull back the bedcovers, and so James stood and stared at the length of her body a full minute before he lent his voice to the necessary process of waking her. She was so mind-numbingly beautiful that his fingers twitched to touch her.

But beauty had no place in this debate. A lioness could be beautiful, and still rip out your throat before feeding on your carcass.

He sat down on the bed. The mattress dipped under his weight but she did not stir. He drew a deep breath, filling his lungs with air and purpose. "Wake up, Georgette."

Chapter 30

A VOICE HISSED AT her through terror-filled dreams, bidding her to obey in a tone that brooked no argument. *Wake up.*

Georgette did not even consider ignoring such a summons.

She opened her eyes and found a stranger sitting on the bed next to her. She pushed herself up on frantic hands and scrambled backward, unsure of where she was, which bed she was in, and whose angry face scowled down at her. She felt as confused as she had on waking this morning. The circumstances, and her surroundings, were so eerily familiar she almost closed her eyes, just to see if she was dreaming.

Only one thing stopped her. The eyes. Those haunting green eyes, this time illuminated by lamplight instead of sunlight. They were the same, and yet they were different.

This time, they were not inviting her to come closer.

"James!" She swallowed her gasp of joy, ignored the dark look on his face in favor of focusing on the fact that if he could glower, he could breathe.

His expression was not surprising. He was mad at her. She had known he would be, for leaving the library in such a cowardly way, but she would address his grievance later.

For now, her heart skipped its gladness.

He was alive.

She launched herself at him, her arms wrapping themselves around whatever piece of him she could reach. How could she have fallen asleep? The last thing she remembered was promising herself she would not. She let her nose rest there in the curve between his neck and shoulder. He smelled the same, soap and old blood and warm wool and hard-ridden horse. He felt the same too, his muscles strong and tense beneath her hands as she rested her palms against his back.

But he looked like someone else entirely.

She pulled back and studied the new architecture of his skin, where once his beard had been. She cupped the smooth surface of his injured cheek with one shaking hand. "I thought you were dead," she whispered.

"Indeed." He did not speak in the same hushed tones her own voice offered. His tone, and the guttural way he rolled his vowels, sounded like thunder in her newly awakened head. "Does the fact I am not come as a surprise?"

It should have been a question. But the way he said it, grave and hard, made it clear he did not entertain the idea.

He blamed her. Her body began to shake. It hurt, those words, the culpability he obviously placed in her. But how could he not blame her, when she also blamed herself?

"Randolph said . . ." Georgette swallowed and shook her head against the terrifying memory. "He said . . . you were dead. I did not know what to think."

I was so scared. But uttering the last of it would not erase the accusing look on this man's face. And so she chose to keep it inside, where she could nurse it, protect it.

Cherish it. Fear was an emotion she had long held of a husband, but it was not something she had ever imagined feeling *for* one.

His eyes flashed at her. "Pretty lies, Georgette. But dinna—" He seemed to catch himself, though the brogue he kept hidden made her heart stutter. "*Do not* sit there and pretend you don't know what happened. I saw your note. My only question is, did you pull the trigger or did you set Randolph on me to do your dirty work?"

She shrank back on the bedcovers. "Neither," she whispered.

"Did you leave the safety of Kilmartie Castle and my brother's protection for a reason? Or did you merely fancy a bruising walk through dark woods to cap off your eventful day?"

"Neither, I tell you!" Anger reared its curious, misshapen head. She pushed against his chest, sucking in a breath as he winced in response to the press of her palm. There was scarcely an inch of him she could touch without hurting him in some way. "I left, damn you, but you left me first."

He leaned back, giving her an inch more room in which to find air. "Where did you go?"

"I went . . ." She swallowed, not wanting to give voice to the illogical thoughts that had driven her on her ill-considered flight out the window. "I went to gather my things. At the hunter's cottage."

His face darkened. "Why?"

She cursed under her breath, one of Elsie's choicest words. This, then, was James MacKenzie, solicitor. Tossing out questions, demanding answers. Thinking the worst of her.

Only she might deserve this bit that was coming.

"I was going to return to London, on the morning coach." Her voice cracked, though she lifted her chin in defiance.

Her words scraped at James's already raw heart. "You were leaving me? Without *shoes*?" The thought she had planned to leave him, without even a word of good-bye, hurt as much as the thought that she might have a hand in his attempted murder.

"Yes." She straightened her shoulders. "But not without shoes. That was what I went to the cottage to fetch."

"Why would you do something so stupid?" he demanded.

She raised a brow, a gesture at once infuriating and heart-warming. "London is a filthy place. Shoes are not optional for the journey."

"You could have waited for my return," he pointed out.

"It was no more than you deserved, locking me in the library, stealing my things. That is no way to treat someone you claim to care about. I would have treated you far better, had the situation been reversed."

His already confused feelings scattered like ashes tossed into the wind. It was difficult to trust his ears, much less his instincts. "You . . . *care* about me?"

Georgette nodded, swiping at a lone tear with the back of her hand. "Clearly, I am not thinking straight."

James leaned back, resting his hands on his thighs and staring at the lamp beside the bed. "Clearly, neither am I." He felt as if she had picked him up and tossed him against a wall. He wanted to believe her. Desperately. But the facts were rather damning.

"How did you know where to find me?" Georgette's voice wound its way around the cracks in his heart, honing his thoughts back to his original purpose.

"Cameron found me and showed me your note. He said he had left you here, so it was the first place we looked." His chest felt squeezed in a too-tight belt, and the air seemed trapped in his lungs. "How did *you* know I had been shot?"

She released a long, shuddering breath. "Randolph came upon me in the cottage, brandishing a rifle. He told me he had killed you. I was terrified for you, afraid to listen to him. But then, when I found a pool of blood and your money purse along the road, I realized Randolph had been telling the truth. I found the magistrate and wrote the note to aid his search. But I did not do this thing you are accusing me of. I would *never* hurt you."

James no longer knew what to believe. He only knew that the thought of Georgette meeting her cousin, alone and unprotected, sent his pulse into a mad gallop. "Did Burton hurt you?" His voice came out hoarse, as if someone had put a hand to his throat and squeezed.

"I am untouched," she told him, a smile flirting about her lips. "I cannot say the same about my cousin. I took care of him."

A noise came out of him then, something strangled and desperate. He regarded her a long, wide-eyed moment. "Christ, Georgette, you don't do anything by halves. Where did you leave the body?" He held up a hand as she opened her mouth. "No, don't tell me. As your solicitor, I think it's best if I don't know. We'll claim you acted in self-defense, and—"

"I did not kill him," she interrupted. "I may have knocked him in the head with a fireplace poker. Left a fearsome imprint, that bit of iron did." She nibbled on her lower lip. "And I *may* have threatened to kill him if he harmed you."

James looked at her, admiration breaking through the former bleak plains of his mind. It was not evidence, not anywhere close. But it was an explanation that made sense. He found himself grasping on to it as if it was flotsam and he was a drowning man. She knew he had been shot because she had confronted Randolph. There was no conspiracy on her part, no plot to kill him or blackmail his family.

She *cared* about him.

This was the truth he wanted to believe.

He ran an awkward hand through his hair and offered her a slantwise glance. "It takes a strong woman to handle herself so well."

"Does this mean you forgive me for leaving?" Her eyes were wide. Beseeching.

"I don't know what to think," he told her. His eyes skipped across her face, settled in the vicinity of her mouth. The truth he wanted clicked into place as irrefutable fact.

"Actually, I do," he clarified, the comprehension of his feelings like a warm iron held up to his skin. "I think I might love you."

GEORGETTE'S WORLD, WHICH had been sliding south only minutes before, ground to a halt.

How could he *love* her? They had known each other for all of a day. She had been contrary and disheveled for most of it, two of the very things that had so vexed her first husband. How had she done such an impossible thing as to earn this man's love?

And most important, what was she going to do about it?

She took his face between her hands and splayed her fingers over the angle of his cheekbones, taking care to avoid his injured jaw. "I love you too." There was not the slightest hesitation in offering those words back. It did not matter if their acquaintance was counted in hours instead of months. She had known what she felt since the moment her cousin told her James was dead.

"But I don't know if I trust you," he said.

She was so close she could almost feel the puff of air that came from his mouth on the word "trust." So close, his words hit her like an uppercut. "I . . . I beg your pardon?"

"Trust." He pulled away from her touch. "That part is the hardest for me. I do not know if I can trust you, Georgette. With my heart, my life, my money purse, any of it."

"Your money purse is sitting on the bedside table. Perhaps next time you will listen to me when I suggest it would be safer stashed in an inside pocket." That part was easily solved. But she swallowed against the fear that rose up in her throat over the rest of it. "I suppose, on the matter of your heart, I don't blame you for not trusting me. I am not sure I trust myself, or these feelings you conjure in me." She stared down at the coverlet, picked at an idle threat. "Perhaps it will come. Surely trust takes longer than a day to build."

She heard him draw a deep breath. "I would have said the same thing about love only yesterday, but here we are."

"Where, exactly, are we?" Georgette lifted her eyes.

He held out his hand, and for a moment she thought he would take her own up. Instead, he offered her his palm, face up. "Might I have my ring back, Lady Thorold?"

Her world tumbled then, straight off the edge of reason. He wanted his ring back?

Her heart should have been pounding in her chest. Instead, it fell quiescent, as if it did not quite trust her either. She slipped the signet ring off her finger and handed it to him. He put it on his own hand. It did not spin around, loose, as it had on her own finger. He had to work it over one knuckle, and then push to seat it home.

It fit him like it was supposed to, that ring.

Like it was never meant to be hers.

Behind James's head, the door to the room flung open. Georgette sensed the danger before she saw it, leaped to her feet, coiled and ready to run or fight or whatever was needed. Randolph, disheveled and clearly out of his head, stepped into the room.

And all she could think as he advanced on James was that he might as well kill them both.

Chapter 31

THERE WAS NO prelude, no dancing around words or
threats.

Randolph leaped toward James without provocation
or preamble. Her cousin sported a bruise on his temple
in the perfect shape of a fireplace poker, but it did not
appear to slow him down at all. How he had gotten free
of his bindings she could not determine, but she could
imagine.

Unlike dancing, knot tying was not something she
was qualified to teach anyone.

As Randolph advanced on the man who loved her,
but could not trust her, she felt utterly useless. Except for
one small thing. She knew how to scream.

"James!" she shouted, her heart finding its lost
rhythm. "Watch out!"

But he had already heard the danger, was whirling
before the words were even out of her mouth. He met
Randolph's attack with an upturned arm, then repaid
the man's uncoordinated attempts to hit him with a
single blow to the nose. Incredibly, Randolph did not
go down. He stood there, blood gushing from his nose,
a howl of rage on his lips. Georgette could see that his

pupils were dilated, and from something more than the heat of battle.

Had her cousin taken some of the same herbs he so freely forced on others?

Feet pounded in the corridor outside the room. William and the magistrate pushed their way inside, followed by a tall, thin man Georgette did not recognize. The room seemed to shrink beneath the size and menace of so many bristling men.

"Do you need our help?" William growled, cracking his knuckles and taking a menacing step in Georgette's direction.

James shook his head and stayed his brother with an upheld palm. "I prefer the chance to take care of Burton myself."

"*Burton?*" William spit out. "So this is the blighter who tried to kill you?"

"Aye." James wiped a sleeve across his jaw, smearing blood where one of the sutures had pulled free. Georgette's eyes focused on that bright crimson line. He was bleeding. Injured. He was in no condition to fight off a drug-addled man, even one as slight and awkward as Randolph.

James seemed to either ignore or not notice the blood. He crouched at the knees and lifted his fists, beckoning to Randolph have another go. In another time, or another place, the gesture would have seemed almost playful.

This was not that time or place.

" 'Tis not a fair fight!" Georgette protested. James was injured, every inch of him, while Randolph was crazed and bolstered by the rush of drugs in his veins. Surely the knocked-out dog sleeping on her cousin's hearth had a better chance of winning this fight than James.

Randolph sneered in her direction. "Thank you for keeping him busy here until I could finish him off."

Georgette gasped. She had just worked so hard to convince James she had nothing to do with Randolph's plot. That her cousin could appear out of nowhere and destroy that small step toward trust with a single, well-timed lie brought her near to despair.

"I did no such thing!" she cried, wanting to hit him herself.

But Randolph was beyond listening, to her or anyone else. He advanced on James, swinging.

Georgette turned to William in fury. "Do something!" she hissed.

He did. James's brother crossed his arms. He smiled at her, amusement and warning colliding in a practiced grin. "He does not want our help."

The sound of someone's fist hitting soft flesh spurred her to action. She didn't know who was getting pummeled, but she was not going to let Randolph hurt James. Not again, not while she did no more than stand by, helpless. She looked around for the nearest thing she could find. Not the chamber pot this time, but something equally deadly.

The water pitcher stood at the ready.

She seized it up and tossed the water aside, then similarly threw herself into the melee. She pushed her way between the paired-off fighters, looking for a clear shot at her cousin.

"Now," James growled at his brother, trying to push her out of the way. "*Now* I could use a little help."

She got in one blow, glancing off Randolph's shoulder, before strong arms seized her and dragged her away. She kicked backward, swinging the pitcher wildly. It shattered across William MacKenzie's head.

He proved harder to fell than his brother had this morning. He blinked at her, his face scarlet.

And then he pinned her arms to her side.

"Be still, hellcat." William's voice dug into her ear as surely as his strong arms dug into her stomach. Georgette was caught tight, scarcely able to breathe, much less assist James in dispatching Randolph to unconsciousness. She gave up struggling and closed her eyes, sure that with his myriad injuries James could not defend himself against Randolph's unbalanced zeal.

She heard a sickening gasp. A thud on the floor.

And when she peeked open one eye, it was over. James was standing, not even breathing hard. "The human skull is a bit harder than a sawdust bag," he remarked, shaking his hand.

"Aye." William's voice rumbled behind her ear. "More fun, though." The band of his arms did not loosen around Georgette in the slightest.

"How did Burton even know to come up here?" James asked, irritation singing his words.

"Probably the same way *you* knew where to find me." Georgette found her voice then. "I told the innkeeper to send anyone with news up to my room."

"I'm surprised the whole bloody public room isn't crowding in here," Cameron muttered. He stepped forward and grabbed her unconscious cousin by one limp hand. "A matter for the magistrate, I suppose. Always knew you'd make me clean up one of *your* mistakes eventually, MacKenzie." He began to drag Randolph toward the open door. By the scowl on his face, she wondered if he might not drag the body down that endless stairwell, one jolting, insensible step at a time.

"Where are you taking him?" she asked, her heart straining against her nearly crushed chest.

"A night in Moraig's gaol should bring a return to sobriety, if not civility." Cameron stooped to lift Randolph's body across one sturdy shoulder. "Although I am not sure I'll have a chance to check in on him before Monday. 'Tis Bealltainn, after all."

"Aren't you forgetting something?" William's words were directed at Cameron, but they skittered across the top of her head as if they were meant for her. She was so tightly pinned she could feel the sound being formed in his chest, reverberating against her back.

Georgette closed her eyes. Thoughts of mice and dark cells and a cold stone for a pillow twisted around in her head. She did not worry overmuch about Randolph. The man deserved whatever was coming to him. No, what made her heart flutter was the surety that she was to be the next one taken into custody.

Randolph had implicated her in front of these men. Even if it was a lie, he was out cold and unavailable for interrogation.

And worst of all, James had admitted he did not trust her.

Mr. Cameron's voice floated to her, light as air. "I think I can wait to get her statement on Monday."

Georgette's eyes snapped open. "M-Monday?"

The arms around her loosened, and she found herself actually leaning on them for support. "Aye." William's voice tickled warm against her ear. "We'll need your statement to put him away for good." His voice dropped to a lower whisper. "And thank you for trying to save my brother. It takes a strong woman to deal with him. I think you'll do nicely."

Georgette slowly straightened, her fingers curved against the steel band of William's arm. She looked between the men in the room, who were staring at her with bemused expressions.

James picked something up from the bedside table, which he offered to her like a gift of fine silk. She almost choked on a hysterical laugh as she took the item from his hands.

Her corset. The man was returning her corset. The one she really should be wearing.

William's arms released her, but she scarcely recognized the freedom, so focused was she on disassembling the expression on James's face. There was an echo of feet, filing out of the tiny room.

And then she was alone. With James MacKenzie, surrounded by the shattered remains of the water pitcher, glowering at her as if he could not decide whether she was the most daft or precious female he had ever had the pleasure to meet.

Right back where they started.

SHE STOOD, HER fists clutching the corset, on the other side of the room. Every foot between them was a regrettable mile. She looked like a fierce fairy, her hair a wild ring about her head, her eyes a smoky gray.

"Why?" she whispered.

"Why what?" James took a determined step toward her. He could not sort out what the look on her face meant. She looked . . . confused. He could not blame her. She had seen the worst of him now. He had lost control of his temper and his fists in her presence.

She swallowed once, a wave of motion that drew his eye to the graceful column of her neck. "Why did you not believe Randolph?" she asked.

Why *hadn't* he believed Burton? He wasn't sure he knew the answer, only that he had not given the man's accusation even a moment's consideration. "There was no evidence to support his claim."

"But there is no evidence *not* supporting it either."

James tilted his head, studying her. "Actually, there is," he admitted with a smile, though the evidence he referred to had not been necessary. His mind had been made up from the moment he told her he loved her. "You left a right smart imprint on the man's temple with that fireplace poker. Well-done, Georgette."

She took a hesitant step in his direction. "But you said you do not trust me."

Her pace slowed to a halt. His eager pulse urged her closer. Was she afraid of him? He flexed his fingers, testing the theory in his own mind. It was an abhorrent idea. He had never, in his entire life, so much as considered hitting a woman. Come to think of it, he had never considered hitting anyone who did not deserve it.

She worried her lower lip between her teeth. The front of her dress was stained dark, spattered with water, and his eyes trailed the irregular edges. And suddenly, as he considered how and where she had gotten so wet, he realized what else she had done.

She had struck her cousin. Or she had tried to. Violently. With a water pitcher. And she had done it for him.

His breath whooshed out of him. He stood blinking

stupidly at her. What a spectacular match the two of them made. People everywhere should duck for cover.

He took two steps toward her. He was close enough to reach out an arm and touch her now. She had seen the worst in him, and was still here. He could scarcely imagine why.

"I have decided to trust in *us*." The honesty felt good falling from his lips. "My life, my work, has always been measured by evidence weighed against evidence. You are right there is very little physical evidence here, one way or the other. I have nothing but instinct. My instinct tells me we belong together."

Her mouth opened in surprise. "You cannot be sure of instinct. Your instincts told you I was a thief, not eight hours ago."

"It is a risk," he told her with a wry smile. "But it is one I will take gladly."

She sucked in a soundless breath, her eyes going wide.

And then she was in his arms. The corset dropped from her fingers and hit the floor with a satisfying thud. He remembered a very similar sound from last night, when she had slowly unlaced it, one agonizing ribbon at a time, and then tossed it away.

She was wearing far too many clothes tonight. His instincts told him that too. He cupped her face in his palms, smoothed his thumbs over her cheeks. His fingers felt the warm moisture of tears there. He feathered a kiss over one salt-stung eye, then the other, his tongue brushing against her long, pale eyelashes. "What do you want, Georgette?"

"I want you," she told him without hesitation.

He kissed along her jawline and she tilted her head back to meet him with a happy sigh. "You have to be sure," he growled into her. Citrus and ginger teased his senses, lying somewhere upon her pale skin. "It is your choice to make, not mine."

Another piece of honesty. It had never been his choice, not where she was concerned. He would have given his life just for her smile. And he would give her this chance to refuse him, though his ready body and her willing response told him he could easily have her, choice be damned.

She took a step backward, just far enough to have her eyes search his. "What are you saying? I thought . . . I thought when you asked for your ring back, you meant you did not want this."

James shook his head. Her interpretation of events was so far from the truth he almost chuckled. "You did not read that right, love. If we leap without thinking, your chance for an easy way out is over. You'll be tied to me for life. I want you to be sure of your decision."

He waited, his mind and body squirming at her hesitant response. She had made her wishes clear on so many occasions. His hope that she would want him beyond something carnal seemed a childish dream at this moment.

She reached up and flicked open the top button of her bodice. And suddenly, carnal did not seem such a poor idea.

"Mr. MacKenzie," she told him, her voice as rough as shattered glass. "You make me want to reconsider my position on husbands."

She opened another button, and then another, parting the fabric with sure fingers. Her chemise glowed white, cut daringly low. The shadow between her breasts was a promise and a taunt. He wanted her to keep going, without question.

But first he wanted her to kiss him. Not only to quiet the noise in his head, but also as proof this was her willing choice. Although, if he stopped to inspect it, kissing might not mean as much as he hoped. She'd kissed him before. Three times today, and countless times last night. And here he was, his craving unfulfilled, his body strung so tight he could have shattered from merely her touch.

No, kissing didn't mean much in the way of things.

Unless it led to more.

Chapter 32

SHE DIDN'T KNOW what to expect. Or worse, what to do.

Oh, she had an idea of the mechanics of it. She had lived through the tedious side of coupling for two years. But she had never felt like this, her insides tingling from want, her fingers desperate to tangle up in him.

She finished unbuttoning her bodice. Lifted first one shoulder, then the other. She shifted the fabric down her arms. It hung there a moment, a question gathering courage, before falling to the floor in a graceful rush. She stood shivering in her skirts and chemise, though it was not cold. Her hand splayed uncertainly against her abdomen. His eyes settled on that hand, and admiration played over his clean-shaven face.

She could scarcely believe what she was doing, had no idea if she was doing it correctly. Her long-standing aversion to nudity had never permitted her to strip before a man, to measure her progress by each taut, indrawn breath taken by her partner. James's reaction told her that nudity could be a very good thing, if only she was brave enough to finish it.

Her breasts, normally caged up tight in whalebone, reacted strongly to their uncharacteristic freedom and his none-too-innocent gaze. Her nipples brushed against her cotton chemise with exquisite sensitivity, as if they had been warmed by a fire and then pulled away to be left wanting more.

She closed the distance between them in a rush of skirts and need. He caught her up in his arms but did not kiss her. Instead, he drew her up carefully against the linen of his shirt. She felt sure fingers lift her hair and trail down her neck, and the tiny hairs there prickled in awareness. There was a tug at her waist, and then another, and then her skirts followed the way of her bodice, heaped on the floor. She locked her knees to keep from following them to such an ignoble resting place.

Halfway there, then. This nudity bit was a drawn-out business.

He knelt before her. A singular experience, looking down onto the top of James MacKenzie's head. She did not doubt she might be the only person in Moraig to realize his hair was as thick on the top as it was at the sides. She could see every stitch upon his head, the tanned part along one side where his hair refused to lie flat. His fingers seemed to have their own interests. He unhooked her hose and her garters and pushed them down, pausing over the task of unlacing her boots.

Ah. Now, at last, she understood a new reason why women wore slippers. How much kinder it would have been to the fire building inside her to not have to pause for laces.

She finally stood before him, clad in nothing but thin cotton. He regained his feet and took a half step back, merely looking. Shouldn't he be kissing her?

She was discovering that the things she had once thought she hated could be enjoyed under certain circumstances. Things like husbands. And nudity. But waiting . . . now, *that* she hated. Waiting moved right to the top of her list of things best avoided.

And so she kissed him first.

He groaned his approval, a noise that moved through her body like blood in her veins, pushed farther and deeper by each beat of her heart. Heat streaked through her, melting her limbs and binding her to him. She pressed against him, felt his arousal jutting against the smooth hem of her chemise. Gasped at the intrusion of it.

Cried out from the loss of it.

He had pulled away and was standing a hairbreadth away, breathing hard. He began to shrug out of his jacket, but the motion caught on a low moan as he eased it off his injured shoulder. "I'll need a minute," he told her, his eyes clouded with pain as much as passion.

"Oh. You are hurt." Georgette cringed at the obviousness of it. The wound on his face was no longer bleeding, but now that his jacket was removed, she could see the angry scrape beneath the hole in his shirt, just near his left chest.

She looked around for the washbasin and a cloth. The least she could do for the man who had defended her so gallantly was wash and tend his injuries. But the pitcher lay broken on the floor, the water tossed carelessly away.

"I'll send down for fresh water," she said. "And clean towels."

He tilted his head to one side. His gaze seemed to travel straight through her chemise. The skin beneath prickled with heat and awareness. "You are not dressed for visitors."

Her cheeks flashed hot. "I can put my clothes back on."

He reached a hand out and cupped one breast through

the thin cotton that still, lamentably, covered her. "That would be a wasted effort, love, as I would want nothing more than to undress you again." One thumb rolled over her nipple, a languorous statement of his want. Her body clenched in a reflexive response. "Unless you'd rather call for a bottle of brandy." His smile was pure mischief, starting small and spreading like a fire licking along kindling and paper. "As you did last night."

"I . . . I don't drink brandy." A drum's beat of a pulse started in her belly, fierce and wild.

"Oh, we did not drink it." He ran a finger down one aching, cotton-clad slope of her breast and then inched it, feather-light, up the other side. "Not in the way you imagine. We tasted it." He pointed to her nipple. "I held a bit in my mouth and kissed you here."

Wicked, those words. But not nearly as wicked as the eyes that were feasting on her. He ran his finger lower, reaching under her chemise and brushing against the moist curls between her legs. "And here."

She gasped, as drugged by the shocking portrait he painted with his words as by the touch of his fingers, deftly finding her core and sliding inside her. She sagged against him, almost naked skin against fully clothed male. He chuckled and took her hand, guiding it to the front of his trousers. She felt the hard ridge of his erection, pulsing beneath the flat of her palm. Instinct more than good sense sent her fingers wrapping around the wool-covered length of him.

"And then it was your turn," he whispered. "You tasted it here. On me."

Heat flashed inside her, a lightning-quick moment of embarrassment that was immediately shoved aside by fervent curiosity. He was telling her she had put her mouth on him. That she had placed her lips on the most intimate part of his body imaginable.

She could envision herself doing no such thing last night.

But she could envision wanting to.

She pulled her hand away from his erection. Placed her hands on her chemise. Drew it up over her head in a single, fumbling move. She no longer cared if she was doing it correctly.

She only knew she wanted to do it.

His inhaled breath echoed in the small room. He stared, his appreciative eyes roaming every bare, square inch of her. She let him. A month ago, she would have been diving for the security of coverlet and darkness.

But tonight, she stood bathed in candlelight and let him gaze upon her nudity.

"Beautiful," he murmured. He seemed in no hurry. Then again, he was injured in about ten dozen places. Moving quickly might be beyond him.

"I'm too pale," she told him, strangely unperturbed by the admission.

He shook his head. "Beautiful," he repeated again. "You hurt my eyes with it."

"Perhaps you should shut them, then. I don't think you ought to risk another injury." Laughter bubbled in her chest.

"I'll be the judge of my injuries," he told her, offering her a lascivious grin. He began to work the buttons of his shirt, but she batted his hands away and put herself to a better use than staring. He let her undress him. Let her ease the shirt off his shoulders, let her even unbutton his trousers and push them down, only to get tangled in his boots. She almost giggled at the sight. She had James

MacKenzie, the man every female in Moraig dreamed of, stripped and trussed like a clothing-bound penguin.

A very erect, clothing-bound penguin.

"The bed," she pointed.

He obligingly hopped that way and then sat down while she knelt to pull off first one boot, then the other.

"Not very experienced with the mechanics of undressing the average male, are you?" His eyes glowed hot down at her.

She lifted her chin. "I wasn't aware I needed to be. You are anything but."

He let her pull his trousers the rest of the way off. Sat still even as she peeled smallclothes and socks off his body. And all the while, he grinned at her, the sort of grin that hinted at affection underlying the lust. But his smile vanished as she leaned in close to the flesh rising up between his legs. He hissed through his teeth as her lips made contact. "You really *don't* do anything by halves, do you?"

"Do you really want only half of me?" She flashed him her own wicked grin.

The slant of his jaw mirrored the hardness of the flesh she had just kissed. "I want *all* of you, Georgette. The prim miss. The daring seductress. The fierce protector." His lips quirked upward again. "You've mastered the first two well, but I have a few lessons for you if you are thinking to continue your quest to disable the dishonest men of the world with china."

She stared up at him from her vulnerable position between his legs, so surprised by the first part of what he had said she barely heard the rest. He wanted the prim part of her too? It quite defied logic, especially as she wasn't feeling very proper this instant.

No, in this moment, she felt more the daring seductress. She licked her lips. Watched his eyes follow the line of her tongue. She had no idea what she had done with him last night, had only snippets of insight from everyone with an opinion on the matter.

But her feminine instincts had some ideas. She knew exactly what she wanted to do to him right now.

She kissed him again. Ran her tongue up the length of him and over the smooth surface of the tip. Memorized the scent of him, stronger here than in other places, but no less familiar.

He reached down, hands beneath her shoulders, and lifted her up onto the mattress. "I did not last long with such attentions last night, and I would prefer to make this evening's festivities last awhile longer."

Her body trembled in agreement. He loomed over her, his body close but not quite touching her. He trailed warm fingers across her skin, dipped them beneath her breasts and lifted, swirled and teased the ends. She leaned back onto the bed, guided by his deft touch. The feel of the fine cotton coverlet was like the roughest wool beneath her back, so sensitive did every inch of her feel.

He was busy. Very busy. But her eyes and her fingers were free to roam. She put them to work, cataloging the hurts and injuries he had accumulated today. She feathered her fingers over his face, marveling at the smooth skin she found there. The scrape along his jaw was going to leave a scar, of that she had no doubt. She lifted her hands to his hair, tangling up in the brown locks. The injury along his scalp, the one he had sustained at her hands, would probably heal well. She moved lower. The wound on his chest was shallow, little more than a scratch. Nothing, really, compared to the vicious-looking bruise blooming along one knee. Her gaze hovered there, wondering how he had sustained it.

"Like what you see?" His voice floated down to her, warm and drenched with suggestion.

She looked up, flushing. She had not even realized he was aware of her indecent perusal. "No," she told him. "You have a frightful number of injuries."

"There are places on me that hurt more."

She craned her neck. "Where?"

He shrugged, a thing of beauty in a man without a shirt. The gesture sent hard muscles rippling beneath his skin. "Neglect can be quite painful."

"I don't want to hurt you." She wanted to devour him. Had wanted to do so, she supposed, since spying him in this very bed this morning. But he had been intact and uninjured then. Things were different now. His wounds stared at her accusingly. How he could talk without groaning was a mystery.

"'Tis fine," he soothed, running one hand along her shoulder. "Except for the neglect part. I've a mind to ease that hurt in the best way possible."

Georgette released a tremulous sigh. "I am at your disposal, sir." Who was she to tell him what he was or wasn't capable of? He had surprised her, shifting her intentions at every turn today. She was looking forward to her newest change of mind.

His hands came around her face then, easy and undemanding. His fingers cradled her head, pulled her to him. His mouth met hers, warm and urgent, the hard press of his flesh against her abdomen chasing away any concerns about his condition.

He was very much alive, and very much aroused.

She arched up to meet him, having no idea how her body knew to issue such an invitation. Her breasts made exquisite contact with his hair-roughened chest, and she gasped into his mouth at the sensation. Her legs had their own ideas about how to conduct this business, and stole around his waist, pulling him close.

And then he was pushing inside her, his body shuddering as he found her core.

There was no fumbling. No attempt to force the issue. She was ready and open for him, in a way she had never been before. Everything about this was different, from the scent of his skin to the way his flesh filled her inside. She tipped her head back and held on as he began to move above her.

The feeling should have been awkward. Should have been something to bear silently, praying for speed.

Instead, every inch of her was strung with feeling. Each slide of his body out was a threat to her building emotions, and each slide in an affirmation of his intent. She was coiling there, in that place where they joined, a curling of need and want into something better defined. He was shaping her uncoordinated feelings into a concise geometry, using nothing more than the strength of his body and his hard, labored breathing against her shoulder.

It went on forever. Or it went on a few minutes. She could not tell, lost track of time and space and heartbeats. She closed her eyes to all but the sensation. She was straining for something she had only heard whispered about, the bit of her life she had given up on. There was no doubt in her mind that was where she was heading, or that he would wait for her to arrive. She trusted him, with her life and her body.

And so she took her time, focusing on that dancing, tempting, damning sensation.

She thought it would come upon her slowly, but instead it crashed like a rogue wave, knocking her over and hurling her onto shore. She cried out. She must have. Because he captured her lips in his, as if to silence her from the ears of those who might listen through walls. He held her gently, still inside her, pressing hard up against that place where the feelings were still spooling.

"Good girl," he murmured into her mouth, and that made her open her eyes.

He was staring down at her, his eyes alive with approval and something more. She lifted her chin. "Don't stop," she told him.

He obliged, ever the obedient partner. He began to move again, his body hard and taut above her, great sweeps of physical strength that, impossibly, had her reaching for that place again. This time, it was a longer, drawn-out release. Perhaps one could die only once, and thereafter it was an affair to be savored. Or perhaps this remarkable sensation she had only now discovered after twenty-six years was bound to be different every time.

She only knew that it gripped her again. And that he soon followed, his body frozen inside her, his own guttural cry of release echoing in her mouth.

HE LAY IN heaven, scarcely able to believe his good fortune or his pain. If he hadn't busted a few stitches just now, it would be a miracle. Funny how a body forgot those things, when one held someone he loved.

She lay quiescent in his arms, her skin covered in a faint sheen of perspiration. He knew if he kissed her, he would taste salt. A very satisfied bit of salt. He grinned.

There was no doubt in his mind he had brought her to completion, or that it was the first time she had experienced the sensation.

Well, that she remembered, anyway. She had proven a remarkably fast study last night, albeit under the tutelage of his mouth instead of his member.

Through the closed window, the sounds of the band, which had been so steady this past hour, came to a halt. Shots rang out, first one, then another. His body jerked involuntarily, a hazard of his day's experiences.

Georgette sat upright, her eyes wide. "What was that?"

He sat up too, running a hand gingerly through his hair. "Midnight. They're not supposed to, but every year some drunkard fires his pistols at midnight." He shook his head. "Dangerous, that. Cameron's going to be looking for blood."

She canted her head toward him, her eyes softening. "Midnight. We've known each other more than a day now. It seems much longer, doesn't it?"

"It doesn't seem nearly long enough," he told her. "I don't want a day. I want a lifetime."

He released her from his arms and stood up beside the bed. His legs felt wobbly, but his mind was clear. Good. This next bit required some clear thinking, in order not to make a fool of himself. His trousers lay in a heap where Georgette had tossed them. He picked them up.

When he turned back toward her, she was staring at him, perplexed. "But . . . you took back your ring," she said. "I thought . . ."

James shook his head. "We are married, and I am not letting you go." Her mouth fell open, but he was not through. "And it was your choice. Do not forget that, when you are so mad at me it sends you searching for a chamber pot. You chose me, just now. You've no one but yourself to blame."

Her smile bloomed, slow and easy. Gray eyes, rimmed with tears, peered up at him. He felt his body stirring again. Impossible.

And yet, unmistakable.

"But . . ." Her words fell away, caught up in the catch of her breath.

James pulled the fede ring out of his trouser pocket. Knelt beside the bed and slid it onto her finger. "We just consummated our marriage. It is very nice to meet you, Mrs. MacKenzie."

Chapter 33

He picked up her rigid hand and kissed it, intending to breathe life into her.

At her startled gasp, he said, "This was my grandmother's ring. That was why I asked for my signet ring back. It's time I started acting like a Kilmartie."

"I . . . I don't know what to say," she told him. The tears he had seen earlier swimming in her eyes fell now, one fat drop at a time, their certain trajectory the end of her nose. "Except, I . . . ah, I accept."

He chuckled, burying the sound in the skin of her wrist. "'Tis too late for that, love. We've moved past accepting, I think. There's not a court in Scotland that would undo this marriage now."

She smiled, a shy bit of relief.

"I know your home is in England," he went on, anxious to sort out the pieces now that the important parts were established. "We can move to London, as soon as I earn enough money."

"Money?" she echoed.

His eye fell on the bedside table and the money purse she had placed there. It was lighter than he wanted, but heavy enough for a start. "It should take six months, a year at the most, for me to make enough money to start a practice in London." His gaze fell back on her. "Can you wait with me here that long? We could stay with my family, if you want, at Kilmartie Castle. Or rent a small house near town. Either is fine, as long as you are happy."

She stared at him, her brow pulled down. "You . . . you do not know?"

He paused over her hand. Suddenly, he felt very naked. Vulnerable. "Know what?"

She smiled at him, sheepishly. "I am wealthy, James."

His eyebrows jerked upward. "Wealthy?"

She nodded. "Why did you think I offered you two hundred pounds to procure an annulment?"

He leaned back, still wrapping his head around this unexpected twist. "I did not think you could actually do that. I thought you were making that up."

"Why on earth would I make that up?"

He gripped her hand more tightly. "People being dragged to the lockup often can't be trusted."

She leaned back, smiling more broadly now. "Why did you think Randolph was so desperate to marry me, with or without my consent?"

"You're a beautiful woman," he choked out. "Any man would want you."

She shook her head. "He was after my fortune, James."

He swallowed, his pride shrinking from her words and her offer. "How much?" he whispered.

"Enough that Randolph Burton was willing to kill you to have a chance with me."

James expelled a violent breath. This was not something he had planned for. Not something he wanted. He shook his head, uncertainty shouldering its way to the front of his mind. Things had seemed simpler when it was just about love. "I do not want your money, Georgette."

She leaned forward. One naked breast brushed temptingly against his chest. "I know," she whispered. "That is precisely why I want to share it."

He let her rest against him while alternate possibilities snaked their way through his head. The band started up again outside, to a hearty chorus of cheers. He cocked his head toward the noise, his mind settling on what he wanted. "I want to earn my own way," he told her. "We will put your money in trust, so it is yours and always will be."

She sighed against him, a sound of exasperation but not regret. "But I can spend it?" she asked, her voice muffled against him. "In any manner I choose?"

"Of course."

She pulled back. "Well then, I want to purchase a house for us. After all, I need a place to put my maid." Her smile grew broader. "And my kitten. Mr. MacRory will insist upon it, I'm afraid." She lifted a hand to her temple, her eyes going wide. "Oh, and a dog. I have acquired a dog today. You may not have known that."

James felt the tension leave his body, one long strand at a time. "You've been busy, Mrs. MacKenzie." He pressed a kiss to her forehead. "We'll do whatever you want. As long as we are together, I care not where or how we live."

She regarded him with a salacious gleam in her eye. He knew, in all the years ahead of them, he would never get tired of seeing this woman's personality shift from prim to predatory.

She brushed a none-too-prudish hand over the length

of him. "If you can see fit to hold this thought another hour or so, I've a keen desire to dance with my new husband."

As if in agreement, the band outside swung into a Highland jig.

James helped her to her feet. Laced her into the corset and buttoned her bodice over it with the lightest of fingers. He found he didn't mind covering her, now that he knew it would be his privilege to unwrap her later, one decadent layer at a time.

Finally, she was standing beside him, dressed. She reached up on her toes for a kiss. He was happy to oblige. It occurred to him, as his lips met hers, that this pretty little scene came very close to the ending they *should* have had this morning.

Only, thank God for chamber pots. Without it, he suspected it might never have come to this.

THE CROWD SHOWED no signs of stopping. The rowdy hints of Bealltainn that had reached Georgette's ears through the window could not compare with the intensity of the street-level celebration. The heat from the bonfire was immense, winding its way into every pore and flushing her body from the outside in.

Everywhere she looked, couples were dancing. Embracing. Kissing.

And for once, she felt right at home among them.

She gripped James's hand tightly as they threaded their way through the mob. And then they were stepping up on the wooden platform and he was facing her, bowing from the waist.

"Mrs. MacKenzie," he said, his eyes already dancing. "Would you honor your husband with a waltz?"

James MacKenzie proved less brilliant at dancing than he did at the rougher, more intimate pursuits he had recently introduced her to. Perhaps it was because he favored his leg, or because his head injury left him off-balance. Or perhaps—and this seemed more likely—it was because she made a less than ideal partner, stumbling over the fast strains of the music that were more primal and quick than the graceful dances she was used to in London. She clung to the man in her arms, letting the world spin around her, counting the moments until she could get him back to the little room above the Blue Gander.

A shout penetrated the wild pace of the music. "Glad to see you found your wife, MacKenzie!"

"Tie her up next time, save yourself the trouble!"

"Show her how a Highlander does it!"

"Kiss the woman, why don't you?" The last bit was delivered more solemnly, and at closer range. Georgette turned her head to see the smiling face of William MacKenzie. He clapped James on the back. "Glad you worked it out, Jamie-boy."

And then he disappeared, lost in the couples swinging about in a mad rush. She twisted, trying to see where he had gone. Instead, she saw Mr. MacRory dancing with a stout, fair-haired woman who very much looked as if she appreciated a man who could provide all the beef she wanted. Elsie and Joseph Rothven spun by, locked so tightly, hip-to-hip, that Georgette had no doubt the youth was in for another momentous first experience by the end of the night.

Feet pounded on the wooden platform. Hearts raced in time with the music, sawing its way toward a spectacular conclusion. She stepped closer into her husband's arms.

"Do you regret your choice, now that you have seen my dancing skills?" His words brushed the top of her head.

She shook her head. She had made her choice. And she would never regret it.

His fingers stole up to tip up her chin. Their feet came to a stop, though the music plowed on. "Remember, Mrs. MacKenzie. Kissing is part of Bealltainn."

She closed her eyes as his mouth descended on hers. He might not know how to dance, but he knew how to kiss, James MacKenzie did. Knew how to use his tongue to part a woman's lips and delve into her secrets. She spilled them all, opening her mouth and meeting his tongue's inquiry with her own.

The heat of the fire, the shaking of the wooden platform, the exuberant shouts of the townsfolk, all fell away as her mind coalesced on a series of unshakable thoughts.

She still didn't like brandy, although she found herself more than a little curious about James's recommended use. She was not fond of waiting, although she could allow that a delay might build up a delicious degree of anticipation. She was reconsidering her position on nudity, a point she had already aptly demonstrated.

But husbands . . . now, on that matter she found herself a complete and total convert.

And she could not wait to prove it.

Keep reading for an excerpt from
BRIGHTON IS FOR LOVERS,
another thrilling historical romance
by Jennifer McQuiston

Coming soon from Avon Books

David Cameron stopped dead in his tracks and let memory knife him in the gut.

One moment he was walking that ever-changing line between land and ocean, focused on the act of *not* remembering. It had taken him an hour to hike here today, and much of that walk had sorely tested his athleticism, with sharp rocks and narrow footholds where the ocean encroached on the white chalk cliffs. He had not recalled traipsing such a grueling footpath eleven years ago, but then again, he had barely been walking at the time, and his thoughts had been focused on things more difficult than the landscape.

The next moment he spied her, and those denied memories split open and threatened to swallow him whole. Their only prior meeting had been a chance encounter more than a decade earlier, but there was no denying his Brighton mermaid still haunted the same section of beach he had narrowly escaped with his life.

And apparently his savior, whom he had more than once suspected of being nothing more than a drunken mirage, had been real.

He discerned the exact moment she recognized him too. Her limbs arrested, as if she were suspended in time and place. She stood frozen, leaving it to him to close the distance between them.

David's heart kicked over as she grew larger and more animated in his eyes. Time had a way of taking a remembrance and turning it into a still miniature in one's head, to be tucked away and brought out only on special occasions. When he thought of her at all, it was always as the child who had pulled his sorry arse from the surf eleven years ago.

This was not that child.

Oh, she had the same freckles and brown tresses, although this time her hair was dry and ruthlessly pulled back from her face. She possessed the same sharp nose, the same flat chest. Christ, she had on the same girlish frock, some unfashionably plain thing that came down only to her calves and looked to have seen one too many summers.

But she was far taller now. Lanky, he would have called her, had she been a horse he was contemplating at auction. Her shoulders seemed ill-contained by her clothing, and strained against the seams of her dress. Her expression was different, too. The girl he remembered—although, admittedly, it was a memory distorted by grief and whiskey—had been extraordinary. Full of life, leaking emotion.

The woman seemed better contained.

"Miss Tolbertson, isn't it?" he asked as he drew up in front of her, because really, under the peculiar circumstances, what else could he say?

Her mouth seemed to work around the words she wanted to say. "You remember my name, Lieutenant?"

"A man retains certain facts regarding near death experiences. The name of his rescuer tends to be one of them." He looked down at her, and realized he did not have to look very far. Her nose came nigh up to his chin, a singular experience when one considered he was six-foot-two in stocking feet. "And it's no longer Lieutenant. I sold my commission last year. Please, call me David."

Her eyes widened. "I hardly think . . . I mean . . . I do not *know* you."

"You've known me for eleven years. You rescued me from this very spot, when I should have drowned. Formality seems a little pointless, under the circumstances."

She drew in a deep, audible breath, and then her mouth found a smile that reached her eyes. He recalled that now, too, how one had to search their mind to identify whether her eyes were green or brown or somewhere in between.

"Then you must call me Caroline." She sent a furtive look in two directions before her gaze came back to rest on him. "It is not as if there is anyone to hear our frightful lack of propriety anyway." She assessed him in a broad, hazel sweep. "I confess, you have taken me a bit by surprise. I rarely see anyone on this stretch of beach."

David had not known what to expect on returning to this beach this morning. An epiphany, perhaps. A dark memory of the boy he had once been, and a sharp reminder of the man he must be.

But he had not expected her.

"It *is* a rather isolated bit of coast. And difficult to reach." He glanced down to the high hem of her skirts and the sturdy half boots that graced her feet. She had dressed properly for the walk. *Practical girl*. He was wearing shoes better suited for a stroll along Brighton's Marine Parade, and a vicious blister had taken up residence on his right heel.

"Why did you never return?" she asked, her voice lower and huskier than the one in his memory.

David considered his answer. After the events of that fateful day, he had returned to nearby Preston where his infantry unit had been stationed. He had been close enough to have come back any time he had wanted.

But he *hadn't* wanted. The less he thought of Brighton, and the fewer visual triggers he forced on himself, the easier it had been to go on during those early, guilt-ridden years. He shrugged noncommittally. "I live elsewhere. This is my first visit back since that day."

"Oh." Her wrinkled forehead softened. "I suppose that explains why I haven't seen you again."

"Do you live in town, then?" Though her accent was more educated than the dialect he had picked up from the few local fishermen he had encountered, it seemed too much of a coincidence to see her twice in two visits if she did not.

"Yes, on the far east side. Our house sits right on the ocean." As if prompted by the question, her eyes pulled toward the crashing surf. He followed her gaze and caught the diamond flash of waves peaking before boiling over into gray. The tide was coming in, and it was a fearsome sight. The high cliff walls that surrounded them formed an inlet that seemed to force the water into a constricted space, intensifying the effect.

Had the waves been this rough and the tide this high that day, eleven years ago, when she had swum out to save him? He couldn't remember. But the thought of such danger, heaped on a child's shoulders by his own stupidity, chilled him thoroughly.

"I wouldn't want to keep you." Her voice broke through his thoughts. She motioned toward the footpath down which she had just come. "Not if you have a schedule to keep."

"I am not expected elsewhere at the moment." She seemed anxious to be rid of him. He wondered if perhaps she felt a need to hurry him along, in case he was considering another ill-advised swim off this section of treacherous, rocky coast.

Truly, there wasn't enough whiskey in the world.

"I am visiting Brighton with my mother," he added, "but she has eschewed my company at present."

In point of fact, his mother had practically tossed him out of the room they had taken at the Bedford Hotel, insisting she was fine, snapping at him when he tried to plump her pillow or read to her out loud from the novel she kept on the table by her bed. He might have been plagued by troublesome memories in the three days since their arrival, but his mother seemed better, at least. The physician's prognosis a month ago had not been favorable, but already her lungs sounded clearer. Perhaps there really *was* something to the restorative power of Brighton's sea water cures.

He had initially argued against his mother's suggestion for a recuperative holiday here. He had felt no desire to return to the town of Brighton and the nightmares that he sensed would await him here. But he had not been able to refuse his mother when she told him her heart was set on Brighton. Not when she had been so ill for so long.

And not when she had intonated it might be her last request.

"You are here for the summer then?" Caroline asked, thankfully oblivious to the maudlin direction of his thoughts. "So many are, now. The new rail system even permits Londoners to come for the day, if they want. Can you imagine? London to Brighton and back again, in only a few hours." She wrinkled her nose, stretching a remarkable constellation of freckles far and wide. "Last year they came in droves every Saturday, to soil the beaches and overrun the sewers and generally trample over every blade of seagrass they can find. We have begun to earn the moniker 'London-by-the-sea', I'm afraid. I hope you won't be disappointed here."

A grin worked its way into residence on his face. She was the same, but different, too. She no longer chattered on with quite the same fervor as she had as a child, but she still chattered.

He was fascinated by the changes time had wrought, both in her appearance and her demeanor. Although he would have expected the opposite reaction, given the circumstances of their history, her voice drew him from his self-flagellating thoughts and diverted him from painful memories.

Suddenly his month's penance in Brighton no longer seemed so long, or so threatening. He offered her the full force of his smile. "I have not been disappointed in the least. And while Brighton's popularity among Londoners is certainly a diverting topic, I would really rather talk about you."

CAROLINE DREW a deep breath, wondering why her stomach skittered so at the sight of one man's straight, white teeth.

David Cameron was not quite as handsome as she remembered. Although his shoulders were every bit as broad as they had been eleven years ago, today they were covered in a brown wool sack coat instead of a diverting military uniform. His unruly curls were the color of new straw, and seemed to mock the shimmering spun gold of her memory. His face had lengthened into the hard planes of adulthood, framed by tiny lines etched by sun and experience, there at the corners of his blue eyes.

Handsome, to be sure, but not that handsome.

Of course, David Cameron *was* the man she had fallen a little bit in love with before she was old enough to know better.

When she had first caught sight of him, framed by scrub and seagrass along the eastern edge of the white cliff walls, she felt as if she had been slammed against the rocks that broke the waves into fragmented pieces, a dozen yards or so from shore. She could still scarcely believe he had appeared after eleven long years. Even more astonishing, he was speaking to her as if he was *enjoying* the conversation.

And so, despite his kind teasing, she was going to do anything it took to prevent the conversation from turning to her.

"You're from Scotland?" She wet her lips, wishing she didn't feel so nervous. "Although your brogue is not so strong as my memory."

He grimaced. "Ah, I treated you to my brogue during our last meeting, did I?" He leaned in, one conspirator to another, and she felt his nearness as surely as if he had pressed himself against her. "I'll share a little-known secret. My accent tends to come out when I have had too much to drink."

She pursed her lips around a smile. "Well, that certainly explains it, then. You smelled like a distillery the last time we met." She took an exaggerated, indrawn sniff. "Not today, however." In point of fact, he smelled . . . interesting. Like salt and ocean and, ever so faintly, freshly laundered cotton that had been heated by exertion.

Her cheeks heated at the audacity of such an inappropriate thought, and she cast about for a diversion. "Why does your mother not wish for your company today?"

He sighed, and she could pick apart the different tones of worry and exasperation that formed the sound. "She has been ill, and the doctor prescribed a rest cure. I brought her to Brighton with every expectation of serving as a doting son during her convalescence. But since our arrival, she seems to harbor other opinions for how I would spend my time."

Caroline suppressed a smile as he ended the explanation on a not-so-silent groan. "Oh?"

"Social engagements." He made it sound much the same as one might say the word "manure."

"We should probably keep our mothers apart then," she observed dryly. "Because mine is possessed of similar intent."

He laughed then, a spontaneous burst of mirth that the wind snatched up and tossed against the cliff walls. "The baroness harbors aspirations of a social agenda that eclipses anything to be had in my hometown of Moraig. I really don't understand the fuss. I am only a second son."

Caroline's heart thudded in the direction of her knees. She had not known of his status, that day eleven years ago. She had seen his military uniform and presumed him a common soldier, but by Brighton standards, he was borderline royalty. "Well, the son of a baron attracts some notice, especially in a small town like Brighton." Unfortunately, if he moved in the circles she suspected, he was out of her social sphere.

"I brought my mother here to convalesce, but it seems her constitution is less dire than the pressing matter of her youngest son's lack of marriage prospects. She has already accepted not one, but *two* invitations on my behalf."

Caroline gave an indelicate shudder. "Sounds lovely."

"Truly?" He sounded surprised.

"No." She shook her head. "I confess I would rather play shuttlecock. And shuttlecock is a game I dearly despise."

That had him laughing again, and the sound sent her insides into a heated free fall. "If not shuttlecock, what then? We've established you don't mind a bit of impropriety. Do you still swim, mermaid?" he chuckled.

And just like that, the desire to direct the conversation away from her eccentricities circled full round to take her by the throat. Perhaps he hadn't heard the rumor about her unfeminine proclivities that was circulating like a scrub grass fire among Brighton's summer visitors, but he *had* once seen her swim. Even if it had occurred eleven years ago, even if it was something they had both sworn to silence, that kind of secret was dangerous to a girl like Caroline, who already hovered on the outer fringes of society.

And while she was not sure she *wanted* to be accepted by the summer set, her mother was insistent she set her sights on more than a life of quiet spinsterhood. And that meant Caroline was expected to conform, even if acting the lady felt closer to a stranglehold than a blessing.

"No." Caroline squirmed against guilt in her sweat-soaked dress. For a moment she contemplated changing her answer, telling him the truth. But how to explain that, despite her knowledge of Society's expectations, despite her grudging admittance that her mother's hopes for her future made perfect, proper sense, Caroline's soul—nay, her *sanity*—cried out for something different? The ocean might pull and push her. It might occasionally threaten to kill her.

But it did not degrade her. She felt *whole* amid the waves, in a way she never did amongst the crowd.

And so she swam in secret. Furtively, like one of the silver-finned fishes that darted amongst the rocks, escaping the larger toothed fish that sought to consume her whole.

"Ladies do not swim," she added, weakly to her own ears.

His brow lifted. "You used to swim very well. You had an oddly styled stroke, if I recall, but it was quite effective."

The warm day and the uncomfortable bent to the conversation made the perspiration break out along her forehead in what she had to presume was a most indelicate sheen. The swim she had come for, the swim which was now out of reach, would have helped restore her to rights. But the reality of her circumstances stopped the words from lifting off her tongue.

David Cameron seemed to like her. Why would she destroy that with a bit of uncalled-for honesty?

"You were drunk that day," she pointed out, breathless. "You probably don't remember things very clearly. And I was never very experienced. I doubt I could imagine much more than a bit of uncoordinated splashing now."

He nodded, as if her lie made all the sense in the world, when it didn't even make sense to her. And just like that, the idea of telling the truth shriveled into something unrecognizable.

"I never told anyone, you know," she murmured.

"That you used to swim?"

"That you could not." She swallowed nervously. "I never told anyone about that day, not even my sister Penelope."

He inclined his head, a physical acknowledgement of the courtesy she had shown. "That is a long time to keep a promise. I would not have faulted you if circumstances had compelled you to share such a secret."

"I think someone's word is the most important part of their character," she told him. "A promise is something you must keep."

His mouth flattened into a thin line. "An admirable sentiment. I wish I could claim to keep my promises half so well."

For a moment, fear knocked the base of her spine. "You mean you told someone about me?"

He shook his head. "No. I was referring to another promise I made once. A long time ago."

When he made no move to explain further, Caroline wiped her damp palms on her skirt. The sun mocked the awkward silence. It was always this way, next to the white chalk cliffs, an unexpected blast of blinding color and energy. As a result of this peculiar convergence of sun and wind, she was tanned in places a proper lady should not be, simply from her daily swim. She could feel her nose burning now.

"I must go," she said, already turning toward the footpath that would carry her back. "Mama will expect me home for tea."

"Will I see you here tomorrow?" David called after her, breaking the silence that had engulfed him since his last peculiar statement.

Caroline hesitated. While his unexpected appearance today had gladdened her heart and stirred her hopes, it had interrupted today's opportunity to swim. As long as she could remember she had come to this hidden cove with her father, first to collect shells, and then, in the years before he had died, to learn to swim.

And despite his easy smile, despite the fact he had already seen it, she did not want to share it with anyone else.

Not even David Cameron.

"I don't come here every day," she hedged, chewing on her lower lip. "But you can call on me in town, if you prefer, and we can walk along the Marine Parade, or along the Steine. My house is the large Georgian with red shutters, the first one you encounter on the footpath back."

He grinned, whatever melancholy that had gripped him momentarily tucked away for another time. "I shall do that."

For a maddening moment, a moment she could not regret, but which she wished she could control, her stomach churned its agreement. Did he mean to court her, then? Eleven years of yearning, secret dreams stretching from childish fancy to adult curiosity, rose up in hope.

And then he ruined it. Took her swelling hope in his hands and pressed it flat, as if her dreams were a whimsical castle made of sand and he was the inevitable tide.

"After all," he said, as if the matter of Caroline Tolbertson receiving a gentleman caller was not an astonishing thing. "If I am going to resist my mother's harried matchmaking efforts this summer, I suspect I am going to need a good friend in Brighton to make it through unscathed."

Next month, don't miss these exciting new love stories only from Avon Books

Kiss of Temptation by Sandra Hill
Condemned to prison for the sin of lust, Viking vampire angel—or vangel—Ivak Sigurdsson is finding centuries of celibacy depressing. When temptation comes in the form of beautiful Gabrielle Sonnier—who needs help breaking her brother out of prison—Ivak can't help but give in. But as the two join forces, they both begin to wonder if their passionate bond is really only lust, or something more.

Stolen Charms by Adele Ashworth
Determined to wed the infamous thief, the Black Knight, Miss Natalie Haislett has no trouble approaching Jonathan Drake—reputed to be a friend of the Knight—for an introduction. This may be difficult as Drake is the Knight himself! While traveling together in France as a married couple in search of the Knight, passions bloom and the daring bandit sets his sights on the most priceless treasure of all . . . Natalie's heart.

Sins of a Ruthless Rogue by Anna Randol
When Clayton Campbell shows up on Olivia Swift's doorstep, she's stunned. No longer the boy who stole her heart, this hardened man has a lust for vengeance in his eyes. Clayton cannot deny that the sight of Olivia rouses in him a passion like never before. But as tensions between them rise, the hard-hearted agent will face his greatest battle yet . . . for his heart.

REL 0313